The PREMONITION *at* WITHERS FARM

Books by Jaime Jo Wright

The House on Foster Hill
The Reckoning at Gossamer Pond
The Curse of Misty Wayfair
Echoes among the Stones
The Haunting at Bonaventure Circus
On the Cliffs of Foxglove Manor
The Souls of Lost Lake
The Premonition at Withers Farm

The PREMONITION at WITHERS FARM

JAIME JO WRIGHT

BETHANYHOUSE
a division of Baker Publishing Group
Minneapolis, Minnesota

Published by Bethany House Publishers
11400 Hampshire Avenue South
Minneapolis, Minnesota 55438
www.bethanyhouse.com

Bethany House Publishers is a division of
Baker Publishing Group, Grand Rapids, Michigan

Printed in the United States of America

Library of Congress Cataloging-in-Publication Data
Names: Wright, Jaime Jo, author.
Title: The premonition at withers farm / Jaime Jo Wright.
Description: Minneapolis, Minnesota : Bethany House, a division of Baker Publishing Group, [2022]
Identifiers: LCCN 2022011312 | ISBN 9780764238338 (paperback) | ISBN 9780764240911 (casebound) | ISBN 9781493439164 (ebook)
Subjects: LCGFT: Novels.
Classification: LCC PS3623.R5388 P74 2022 | DDC 813/.6—dc23
LC record available at https://lccn.loc.gov/2022011312

Scripture quotations are from the King James Version of the Bible.

Cover design by Jennifer Parker

Author is represented by Books & Such Literary Agency.

Baker Publishing Group publications use paper produced from sustainable forestry practices and post-consumer waste whenever possible.

22 23 24 25 26 27 28 7 6 5 4 3 2 1

To the Poll family: Tim, Sue, Alex, Zach, Sylvia, and Izzy

I've never been more grateful for the internet,
for blogs, for friendship.
I realize, at first meeting, we both considered the
other's potential to be a serial killer.
This is also how we knew we were meant to be friends.
And once we discovered we had no intentions of enacting
violence toward the other, our friendship has only grown.

Here's to country life, mud, ATVs, homeschooling,
reading each other's minds, bad cooking,
and gut-splitting laughter.
Oh, and here's to cats and chickens.
Lots of them. Everywhere and always.

May 31, 1910

Darkness will be pivotal.
Expect her to scream.
Drink the sound into your soul.

What makes me like this?
The mind of a killer is a journey into chaos.

I do this only for you, sweet one.
For you, I walk with the dark.

1

Perliett Van Hilton

AUGUST 1910

When death came to visit, no one ever prepared tea and cookies. Still, Perliett Van Hilton sipped her tea and eyed the good doctor over the rim of the white china cup. She could read distaste for her in his eyes, but more than that, she could see that death had already begun its mission to etch lines into the corners of his eyes. Age lines. Though he couldn't yet be forty. Surely not. Still, Perliett had a personal theory that if one wasn't death's friend, then for certain they were its enemy. In which case, it aged them faster because they went to war against it rather than falling into death's inevitability, as one might fall onto a feather mattress.

"Did you hear me?" George Wasziak—*Dr.* George Wasziak—inquired of her, decidedly aggravated. Wasziak. He was also decidedly Polish, which meant her decidedly German roots would pit them against each other naturally merely because of their stubborn ancestral tendencies. And that didn't even consider that Dr. Wasziak was convinced she practiced quackery and her mother practiced—

"*Miss* Van Hilton." He demanded her attention.

She took another sip of lavender tea instead.

His eyes were charcoal black. Remarkable. She could barely make out any brown, which meant he looked just shy of possessed. Which also meant George Wasziak was absolutely fascinating to her.

"You say she's dead?" Perliett finally responded, to which George—she preferred to irritate him and so addressed him by his Christian name—raised a very dark eyebrow.

"Deceased," he corrected.

"Departed," Perliett countered, using terminology destined to get under his skin. And for certain it had, as she watched his chest lift in an almost imperceptible sigh. She bit the inside of her bottom lip. It was remarkably inappropriate to laugh considering the topic of conversation at hand.

"How?" Perliett managed to maintain her serious composure.

"How did she die?" George clarified.

"No, how did she brew her tea in the morning?" Perliett thinned her lips, masking a smile. "Of course I meant how did she die."

George's eyes narrowed. "She was . . ." He hesitated.

"Out with it, George." Perliett held her teacup just below her chin to emphasize how casually one could face death if they really wanted to. Though it probably wasn't the wisest or most sensitive of approaches. Were it anyone other than George bringing her this news, Perliett knew her reaction would have been far more weighted down by the gratuitousness of death.

"She received eight stab wounds to the abdomen, one of which severed the abdominal aorta."

"She bled out?" Perliett lowered her cup a tad. She tempered her expression so as not to reveal the horror that raced through her, stilling her morbid sense of humor. To this point, George had not indicated murder. He had—well, he had simply said the woman was deceased. A murder? Here? In this quiet farming community? The impact of such a thing was monumental.

George jerked his head in a nod. "Yes. She bled out."

"I see." Another sip, this time to disguise the emotion that welled in her throat. She didn't need George Wasziak to see her weakness. He was already on the hunt for her vulnerabilities to discredit her medical services further. Contrary to George's belief, Perliett was very empathetic toward those affiliated with death. Even if her view of the afterlife differed from his dramatically.

George stood on the front porch of her farmhouse that was nestled at the edge of the neighboring farm's cornfield, across the road from a large barn that once held three stories' worth of hay but now was empty. The floorboards beneath George's feet were painted gray, the porch railing behind him white, and a massive willow tree rustled feathery yellow-green branches in the yard behind him. The remnants of her father's work. All of it. Now the farm was ghostly in its quietness and yet welcoming all the same. It was beautifully barren of busy work, and home to Perliett and her mother.

Perliett stepped toward George.

George took a quick step backward.

Perliett motioned toward a wooden rocking chair. "Please, have a seat."

"I prefer to stand."

"Very well." Her father had never been so stubborn. Perliett eyed George as she edged around him, still clutching her teacup, and settled herself into the chair. She preferred her father, who had also passed on. His gentleness. His kindness. His everything that George Wasziak didn't seem to possess.

Perliett absolutely refused to be intimidated by the doctor's six-foot-two frame, or by his skepticism of her and her mother's trades, or by his Presbyterian upbringing, which was juxtaposed to her Methodist one. Did he pray the Rosary or was that something only Catholics did? Perliett shook the thought from her head. It wasn't applicable to the moment. None of her thoughts were. They were simply a toy box of thoughts to distract her from the awfulness George had brought to her front porch.

George tipped his head to the left and stared down his nose. An *aquiline* nose. She'd read that description of a man's nose in a book once and had absolutely no clue what it meant. But Perliett assumed his was just that. Because it was straight and perfect.

"Miss Van Hilton—"

"Perliett," she corrected, then sipped her now-cold tea.

"Miss Van Hilton, Eunice Withers has been murdered."

"I would assume such. One doesn't fall onto one's own knife eight different times in succession." She hoped her flippancy hid the fact that her eyes were burning. Eunice Withers. The poor girl. The poor sweet girl . . .

George's face reddened. "I need your services."

"Truly?" Perliett set the teacup on a white wicker side table that also held a small potted fern. She folded her hands in her lap and rested them on top of her emerald-green skirt. "I cannot bring her back to life, you know."

"I didn't mean your *medical* services."

"So, you admit I provide those?"

"I admit nothing of the sort. I merely need your services to clean the body."

"I see. Eliminate the signs of violence before Miss Withers is given over to the undertaker?"

"Yes."

"Yes," Perliett echoed. "I suppose that would be unseemly for your . . . er, delicate sensibilities." She raised her eyes and knew her blue orbs were blinking in coquettish innocence at the man.

He opened his mouth to reply.

Perliett interrupted to spare him the effort of defending

himself. "Absolutely." She pushed up from the chair, and this time Dr. George Wasziak didn't have the opportunity to step back. She tapped the knot of his tie with her fingertip. "I would be more than honored to help prepare Miss Withers for the afterlife."

"She's already entered it," George growled. "Her body needs no preparation for that."

Oh, heavens. She simply *had* to poke at him one more time or she might burst into tears. To mask her emotion, Perliett jabbed at George's tie again, and he stiffened. "My mother might beg to differ, but we'll ask Miss Withers the next time we speak with her."

George's eyes darkened further—if that were possible.

For a moment, he unnerved Perliett. Then she recovered. She knew that most average Christian members of the small Michigan farmland community didn't respond with welcome to the fact that her mother spoke to the dead. *Saw* the dead. Spiritualism, for many, was dabbling in a world one should leave very much alone. For Perliett's mother, it was her livelihood—even her companionship. Especially now that the staying hand of Perliett's father had dissipated with his passing. There was no further influence from the churchgoing man to temper her mother's fascination with the afterlife.

Perliett? Oh, she accepted it. Because it was her mother, and because it was the only way she could stay in communication with her beloved father. The man whom death had stolen, and the only time Perliett had hated death for such an act.

2

Molly Wasziak

PRESENT DAY

Weep for the living, not the dead.

While she related to the sentiment, it did not thrill Molly that it was chiseled into the basement's stone foundation. A foundation made of broken sections of old gravestones. She offered her husband a side-eye. He wasn't looking at her, but instead was studying the old gas furnace.

"It's LP, right?" Trent asked of their real estate agent, Maynard Clapton.

The man dipped his bald head in response. "Oh yeah. No natural gas lines out this way. It's liquid propane all right."

"We'd need to work on insulating the house better." Trent reached overhead and swiped his callused palm along the edge where the joists met the wall.

"It is an old farmhouse, so yes, it's not going to be efficient. As you can see, the basement is more of a cellar." Maynard ducked as a string slapped his face, attached to the lone lightbulb that was screwed into a fixture in the middle of the ceiling. "It's solid, though." He slapped the stone wall, his palm against the half-finished name of *Wilber Smy—*. "Farmers back in the day used fieldstone, but in order to recycle and be frugal, they also used castoff headstones, as you can see. The stone carver made an error, or something cracked, or what have you and the markers were worthless."

"Granite is good in a foundation," Trent acknowledged. He didn't seem bothered by the idea that the farmhouse had been built on the lives of dead people. Their half names and epitaphs intermingling with stones from the fields as though they were insignificant.

Molly looked down at her shoes, now covered in a layer of basement dust. The floor was hard-packed with earth and stone. She didn't dare look up, because between the wooden rafters were so many spiderwebs, Molly was sure you could throw a tennis ball up there and it'd get trapped. Spiders were the spawn of Satan, plain and simple.

Maynard looked between them. Molly knew what he saw without even needing to think about it. A couple in their early thirties, married straight out of high school, and about as close now as two buddies living in a dorm together. Molly called Trent her *roommate*. He hated it, but never said—or did—anything to change it. Maynard was probably wondering why they were bothering to buy an over one-hundred-year-old farmstead as a hobby farm instead of using the money to file for divorce.

She wondered about it too. Not that she wanted a divorce. It was just . . . the next logical step? Isn't that what people did when they coexisted? What once had thrived as two best friends had diminished into an unargumentative silence. It didn't help that she knew a lot of it was her fault. But it also didn't help that Trent had about as many emotions as one of the fieldstones in the basement foundation.

Yet that was Trent. She blamed it on too many hours alone on the tractor, working someone else's fields while wishing he had his own. Not to mention, he was a Wasziak. Wasziak men were known for their aloofness, even their gruffness at times. Men with hearts of gold, but as sentimental as a cement garden gnome.

Still, Molly could see this house through Trent's eyes. A place like this, with an old farmhouse, a barn, a chicken coop, and miscellaneous outbuildings, not excluding a half-falling-down outhouse, and Molly knew Trent was sold. The place was theirs. Even if she hated it.

Molly buried her dreams of marble countertops and white trim work in every room. Instead, the kitchen upstairs was a galley style with enough counter space for a toaster and maybe a kitchen mixer. The appliances were white and old. And a master en suite that was a must-have for all those house-hunting couples on HGTV? Yeah, she was going to get a square bedroom on the suffocating second floor of the non-air-conditioned farmhouse, with a blue shag carpet from the eighties. She didn't even like blue. Oh yeah, and no bathroom connected. She'd have to traipse down the tilted floor to get to that.

Molly tried to still her tempestuous, almost bitter thoughts. It wasn't fair to Trent. It wasn't fair to her.

"So, what do you both think?" Maynard crossed his arms over his polo-shirt-clad chest. He looked from one to the other.

Trent shot a searching glance at Molly. He said nothing except with his eyes. Clear blue-gray. His *Clapton Bros. Farms* baseball cap was flipped backward, and his longish, light brown curls looked like they were trying to escape the confines.

"It's fine," Molly agreed. Yay! She got to make the life-changing decision to buy their first home in a basement made of gravestones.

Maynard ping-ponged a glance between them.

Trent gave a brief nod.

The real-estate agent clapped his hands together. "Great!

Let's head upstairs. We'll discuss the offer you'd like to make and get this baby turned over to you as fast as we can."

The men moved past Molly. It was possible for feet to become permanently attached to the floor, right? Because she couldn't move. Couldn't process.

Her first house.

Their first house.

Built in 1867, added onto at the turn of the century, and updated in 1992.

She should be excited, grateful, overjoyed that Trent was realizing his dream, and that she could be by his side as she'd wanted to be so badly when they were in high school. Back then, her dreams were of marriage, home, and family. She now had the first two—it was the latter that spiraled her into this darkness. This place that was impossible to crawl out of. It was the word *family* that crushed every speck of hope, stole joy like a hole in a bucket, and made grief her constant companion.

The stairs leading up to the ground floor were nothing but bare wooden steps. Molly eyed them even as Maynard and Trent reached the top and moved toward the kitchen without her. Trent didn't need her for this. This was his thing—his place—his dream.

Molly cast a resigned smile toward poor William Smy—'s gravestone. "Guess you and I are going to get better acquainted, Willie."

Great. She was already talking to dead people. The thought made her breath hitch and her foot pause as it hovered over the bottom step.

Dead people.

The room tilted, making Molly stumble and reach for the railing. She felt the icy whisper of air on the back of her neck. Taking a breath was like trying to draw in air while having the house settle its full weight on her chest. She wasn't alone. She could sense it. Feel it. Everything but *see* it.

"Go away," she whispered.

The basement lightbulb flickered.

An electrical buzz crinkled in the air.

The basement went dark.

Molly barreled up the stairs, her feet clomping on the wood boards. She would have to give that dream up as well. The dream that she wouldn't be haunted in a new place. Followed. By people just beyond who wanted her to listen, to give them her attention. People who were restless, anxious, and persistent. People who were dead.

I killed her.

It came out from inside of me, and I could not condemn it.

Someday, someone will find this. They will read it.

And they will discard it when they realize they have touched words written in blood.

3

Perliett

Perliett plunged her pale hands into the cleansing water in the basin, rubbing goat's milk soap on her skin and then holding her flesh under the coolness. Her throat hurt from holding back emotion. Emotion she shouldn't feel—or should she? That was only one of the conundrums of being the offspring of a devout Christian and a devout spiritualist. Death was eternal, that was agreed upon. But the finality of it, the security in it, or the desperation of it? Her mind always whirled with the unanswered and the mysticism that seemed to coincide with faith. That she was shaken was not something Perliett had any intention of revealing to George Wasziak. Thankfully, there was a distraction from her own empathetic emotion.

"Saints above!" Kenneth Braun gagged again, but this time he was holding his nose, blood seeping through the cracks between his fingers.

"Open my apothecary chest. There." Perliett tilted her head toward a wooden chair flush against the wall on which rested her dearest possession. "In the top drawer you'll find a small burlap bag. Open it. Press the moss into your nostril and it will stanch the bleeding."

Kenneth hurried toward the chest.

A bloody nose. He was terribly worked up, yet she couldn't blame the farmer who had the misfortune of stumbling upon Eunice's mutilated body as well as assisting in its retrieval. Perliett related to some of his angst, for she herself would have loved nothing more than to rest her forehead against the strong shoulder of a handsome man—*not* George Wasziak—instead of tending to Eunice Withers's dead body, but there were simply none available. So she stiffened her upper lip while Kenneth allowed his own angst to flow forth from his nostril.

"If you're giving Kenneth skull moss . . ." George's growl from the doorway stilled Kenneth's rummaging through the chest.

Perliett flicked her wrists, letting droplets fly from her wet hands. She lifted the cotton towel beside the basin and dried her skin as she turned. "It *is* moss."

"Scraped from a dead body's skull? That practice ceased centuries ago. It's defilement of the deceased." George pushed between Kenneth the farmer and Perliett's apothecary chest. He snatched the burlap bag from the man's hand. "*Don't* follow her instructions. By the time she's finished, you'll wind up with leeches crawling all over you in a bloodletting."

"Why would I blood-let someone already letting their blood?" Perliett finished helplessly. She didn't bother to correct him that she had in *no way* scraped the moss from a dead person, although that was how it once had been done. She simply thought moss was a good application of a natural product versus wasting a perfectly clean white piece of cotton.

George marched across the small examination room and dropped her bag of moss into a garbage receptacle. He retrieved a clean white bandage, pressed it against Kenneth's nose, and encouraged him to tip his head back.

"He'll choke on his blood," Perliett warned. "It will run down the back of his throat and—"

George silenced her with a look.

With George preoccupied with Kenneth, Perliett returned her attention to the indecently naked body of Eunice Withers, now covered with a sheet. They had held a tentative truce as they attempted to dissuade Kenneth Braun from hovering as they cleaned Eunice. It was unseemly and wrong that he remained. Still, he had been insistent, and to George's chagrin, Perliett had no patience for arguing with a man who had obviously not only discovered the dead woman's body, but likely was more familiar with it when she was alive too. That was obvious if George had even a lick of deductive reasoning, which apparently he did not. He didn't seem to notice the way Kenneth bit at his fingernails, blinked back tears, and trembled like a man who'd just lost his dearest possession.

That Kenneth and Eunice had been having an illicit affair was more than likely the reason Kenneth hovered. That she had announced earlier her conclusion that Eunice had *not* been with child also explained the drop of weight from Kenneth's shoulders and then the nosebleed.

Perliett bent over Eunice, studying her small nose, her ghostly pale skin, her thick lashes and dark hair. She was brunette—like Perliett herself—that dark German brunette with the deep skin tone and a delicate chin that hinted of obstinacy. Eunice Withers was known in Kilbourn as one of the most eligible women of marriageable age. An affair with a farmer would have surely infuriated her father, but then it would have made more sense for Mr. Withers to take a knife and gut Kenneth Braun rather than his own daughter. So the affair, assuming Perliett's theory was correct, did not answer for why Eunice had been brutally murdered, and—Perliett dared a look at Kenneth, whose nosebleed was coming under control now—no one could fake a nosebleed to appear innocent of murder.

"Keep pressure on your nose," George directed. "Head home. There is no reason for you to linger here. I'm certain the police will inquire of you this evening, and the circumstances in which you found Eunice will need to be recounted more than once."

"A stiff drink may calm your nerves," Perliett offered.

"*Or* a warm cup of peppermint tea," George added sternly.

"That too," she nodded. Fine. George couldn't argue that brandy would be far more valuable in calming one's nerves than peppermint, but then he had the unspoken point that it might inhibit Kenneth's ability to relay facts of the day to the police, who were still scouring the cornfield for any clues. Not to mention, word was spreading fast, and Kenneth had stated the police were spending as much time investigating the crime scene as they were trying to keep curious onlookers from engaging in their own amateur investigations. Murder in Kilbourn was entertaining, if also horrible. Many wouldn't sleep well in their beds tonight, and Kilbourn was now minus one of their prettiest young ladies.

The door closed behind the farmer, leaving Perliett alone with George, who continued to glower at her as she gently ran a comb through Eunice's snarled hair. She didn't bother to look at him, instead noting the threads of corn silk that fell from Eunice's hair down onto her shoe and then slid off to the wood floor.

"I would assume she was killed in the cornfield and her body wasn't just left there," she ventured.

"Why is that?" George growled. He was a bear. No. No, a bear was too coarse and rough. He was a . . . lion. A proud lion with absolutely no sense of imagination whatsoever.

"Because there is corn silk in her hair." Perliett lifted a strand and held it toward George. "And there were some silks encrusted in her wounds. If she had been left in the cornfield but not killed there, any silks would merely be on top of the wound, not intermingled. It's as if her assailant's knife had silks sticking to it as he—stabbed her." She choked a little on the ending of her observation.

George took the offered corn silk, eyed it, then flicked it away. "This is farmland. It could have been stuck to the knife long before they used the weapon on Miss Withers."

"She died in the cornfield," Perliett muttered under her breath.

"Pardon?" George was quick to respond.

"I said, 'You're the master of your field.'" She met his eyes. His narrowed. God had made a few errors when He'd created George Wasziak. One, He'd forgotten to give the man a smile, and two, why the last name of Wasziak? No woman in her right mind would want to adopt that surname as her own.

Her random thoughts, however insulting to the sovereignty of God, were of no help when George cleared his throat.

Perliett ceased combing Eunice's hair.

"You are not here to sleuth out the reasoning behind Miss Withers's passing," George corrected. He was so lofty and pompous, Perliett wanted to stick a pin in him and watch him deflate. "Finish cleaning her hair and then I will send someone to contact her family. They will want to dress her for their parlor and prepare for the wake."

"If they dress her, they will see the wounds. I cleaned them, but they're still there." Perliett couldn't imagine being Eunice's mother and wrapping your child's body in a dress meant for Sunday church and now clothes she would take with her to the grave. They would decompose there. Become worm-eaten rags. And then—

"Perliett." George stated her name with an unfamiliar tempering of his tone.

She snapped from her thoughts, noting that her hand rested on Eunice's forehead, and her eyes were blinking rapidly. Empathy. Empathy was the emotion that warred with the brutality of death.

"Are you all right?" His voice was doctoral.

Perliett coughed gently to clear away unwanted tears. "Yes. Yes, I'm—merely worried about the wounds to her abdomen and her mother seeing them."

"They are small, as stab wounds typically are," George observed, but he appeared to be pondering a solution.

"Small on the outside, vicious on the inside." Perliett stroked some hair from Eunice's face. "Perhaps a wrap around her abdomen? We could advise the family that it must stay there to . . . well, to preserve the body for burial? A form of mummification?"

George was expressionless as he stared at her without blinking. One minute. Perhaps another. Then, "*Mummification*? Are we Egyptian now?"

"I merely suggested it to offer an excuse for why they shouldn't remove a wrapping." Perliett could feel the hot blush creep up her neck. George Wasziak thought she was a quack, and sometimes her impulsive suggestions certainly reinforced that idea.

"Perhaps we merely state that the wrap is to be kept on to avoid shock and potential trauma to the family?"

"Yes. Yes. That," Perliett said with a nod.

The house was dark when Perliett arrived home. She was accustomed to this, in the evenings, after the sun had dipped below the horizon. The screen door squeaked as Perliett opened it. She hefted her apothecary chest onto a shelf just inside the entryway. It had been a gift from her beloved father. She'd wanted to attend medical school one day. Father hadn't been fond of the idea, instead encouraging her to dabble in medicine. Perliett would do anything for her father, including deny her own dreams. So she dabbled. She studied old medical journals, and since the age of nineteen she had begun to help others who simply couldn't afford

Dr. Wasziak's fees. Which had helped to form the Grand Canyon in their five years since acquaintanceship. George didn't trust she could learn from books alone. Truth be told, sometimes Perliett questioned whether he was right. But it wasn't as if she had attempted to perform surgery on anyone.

"Mother?" Calling softly so as not to startle her, Perliett unbuttoned her light overcoat and hung it on a coat-tree. She unpinned the hat from her hair, setting it atop the same shelf as the apothecary chest.

Perliett tiptoed quietly through the front entry of their house, her shoes making tapping noises on the wood floor. She peeked into the sitting room. It was empty. The study then. PaPa's study. It was inevitable really. She shouldn't have bothered to check anywhere else.

The door was slightly ajar. Candlelight flickered and created shadows across the floor, and as Perliett pushed the door open, more shadows danced on the dark wood-paneled walls. The curtains hanging over the window that overlooked the front garden were a heavy green velvet. They were closed, a funeral-like shroud over the room. Perliett heard the clink of crystal, as though someone's ringed hand had bumped into a decanter. A round table sat in the middle of the room, having replaced PaPa's desk over a year ago.

Four people sat around the table. One, Perliett did not recognize. Two, it surprised her to note due to their religious affiliations, were Mr. and Mrs. Hoyt from the First Baptist Church. The fourth was Mother—Mrs. Van Hilton to most—Maribeth to those who knew her closest. Even Perliett thought of her mother as Maribeth more often than not. Her mother was more of a peer. A mixture of a friend, a mother, an equal, and a mystery. She could be the proper wife of a Christian church elder, and she could rival any turbaned seer for the ability to speak with the dead. Perliett loved her mother, admired her mother, and was also—if she was being honest—a bit afraid of her mother. Especially now that PaPa was no longer there to temper Maribeth's behavior.

Eyes closed, head of full black hair tipped back, Maribeth Van Hilton raised her face toward the ceiling. The candlelight created hollows beneath her eyes and in her cheeks, which made Maribeth appear haggard, even though her natural beauty was still apparent. She had become Perliett's mother at the age of twenty, so now her forty-four-year-old widowhood made her alluring and mysterious and even a bit sensual—or so Perliett had heard whispers of from others in town. A bit awkward to hear of such, considering it was her own mother, but then Maribeth was Maribeth as much as she was Mother. They were two separate personas in the form of one being.

A circle of smoke spiraled from four candles in the middle of the table. A chain of emerald beads wove in and around them. A tall cabinet stood against the far wall, its doors open. Curtains hung inside, golden tassels holding them back. There was a chair, empty, but Perliett knew what it was for. Closet visitations weren't uncommon for Maribeth to pursue, though Perliett had never witnessed an apparition actually *use* the chair—or appear for that matter.

Perliett could hardly subdue her own shudder. She'd never forget the moment she had sequestered herself inside the study at the circular table, shortly after her father had died, as her mother summoned the afterlife. She would never fail to recall that moment in the darkness when a man's hand gripped her shoulder and squeezed it three times, just like PaPa had always done. To reassure her. In her shock, Perliett had slapped at the hand instinctively as her feet kicked outward, just before the wardrobe doors burst open to reveal nothing at all, and still somehow an energy was released into the room that curled into Perliett like a ghost's whisper. Her mother had stared at her, skin pale—almost luminescent—and their eyes had met. Perliett had run from the room, the chair toppling over from her sudden movement. Feeling her father's familiar grip should have been comforting, but somehow it wasn't—because he'd been dead for six months.

Now she scanned the room again. All the participants seemed to be in some sort of trance. She wondered sometimes if it was simple human fear that put them into such—or perhaps it was intense curiosity? An impulsive desire to utter the most horrific scream she could muster came over Perliett. Merely to see what would happen. More than likely, Mrs. Hoyt would engage in an instant attack of the vapors. Mr. Hoyt's rotund belly would smash into the table, making a candle knock over, which would set the doily under them aflame. At which point, the stranger at the table would bat at it with his massive hands he already had folded in front of him. The flames would go out. His skin would blister. Perliett would treat burns without George Wasziak glowering over her shoulder, and through it all her mother would be—

"Perliett." Maribeth's voice interrupted Perliett's imaginary circumstances. Her tone was polite but carried a thin cord of stress running through it.

Perliett blinked. She had fallen into her own sort of trance. A thick smell of incense burned her nostrils. She met the eyes of the stranger, who appeared younger than she'd first thought, but also was more likely closer to her mother's age—or George's age—than her own. She swallowed back the weirdest sensation that had risen in her throat. A heaviness on her chest . . . breathing was a challenge . . .

"Perliett." Maribeth pushed off the table, rising to her feet. She held her hands over the table to still her guests and whatever spirits lingering who Perliett had disturbed. "Darling, are you all right?"

What her mother was really asking was *Why did you disturb my séance*? But that was hardly appropriate for the time being.

Perliett cleared her throat, no longer entertaining the idea of screaming for a lark and intending to startle, but instead realizing her immature thoughts had been selfish and costly to her mother.

She dipped her head in apology. "Forgive me. I was not aware you had guests."

A candle flickered.

Mr. and Mrs. Hoyt eyed her with a stern expression. Mrs. Hoyt's lips pinched, sending wrinkles reaching out from the corners of her mouth like minuscule tree branches clawing at the rest of her pudgy face.

"I'm sorry if I have disturbed . . . anyone."

Maribeth drew in a controlled breath, her nostrils flaring a bit. Her sculpted features took on more definition as she crossed the room and engaged the gaslights. The chandelier above the round table burst into light, transforming the room from a spiritualist's cave where departed spirits converged with the living to a simple study, where bookshelves along the far wall became clear enough for titles to be read.

"I am afraid that we are finished for the evening." Maribeth's announcement was met with a mixed reaction.

Perliett managed through the sting of guilt as Mr. and Mrs. Hoyt stood. Mrs. Hoyt adjusted her skirts and tugged gloves onto her hands, and Mr. Hoyt puffed out his chest.

"We've already paid you for an evening of—"

"Yes." Maribeth dipped her head in a gracious nod. "And you shall have one. However, once the spirits have been disturbed, summoning them back is quite difficult. I'm afraid *if* your niece were to have made an appearance, her spirit has already taken respite for the night."

Mrs. Hoyt whimpered.

Mr. Hoyt grumbled under his breath.

"Thursday evening perhaps? At nine? I shall extend our gathering for an additional fifteen minutes." Maribeth did not offer other promises. One couldn't promise much on behalf of the dearly departed. They did in death whatever they wished, the same as they had in life.

Mr. and Mrs. Hoyt pushed by Perliett, who moved to the side to allow them space to exit.

Mr. Hoyt gave her a dark glare. "We'll show ourselves out." And they continued down the corridor, where it opened into the front entrance. Mr. Hoyt snatched his hat from the hall tree, his umbrella from the stand, and then draped a cloak over Mrs. Hoyt's shoulders. Front door opened, they departed, not unlike a spirit. Blustering, incomplete, and wholeheartedly unsatisfied.

"Mr. Bridgers." Maribeth addressed the stranger who had yet to rise. Perliett noticed, as she turned back to the room, that he was watching her. Assessing her if she wasn't mistaken. His dark eyes drilled into hers with the ferocity of someone who was certain she was hiding something. Perliett furrowed her brow in a questioning scowl, and Mr. Bridgers broke their contact by addressing her mother.

"Mrs. Van Hilton." He stood. His large hands matched his torso, which was broad. Muscle encased in a tailored suit. Once he finished rising to his feet, he towered over Maribeth's petite form by a good twelve inches, and over Perliett by eight. "Thank you for your time tonight."

"I assure you"—Maribeth cast Perliett a quick look to communicate her need to remain silent—"this is a rare occurrence. My daughter is very sensitive to these gatherings, and she simply wasn't aware tonight."

Perliett met Mr. Bridgers's brooding heavy-lidded eyes again. He spoke to Maribeth but refused to look away from Perliett. "I'm certain you are correct." His voice was a low rumble and sent rivers of intrigue mixed with nervous energy through her bloodstream. "I truly did not expect any grandiose visitations."

"But your aunt—" Maribeth began.

Mr. Bridgers interrupted. "My aunt has been dead going

on four years now. Another evening of silence will not make our separation any less unusual." At that, he tipped his head in dismissal at Maribeth and strode toward the door as if this study were his own, he was master of the house, and Perliett and her mother merely his house servants.

Pausing, he looked down his nose at her. "Please see me to the door." It was a command, not a request.

At Maribeth's quick nod, Perliett obeyed and despised herself for her quiet obedience. She could sense his presence looming behind her as she steered him down the hall. The front door ahead was a beacon of escape. Send the man on his way. If he were cloaked in black and hiding in a dark alleyway—if their farmland community *had* alleyways—Perliett determined he would feel far more at home.

"Where do you hail from?" she ventured. It struck her as oddly coincidental a stranger would appear in her home the same day she'd ministered to her first murdered corpse. Perliett was thankful for her long sleeves, which hid the nervous bumps that dotted her skin.

"The windy city" was all he offered in response.

Chicago.

"And you've been in Kilbourn since . . . ?" She let her question hang, daring a quick look over her shoulder. My, he was towering over her and very close.

"Since this past weekend." He reminded her of barely constrained thunder. The kind of thunder that both exhilarated you and terrified you simultaneously.

"Did you bring a hat?" Perliett noticed the hall tree was empty now that the Hoyts had departed. "Sir." She added the word because his mere presence seemed to demand it.

"I did not."

"Very well then." Perliett twisted the doorknob, opening the way to her beloved porch overlooking the yard. Moonlight made it all appear various shades of blue. Eunice Withers's image flashed across her mind again. Had she run through the dark? Illuminated by moonlight, shooting panicked glances over her shoulder before she was—

"Jasper."

"Excuse me?" Her voice squeaked.

"You may call me Jasper," Mr. Bridgers said.

"I'd not inquired, nor had I intimated that I was concerned with your name." The words escaped her as easily as if she were goading George. But Mr. Bridgers wasn't George. Not in the slightest. He wasn't irksome or even arrogant. He was . . . superior. Even she knew it, though she had no idea why.

There was a flicker of a twist at the corner of his mouth. "Very well . . . Perliett."

It was bold. Offensive. And too familiar. Yet he used her name anyway, though they'd never been properly introduced. He used it as if he knew her better than she knew herself. Only he didn't.

He *didn't.*

Perliett assured herself of this as the man descended the porch steps without another word and disappeared into the moonlight.

4

Molly

The gravity in Trent's voice negated the hurt Molly was already drinking away with her morning coffee. Their first night in the farmhouse had been unromantic. She'd allowed herself the teensiest smidgeon of hope, which dissolved when she crawled into a sleeping bag on top of their bare mattress at midnight. She'd even waited to take her bedtime prescription. The one that helped her sleep. But Trent had stayed in the shed outside long past midnight, cutting a sheet of drywall to patch the downstairs bathroom wall. A pipe had leaked eons before they bought the place. It'd been fixed. The wall hadn't.

Now Molly sucked down one more gulp of coffee and her morning prescription—an antidepressant—and muttered "I'm on my way" into the phone before hanging up. Trent had called her from a neighboring farm where he was, out of the goodness of his heart, helping with chores while their neighbors were out of town. This before he continued on his way to his job at Clapton Bros. Farms, the monopoly of farmer families in Kilbourn, Michigan. There were Claptons everywhere in Kilbourn. The first farming Clapton had arrived there in the 1940s, and since then it seemed a mass migration of them had descended on Kilbourn so that anyone who was anyone was related to or bore the name of Clapton.

Molly snatched a stocking cap from the table where she'd thrown it last night and tugged it over her hair. It wasn't cold out. Her hair was just awful. Half curly, half straight, half frizz. If a troll and a princess had a child, Molly would be it. She was reminded of this when the screen door scraped against her backside as she crossed the threshold to hurry outside. Her rear had inherited the genetics of the troll—unfortunately.

She rammed her feet into rain boots with bumblebees in plastic print all over them and pushed open the exterior screen door. Humid August heat slammed into her face—Florida had nothing on Michigan—along with the familiar but pungent scent of manure from the neighboring farm's field. Corn stretched in rows across the road. Their own white barn heralded nothing but the omen of future chores.

The neighboring farm wasn't that far away, and Trent hadn't gotten their ATV up and running since it needed a new spark plug. She'd have to use her legs. Curse exercise. It was hard enough to rise and get going in the morning, let alone trudge down a country road. Gravel crunched under her rubber boots as Molly hiked down the road, careful to stay on the side in case of oncoming traffic. Traffic? It was six-thirty in the morning. The only traffic out there would be local. She neared the driveway of the farm. Trent's truck was idling at the end. He stood at the culvert, hands on his hips.

Ten years ago, Molly's heart would have stopped at the sight of Trent Wasziak. Tall, muscled, wearing beat-up jeans with a navy-blue T-shirt hanging on his hips and barely skimming his biceps. Tan arms. Brown hair streaked with blond, with a baseball cap boasting the brand of farm machinery preferred by his employer. But now? She knew what it was like to have his body wrapped around hers, to be held by him, to have him kiss her just behind her left earlobe where it both tickled and entranced. It was heart-stopping . . . she missed him. Did he miss her?

"There's a body in the ditch." Trent held his palm out toward her to slow her, his phone held to his ear.

He said it so matter-of-factly that it took a few seconds to register. A body in the ditch. Not roadkill like a dead deer or possum, but he'd said *body*, implying it was a human. Molly froze, not so much out of respect for his outstretched hand, but because the impact of what he said cleared her mind of anything related to them.

"A body?" Molly heard her voice squeak.

Trent waved her off as he spoke into the phone. 911. Body in the ditch. No, he just found it. Sparrowtail Road.

Trent was giving the fire number to the farm.

Molly inched closer.

A culvert skirted the driveway on both sides. Anyone driving off the edge would have their vehicle tilting dangerously and their tire lodged in such a way they wouldn't have any traction to drive out of the predicament. Tall grasses, including dandelions, thistle, and some wild parsnip grew waist-high. Weeds tangled around an old beer can, and a receipt someone had tossed from their vehicle was muddy and pressed around the stem of a thistle.

There it was. Death.

And she hadn't sensed it.

Molly drew her hand over her mouth as she leaned over the culvert to stare into the ditch. The wild plants were matted down, then bent around the body as if to create some sort of barely there shelter against the elements. Sirens in the distance met Molly's ears, but she had difficulty compartmentalizing them as she stared into the gray face of a young woman.

"Yeah, I can hear them coming," Trent responded to the 911 operator.

Molly took a step toward the culvert.

Trent's hand grasped her elbow to hold Molly back. "Correct," he said to the operator. "I can tell that she's dead."

She.

Molly's gaze grazed the snarled long hair that fanned over the face with the open eyes, a now-milky blue. Staring into the sky with a startling blankness, the corpse was spattered with mud, both arms at odd angles where her body had fallen. The woman was dressed in blue shorts. Her shirt was a button-up oxford now pulled halfway up and revealing her midriff. There was no purse beside her. She did have one flip-flop on her left foot, but it was missing from her right, and Molly couldn't spot it in the weeds.

"Someone dumped her here," Molly muttered. She squatted at the culvert's edge. The dead gaze of the girl didn't waver, didn't move.

"Don't touch anything," Trent warned.

Molly nodded without looking at him. Of course she wouldn't. Not a thing. She fixated on the dead woman's eyes. Eyes that seemed to be frozen with their last vision burned into them. Nausea coiled in Molly's stomach. This was someone's daughter. Someone's sister. Somewhere someone was looking for her.

She heard a snap beside her, like a light footstep. She felt the brush of a breeze on the back of her neck, and Trent's voice waned into a distant echo. Still fixated on the body, Molly's breathing became a cadence, *one-two-three-four* in, *four-three-two-one* out.

Find her.

Molly heard the voice of the dead girl. Like a whisper, a breath in her ear, she heard the woman's voice.

Find her.

Molly's heartbeat pounded, thrumming against the words. The dead don't speak. They don't talk. They don't interact with the living.

She squeezed her eyes shut, blocking out the vacant stare of the young woman who hadn't really just blinked. She hadn't. Molly was certain of it.

Find her.

This time the voice was clear. Molly's eyes snapped open. "Find *who*?" she answered.

"Molly?" Trent interrupted.

The moment broke. The breeze dissipated.

"Molly!" Trent hauled her to her feet as she rocked forward on her tiptoes, her squatting form losing its balance and falling forward toward the corpse twisted in the grass.

Molly fought against black shutters that were closing over her eyes. She clung to Trent's arm as he pulled her up.

"I shouldn't have called you." His blue eyes burrowed into hers, concerned and asking so many unspoken questions. But all he said was "We can't disturb the body."

"I have to find her," Molly whispered. She reached up and fingered Trent's chin, rough with whisker stubble, her thumb and forefingers moving together. "I have to," she repeated.

"What are you talking about?" Trent's brows furrowed in concern and confusion. His fingers on her arm squeezed until they pinched her skin just enough to startle Molly from her stupor. She blinked rapidly, pulling away from her husband. His touch was like fire on her skin. He had no idea how he awakened her, sharpened her nerves. The good ones and the bad ones. The ones that revived the fantastic memories of puppy love and sweet, sexy romance, and the bad ones that brought back the memories of dark nights curled on the bathroom floor, Trent's agonizing silence, and the endless calls to the doctor.

"Please don't touch me," she said, squirming away from him. From all Trent represented. Happiness she didn't deserve to have. Sadness she was cursed to live in.

He didn't know. He couldn't know. Not what it was like to see their faces every day. Hear their cries. Yet they weren't there. The dead. *Their* dead. Hers and Trent's. Their babies had left them forever.

Trent had moved on.

She would never.

Molly stared into their past with the filmy-eyed gaze of the corpse in the ditch. Unblinking, unmoving, unwilling to close her eyes to rest.

Hours drifted by. Molly watched from the window of Trent's truck as the forensics team lifted a black body bag from the ditch, its midsection lower as they hoisted it onto a cart. Yellow tape cordoned off the area. Three different news teams were half blocking the road, their cameras held by eager operators. A reporter stood under the maple tree that bordered the lawn and the road. She hadn't asked if she could stand on private property, but apparently was opting to ask for forgiveness later if reprimanded.

Molly glanced at her phone, which she'd laid on the passenger seat. She'd just gotten off a call with the Bensons, who owned this small hobby farm. They were away on vacation, and boy, they had not expected their travel to be so overturned. Yes, they would continue to feed the animals until the Bensons returned home. Yes, she and Trent were okay. Yes, they'd given the police the Bensons' contact information. That they were away on vacation instantly cleared them of suspicion. It'd been an awkward call nonetheless, but with Trent preoccupied with the police, Molly had been the one available to take their call.

Molly knew she'd learn nothing from the investigation. She chewed on the end of a stick of beef jerky she'd found in Trent's lunch box, her other arm hugging her middle. The window was like a television, and the scene outside some sort of wreckage she couldn't peel her eyes from. She'd never forget the young woman in the ditch. Never forget the staring eyes void of soul and life. A story violently cut short—

A knock on the driver's side window startled Molly from her stupor. She rolled it down—that was how old Trent's truck was. No bells or whistles at all.

"Hi." She met her husband's squinted gaze.

"You doing okay?"

"I'm fine." She was better than the girl in the body bag.

Trent mustered a smile. He patted the truck door. "They've released me to get back to work." That was the pitfall of farming, and even local law enforcement understood. You couldn't just not show up at the farm. The cows would suffer, crops, chores . . . they all had to be done. Rain or shine. Sick or well. Alive or dead. It was like a marriage—only better in some ways. The animals appreciated you. The land—well, the land took more often than not.

"I need to get the horses fed here and then head to the farm." *The* farm. The big farm. His employers, the Clapton brothers, had a massive farm—three actually. It was a multimillion-dollar family estate, and it made every other family farm in the region seem paltry by comparison.

"Okay." Molly nodded. "I talked to the Bensons," she added.

Trent nodded. "Yeah, the cops will be in contact with them too. I'm guessing they'll need to come back home. Sucks to have a vacation end like that."

"It's not their fault someone chose their ditch to dispose of the body."

"Investigations don't play favorites" was Trent's only reply. He studied her for a moment. "Want to wait for me to finish the chores and then I'll give you a ride back to the house?"

"No." She shook her head and mustered the willpower to shake herself back into the mental capacity to live today as it was, not dwell in the past and on what she didn't have, all that they had lost. "I'll walk."

"'Kay." Trent stepped aside and opened the door for her.

Molly jumped down, and her boots ground against the

gravel. She looked up at Trent, who was a few inches taller, and for a moment she almost had the courage to just meld into his chest and wrap her arms around his waist. But that invisible, awkward barrier was between them. She chose not to, but instead tugged her T-shirt down to hide her oversized backside and hoped Trent didn't have any hot female farming co-workers she didn't know about.

"The police said they'd call if they have more questions, but that you can go for now. I doubt they'll need you. You didn't find the body." Trent shut the truck door behind her. "Still, keep your phone on you."

"I always do." And she did.

Trent's hand came up, hesitated, then fell back down at his side.

The absence of his touch made her ache.

"Well—have a good day then." He ended with a lame raising of his eyebrows.

A good day. Sort of hard to do as she passed the cart with the dead woman's body encased in plastic. Molly paused and stared at it, as if she could see through the bag to the person beneath it. Her eyes would be closed now. The forensics team would have made sure she was transported properly, all evidence being acquired here at the scene and what was left on the body waiting for the medical examiner's assessment.

Find her.

Molly froze, staring at the body bag. The voice again. So clear. So urgent. She looked around her. Authorities milled around, all with a purpose. Detective. Police. Forensics. Had no one heard the voice?

"Ma'am."

Molly jumped.

A police officer looked kindly at her. Kindly but firmly. "We need you to move along now."

"Yes." The moment felt out of body. It wasn't she that moved her legs forward, acquiescing to the instructions to leave the scene. It wasn't her breath that filled the surrounding air, echoed in her ears, and captured her focus. She could feel herself staying behind, holding hands with the dead woman, even as Molly's feet moved her body toward the road. Toward the farmhouse she never wanted. Toward her life that was haunted by ghosts of her own.

5

Perliett

Funerals were, after all, a necessary inconvenience. This was Maribeth Van Hilton's mantra, and Perliett could see it barely concealed behind the sorrowful expression carefully positioned on her mother's face.

Eunice Withers was to be buried in the middle of the cemetery. A mound of dirt mixed with green sod had been ripped from the earth to make a place for the unfortunate young woman. Perliett lifted her eyes, Eunice's casket a barrier between herself and the man her vision locked with. George. He was a nuisance, and even now he glowered at her. It wasn't as if *she* were the one who had stabbed the very life's blood from Eunice and thrown her in the cornfield like a forgotten sack of potatoes.

Perliett winced. Sometimes she was very glad people could not read her thoughts. A sideways glance at her mother affirmed Maribeth couldn't read them either. Which was helpful, considering her mother could *hear* many things otherworldly that no one else could. She knew Maribeth was attuned to the spirits even now. Perhaps Eunice would step forth, speak to Maribeth, and provide an element of comfort to Eunice's grieving family. This was why Perliett's mother wasn't overly fond of funerals. For Maribeth, communication did not cease with the dead but only shifted into a different medium.

The reverend's baritone voice droned on, reciting Scriptures Perliett could barely remember, let alone abide. Paltry comforts, words were, when faced with the loss of a precious one. It didn't matter who spoke them either. Whether coming from a fellow mourner or God himself, words were hardly comforting when the heart had shattered into a thousand pieces.

Perliett scanned the guests. The shroud of black was dismal, and Perliett shifted, listening to the soft rustle of her own silk dress that flowed straight to the tops of her black-leather-clad feet. Eunice Withers's family was comprised of three girls: Angelica, the eldest; Eunice, the now-dead middle one; and Millie, the youngest. Perliett noted the consternation on Millie's face. She was perhaps seventeen? Porcelain-faced, rose-lipped, delicate features, not unlike Eunice's. It was Angelica who'd inherited her father's less fortunate genes with the mousy-brown hair and homely features. Yes, it would be Millie's beauty that would now step into Eunice's shoes as a desirable and marriageable young woman coming into her own. Poor girl. That a death would be responsible for ushering Millie into life's experiences was disheartening.

"Did you ever notice you resemble a Withers daughter?" Maribeth's whisper shocked Perliett, and she jerked away from her mother.

The reverend continued speaking as the two women exchanged harried glances. Maribeth's beseeching Perliett to consider her observation, and Perliett's pleading for her mother not to disturb the peace with her superstitions.

"It was merely an observation," Maribeth whispered again.

Perliett squeezed her mother's hand, which to anyone else

appeared to be offering comfort, yet the squeeze was entirely too tight for that. Dark hair and blue eyes did *not* constitute a resemblance, and why Maribeth found it fascinating enough to compare her own daughter to a dead woman was a bit disconcerting.

Thankful that Maribeth seemed to be biting her tongue, Perliett allowed herself to renew her observations of the funeral-goers. A man mingled with the church guests. His head was bare, unlike the other men in attendance. His dark overcoat was familiar, and in the daylight, though the sun was currently behind the clouds, his features were more definable than the other night during her mother's interrupted séance. Why in heaven's name was Mr. Bridgers attending the funeral of a young woman he couldn't possibly know? It was beyond Perliett's imaginative abilities. She narrowed her eyes, clutching at her handbag's strings, her gloved fingers toying with its tassels. He was staring directly at her. Jasper Bridgers's deep-set eyes were black. Probably a dark brown, really, but from where she stood, they appeared to be black. His angular face was chiseled, his forehead broad, his dark hair rakish and boldly unkempt. She refused to look away, though every ounce of the blood in her body had thickened to a nervous *chugalug* through her veins.

Perliett.

To her chagrin, Mr. Bridgers mouthed her name, drawing attention to his fine mouth, his clean-shaven face, and her own name on his tongue, though the word had not been spoken.

The reverend had reached the "ashes to ashes" part of the eulogy, but Perliett barely heard him. She looked down at her shoes in a hurry, desperate to break the penetrating stare from the stranger, which was so much more unnerving than that of George Wasziak's. At the thought of him, Perliett searched out the doctor, only to find he was eyeing Jasper Bridgers—no, he was surveying all the attendees. Perhaps his thoughts mirrored her own. That the murderer might have joined the mourners to gloat over his handiwork in anonymity.

That she might share a thought with the doctor irritated Perliett. She made the error of offering a soft snort of derision, which earned her quick looks from those around her. Their censure brought Perliett back to the reality that she stood at the graveside of Eunice Withers. Slain Eunice Withers. Death from tuberculosis would have been far more tolerable than this. Murder wasn't palatable to anyone.

Finally, the reverend ended his sermon about eternal life, and a man at each corner lowered the casket into the open grave. It settled into the earth with a thud that made the finality of Eunice's current condition that much more burdensome. Mr. Withers, Eunice's father, tossed a handful of dirt onto Eunice's casket, and then her other family members followed suit. Such a mournful sound, the dirt colliding with the lid that covered the woman's corpse. Mrs. Withers appeared to barely stand as she hung on Angelica's husband's arm. Her son-in-law, Errol, was helpful to Mrs. Withers, and he even offered Angelica his other arm.

Condolences were mumbled next, embraces offered, handshakes, and the like. All habitual ways humanity offered some sort of physical connection to those left behind, who could no longer reach their loved one. Could no longer feel the warmth of their skin or the beat of their heart.

"It makes one wonder what her last thoughts were." Jasper Bridgers's voice rumbled in her ear and moved a curl at the base of her hairline. He had come from nowhere, or so it seemed.

Perliett didn't gift him with the grace of her focus, mostly because she was a puddle of nerves. She let him interpret it as indifference.

"What a morbid thing to say, Mr. Bridgers."

Her rebuke had little effect on him.

"And yet everyone considers it. That last thought, that moment before the soul slips away from the body and becomes what it was meant to be. Free. For eternity."

"Or"—George Wasziak's baritone burst into the moment with the rudeness of, well, George Wasziak—"the soul faces the good Lord only to find there's no recompense great enough that can be offered and thus the person is rebuked from God's presence."

"To then burn in the lake of fire?" Mr. Bridgers's tone didn't change.

They sandwiched Perliett, both their shoulders almost touching hers with the three of them looking forward, observing the gatherers as they dispersed.

"Or perhaps such souls linger here, left with unfinished business." Perliett's offering to the conversation was met with a snort from George and a nod from Mr. Bridgers.

"Absent from the body is to be present with the Lord," George said.

"Or to burn to a crisp in hell, according to your theory," Mr. Bridgers goaded. "I prefer lingering with unfinished business."

"As would most," George didn't hesitate to add, "were it an option."

"Come now." Perliett gave a small wave of her gloved hand. "Sparring about the afterlife is as ludicrous as assuming one can pinpoint the moment the world began."

"Was created," George corrected.

"Or evolved," Mr. Bridgers said. "Darwin has his merits."

"If you're a fool." George stiffened, and Perliett felt it. Felt the warmth of the doctor next to her and the searing heat from the presence of the man on the other side of her.

"For pity's sake!" Perliett denounced them both and then clapped a hand over her mouth as several of the gatherers jerked their heads up in surprise at the outburst. "For pity's sake," she repeated, this time hissing at both men. "You are sparring like schoolboys. This is a funeral, and you should both respect it as such."

Mr. Bridgers agreed to Perliett's rebuke with a nod of his fine head.

George stared down his nose at her. "Who is this *friend* of yours?" He gave a cool tilt of his head toward Mr. Bridgers.

Perliett drew back. "He's not my *friend*, and I've absolutely no idea why he's at Eunice's funeral."

"I'm hurt," Jasper Bridgers said. "As a new member of the community, isn't giving condolences, even to strangers, my due diligence?"

"He . . . you . . ." Perliett fumbled for words.

"Due diligence or intrepid curiosity?" George said, echoing Perliett's unspoken thoughts.

"Is it a sin if it were a bit of both?" Mr. Bridgers's thick dark eyebrow quirked upward.

"It most definitely is not." Maribeth stepped into the conversation, directing her attention to George. "As for *who* Mr. Bridgers is, he is associated with my work."

"Your work?" The raised eyebrow said all it needed to. The good doctor had made no secret that he disapproved of Maribeth's spiritualism with about as much fervor as he did Perliett's "quackery." He was thoroughly unlikable and on so many levels.

"Have the authorities considered," Maribeth said, ignoring the doctor's censure, "consulting with me regarding Eunice's passing?"

It had crossed Perliett's mind, but suggesting it to George was not whom she'd imagined first raising the idea to.

He frowned.

"Perhaps she herself would share with us her last thoughts," Mr. Bridgers said, breaking in.

"And who was responsible for her demise," Maribeth added.

"Have you ever attempted to contact a murder victim before?" Mr. Bridgers asked.

"I have not," Maribeth answered.

George tilted his chin up, lofty in all his religiously pious airs. "The devil can communicate whatever he wishes to you in whatever form he takes. I would no sooner trust his witness through an apparition than that of someone who is a perpetual liar."

Perliett had had enough of George, frankly of the entire conversation, and she was determined to end it.

But Mr. Bridgers interrupted before she was able.

"I shall discuss this with the authorities. It is a curious and most interesting idea, Mrs. Van Hilton." He offered Maribeth his elbow, and Perliett's mother took it. Leading her forward, he engaged her in a conversation that drifted away with them but was as purposeful as the steps they took.

This time, George's shoulder did brush hers, and Perliett would have stepped away had his fingers not grazed her elbow in what she was certain was an absentminded gesture meant to stop her. His touch irritated her skin while at the same time she noticed he was wearing cologne. Something he never had done in the past, and it smelled like . . . cedarwood and juniper? Masculine. Disturbing.

"I would advise your mother not to become involved in the death of Eunice Withers."

Perliett turned to look across her shoulder at the doctor. "Whyever not? If she can help—"

"Help? *Hinder* is the more apt description. Not to mention, if the killer believed there was any credence to her séances, then she may position herself in the center of his attention."

Perliett winced at his logic. "My mother is a powerful woman."

"In her beliefs, yes, but physically? Could she ward off a stronger person wielding a knife with the force of the man who attacked Miss Withers?" George turned to her then, his fingers releasing their light hold on her elbow. Perliett felt their absence. He tipped his head toward her, and for the first time, Perliett had to credit him with genuine concern and not simply arrogance. "We disagree on most things, Perliett, but even you must admit there is danger in seeking after the dead. Their spirits. Whether from the devil himself or from his ambassadors here, who are very much alive and very deviant in their intent. Must you toy with either of them?"

Perliett had nothing to say. She stared into George's black eyes and wondered, for the first time perhaps, if Dr. Wasziak might actually be making a valid point.

Thunder rumbled through the night sky, but the pounding on the front door had stolen Perliett's attention. She tied her wrapper around her, passing Maribeth in the hallway. After an exchange of concerned looks, both women moved in unison.

Gaslights illuminated the hallway, making the furniture cast angular shadows across the floor. A large portrait of her grandfather eyed her like a ghoul as she passed him. She felt certain, as always, his eyes followed her from his frozen position within the frame. She met him only once as a child. He had made a dark impression on her. Even now, her mother's father seemed to know things he shouldn't—and he was dead.

She reached the door, Maribeth on her heels, just as another pounding added to the sudden downpour of rain.

"It's Mrs. Withers." The messenger was a gangly young man, puffing from his urgency. His hair was damp from rain. "She's crying nonstop. Mr. Withers sent me to get help. We don't know if she's in pain or losing her mind since Eunice was killed."

Perliett recognized the messenger as one of Mr. Withers's

few farmhands. She waved him off the front porch and the rain that was spattering them from its ricocheting off the steps.

"Give me a moment. I will change and get my things."

Maribeth interjected, "There's lightning and it's pouring rain out there. I should come with you."

Perliett paused for a moment, considering. Then she shook her head. "I doubt tonight would be wise to approach Eunice's spirit on behalf of her mother."

Maribeth toyed with a ribbon at the neckline of her housecoat. "But if it would bring her comfort . . ."

"Or perhaps upset her further?" Perliett wasn't of a specific opinion as much as she questioned the wisdom of the timing. For some, seeking the other side brought immense comfort, while for others it could be upsetting. And also upsetting if the deceased loved one determined not to make a connection.

"Do as you feel is right." Perliett left it to Maribeth's discretion and hurried toward her room, leaving her mother behind with the young man.

Several minutes later, she'd slipped into proper clothes, rejecting her corset for reasons of time. Perliett gripped her apothecary chest and hurried back toward the front door. Maribeth waited there with the lad, who shifted his weight from foot to foot. His expression was worried and then relieved when Perliett came into his view.

Maribeth was still clothed in her nightdress. "I've decided to stay. My very presence may upset Mrs. Withers with the potential of what I bring with me. Perhaps it's best if you find out her state of mind before I offer my ministrations."

"Very well." Perliett experienced a slight pang of disappointment. She would appreciate her mother's company since it was the dead of night. Yet it was too urgent to voice that concern now. Besides, if she was being honest, nighttime house calls were few and far between for Perliett. Most preferred George—*Dr.* Wasziak—simply because of the letters following his name, the university education, and the fact that he was a man.

It did come back to bite when Perliett realized many considered her more of a health enthusiast than someone qualified to help. Certainly, for years, home remedies, scientific remedies, and even mystical remedies had assisted in an individual's healing.

"Ma'am?" The lad waiting to take her to the Withers farm interrupted her meandering thoughts.

"Yes." She nodded. "Yes. Urgency. I'll need my cloak." Perliett wasn't wasting further time on justifying why she was qualified to make a middle-of-the-night house call. Mrs. Withers wasn't injured, she was grieving. It didn't take an M.D. at the end of one's name to assist with grief.

Maribeth helped Perliett slip into it, buttoning it at her neck. "Take my hat." Maribeth's black veiled hat from the funeral still hung on the hall tree. Perliett accepted it, pinning it to her haphazard updo.

"I'll be fine, Mother," she reassured Maribeth. They met each other's eyes, and Maribeth's reflected her concern.

"I don't have a good feeling . . ." Truth be told, Maribeth rarely had good feelings. Instead, she relied on her senses and influences, and Perliett respected that.

Then come with me. Perliett's thoughts were too belated now to do any good. The waiting lad was dancing from foot to foot with impatience. "I'll be fine," she voiced instead.

The farmhand ushered her toward a buggy, and within minutes they were careening through the thunderstorm toward the Withers farm.

Lightning streaked the sky as they hurtled down the driveway. Perliett clutched the seat for fear of catapulting off, and while she appreciated her driver's devotion to meeting the emergency, the speed at which he pushed the horse was breakneck.

They rolled to a stop in front of the farmhouse. Rain pelted Perliett, as she didn't bother to wait but climbed from the buggy on her own.

"Thank you!" she called to the lad and hurried to the front door. It opened almost immediately, Millie's pretty face greeting her with tear stains on her cheeks.

"Oh, I'm so glad you're here." She ushered Perliett inside. "Papa is with Mama in their bedroom. Errol says that Angelica wasn't in much better condition, only she finally fell asleep, so my sister is no help to us. Mama is inconsolable, moaning and writhing. We don't know what to do!"

Heavy footsteps sounded on the stairs. "Is the doctor here?" Mr. Withers's deep voice rivaled the thunder for its low rumble.

Perliett met the frantic face of Mr. Withers as he appeared on the stairs. He froze. His graying hair stood out in spikes around his head from ruffling it with nervous fingers. His face was as white as a sheet, and his eyes darkened at the sight of her.

"I told that boy to get the doctor!" he barked.

"Miss Van Hilton is less expensive . . ." Millie started.

Perliett felt her face droop with hurt at the unintended insult. Less expensive. Mr. Withers was a well-known miser of a farmer, but the idea she was chosen because she cost less than George was disheartening. It had nothing to do with faith in her abilities. Equally disheartening was that the Withers family was even willing to consider cost at the peril of their mother and wife's welfare.

"Take her to your mother." Mr. Withers barreled past them and disappeared into another room.

Perliett exchanged glances with Millie, tightening her hold on her box of supplies. They maneuvered the stairs quickly, reaching the upstairs hallway. She tried to gather her wits after having her pride trampled on by Mr. Withers.

Mrs. Withers writhed on her bed, the sheets torn from

the bottom of the mattress and rolled into a ball. Her body was damp with sweat, her graying dark hair sticking to her cheeks. She clutched a shawl and moaned, pressing it into her nose and mouth as if she intended to suffocate herself with it.

"It's Eunice's shawl," Millie explained in a whisper. Her blue eyes grew more wide and more worried. "She won't let it go, and she keeps weeping into it."

"I understand." Perliett moved to the edge of the bed, setting her box on a nearby chair. "Mrs. Withers?" she inquired.

The woman only moaned into the shawl.

"Mrs. Withers," Perliett tried again, "I am here to help you. Are you in any pain?"

Mrs. Withers opened her eyes for a moment, focused a cloudy gaze on Perliett, then closed them again. Perliett bent over the woman, whose moaning only continued, muffled by the violet-colored shawl pressed against her mouth.

"I need to know if you're in pain," Perliett said.

This time, Mrs. Withers mumbled through an agonizing sob, "My girl. My *girl*!"

Perliett took the liberty of running her hands down Mrs. Withers's body. A quick examination revealed no wounds and drew no cries of pain from the woman.

"Is she going to be all right?" Millie breathed.

"Oh yes." It was a flimsy reassurance, and Perliett knew Millie recognized that. Still, that was more comforting than *No, your mother is losing her mind with grief*. And she was. That much was apparent, and there wasn't much medically she could do outside of . . .

Perliett straightened and looked to her apothecary chest. Flipping the latches at both ends, she opened it. There. She reached for the brown bottle, its label printed in block letters.

"What is that?" Millie asked over her shoulder.

Perliett didn't mind. It was natural for Mrs. Withers's daughter to be so concerned, especially considering all they'd been through this last week.

"Heroin," Perliett answered as she prepared to uncap it. "We use it for various things, but one is to 'give optimism to the mind,' as the maker here claims." She tapped the bottle with a well-trimmed fingernail.

"Oh." Millie's voice was small because of her lack of comprehension. "I've not heard of it."

"As you shouldn't have!" George Wasziak's voice filled the room with his offended tone. He pushed his way in with an explanation to Millie's shocked expression. "Your brother-in-law, Errol, had me fetched after he realized your messenger was retrieving Miss Van Hilton."

At Millie's concerned "Oh," he added, "Errol will cover my fees. You've no need to concern your father with them."

Millie visibly relaxed, but Perliett stiffened. She stood poised with the bottle of liquid heroin in one hand, a spoon in the other.

Mrs. Withers curled into a fetal position, pressing the suffocating shawl against her face.

George glowered. Well, he always glowered, but this time there was a dark ferocity to it. "I recommend capping that monstrous liquid instantly."

"Would you prefer I use the tablet form?" Perliett couldn't help but poke at him, even though it was highly inappropriate at a patient's bedside.

"For all that's holy!" The man had the audacity to snatch the bottle from her hand. A small amount of liquid dripped from the bottle.

"Return that at once!" Perliett could match his glower and it took little trying. He brought out the worst in her.

George fisted the bottle and held it up with a singular firm shake for emphasis. "Any good doctor knows this has a darkly addictive side to it."

"Do they? Really? And yet it's still available to doctors to administer and even sell to their patients?"

George's eyes blackened more than they already were.

"And *you* obtained your own bottle *how*? You're not a licensed medical practitioner. You're not even a *practitioner*."

Perliett tilted her chin upward. "That is no business of yours."

George strode to the window, shoved it upward, and in one swift motion tilted the bottle and allowed the heroin to drain out.

"How dare you!" Perliett chased after him but was too late.

"How dare *I*?" George stuffed the empty bottle into his coat pocket and waved his hand toward Mrs. Withers. "You're the one masquerading as a doctor—which she is *not*!" He shot his last comment at Millie. "The sooner you accept that your abilities are limited, the better." This was directed to Perliett.

She had nothing to say.

No. No, that wasn't true. She had plenty to say, but not in front of poor Mrs. Withers or Millie. She allowed George to step between her and Mrs. Withers's bedside. He bent over her, checked her pulse and other vitals, then opened his own bag of treatments.

"Have you administered any medications to Mrs. Withers at all?" he barked.

"No." Perliett pursed her lips and crossed her arms over her shirtwaist. If disdain could ooze from her body, it would be a goopy mess trailing along the floor. But she held it in and allowed *Dr.* Wasziak to do his thing.

The painfully honest truth was, he was a very good doctor. There was no reason not to trust his expertise. He just butted in when he felt he had precedence—which was *always*. She didn't mean her patients any harm, and heavens knew heroin was a perfectly fine treatment for many ailments! Cocaine was more typically used for pain or coughing, and it treated well but had its own set of other ill effects. Heroin was an appropriate replacement and—

Perliett snapped to attention as George initiated his instructions. He was gentler with Millie. The lines on his face softened. His voice tempered. Even his shoulders stooped in concerned care.

"I know we'd like to give her a sleeping aid or something, but I am very hesitant to attach a patient to those. They have many qualities that worry me. I would recommend lavender tea instead, and I will give you a small vial of frankincense. Apply the frankincense every few hours to her wrists, her nostrils, the base of her ears and throat."

"And what will that do?" Millie breathed.

"It will help calm her," Perliett interjected. She would have suggested it herself, but she felt so awful for the grieving mother that heroin seemed far more merciful than the oil derived from dried tree sap.

George muttered a few more instructions, with the young woman nodding in agreement. Within moments, Perliett found herself ushered from the room, George carrying both his bag and her now-closed box. They passed Mr. Withers on the stairs. The man gave George a nod and a grumble of thanks, completely ignoring Perliett, his shoulder nudging hers as he passed her on the staircase.

"Your cloak?" George looked around the front room.

"I am perfectly capable of donning my cloak." Perliett tilted her nose up. She didn't want to match the man's arrogance with her own, but he was so vexing! She snatched her cloak from where it hung over the back of a chair. Draping it around her shoulders, she fastened the button at the neck. A black button with a delicately braided rope to attach it to the garment. She was proud of this cloak. Even if it was black.

"I will see you home." George opened the front door, apparently accepting that none of the Withers were in any frame of mind to bid them farewell or think of offering transport back to her home. Their farmhand had long since disappeared, probably already tucked into his bed.

Perliett eased past George and onto the Withers front

porch. Crickets sang in the bushes that pressed against the porch rail. A tin bucket—probably used by Mr. Withers as a spittoon—reflected what little moonlight was in the sky. The barn loomed large across the drive. A dark shadow against an equally dark sky where only slight, puffed edges of clouds could be seen. Starlight had been snuffed by the oppressive blanket of dew in the air now that the ferocity of the storm had passed.

She took the porch stairs with confidence, even as Perliett eyed the driveway, the road, and the copious miles of cornfields that bordered the sides. It was a mere two-mile walk to her house. The sky spat a bit of drizzle, but wetness didn't cause her to melt.

"I'm quite capable of walking home." It was a late opposition to George's high-handed declaration, probably meant with the intent of a gentleman. Perliett reached out to take her apothecary chest.

He held it hostage, and the darkness did nothing to enhance his already-stern features.

"And what other *remedies* do you have in here?"

Perliett took a step toward him, reaching for her belonging. "I have frankincense."

"Mmm."

"Among other things," she added unnecessarily.

"Let's see you home." He refused to relinquish her case.

"My house is not far. The walk will do me good." Perliett gave the yard a nervous scan. As much as she disliked the man, there was something to be said about riding in his buggy versus hiking down a deserted road lined with corn higher than her head in the middle of the night.

George started for his buggy, which instigated her to follow since he still had her apothecary chest in hand. "A week ago, you and I spent time together—"

It irritated Perliett that she could feel herself blushing.

He was still talking. "—over a dead woman's corpse.

Brutally murdered, and you yourself counted eight stab wounds. This tells me that the killer was very aggressive or very angry."

"Why?" Perliett danced around to his left side, where her box swung from his grip.

George didn't bother to offer her any looks at all but fixed his gaze on the darkness beyond and the outline of his horse and buggy. "Because one stab to her aortic artery and she would have bled out. It hardly required seven more thrusts."

"But if the killer knew nothing about the artery . . ." She let her words hang as she moved to take her box from him.

George tugged it away. "Even if he didn't, why so many wounds? Why not a gunshot? Poison? Something less personal?"

"For heaven's sakes, I don't know." Perliett leaped forward to retrieve her supplies as George hoisted the chest onto the seat of his buggy. She pulled it toward herself, banging it into her thigh. "And I will walk."

This time, George's hand settled on her wrist.

"Unhand me!" she protested.

There was irony in his voice. "Unhand you? How very Shakespearean of you. Perliett, use that head of yours that you're so proud of and consider the fact that there is someone still walking free who has more than once plunged a knife into a woman's midsection."

He used too many words.

Perliett allowed herself the privilege of a delicate snort. "There's a killer who stabbed a woman. I comprehend this."

George tugged her closer, and this time Perliett's breath caught. She felt his glare, even though the night shrouded it.

"I do not want to retrieve your mutilated body from a cornfield tomorrow morning. Do as I ask."

She gaped at him. How stupid. How stupid her own stubbornness was. Hearing it so bluntly put brought common sense swooping in and made her feel very foolish.

"Please," George added, though it was choked and sounded as if it pained him.

Perliett scanned the darkness. The shadows. The cornstalks weaving back and forth in a subtle motion like the thin arms of a skeleton man. She could imagine them reaching for her, straining through the night, until bony fingers wrapped around her, digging into her skin. She felt him—the Skeleton Man—pull her toward his maze of stalks. An abyss where corn spiders hung off sticky leaves, and where he shoved corn silk into her mouth to silence her. Silks that dangled down her throat, gagging her as he drew back a bony arm, knife glistening in the brief shaft of moonlight—

"Yes. Yes." Perliett half threw her box into the buggy and hurried to climb in. "Take me home, George."

6

Molly

Her eyes snapped open, greeted only by the dark silence of their bedroom. Molly turned her head on her pillow. Trent was beside her. Asleep. The scruff on his face barely visible in the darkness. The window was directly above them, their headboard peeking over the sill. A four-paned farmhouse window with flimsy curtains. Through them she could make out stars in the night sky and see a large branch of the maple tree that swooped over the yard.

Molly jerked her attention to the door on her side of the bed. There it was again. A scraping sound. She was frigid under the sheet and blanket. Chills swept down her arms and legs. A general coldness settled over Molly. Why did everything creepy have to happen at night, in the dark? She should feel safe—Trent was right beside her. But he would sleep through the end of the world. In fact, he hadn't moved since he'd come to bed.

The old farmhouse was full of strange noises. That was it, Molly reassured herself. With the floors being so uneven, a draft could make a door close. Ghostly but explainable.

Even breathing sounded loud to Molly. She held her breath,

straining to hear whether the farmhouse was groaning its protests from being shifted in the night, or if—

The floorboards outside the closed bedroom door creaked as they argued against some force pressing down on the hardwood. Molly clenched her teeth, willing her breaths to remain silent. Someone was there. In the house. The floor wouldn't groan on its own. They had no pets roaming the house.

Molly reached under the covers and poked Trent. He grunted, rolled onto his side, his back to the door. The chills hadn't dissipated. If anything, she had gotten colder. Molly stared at the door, its antique hinges, the beveled edges. It was a heavy bedroom door, unlike the hollow modern doors. But there wasn't a lock on it. She hadn't wanted to sleep closest to the door. When she was a kid, she'd always chosen the bed farthest from the door. For whoever slept closest would be the first to die if some unknown entity broke in with malicious intent. It wasn't heroic of her by any means, but it was her reasoning nonetheless. Molly regretted that Trent had arranged the bedding and positioned her where she didn't want to be. Now she was stuck, every night, sleeping by the bedroom door. The first to die . . .

She sat up. The floor creaked again, and then suddenly the chill dissipated. The oppressive weight of the unknown seemed to flee.

"What's wrong?" Trent's groggy voice broke through the terrifying stillness.

Molly jumped, clutched at the blanket, and flung out her hand to slap her husband. It was instinctual. Driven by surprise and pent-up fear.

"Ow!" Trent ducked away, trying to dodge her open palm that connected with his shoulder.

"Someone's out there," Molly hissed. "Get your gun."

Trent was instantly alert. His hand came up, warning her to be silent. He was listening. Reaching for his nightstand, Molly saw Trent's fingertips rest on the lockbox he kept there. The latch released, and the hinged door opened. He drew out his handgun like any typical country boy from the Midwest would. Heck, if it was safe, he'd probably sleep with the gun tucked under his pillow.

There were no more sounds except the rustling of the sheets as Trent eased himself from the bed. Palming the grip on the gun, he held it pointed up and close to his shoulder as he made his way to the door. With caution, he opened the door, now leading with the gun, aiming to clear the hall. Minutes clicked by. Molly heard Trent's movements. Checking the rooms upstairs, followed by his light footsteps down the stairs to the main level. Then there was nothing. Silence.

Molly knew better than to follow Trent. But perching in bed helplessly didn't rest well with her either. Especially in this place. This place that wasn't home yet, but a foreign house that had given respite to others for over a century. Souls that had passed through it, born here, died here. They lingered—or maybe it was their memories that lingered—in the framework. Lost voices, stilled by the silencing of time. Death was a necessary evil. No one's story remained forever, and even if something had embedded the memories in the walls, they didn't put out a welcome to anyone who was a stranger here. Instead, Molly could *feel* them eyeing her, staring at her from the shadowed corners. Questioning her.

Why have you come?

What is your purpose here?

What will you do to mar this place for the next generation?

Somehow, old farmhouses weren't warm and inviting like the magazines made them appear. No Pinterest board of creams and beiges could serve up enough inspiration to convince Molly that this place wasn't filled with secrets. Dark secrets. The kind that old places like this tried to hide but that came alive in the dead of night. Hunted by a husband with a gun that would have absolutely no impact if the sounds were from another entity altogether.

Molly snuggled into the bed, childishly pulling the blankets up over her ears and covering half of her face. She knew the truth now. She'd sent Trent on a goose chase for someone made of flesh and bone. Someone Trent was sure to think was associated with the dead girl he'd found that morning. Her vacant eyes, life stolen from her. Trent would be on alert for a killer.

But the floor creaking . . . the scraping . . . Molly knew—or she fought against the knowing—that it was the house itself. Speaking to her. Stalking her. Letting her know that even in her sleep, they would follow. The voices. The spirits. The ones clamoring for her attention that she so ardently fought to silence, and the ones she so desperately kept secret from her own husband.

Molly cupped her coffee mug with both hands as she watched Trent through the window. He strode across the gravel drive and climbed into his truck parked outside the barn. White paint chipped off the barn's side. Weatherworn. A tin roof dented and scarred by time. He didn't know. He *couldn't* know. For one thing, she was on antidepressants. She'd not been the same since their miscarriages, and though difficult, it was accepted by both of them. It was one of the reasons she didn't work. Trent wanted her life to be as anxiety-free as possible. Too bad he didn't realize *he* caused at least fifty percent of her anxiety by living so platonically. Passion had fizzled with the onslaught of grief.

But—Molly took a sip of coffee—she would never, *never* tell Trent what had developed since they'd lost their babies. The visions. The sounds. He'd have her committed. He'd race her to a hospital, have her put in a straitjacket. Lord knew what exactly he would do, but she was certain Trent would not just sit back passively and accept that she heard voices. She could keep up with the façade. She had for the last year anyway. Since miscarriage number four. She could live alone in silence with her ghosts.

Molly watched Trent drive away, pausing long enough for another vehicle to squeeze beside his truck.

Sidney was here. Sidney didn't know either.

And Molly was determined to keep it that way.

She went for more coffee, feeling the familiar resolution. Within minutes, the screen door in the mudroom slammed. She heard shoes being kicked against the wall, and then—

"When are your chickens coming?"

Molly met her best friend's animated face with a confused smile. "Chickens?"

Sidney—or Sid as Molly always called her best friend since the third grade—was busying herself by pulling her long, curly burgundy hair into a messy bun. The same color as Molly's. Granted, they used the same color hair dye, but that was neither here nor there. They used pretty much the same everything.

"Sure. Every farmer's wife needs to have chickens. Heck, every woman who lives in the country should have them."

Molly didn't bother to ask if Sid wanted coffee. Instead, she retrieved one of the mugs she'd unpacked and put in a cupboard. "I don't know the first thing about chickens."

"I do." Sid helped herself to the fridge, snatching the hazelnut creamer from the door. "And with a place this ancient, there *has* to be a chicken coop."

Molly poured the coffee as Sid added the creamer. It became a sugary drink in no time flat, emphasizing one of the few differences between her and Sid. Molly preferred hers just barely creamy and with no sugary flavors. The hazelnut creamer was solely in the fridge for Sid.

"Think of it." Sid sipped her morning brew and leaned against the counter. "You could wake Trent up in the morning with a fresh quiche made from your own chicken eggs."

"I don't know how to make quiche."

"An omelet then."

"Sid."

"So, you can't cook? What does that matter? Watch the Food Network for a while. Buy a Betty Crocker cookbook. You'll figure it out!"

"Or I could just put out a box of cereal," Molly teased.

Sid tilted her head, narrowing her hazel eyes in exasperation. "Wow, you're even killing me with your lack of romance. Besides, chickens, eggs . . . country life"—she spread her arms wide—"it's all heaven!"

Molly laughed, but inside she felt the pang of truth in Sid's words. She didn't want to be reminded of the lack of romance in her life.

Sid broke the brief silence. "I need the grand tour! First inside, then outside."

"I haven't really bothered with outside yet." Molly tried to muster some of the happiness that had flitted through her on Sid's arrival. "Or the inside," she admitted. She hadn't been in the mood to unpack. "It's actually a mess inside."

"Okay. Then let's go outside first."

"And avoid the creepy gravestone basement?" Molly teased.

Sid paused, her mug midway to her mouth. Her eyes widened as she stared at Molly over her coffee. "The what?"

"Botched gravestones bolster the foundation," Molly informed her bestie. "They're antique."

"Sooooo, your house is a graveyard?" Sid grinned. "It *has* to be! Bodies hidden behind the walls. Ooh, how deliciously creepy."

Molly knew Sid was joking, so she ignored the previous night's events and stuffed away her own personal superstitions. "Doubtful." That was the appropriate response anyway. Keeping up the charade wasn't hard. Sid and Trent weren't naturally superstitious people. They mocked the concept of ghosts and hauntings, having no idea how it made Molly's insides churn with nervous energy.

"'Kay. Time for chickens!" Sid's announcement was coupled with her take-charge stride into the mudroom.

Molly followed, and they bantered as they pulled on shoes. It was warm already. Molly could feel the sticky humidity the moment she stepped outside. An image of the young woman's corpse in the ditch brought her up short. She squinted into the morning sun, toward the Benson farm in the distance. Cornstalks and trees mostly hid it, although she could make out the roof of the barn.

"They still have crime-scene tape up this morning." Sid read Molly's thoughts, her voice grave. "It was on the news too."

"They haven't figured out who she is?" Molly hadn't had the gumption to tune in to the news, whether TV or radio.

"No. At least they're not saying." Sid shook her head. "Are they allowing Trent to get in to do chores?"

"Yeah. And they called the Bensons, and they're on their way back. I guess the authorities have a lot of questions for them."

"But they were gone, so how could they have anything to do with it?" Sid frowned.

"I think it's probably more about what connections there may be—not to mention it was on their property that the body was found."

Sid nodded. "I suppose." She sipped her coffee as they walked toward the barn. "Outside of old gravestones in your basement and a dead body down the road, what else do you have to reveal to me?"

Molly missed a step but recovered. "Nothing." She could feel Sid's sensing stare. The woman always knew when Molly was hiding something. Especially lately. She'd pulled away from Sid too. Maybe not as severely as she had from her own husband, but . . .

"So, there's the barn." Sid saved Molly from having to answer. "We definitely need to explore that. I should bring my metal detector. Who knows what we'd find in the ground around this place!"

For a moment, Molly forgot herself as the idea piqued her curiosity. "Ooh, yeah!"

"Let's go behind the barn. I see other outbuildings." Sid took over the tour. Molly followed her friend, who years ago had embraced country living. She and her husband, Dan, and their four kids made it practically a work of art. Horses, chickens, a garden, canning, homeschooling . . . Sid was the epitome of a woman in her mid-thirties who had fully embraced the heartbeat of Michigan country.

Then there was Molly. She was still trying to figure out who she was. Sometimes Sid's stability made her envious. Sometimes it made her ache. Most of the time, Molly relied on it, more than Sid probably realized.

"Okay, that building there I bet was used as a toolshed." Sid eyed a medium-sized building off to the side and behind the barn. It appeared to be newer than the barn. Its foundation was made of cinder block, its doors more modern but with tarnished knobs. The elements had been tough on it, leaving the siding weatherworn and the tin roof rusty. Two windows were intact, though some of their panes were cracked. Sid set her coffee mug on a rusted metal barrel that sat beside the door. She tried the doorknob, and it opened. Poking her head in, Sid's words echoed from the empty innards of the shed.

"Yeah, I can see where they probably had some small machinery in here too at one point. There are grease and oil stains on the floor, and it smells like oil."

Molly followed Sid into the shed. The floor was rough cement with dirt ground into its crevices. The corners of the shed were piled with leaves, debris, old nails, and there were cobwebs. Many, many cobwebs. Dead wasps were crispy in the windowsills, their yellow bodies faded from months of baking in the summer sun. She remembered now. Trent had said something to her about wanting to clean out the back shed so they could build shelves and store his "stuff" in here. Meaning a push lawn mower, tools, his copious numbers of coffee cans filled with nails and screws, quarts of oil, and so on. Basically this place would become a garage without the vehicle storage.

"Nice but not your chicken coop." Sid was on a mission. She charged from the shed, ducking so as not to hit her head on the doorframe that was sagging. Molly followed, vaguely curious but mostly preoccupied with her own thoughts. They swirled in her mind, making focusing on the moment at hand difficult.

"Aha!" Sid pointed. "Chicken coop!"

What Sid was pointing to appeared to Molly to be just another outbuilding. More squat, one level, and a peaked roof with a small square window that hinted of an attic of sorts. The foundation was of fieldstone, with wood siding turned gray by the elements. A fence ran from one corner, creating a square with the main entrance to the building inside the fence.

"Aren't chicken coops . . . cuter?" Molly recalled pictures of angular little buildings on stilts, at least three-quarters the size of this building, and definitely not capable of having a human enter it.

Sid gave her arm a playful slug. "C'mon, this is country living, Molly, not suburban chickens. We use outbuildings and make them into coops around these here parts." Her exaggerated redneck accent made Molly grin.

"I just thought—"

Sid interrupted with exuberance. "You can get a cutesy coop if you want a few chickens. But if you're going to *raise* chickens, you need to go big."

Molly raised her brows. Raise chickens? The idea of a few chickens and a cute coop seemed more manageable to her.

"I love it!" Sid was beaming, excitement oozing from her

eyes. She cast a contagious grin in Molly's direction. "Check it out! You have an entire *building* for a coop!"

The fence was gated, but the gate was hanging from one hinge and in need of repair. Sid pushed it to the side and crossed the fenced area, manhandling the door to the coop that was apparently swollen from time and weather and sticking to the floor.

Molly moved to follow, reaching the fence and holding out her hand to the wobbling, lopsided gate. Her fingers touched the metal, and she stilled. A zinging sensation drove through her fingertips, up her arm and into her face. She could feel the tingling on her skin—no, it was *behind* her skin—it was inside of her. Molly stumbled and grabbed hold of the wooden post the gate was attached to. As she did, her body leaned into it, her shirt soaking up dampness from the humidity.

Don't go in.

The humming reverberated in her head, causing a rush of throbbing pressure that made Molly squeeze her eyes shut.

Stay out.

"Molly?" Sid's voice overwhelmed the subtle murmur in Molly's mind. "Molly." Sid's tone was sharper this time.

Molly opened her eyes, groggily taking in Sid's concerned expression. The door to the coop stood open. Molly stared at it, studying the darkness beyond it, straining to see inside while everything in her urged her to drag Sid far away from it. To slam shut the door on its old-time chicken nests, its dust and cobwebs, and whatever other secrets it held inside.

"Molly, are you all right?" Sid held her hand up as if to touch Molly's cheek, but she didn't. It hovered just beside Molly's face. "You're pale as a ghost."

Ghost.

Who had warned her to stay out?

"I-I'm fine," Molly muttered, pushing off the wood post as she attempted to find her balance on her own feet. The thrumming had stopped as quickly as it started, leaving her woozy.

"Are you sure?" Sid's brows pulled together.

Molly looked around them. Someone had to have been here. Just behind her maybe. Or inside?

"Y-yeah. Yeah, I'm fine. I just didn't eat much for breakfast and got a little dizzy," Molly lied. She could feel Sid searching her face, trying to decipher what was going on in Molly's mind.

Sid shot a glance back at the coop. "Do you want to go in or head back and get something to eat?"

"I'll be fine. Let's go in and see what's there." Molly pushed past Sid and stalked bravely toward the chicken coop. Worst case, it housed the ghosts of dead chickens. How bad could they be? Little apparitions with feathers, clucking and pecking at the ground? The absurdity of a ghost chicken almost made her laugh, and the absence of the tingling sensation she'd felt just moments before made relief almost palpable.

Sid followed Molly's lead, accepting her explanation and chattering on about making something more substantial than cereal when they returned to the house. Molly let her talk. It calmed her nerves to have some normalcy, and, if she was being honest, cereal *was* a paltry excuse for a breakfast anyway.

7

It was stifling inside the chicken coop. Having been closed up, the windows boarded, the doors barred, it was as though the air inside had been captured the day the place had served its last hen. There was a thick layer of dank, musty straw with patches of the old wood floor underneath. Nails protruded from some boards and up through the straw. Molly and Sid stepped carefully, both lost in their own worlds as they examined the interior of the coop.

"Those are the nesting boxes." Sid pointed to a row of empty compartments, once filled with hay, where the chickens had nested. Eggs would have been laid here, then collected, with a few chucked back onto the ground for the chickens to eat. "Chickens are cannibals," Sid mentioned. It was so offhanded that Molly was surprised how in line the comment was with her own thoughts. She'd seen chickens eat their own eggs before. It was gruesome, in a way. It also kept Molly from having any nurturing emotion toward the birds.

But not Sid. Sid loved her chickens, and apparently she thought it was her duty to convince Molly to feel the same way.

"All we need to do is rake this out." Sid toed a pile of straw, dust particles pluming upward. "It's moldy and worthless. We can bring in new bedding. We'll need some water stations. The windows should be opened. Do you think Trent could install chicken wire across them? In fact, if he could make shutters, you'd be able to lock them up at night to keep out the critters and weather, and they could be left open during the day. This place definitely needs airflow."

Sid approached a boarded-up window and tugged at the wood nailed across it. A corner busted off. "It's rotted. I wonder when this got closed. I bet it wasn't always a chicken coop because there's an attic. Chickens don't need attics. But then, back in the day, a building like this might as well be functional if you ever needed it for something other than chickens."

Molly nodded. Sid would know. She eyed the narrow ladder at the far end of the coop. It had eight rungs and then disappeared into the attic.

"Remember when we were kids," Molly began, "we always wanted to play in the barn at my cousin's? In the loft?"

Sid stilled. Molly could feel her eyes on her and not the ladder.

"I remember," Sid answered. "We were going to turn it into a clubhouse. With hay bales for walls. That's when I first wanted to marry someone and live in the country. I fell in love with farm life."

Molly met her friend's eyes as Sid approached. "I fell in love with Trent."

It was an honest confession, and it was one she'd been resistant to voice lately. The irony was also that *she* had married the farmer. Sid had married a computer nerd, who worked out of the upstairs office of their own remodeled farmhouse. They were hobby farmers.

"Molls . . ." Sid's hand rested gently on Molly's arm. "Listen. I'm worried about—"

"I wonder what's in the attic," Molly interrupted. She should've kept her mouth shut. Shouldn't even open the door a bit. Molly tested out the first rung on the ladder. She could feel Sid's concern burning into her as she climbed and was determined to prove to Sid it was nothing. Truly. Nothing.

"It's dusty," she called down to Sid, forcing cheer into her voice.

Sid stood at the bottom of the ladder. "Is there anything up there?"

Molly glanced back at her and waved her up. "C'mon. It looks empty, but who knows?" Molly hoisted herself onto the attic floor. The roof slanted so that standing to her full five-foot-seven height wasn't possible. Molly tapped the floor ahead of her with her foot to check the stability of the floorboards. Like any good farm building, they were thick, solid, and fabulously built.

She swept the room with her gaze as she waited for Sid to climb up. When her friend reached her side, they gave each other a meaningful look.

"This place would've been outstanding as kids," Sid breathed.

"The perfect clubhouse," Molly agreed. "If we were kids, we could put a few beanbag chairs under that lone window that looks over the yard. And we could put up posters of our heartthrobs Jonathan Taylor Thomas, Luke Perry, or *my* favorite, Will Smith."

"Oh, gosh no." Sid clucked her tongue. "No, that would've been *your* side of the clubhouse. I'd hang posters of furry heartthrobs, like *The Black Stallion* or *Misty of Chincoteague*."

Molly laughed, running her fingers along one of the rafters. "Think about it. Back in the day, kids playing in here above the chickens, in their little prairie dresses, and little boys in suspenders?"

"Oh yes. Outside the window would be Pa and his plow," Sid added. "Of course, there were probably a few other kids, and farmhands, and ooh, just imagine—some *dogs*!"

Molly could imagine. That was part of the problem. Her vision glazed, then cleared. She reached out her palm and pressed it against the wall, the rough wood beneath her hand poking her skin. Sid was saying something, but her voice came as if far off in the distance.

". . . must have been neat with horse-drawn plows and . . ."

Sid's voice was overwhelmed by that of a child. Audible or in her mind, Molly couldn't differentiate. The voice was whisper quiet, with an ethereal note to it, watery with childlike emotion that was coupled with worried fright.

Who killed Cock Robin?
I, said the Sparrow,
with my bow and arrow,
I killed Cock Robin.
Who saw him die?
I, said the Fly,
with my little teeny eye,
I saw him die.

"I saw him die." Molly repeated the words that ricocheted through her daze. "I saw him die."

"Molly?" Sid's fingers dug into Molly's arm. Maybe it was the sting of their pinch that brought Molly back to the present, but she was certain she saw the little girl in the far corner of the coop's attic. The girl wore a rueful smile as she clutched a book to her chest. Her lips moved as if she continued the ancient nursery rhyme, but then—

"Molly!"

Molly jerked at Sid's sharp demand. She locked eyes with her friend, then strained to see over Sid's shoulder. But the image was gone. A wisp that had vanished, along with the sound of her questioning voice.

Who saw him die?

I . . .

This was not cool. Molly's hand shook as she pushed hair back from her face, staring into the bathroom mirror. Her reflection was pale. She hadn't realized she'd put on as much weight as she had either. Her face was fuller. She was curvier.

A knock on the bathroom door interrupted her self-critique and stilled her thoughts from going in a direction she would have avoided anyway.

"Open the door."

It was Trent.

Sid had brought Molly back to the house after the debacle in the coop. Apparently, Sid was either convinced Molly sorely lacked protein for breakfast or Molly needed to see a doctor. *"Iron deficiency maybe?"* Sid had offered. She had no idea that Molly hadn't been close to passing out like Sid believed. Sid obviously hadn't heard the quivery whisper of a creepy child's nursery rhyme. Sid hadn't seen the little girl either—she would have said something if she had.

Which meant Molly was losing her ever-loving mind.

"Please open the door." Trent was stern.

Molly smiled a little, even as she berated herself. He also knew that stern tone would get her to respond. Maybe it was instinctual, as a woman, to respond in obedience to a male voice that oozed authority. It was offensive to any strong-minded feminist out there, but Molly couldn't help it. She'd been raised in the Midwest, where families were still patriarchal and good country men were good strong fathers, and good strong husbands, with wills stronger than the axles on their tractors.

She opened the door. Or tried to. It stuck because it was old, so she had to tug on the door for it to give way from its tight fit against the frame.

Trent's left arm was braced on the upper corner of the doorframe, and that meant his T-shirt sleeve had pulled down, revealing his farmer's tan. Dark olive skin until a clean line defined where the sun hadn't been able to shine, leaving behind "skin so white it'd make a snowman blink twice." Or at least that was what Molly's grandfather used to say years ago.

Concern was etched into the creases by his eyes. He'd

flipped his cap backward on his head. There was dust on the bridge of his nose—dirt and dust from working in the barn. A waft of pungent manure met Molly's nose. It was Trent's cologne. Cow poop. The romance was likely to kill her because of its fumes if not its lack of effect otherwise.

"You're avoiding me." Trent stated the obvious with the talent of a man.

Molly waggled her brows at him, squeezed under his arm, and moved past him. Trent followed, and she heard him sigh.

"Can we talk?"

"Sure." Her voice was abnormally peppy. Fake. She knew it. Trent knew it.

"Molly, I'm worried about you. Sid called me. She's worried too. Why aren't you eating? You know it's important. Especially with your—depression."

Molly didn't miss the hesitation in his voice. This wasn't new. This was a recurring conversation. Molly stopped in the living room. Their couch was against the wall. A recliner. A trunk filled with blankets. The TV was in the corner. The bookshelves were empty. She made a beeline for the boxes stacked on the floor next to the shelves and tugged open the top one.

"What do you need me to do?" There was desperation in Trent's voice.

"Nothing. I just need to remember to eat better." Yes, go with Sid's explanation that Molly had almost passed out. Trent didn't need to know about the vision any more than Sid did. Molly hid her face in the box of books, squeezing back a sudden surge of tears.

She wanted to be able to tell her husband. Tell him without the threat of being treated like she was having psychological issues—which was unrealistic to wish for, considering that *had* to be what it was, wasn't it? She was already depressive. Already anxiety-ridden. Already an insomniac depending on a prescription to help her sleep. Doctors would be concerned about psychosis. She'd have to test for bipolar, or borderline personality disorder, or—

Trent was talking. "I'd hoped a new house—a new place to begin—would inspire you."

"Inspire me to eat better?" She would go with the food thing. It was safer. "Trent, I'll make it a point to pay more attention. And the farm here, it's—it's nice." Molly straightened, a stack of books in her hands. She addressed Trent, forcing a casual nonchalance into her words. She even managed what she hoped was an encouraging smile that showed him she didn't hate the house and she didn't hate him.

"Nice," Trent repeated. He leaned against the couch, his arms crossed over his chest. "Molly, we've been here a week and you haven't even started to unpack."

"That's not true." Molly slid the books onto an empty shelf. "See?"

"Molly."

"What?" Another handful of books landed on the bookshelf.

She heard Trent heave a tired sigh. She heard his footsteps behind her. She felt his hand reach out to close over her arm, only he didn't touch her. He dropped it instead to his side, leaving her skin bereft of the tenderness she craved and resisted simultaneously.

"I'm sorry." The resignation in Trent's words dropped like a lead weight onto Molly's conscience. She spun around, mouth open, ready to refute his apology.

No! It wasn't him, it was *her*. It was *God*! It was the abhorrent aspects of life and then death. Uncontrollable, undeniable, but also unforgivable. She couldn't move on—that was it. That was the problem. If she could somehow transfer into Trent's soul the nauseating pointlessness of existence now, then he would understand why this new house, this change in life, this—well, *everything*—meant absolutely nothing. He was lucky she wasn't rocking aimlessly in a chair with a blanket over her lap. That was about all the motivation she had these days.

"Trent, I—" Molly's words stuck in her throat as she looked for Trent. His retreating form met her as he exited the living room, leaving her alone. She tossed the book she was holding onto the couch, a sudden urgency to find some sort of resolution with Trent taking priority. She chased after him, her bare feet padding on the wood floor.

"Trent, please."

He was in the kitchen, standing in front of the open fridge door, staring into the fridge as if a French silk pie would magically appear.

Molly tried again. "Trent, I'm sorry I'm not the woman you married."

He dared a look at her.

Okay. Yes. That sounded manipulative. Victim mentality. Their grief therapist had walked her through that after the second miscarriage. She squeezed her eyes shut and searched for better words. "I'm trying to redefine who I am now, and I—"

"It's okay." Trent's palm raised toward her told her he didn't want more psychobabble tonight. This was the part of Trent that irritated her. He loved so hard but was so . . . aloof. Impenetrable. A realist.

He shut the fridge door and faced her, the dirt still smudging his nose, his hat still on backward, his frame still tempting in spite of the farm smell that clung to him. "I need to be able to go to work and not worry about you collapsing because you forgot to eat."

Molly grimaced internally. If it were only that. That she could resolve. She let Trent believe the lie and tried to reassure him. "You can. I promise. I'll eat." Steak and potatoes if she had to.

Trent's mouth worked back and forth as he assessed her. She could tell he wanted more.

"What is it?" she pressed.

He cleared his throat. "Nothing."

"It's not nothing," she argued.

Trent offered her a lazy shrug. "It is to you." His eyes grew serious. "It is to you," he repeated.

She knew what he was referring to. Knew what Trent targeted and Molly's ire rose. "So I'm not allowed to grieve the loss of our children? I need to just—just move on like they were blips on the map of our lives?"

Trent hefted a sigh and scratched the back of his neck, irritation palpable. "It's been two years, Molls. Two years since the last miscarriage."

"So?"

"At what point do we heal and move on?"

"Move on," Molly repeated lamely. "Move on." It sounded harder to her than climbing Mount Everest without oxygen.

"Never mind." Trent waved her off and straightened. He pushed past her, leaving behind his farm cologne wafting in the air. Leaving behind the memories of lost dreams. Leaving behind Molly.

She stood in the kitchen, alone, with only the voices to wrap around her empty soul.

In which we choose to die.
Do we choose it?
Death.
I see it in her eyes.
I saw it leave her eyes.
Death is a powerful thing.
It makes me hunger for more of it.

8

Perliett

"You absolutely mustn't!" Perliett's urging fell on her mother's deaf ears.

Maribeth offered Perliett the same look she gave her during her séances, this being the silent stare down her nose and over her shoulder until her gaze collided with Perliett's. It was the somber look of a staunch believer.

"Mr. Withers has requested it. Along with his daughter, Angelica."

"I know, and I may have agreed with you, except after tending to Mrs. Withers, she is not of the mind to manage disappointment should Eunice not make a connection." Perliett didn't have confidence in the spirits to come when called. Curiosity or even an aged grief made the risk less impacting. Then there was the element that Perliett didn't want to admit and that was the smidgen of doubt she carried toward her mother's practice of spiritualism. The spirit world was impossible to predict, and yet . . . there was such confidence in her mother.

She tried again. "Does the Withers family understand it is unlikely Eunice will appear in bodily form? That they won't be able to interrogate her and watch her dead lips mouth the name of her killer?"

"Oh, don't be morbid, Perliett." Maribeth waved her off and focused on straightening the black lace cloth that covered the round table in the study. "We are merely going to attempt to make a connection. For the sake of Mrs. Withers."

"Who won't even be in attendance!" Perliett recalled the poor woman from last night, with her grief having crowded out all sense of living for herself.

"Precisely why you've little to worry about." Maribeth tugged a candle nub from its brass holder and replaced it with a new white stick. "But to let a mother know that her daughter is at peace in the afterlife, wouldn't you wish that? For me? If I were Mrs. Withers?"

She would. Perliett nodded.

Maribeth smiled then. "And so Angelica and Mr. Withers wish to take that thread of hope to Eunice's mother. They don't need Mrs. Withers handicapped by the daunting reality that her daughter was . . . was mangled like a pincushion."

"And *I* am the morbid one?" Perliett retorted.

Maribeth's black brow winged upward, reminding Perliett of a raven. "Would you withhold hope from the grieving and heartbroken?"

No. She wouldn't.

Perliett stifled the niggling sense of disquiet in her spirit. "No, Mother. But I would be cautious not to offer it senselessly—Mrs. Withers isn't of sound mind."

"We've already established that Mrs. Withers will not be in attendance."

"But she'll hear of the evening's experiences and—"

"*If* Eunice even makes a connection. All may be silent." Maribeth straightened a chair that was positioned too close to its neighbor.

"And if Eunice isn't at peace?" Perliett asked.

Maribeth stilled, then raised her eyes to her daughter.

They were firm but gentle. They carried that distant vagueness in them that kept Maribeth just above Perliett in understanding. "Then we should know that."

"And do what? How do you rescue someone in the afterlife?" Desperation was leaking into her tone. Perliett could hear it. But she was also seeing someone other than Eunice. Someone *she* wished to hear from. Someone who had failed her miserably by refusing to visit from the afterlife no matter how many times Perliett pled with Maribeth to attempt a summoning.

PaPa.

Maribeth neared her, reaching out and gently stroking Perliett's upper arm like a mother would—should—comfort their child. Her face was gentle, her eyes searching Perliett's. "Darling, I know you wish to hear from him, but he is silent. I can only conclude his soul is at peace."

"Of course his soul is at peace." Perliett sniffed, and Maribeth offered her a handkerchief pulled from the waistband of her skirt. "But I miss him so."

"I know." Still, Maribeth didn't add her own shared empathy. She never did. PaPa's passing had almost seemed to set her free in a way. To do as she pleased without the restraints of her pious husband, who followed the Scriptures and believed the Old Testament's warnings against beseeching the spirit world.

Maybe that was why PaPa didn't come forward now. He was as firmly convicted in death as he was in life. Honor God's commands.

Perliett grimaced, feeling quite stuck between her living mother's and dead father's beliefs. If she could find a compromise of sorts . . .

She snapped back to the present conundrum. "What will you do if Eunice is like PaPa and remains silent? Tell Eunice's family that she is not in distress? Or tell them that her soul lingers, incomplete and unfulfilled?"

"Whatever my spirit senses, I will communicate." Maribeth moved back to the table, positioning her items with an eye to detail.

"But how will that *help* them?" Perliett slapped her palms on the table, demanding her mother's undivided attention. "If Eunice stays silent like PaPa?"

"Your father"—Maribeth swallowed her emotion—"is as stubborn in death as he was in life, Perliett. It is *his* choice to remain silent from the beyond."

"And it is *my* agony that must bear it repeatedly." Perliett clutched the lace tablecloth in her fingers, causing the candlestick to tip and fall. "I'm not convinced—"

"You don't believe?" Maribeth sucked in a shocked breath.

Perliett flattened her lips as she drew a breath and released it. "I'm not convinced conjuring the spirit of a murdered woman is the wisest thing to do at present."

"But if Eunice *can* provide a clue? Should we not assist the authorities?" Maribeth's expression was so open, lacking in judgment and instead shrouded in sincere concern. "Why would we silence the voice of the dead if they wish to speak?"

Maribeth reached out and righted the candlestick. She smoothed the tablecloth, then left Perliett with a plea. A plea to believe in full and to remain silent about her misgivings.

Her mother paused at the doorway, looking over her shoulder at Perliett. Her countenance was one of concern, almost disheartened. She opened her mouth, closed it, then tried again, speaking words that Perliett could tell her mother didn't wish to speak.

"Perhaps it is *you* who silences your father, Perliett, and not his own spirit. Until you *truly* are open . . ." She breathed in a sad breath through her nostrils. "Well, I will not withhold hope from the Withers family. Not in their time of grief."

Perliett had no argument against showing compassion. One could not resist it. Compassion trumped moral code, did it not? Because the intent was good, and therefore any action ladened with it followed suit.

The sitters had arrived. Of course, it was after dark, just as her mother preferred. Darkness seemed to assist in the summoning, although Perliett wasn't sure why.

She stepped aside as Mr. Withers entered through the front door. He immediately swiped his hat from his head, twisting it in his hands, his nervous energy evident. His daughter, Angelica, entered behind him. Her hazel eyes were wide and surveyed the corners of the entryway as if ghosts already hovered there, waiting to greet them. Her husband, Errol, accompanied them. He met Perliett's eyes directly, and she saw her own misgivings reflected in his. She dropped her gaze before her unspoken questions discredited her mother.

Another body entered, squeezing broad shoulders in between Angelica and Errol. His dark hair was combed neatly, but no hat covered it. There was a darkness over his features that created a niggling of doubt in Perliett. He leveled his eyes on her, and she was sure all reasonable thought fled beneath the smoldering gaze.

"Mr. Bridgers." Her voice was breathier than she'd intended.

The corner of his mouth turned up. A carved mouth. With a strong jawline, colored by shaved whiskers whose shadow refused to flee after the razor had done its work.

"I-I didn't realize you were coming." Bother. She was acting like a twitterpated schoolgirl, not a strong woman who was called upon for her medical expertise.

"My apologies." He tipped his head. "I communicated with your mother."

"You are now acquainted with the Withers family?" Perliett challenged. Giving his condolences at the funeral as a member of the community was one thing. Attending a private séance intimated a far closer relationship.

"I invited him." Angelica's voice quavered with a nervous energy that seeped into Perliett and made her uneasy herself.

"Oh." Perliett accepted Angelica's insertion, but she still had no conception of the relationship between the Withers family and Mr. Bridgers. It made little sense to her. That he was acquainted with her mother, and Maribeth seemed to welcome him . . .

Perliett shook her suspicions away and made sure her smile enveloped the Withers family, if not Jasper Bridgers. Maribeth had instructed her to show them to the study. She was preparing herself for the séance. Mustering the fortitude to beseech the dead and to commune with them took focused concentration.

"Please." Perliett motioned. "Follow me."

There was an oppressive darkness as they entered the study. Draperies were drawn over the windows. A lone candle in the middle of the table was lit, its flame flickering back and forth.

"Welcome." Maribeth opened her arms. She dressed simply. Nothing exorbitant or showy. "Please, be seated."

Mr. Withers cleared his throat nervously. He pulled out a chair and slid onto it, gripping the edges and hopping it forward so his knees were under the table. The black lace tablecloth covered his lap, and he pushed it away with callused hands.

Angelica and Errol also took chairs. Mr. Bridgers waited until they were seated before taking his own.

Perliett hesitated. Sometimes her mother preferred that she leave, other times that she stayed. They'd not discussed it, nor was she certain which was the preferred conduct tonight. Curiosity compelled her to hesitate longer. *If* her mother made a connection with Eunice . . .

"Perliett?" The question in Maribeth's voice, as well as

the extension of her hand toward an empty chair beside Mr. Bridgers, brought the answer to Perliett. Grateful to be included, Perliett rounded the table and eased onto the chair, careful to hold her knees together so as not to brush against Mr. Bridgers. She could smell a spicy ginger wafting from his clothes. Warm. Intriguing.

"Have you brought the items I requested?" Maribeth kept her voice modulated.

Angelica nodded silently and opened the drawstrings of her handbag. She pulled out a yellow ribbon, a cameo, and a small photograph of Eunice.

Maribeth dipped her head in acknowledgment of the items, drawing them toward her. She laid them at the base of the flickering candle, which produced a macabre glow on the faces of those around the table. Maribeth ignored the atmosphere, instead drawing her fingertips over Eunice's face in the photograph. It was hardly apparent in the depth of the room's shadows, and because of that, Perliett was drawn back to the memory of George's office when Eunice had lain on his table.

Perliett could almost hear the water as she wrung the towel over the tin bowl of pink-tinged water. Washing the blood from the abdomen's wounds was gruesome. In death, Eunice had already lost much of her beauty, her eyes sunken by the trauma she'd endured, her jaw slack and mouth hanging open with no breath coming forth.

Eunice had been so still, so—so *dead*—as Perliett had washed the corpse's arms, her hands, her chest. It was intimate, the washing of a dead body, and with the act brought the memories of the deceased in life. Eunice's infectious smile, her laughter, her kindness, the way her eyes twinkled, how everyone was proud to know her, even if—as it was with Perliett—they weren't close. But she had been flirtatious also. Perliett considered Kenneth Braun for the first time since that day he'd discovered Eunice's body. He'd not attended the funeral. That was odd. Had Eunice and Kenneth's relationship been a clandestine one? Perliett bit the inside of her bottom lip as she considered. Was she the only one who had suspicion that Kenneth and Eunice had been having a love affair?

The realization made Perliett lift her eyes. Maribeth was reciting a prayer, her lips moving with fervency as she breathed the words.

"Amen," Maribeth finished.

The Witherses and Mr. Bridgers all appropriately echoed the amen with one of their own.

"We shall join hands," Maribeth instructed.

Perliett tried to push the image of Kenneth's distraught face from her mind so she could focus on the present. The outlines of the table members were apparent in the dim light. Perliett's breath caught as she lowered her eyes to see Mr. Bridgers's hand open, waiting to accept hers. It wasn't particularly appropriate to take hands with the stranger, especially ungloved, but Perliett had no choice but to do her mother's bidding or else risk causing a scene.

So she slipped her hand into Mr. Bridgers's. Instantly, her skin became warm as their palms connected. Perliett closed her eyes, aware that no one was watching her, so consumed by the air that seemed to swirl around them. For a moment, Perliett was certain she could feel Mr. Bridgers's pulse against the tender skin of her hand, telling her things she shouldn't know about him. That he was calm. Unafraid. Terrifyingly real and terrifyingly male.

As if Mr. Bridgers knew Perliett's instinct would be to withdraw, he tightened his grasp on her hand, his thumb giving her skin a delicious stroke meant to calm but succeeding only in sending shivers through her.

"Eunice?" Maribeth's head was tilted back, her eyes closed, face directed upward. She continued to summon the dead woman. The air grew denser, thicker around them.

Perliett was accustomed to the weighted feeling that lowered onto her chest, suppressing her breaths as the darkness suppressed the group.

Angelica gasped softly. "Who was that?"

"Tell us what you heard," Maribeth prompted.

"I felt—I—" Angelica sputtered.

"Go on," Maribeth encouraged, never changing from her modulated tone.

"I felt fingers brush the back of my neck!" Angelica said, hurrying to admit the phenomenon.

"Eunice is here," Maribeth breathed. She tilted her head back again.

"Ask her who killed her!" Mr. Withers blurted. "I'm paying for this. Tell her I'm paying good money to hear from her!" Apparently, even in death, Eunice was being held to a conscientious financial standard.

Perliett stiffened.

"We must be still," Mr. Bridgers's calm voice advised.

"Is this you, Eunice? Declare yourself, please. Tap thrice if you are in the room."

A definitive three taps echoed in the room, stealing the breath from all the participants.

Perliett couldn't help but grip Mr. Bridgers's hand tighter.

"Yes. She is here," Maribeth whispered. "Eunice, will you show yourself to us tonight?"

Silence followed.

The flame of the candle flickered erratically.

Angelica squeaked again. "My hand. She touched my hand!"

"Ask her!" Mr. Withers insisted.

Maribeth opened one eye and gave a small nod. "Eunice, if your spirit is disturbed, tell us of your distress."

Three knocks followed.

Errol swore softly.

Perliett dared a sideways glance at Mr. Bridgers. She could

only make out his profile, sharp in the dim candlelight. He was staring at the flame, his eyes fixated on it as if in a trance.

"Does your killer go free?" Maribeth inquired through the thick air.

No response followed.

"There is no need to fear us, Eunice. We only wish to help you find peace. Your killer, is the person still among us here in Kilbourn?"

Glass shattered from the front window, sending shards spitting into the room with the ferocity of an explosion. The draperies winged inward toward them, as if someone were running from behind them and pushing them out. A burst of fresh air, sticky but cool from the summer night, whipped across their faces. Angelica's screams rent the air, followed by the curses Errol dropped liberally. Mr. Withers fell backward, his chair crashing to the floor. He scurried backward on his bottom, palming the floor as he half dragged himself away from the table. Maribeth's shocked wail helped none of the guests find reassurance, as she herself launched forward against the table, her head cracking against the wood.

Mr. Bridgers yanked Perliett against him, shielding her belatedly with his body. As his arms wrapped around her frame, Perliett noticed the flame of the candle still glowed despite the burst of wind and broken glass. Then, in the inexplicable shadows, Perliett saw two ghostly white fingers reach out and snuff the flame, plunging them all into complete and utter blackness.

9

Molly

"You brought your metal detector?" Molly laughed as Sid pulled it from the back of her Suburban.

Sid didn't bother to look up as she reached for the hatch to close it. "Sure I did! Old farmsteads like this? You could have treasure buried somewhere in the backyard. You could be rich by the end of the day! Not to mention, my mom took the kids for the weekend, so I have all day today until Dan finishes his work projects."

"Dan going to wine and dine you since you're sans kids tonight?"

Sid waggled her eyebrows. "Probably frozen pizza and Coke, but hey, we're simple folk."

Molly couldn't respond with any criticism. The last time she and Trent had gone out on a date was maybe two years ago? Like an actual *date* night. She didn't count the endless evenings they had spent alone together and barely spoke.

Sid made a few adjustments to her detector and within seconds was waving it around the driveway. It beeped a steady cadence as she moved toward the barn and the shed out back. "Chicken coop time!" she announced.

Molly followed, hiding her hesitancy behind a smile. It was good to be outside. Good to do something other than unpack books and knickknacks, and wonder why on earth she'd bothered to pack a box of old ticket stubs and other sentimental paraphernalia from her youth.

The sun was already warming the air, sending waves of humidity thick with heat across her bare legs. She adjusted the waistband of her cutoff shorts and wondered for the thousandth time how the extra weight had crept up on her.

Sid was energetically sweeping the lawn, brushing the tips of the green grass with the detector. "I want to find a time capsule someday."

"With a metal detector?" Molly challenged, grinning.

"If there's metal in it, this will find it." Sid touched the brim of her baseball cap, smashed over her burgundy curls that were pulled into a ponytail. "Hey. Don't knock my motivation."

The detector went off with a rapid series of beeps as Sid approached the dirt near the fence line of the chicken coop.

"Ooh!" Sid immediately dropped to her knees. She was wearing shorts as well but didn't seem to mind the earth as it dug into her skin. "Help me," she directed.

Molly followed suit, a bit more gingerly, but soon she too was fingering the ground, attempting to uncover whatever the detector had located. She tugged a spade from the small of her back, where she'd tucked it into her waistband.

Sid eyed it. "Packing a shovel, eh?"

"Better than a pistol," Molly quipped. "And you can't dig with a metal detector."

"Truth!" Sid gave her an appreciative look as they settled into their familiar camaraderie. It was at least the millionth time Molly had issued a silent prayer of thanks for Sid's friendship. Any other friend would have abandoned her by now. Her mood swings, her morose personality, her unpredictability . . . instead, Sid brought normalcy into her life.

If one could call digging a hole behind a barn normal.

"Aha!" Molly's spade hit something metallic. She pulled it out and dug deeper with her fingers into the hole.

"What is it?" Sid leaned forward eagerly as if Molly might bring up a Roman coin from the soil of a Michigan homestead.

"A button." Molly rubbed the soil from the object, revealing a dirt-encrusted emblem of some sort. An American bald eagle with wings outstretched.

"I bet that's a military uniform button." Sid held out her hand with anticipation that Molly would share the intoxicating moment of unearthing a historical object.

"Is it worth anything?" Molly watched as Sid took the button and studied it. Her brows drawn, her eyes narrowed, she thumbed it for a moment.

"Probably not. Looks just like that other World War One button I found a few years ago. Standard military issue. It's not uncommon to find them."

"Why would it be in the yard behind a barn?" Something about the item gave Molly an unnerving jolt. A man had fingered the object many times, sliding it through a buttonhole, marching into war, diving into a foxhole. Somehow, it had ended up a relic with no remaining story to be told, buried in the dirt of a farm.

Sid shrugged. "My great-grandpa wore his old military jacket to do chores sometimes. My mom has pictures to prove it. People reused things back in the day. It was wasteful not to."

"I suppose." Molly eyed the button.

Sid held it out to her. "Want it? It's your property."

"No," Molly answered, a bit too quickly. She didn't want to explain to Sid that the button felt alive to her. That somehow the wearer's spirit was attached to it, aching to be summoned, to tell his story, to be remembered. "You keep it," Molly finished with a wobbly smile.

Sid pocketed the button. "Score! Thanks!"

Molly sprang to her feet, feigning anticipation. "What's next?"

"The chicken coop." Sid swung the metal detector around.

They headed for the outbuilding that was supposed to house chickens. Molly tamped down the memory of the vision of the little girl in the attic, smiling as if she knew some wicked little secret. Attempting to redirect her thoughts, Molly grasped on to the closest possible subject she could think of.

"What breeds should I get?"

"Of chickens?" Sid walked with her to the coop. "Well, there are Bantams."

"They're smaller, right?"

"Mm-hmm, and their eggs are small. I like Ameraucana chickens, or Buff Orpingtons are pretty. They're gold."

"Do they lay golden eggs?" Molly tossed Sid a wink.

"No."

They shared a laugh as they ducked into the coop, careful to avoid hitting their heads on the lower doorframe. Sid went to work, waving her magic wand over the floor. Within minutes, she'd collected several nails, dug a tin can from beneath the molded straw, and retrieved an old pop bottle cap.

Molly wandered, toeing a wooden box and grimacing when she uncovered a nest of dead mice babies, their bodies mostly skeletons. The ladder into the attic loomed in the corner, teasing her senses.

Run away, it seemed to mock. *Before the girl comes back.*

Molly wasn't sure why ghost girls were the creepiest sort of spirits. Something about a little girl in a white nightgown, barefoot, with hollow black eyes was far more terrifying than a cute little ghost boy in overalls. Too many horror movies and novels had sensationalized ghost girls. Molly shivered at the thought.

"You going up?" Sid's voice at her shoulder made her jump.

Molly hesitated. "Um . . . I probably should see what needs cleaning out up there."

"The chickens won't go up there. You don't need to clean it to get your flock started." Sid's observation gave Molly an out.

She probably should take it. Molly shook her head instead and obstinately gripped the ladder.

"You *did* eat breakfast today, didn't you?" Sid's response was laced with teasing but with a bit of seriousness tacked to the end of it.

"Venison sausage *and* a scrambled egg," Molly lied, then climbed into the attic. She'd eaten a few bites of a banana, but Sid didn't need to know that. She also didn't need to know that her eating habits had absolutely nothing to do with what had happened the last time Molly was in the attic.

Molly hesitated on the ladder. She could already envision popping her head up through the floor to be greeted by the little girl, her black unblinking eyes staring at her as she crouched by the opening. Small white hands reaching out, grasping at Molly's throat. The slow suffocation of an evil spirit determined to murder the living.

No.

There was no ghost.

Molly released her breath, not realizing she'd been holding it. The attic was blessedly empty. Wood flooring stretched in front of her. Boxes in the corners. Cobwebs. Mouse droppings. No spirits. No poltergeists. Only silence.

"Are you all right?" Sid called from below.

Molly coughed, clearing fear from her throat. "Y-yeah. All good."

"I'm going to keep sweeping down here. There are a lot of nails that need to be cleared."

"Yep. Sounds good." Molly stood slowly, bending so she didn't collide with the slanted roof. She heard Sid's metal detector begin its detecting. A slow, rhythmic beeping that brought a semblance of steadiness to Molly's wildly beating heart.

She wasn't sure why she was so compelled to face terror head on in the chicken coop attic. There was nothing there. Nothing at all. Maybe that was why. Facing it would disprove her memories. Disprove what she thought she'd seen, what she thought she'd heard.

Molly's footsteps echoed as she crossed the floor to peer out the far window. It was small, square, and squatting in front of it, Molly could make out the bedroom window in the farmhouse. It peeked above the barn's roof. She could see the outline of her and Trent's bed with its worn but vintage headboard. The sun bounced off the lower part of the window. The curtain fluttered, as if a breeze were moving it from the inside.

She grasped the attic's wooden wall frame.

No one was in the house.

The windows were closed.

There was no reason for the curtain to move like that.

Molly strained to see clearer, the window being far enough away from the coop to make it difficult to see anything else. She leaned into the attic window, her nose almost pressed against the dirty glass. Her heart thudded in her chest and reverberated in her ears. Her breaths came shorter.

Placing her palm against the window, Molly tried to steady herself as she made out the form of an indistinguishable person staring back at her from her bedroom window.

"Molly!"

Sid made quick work of climbing the ladder after Molly's uncontrolled garbled scream.

Molly hated herself. She sat against the attic wall, hunched below the windowsill, her knees pulled up against her chest.

Sid scurried to her side and crouched in front of her. Concern etched into every crevice of her face. "What is going on with you?" Her tone wasn't one of condemnation but of real worry. Sid rested her hand on Molly's knee.

Molly shook her head. "I'm fine." At least she thought so. Who knew who was in her bedroom? She'd blinked a few times, and the vision had disappeared. The curtain was still. Once again, there was nothing to tell Sid—nothing she *wanted* to tell Sid. "I saw a mouse." She excused herself, but noted her hands were shaking. She tucked them under her rear so Sid wouldn't notice.

"A mouse?" Sid gave her a look of disbelief. "You haven't been afraid of mice a day in your life. You're pale as a ghost."

The words drained more color from Molly's face, she could feel it.

Sid pulled her phone from the back pocket of her shorts. "I'm calling Trent."

"No!" Molly's hand shot out and landed on Sid's, halting the trajectory of the phone to Sid's ear. "Please. Don't. There's no reason to."

Sid's mouth scrunched back and forth as she considered. Her eyes glowed with consternation. "Molly, you're acting really strange. You're worrying me."

"I'm fine." Molly had to give Sid something to appease her. "I just—the mouse ran across my foot. I need some time." Time to get her story straight before she cornered herself in her lie. Time to erase the voices and sightings of spirits wallowing in dark corners. Leave it to Trent to move her into a haunted farmhouse. To disrupt an already-disrupted life.

Sid readjusted so she was sitting in front of Molly, cross-legged, her phone resting on her knee. "This seems like more than a mouse." She was picking her words carefully. "You seem . . . troubled."

"I haven't been sleeping well." Another lie. Her medication knocked her out most nights, but it would pass as a good reason to be on edge. "There's a lot of change with a move," Molly justified.

Sid tipped her head to the side. "You moved five miles out of town to a farm. You didn't move to Papua New Guinea, or something."

"Papua New Guinea?" Molly's mouth quirked in a slight smile.

Sid waved her off. "It's the first place I thought of that sounded shocking. The point is, I know a move can be stressful, but isn't this your and Trent's dream? I mean, maybe I'm overreacting, but the last time we were here, you almost passed out on me, and now—heck, girl, you can *scream*!"

Molly managed a wobbly laugh. She hated lying to Sid. Hated being dishonest. But what was she supposed to say? *Hi! I see dead people!* She'd heard that line before. It'd been popularized, and it wasn't a sign of mental stability. They'd commit her. Or worse, arrange for some modern-day exorcism. Okay, she was being extreme. Trent and Sid wouldn't do that.

"Molly?"

She snapped out of her mental spiraling. "What?"

"Are you and Trent . . . you know, okay?"

Molly leaned her head back against the attic wall. She sucked in a deep breath, filled with the pungent mustiness of the old building. She couldn't answer. There was too much—*so much*—that was twisting her mind into an uninterpretable mess.

Sid took Molly's silence and seemed to accept it, yet Molly didn't miss her friend's suppressed sigh.

"I know that since the miscarriages . . ." Sid paused. Hesitant. "But getting this new farm and starting fresh . . ." Her words then drained away as if she had a point but was afraid to say it.

Molly stifled a laugh. "It's more Trent's farm than mine."

"But—"

"Sid." Molly opened her eyes and leaned forward, earnest, catching her friend's gaze and holding it. "Seriously. I know I'm not as fun as I used to be."

"I never said that—"

"But it's true." Molly struggled to her feet, wiping dust from her bare legs. She ignored Sid's beseeching look from her position on the floor. "We lost the babies, Sid. Four of them. You have your children. Breathing, *alive*. Mine are dead. There's no more of them, and there won't be, and I have to live with that. So, no. Trent and I aren't okay. He wants to move on."

"And you don't?" Sid rose to her feet as well.

Molly ducked her head. She watched a tear fall, dropping onto the wood floor, staining it. Yes. She knew. She knew, deep in her heart, she had to move on. To be healthy again. To find healing. To find . . . meaning. But when an earthly hell came to visit you, it didn't just go away. It dogged your feet until—Molly glanced at the attic window—until maybe you actually started to see physical ramifications of it. Evil. Abandonment. Loss. It haunted you until it enveloped you entirely.

10

Perliett

George dabbed at the blood that ran down her cheek. Perliett eyed him cautiously. She'd never had George Wasziak offer her any personal ministrations, but now she could hardly argue against it. It was difficult enough to begin the removal of glass shards from human skin, let alone on one's own face.

His eyes narrowed. Whether in concentration or sheer repulsion from the evening's events, Perliett did not know. She was, however, very aware that Mr. Bridgers—Jasper, as he'd insisted after the mayhem that she dispense with formalities—sat quite close to her. Possessively almost. His own hands were bloodied, though he'd made George tend to her first.

"You've a shard of glass just below your eye," George muttered. He dropped the cloth into a bowl of water, not taking his eyes off the glass shard lodged in her skin. "Miss Petra?" He directed his words to his nurse, who was in her fifties and unmarried. The town of Kilbourn knew Petra Adams as the proverbial spinster who was happy to be such and independent enough to be helpful to Dr. Wasziak.

"Yes, Doctor?"

"I need my tweezers."

"Of course."

Perliett had nothing to say. She could feel George's breath on her skin, his eyes concentrated on the glass in her cheek. He'd yet to ask what had occurred. Ascertaining the injuries, George had hustled into the Van Hilton study, took a quick inventory of the shattered window, the glass strewn across the floor, and the gaslights around the room, now lit, which revealed the evidence of the thwarted séance.

"Can you remove it without scarring?" Jasper's words split the tenuous silence between George and Perliett.

Perliett lifted her eyes to George but saw mostly his hand as he prepared to eradicate glass from her face.

George grunted.

"Ah, well then, do your dandiest."

Perliett heard the goading in Jasper's voice. She was well aware there was some sort of competition growing between the men. If George had anything other than sheer abhorrence toward her, Perliett would have suspected *she* might be the cause. So, knowing it wasn't her, she was clueless as to why the two men would circle each other in verbal fisticuffs.

"Ow!" Perliett sucked in a breath as George closed the tweezers on the shard.

Miss Petra rested a stabilizing hand on Perliett's shoulder.

"At least it's small." George's breath whispered across her face. "Hold steady, Perliett."

There was a familiarity in his tone, and a bit of warmth she wasn't accustomed to.

"I'm going to extract it now." And without hesitation, George did just that.

Perliett sucked in a breath as she felt the glass slide from her skin just above her cheekbone. Blood left a trickling path down her cheek, but George was fast to exchange tweezers and glass for cotton gauze, which he pressed there to absorb the blood.

His eyes met Perliett's, and she swore the rest of the room

drifted away until it was just the two of them, alone. There was a spark in his gaze. Something she couldn't interpret. He was both bothered and worried and . . . uneasy about something?

"There will be a small scar," George said, although the dark abyss of his eyes didn't flicker. "I can do nothing about that."

"I understand." And she did, only she wished it wasn't so.

"I'm sorry."

Perliett stilled.

George stilled.

"You're sorry?" she squeaked.

He nodded almost imperceptibly.

Jasper cleared his throat, and the room rushed back into view, leaving Perliett staring helplessly at George as he turned a shoulder to her to dig in his bag.

"I'll need to administer a stitch or two." George straightened, needle and thread in hand. He directed his attention to Jasper, but his eyes visibly darkened. "Then I will see to your hands."

"I'm sure there's not much to tend . . ." Jasper redirected all their attention to the door. "They need to be taken home, and I'm their transportation."

"Fine." George didn't seem to care about Jasper's condition too terribly. He nodded. "Miss Petra, would you mind cleaning off his hands? Swab the wounds and verify there's no glass embedded."

"Certainly." Miss Petra rounded Perliett and motioned for Jasper to rise. "Come. We'll run water over your hands in the kitchen sink."

Jasper followed Miss Petra, giving Perliett a formal nod. There was something about his expression that drew Perliett toward him, sucking her into the depths of whoever Jasper Bridgers was. Mysterious. Intriguing. Desirable. Altogether—

"A pompous oaf," George muttered under his breath as Jasper and Miss Petra exited the room.

Perliett snapped her focus back to George. "You're quite rude."

"At least I don't pretend to be otherwise. I don't weasel my way into people's lives who are grieving or infiltrate the home of two single women," he groused. Then, "This will sting." The needle poked into Perliett's cheek.

She bit back a whimper.

George pulled the thread through.

Heavens, Perliett was growing clammy. The last thing she wanted was to faint under the ministrations of George Wasziak.

He seemed oblivious to the fact that Perliett was measuring her breaths to maintain her stability of mind.

"Aside from the ever-present Mr. Bridgers, I'd say your little gathering didn't go as expected?" George's words brushed her cheek, following the path of the thread.

Perliett closed her eyes, biting the inside of her lip. It hurt worse than she'd imagined stitches would. "Spirits aren't always pleased to be disturbed," she retorted through gritted teeth.

Another poke. "Or maybe you're testing spirits entirely different from what you believe them to be."

"You truly cannot give my mother any credibility, can you?" Perliett winced.

George paused, waited for her to straighten her face, then continued with the second stitch. He was leaning close, and she couldn't help but notice his mouth. Lips carved and bordered by whiskers.

She realized he had stopped. Perliett lifted her eyes.

George was studying her, the needle and thread in his hand, already cut with her cheek sewn.

Perliett sensed a furious blush creeping up her neck, going to war with the cold desperation of feeling faint.

George raised an eyebrow. "Your mother . . . is none of my concern." It was a cool dismissal, but for some reason it did not convince Perliett that he was as detached as he made himself out to be.

They emerged from the room where George had embroidered her face. Perliett dabbed the stitches and wondered if he'd ever practiced by needling a sampler.

He gave her a sideways glance as they reentered her father's study. It perplexed her that George felt the need to follow her. She was well now, and it appeared Jasper had left with the considerably shaken Withers family.

Maribeth stood in the middle of the mess, the night air blowing through the shattered window. Crickets were chirping again and seemed especially loud without glass to separate the outside from the indoors.

Detective Poll circled the room, eyeing the broken glass that littered the floor. "You say it just exploded?"

Maribeth nodded, her hand clutching her throat. Her hair was in disarray. Thankfully, she had not been harmed, although glass had most definitely dotted the back of her dress in small tears, and Perliett was positive there had to be some tiny slivers stuck in Maribeth's hair.

"It was an unseen force hurtling angrily toward us." Maribeth's eyes were wide with conviction and terror. "I've never seen anything like it before in my life."

George joined the detective, and Perliett frowned at how they so quickly excluded them. The women. The ones who had been there for the event itself.

"Have you found a rock?" George's question made it to Perliett's ears. She exchanged a look with her mother. No paltry rock had caused such a chaotic scene!

"No." Detective Poll toed some of the shards as he made his way to the window frame. The gaslights made the room glow warmly, and he looked like a dark silhouette as he reached the opening. "Part of the window is still intact."

He eyed the strewn glass and the table they'd used in the séance. "It's puzzling. There should be something responsible for this."

"There is," Maribeth piped up, even though the men were exchanging ideas. "Eunice Withers."

George leveled his dark gaze at Maribeth.

Detective Poll met Perliett's eyes, then looked to Maribeth and finally cleared his throat. "Miss Withers—she is deceased."

"But her spirit is very, *very* disturbed." Maribeth made a broad sweep of her arm. "As you can see by the mess she has made of my late husband's study."

Detective Poll scratched his head. There was a helpless desperation in his expression, Perliett noticed, when he glanced at George.

George stepped forward. "There must be explainable reasons for a window exploding."

"Such as?" Perliett stepped forward also, and she heard glass crunch under her shoe.

He glared at her, visibly irritated by her challenge. Well, he should be used to it by now.

"Compression on the glass, for one thing." George redirected his attention to Detective Poll. "Improper installation could apply exponential pressure on the window to cause it to, over time, bow inward and thus explode from the stress."

Detective Poll pursed his lips and nodded. "Good point."

"Or . . ." George darted a look to Perliett, and she crossed her arms. Irritated. Really she should be grateful there might be a human explanation for such a spiritual occurrence. George continued. "Or," he repeated, "a nail meant to hold the window in may also have been erroneously putting pressure on the glass. Perhaps even having nicked it during installation. Eventually, the glass was bound to shatter."

"Explode," Maribeth supplied.

"Combust," Perliett challenged.

"Shatter," George said once more. "Had it been an explosion, you can be assured you would all have glass skewering you and I'd be stopping far more blood flow than a sliver in your cheek could cause."

Detective Poll cleared his throat again, attempting to command the discussion once more. "Regardless, I don't see anything criminal behind this. Whether happenstance"—he shot a look at Maribeth—"or something else, I see no signs of foul play."

"Eunice never meant it to look like foul play." Maribeth had adopted a stern demeanor. "She was trying to tell us something. Tell *me* something. There is violence at play here. In Eunice's death."

"Mrs. Van Hilton," Detective Poll said and held up his hand, "it doesn't take anything other than common sense to know that. Miss Withers was—"

"Miss Withers was brutally murdered," Maribeth interrupted. "Her mother is beside herself, and now the family has no less agony surrounding Eunice's death than before. More agony, I daresay, after tonight."

"And what would you have me do about it?" the detective retorted, obviously annoyed.

"Solve it," Maribeth snapped in uncustomary sharpness. "She deserves to rest in peace. Eunice *wishes* to rest in peace." She swept a critical glance around the area. "She has made that very clear."

There is another.
She is beautiful.
She is mine.

11

Sleep had been stolen from her. Perliett's tossing and turning the last few nights since the debacle during the séance had left her bleary-eyed, achy, and downright irritable. Now she stuck another pin into her hair, adjusted the sash around her waist, and lifted her gloves from her bureau.

It was Sunday. Time for services at church. A day of rest. A chance during an eventful and gory week to have things set back to rights in the eyes of God and man. The line between them—this veil that separated the spiritual from the earthly—was ever so thin. This Perliett knew. But she also knew that God all too often seemed to toy with humanity. Giving them small glimpses into the other side, but never really revealing its true nature.

Today would be no different. She would ride alongside her mother in their carriage. They would sit in the fifth pew from the front, left side. Hymns would be sung mechanically—not unlike the clickety-clack of a train on its tracks—habitual and rhythmic. The reverend who had officiated over Eunice's funeral would now gab prolifically on the nature of God, or the damnation of humanity, or as he so often did, the vices of men, such as the demon liquor.

At the end of his profusely disparaging sermon, churchgoers would remove themselves from the sanctuary with solemnity over their sins. Once outside, all would return to normal. God would be appeased for the rest of the week, and then they'd repeat the process. The church members might have a twinge of conscience, but even Perliett knew that no one would transform the course of their life or the decisions they made. Thus it made going to church every Sunday feel useless to Perliett, the experience leaving her in the doldrums. There was nothing real in church outside of censure from others and God, and a part of her wished it were more than it was. That God was more infinite than the mental boxes the reverend put Him into, and that hope was something immeasurable instead of being carefully doled out in tiny portions.

"Are you coming?" Maribeth called up the stairs.

Perliett dared a glance into the mirror. She looked respectable. Pretty, perhaps, but certainly not beautiful. Her raven hair was dulled due to her not being able to wash it the night before, for her mother had sat in the tub until the water was cold. She wasn't fond of cold-water baths or hair washing. Her stitches looked clean. George had done a fine job. No swelling or redness was a good sign. Of course, the paste she'd been applying at night might not be something Dr. Wasziak approved of, though it was obviously working.

Within minutes, Perliett was seated next to her mother in their carriage, and shortly thereafter, Perliett and her mother slipped into their usual pew with grace and dignity. She noted that the Witherses were not in attendance. Allowing her eyes to roam the room, Perliett mouthed the words to a hymn as she made out the stature of George, stiff-backed in the second row, standing next to his widowed mother. A few rows behind him was Kenneth, the thwarted-in-love man whom Perliett once again considered. Truly no one knew he and Eunice had been lovers? Perliett scolded herself quietly. She was crafting stories where perhaps there were none. Perhaps Kenneth had just been a remarkably empathetic discoverer of Eunice's body? His relief at the verification there was no pregnancy to contend with as a second death, pure chance? Or maybe—maybe the Withers family *did* know about Kenneth. Maybe they kept quiet so as not to add scandal to Eunice's name in the wake of her death.

Perliett noticed Detective Poll was there as well, along with his wife. She would relieve her conscience by telling him her suspicions about Kenneth Braun. At least her suspicion that he was in love with Eunice Withers, not that he had murdered her. Heaven knew that Kenneth had barely been able to hold himself together the day of Eunice's discovery. He certainly had no stomach for angrily skewering her multiple times with a knife.

Yes, that was the next course of action. Discuss this with Detective Poll so she could stop worrying over the idea of Kenneth Braun somehow being important to the mystery of Eunice's death. It would be Detective Poll's problem to address—if it was a problem at all. The past *was* the past, after all. Maybe she was overthinking it all?

Easing onto the pew at the reverend's bidding, hymnals closed and returned to their places, Perliett prepared to be lambasted with the glory of God. She felt her body grow weary from her fitful sleeps of late. She couldn't help but be a tad annoyed that her mother sat beside her, with an inch of space between her back and the pew. Alert, composed, and for all sakes and purposes, as invested in the sermon as she was on an evening in the dark when she summoned the spirits.

Perliett's gaze drifted to the long oval window at her end of the pew. The trees outside were full and luscious with green summer growth. She could see the churchyard, stones from the cemetery, and beyond that, cornfield. Across the street from the church was the narrow street's lineup of critical places of service: the drugstore, the post office, the mercantile, the feed and seed. Kilbourn was a homey little town on a Sunday, and if the reverend would summarize God in a paragraph instead of pages' worth of vocabulary, Perliett could go outside and enjoy it. That was if—

A scream from outside ripped through the congregation and made the reverend's mouth remain open mid-sentence. His eyes sharpened under bushy white eyebrows, and he raised an arm, his clergy weeds bagging down to his elbow.

"Someone will investigate. All remain seated, please," he instructed.

Detective Poll shot to his feet, as did George. Not to be outdone, Perliett did so as well and ignored Maribeth's urgent insistence to "sit down!"

The three of them hurried up the middle aisle of the church. Perliett noticed Kenneth slipping from his pew and following them, his lanky frame awkward as he dogged her heels.

Murmurs broke out all around them. A few well-meaning men had also stood and were moving to join them, but were waved back by Detective Poll, who seemed not to have noticed Perliett or Kenneth behind him.

They burst through the front doors of the church, and, had Perliett been in a better mood, she might have been overcome with curious shock and dismay. As it was, she knew her own expression now mimicked the reverend's as she took in the sight in the churchyard.

Mrs. Withers was kneeling on the lawn. Clutched in her hands was the violet shawl that belonged to Eunice. Her face was drawn, visibly haggard and pale, her mouth open in a silent wail. All Perliett could hear was a guttural gasping for air as Mrs. Withers's lungs competed with the need to sob.

George pushed past the detective, his long strides eating up the earth between himself and the mourning mother.

"Mrs. Withers." He was gentle as he approached her, his hands out with palms upward. "Mrs. Withers? It's me, Dr. Wasziak."

The woman rocked back on her heels, the shawl over her open mouth. Her eyes were wide and beseeching, and Perliett could see that she didn't register who George was.

"Mrs. Withers?" George prompted again.

Detective Poll gripped George's arm. "I'm going to calm the congregation down. They're already on edge because of Eunice's . . ." He paused and glanced at the distraught mother. "Well—"

"Yes, do," George agreed.

Detective Poll breezed past Perliett, giving Kenneth a frown as he hurried back to the church. Perliett had gone all but unnoticed, and now, as George cautiously knelt beside Mrs. Withers, she noticed the woman fixating on her.

"Eunice?" Her daughter's name floated across the air between them.

George looked over his shoulder, his gaze darkening as he noticed Perliett for the first time.

Mrs. Withers's eyes clasped onto Perliett with an insistence that made Perliett question her intentions to follow George and investigate the scream. The expression on the lost mother's face made her skin crawl and a shiver of apprehension slither up her spine.

"You're not Eunice," Kenneth muttered to Perliett with a shake to his voice that indicated he was twitchy and nervous.

Mrs. Withers struggled to her feet, the shawl still gripped by wiry fingers that had worked hard over the years to raise her precious children. Her hair hung over her shoulders, oily and unwashed. Perliett mentally vowed to wash her own hair that night, cold bathwater or not.

"Eunice." Mrs. Withers took a wobbling step toward Perliett, noticed Kenneth, and stopped so suddenly she almost fell over.

George's hand shot out to catch her.

"Kenneth Braun." Mrs. Withers looked between him and Perliett. Her eyes narrowed. "You leave my girl alone."

"I did nothin' to Eunice!" Kenneth's voice turned whiny.

Perliett gave him an impatient motion of her hand to stay quiet.

Mrs. Withers took another step, shrugging off George's steadying hand. "I told you . . ." Her words ended in a wail. "Ohhhhh, I told you!" She dropped to her knees and shook Eunice's shawl toward Kenneth. "Sin ends in judgment. Away from my daughter before you kill her!"

Kenneth released a guttural groan, and without pause, the man spun and ran across the churchyard away from them. His body was hunched as if he too were buried under the heaviness of grief.

Mrs. Withers reached toward Perliett, her eyes widening with earnestness. "Come. Come to me, my beautiful girl."

Perliett mustered her gumption. Mrs. Withers was clearly at the point of grief where a mother lost her mind and could not translate death into something final.

"I'm here," Perliett answered, hurrying toward the pathetic woman, every ounce of her heart aching for the loss Mrs. Withers experienced.

George scowled. "Perliett!" he hissed under his breath, clearly not a fan of her allowing Mrs. Withers her delusions.

It was too late. Mrs. Withers allowed the shawl to flop to the grass at her knees in a pile. She wrapped her fingers around Perliett's wrist, squeezing tight enough to pinch the skin, pulling Perliett down to her own knees.

Perliett winced under the woman's assertive grasp.

"Eunice . . ." Mrs. Withers's eyes had gone wide. She was seeing Perliett, and yet she wasn't. No. She was seeing her daughter. "Are you all right? Where have you been?" The woman lifted her free hand to brush cold knuckles down Perliett's cheek.

Perliett fought back a cringe. "I'm fine," she answered. She could sense George stepping closer to her. She knew his intentions were to stop the woman's delusions.

Mrs. Withers yanked on Perliett's wrist. Perliett bit back a whimper as the older woman sidled close, her mouth against Perliett's ear. Her whisper was hoarse, meant only for Perliett, which she could ascertain as the woman's warm breath traveled into her ear canal, along with words that crawled under Perliett's skin like a thousand flies on a corpse.

"He likes girls like you. I didn't know. I didn't." Mrs. Withers's nails bit into Perliett's wrist. Her cheek brushed against the stitches that George had left behind only days ago when Eunice herself had been summoned. "Don't dare rest your weary feet, my darling. When he comes, you must be ready."

Perliett drew back, searching the woman's face. "Who? Kenneth?"

"Mrs. Withers." George was at Perliett's side, breaking the spell. He dislodged Mrs. Withers's grip on Perliett's wrist, but the woman refused to release Perliett's gaze.

"Mind me, girl. Be ready."

Perliett nodded. More because she needed to convince Mrs. Withers so she would back away and allow George to assist her to a safer place. A place where she could grieve and lose her mind in privacy. A place where she could follow delusions of seeing her daughter without mistaking Perliett for her.

Perliett wasn't averse to speaking with dead people, but she wasn't keen on being spoken to as if she were the next to die.

"This has gone far enough." Maribeth ran her motherly hand down Perliett's arm as if she were a young child instead of an independent woman. There were moments when Maribeth became a bit like a mother bear, and Perliett would be remiss if she didn't admit it warmed her. Maribeth eyed Detective Poll. "Do you have *any* clues as to who is responsible for Eunice's death?"

The churchyard had finally emptied after Mr. Withers had been called on to retrieve his wife, after the reverend finished calming his congregation with the reading of a psalm, and after Detective Poll had reassured anyone who lingered with questions and concerns.

"We are following up on several suspicions." It was all Detective Poll was going to offer them.

"Such as?" Maribeth insisted.

"It's not for you to know," Detective Poll said firmly. His wife sidled up next to him, her brown eyes soft and understanding. Perliett had always wished that they could become friends, even though Evangeline was ten years her senior.

"It *is* so upsetting, though." Evangeline attempted to soften her husband's words.

George sniffed. "I find it upsetting you keep inserting yourself into the middle of it." His stern focus leveled on Perliett.

"As if I purposefully made myself the center of Mrs. Withers's attention?" Refusing to be chastised like a child, Perliett stiffened her shoulders. "*I* was brought into the middle of it when you requested my assistance with preparing Eunice's body."

Evangeline blanched.

"And when Eunice shattered our window," Maribeth added, "which you all seem delightfully disposed to ignoring."

"Eunice did *not* shatter your window." George rolled his eyes in no attempt to disguise his irritation.

"Then what caused it?" Maribeth challenged. She tipped her head and attached a patronizing tone to her voice that made Perliett wince. "Oh yes. That's right. You believe a nail was putting stress on the glass and it suddenly *popped* after years of pressure and at *just* the right moment."

"Everyone stop! Immediately." Detective Poll raised his hands, his expression commanding. "First and foremost, I must ask that you cease and desist from any *assistance* you are trying to offer. We do not need to contact a dead woman for her advice." A severe glance was leveled on Maribeth.

"The law will continue to investigate her slaying without help from the outside. In the meantime"—he turned his attention to Perliett—"you are not helping Mrs. Withers's state of mind when you allow her to believe you are Eunice."

"Precisely," George grunted.

"My recommendation is that you step back and allow Dr. Wasziak to minister to the physical needs of the Withers family and remove yourself entirely."

"I beg your pardon?" Perliett tipped her chin up and hoped she looked as severe as she was going for. A snuck glance at George told her she hadn't quite achieved it. "The Withers family specifically requested my help. How can I deny them my ministrations should they ask again?"

"You were going to give them *heroin*!" George spat.

"Oh no! Is that bad?" Evangeline's hand rose to her throat.

"Why? Have *you* taken some?" Detective Poll shot a worried glance at his tiny wife.

"It's not good," George asserted.

"No, I haven't," Evangeline said to her husband.

"According to *you*," Perliett snapped at George. "Many recognize it as a leading source of effective treatment for people with medical addictions, such as overuse of cocaine. Heroin is also quite effective as a calming agent."

"I hardly believe it's effective to treat one drug with another drug and assume they will cancel the other out!" George groused.

Perliett stiffened and met George's stance. He stepped closer to her, staring down that aquiline nose of his like a Roman centurion ready to feed her to the lions. She would not back away.

"Bayer produces it."

"For *doctors* to prescribe."

"And I am a medical practitioner!" Perliett insisted. The man was daft.

"Show me your diploma. Your medical license." George

glowered. "No? Oh, that's right. You don't *have* one. You have an *apothecary* box with home remedies! You, Miss Van Hilton, are a *hobbyist* playing doctor with other people's lives! Something to toy around with in your spare time since it's more than apparent your father left you well enough off where common daily necessities are not a hardship." His countenance had grown dark like a thundercloud, and Perliett couldn't retort due to the large lump gathering in her throat. She blinked back tears, yet George didn't seem to notice. Instead, he barreled on as if the doctor in him couldn't see that more than tangible items could wound a person, but also words. "I would trust a veterinarian over your unschooled practices. Blast it! I would trust a *woman physician* were she schooled properly. You, however, have not been, and it is beyond my understanding why you pretend to be!"

"Oh, for the love of all that is holy!" Maribeth's unorthodox exclamation commanded all their attention. "A woman was *murdered* and you're prancing about like a peacock showing his colors in order to gain a mate and in the process making her look like a brown ugly duckling! Be a gentleman if not the Christian you claim to be and show some human kindness."

George sputtered.

Evangeline hid a smile behind her gloved hand.

Detective Poll heaved a sigh that could have been heard in the next county.

Without pause, Perliett retorted, "I'm far prettier than an ugly duckling."

A musical laugh escaped from Evangeline, and Maribeth patted Perliett's arm. "Of course you are, but having a standoff with the doctor is akin to going to war with Poland. It won't work. Have you noticed how stubborn the Polish are?"

"I take offense to that." George's eyebrow winged upward.

"I'm sure that you do," Maribeth said, patronizing him with a lovely smile. "Now, back to the topic at hand. Eunice

Withers is not resting in peace. Her mother is losing her senses from grief and believes *my* daughter to somehow be in danger of this . . . this hellion! We have a killer running loose, and to be frank, I've heard very little about what is being done to resolve the situation. Should we lock our doors at night? Are other young women in danger? From what I've heard, he isn't much different from that Jack the Ripper killer in London, disemboweling poor Eunice."

Evangeline's hand shot out to grip her husband's elbow.

Detective Poll opened his mouth to retort, but Maribeth continued without pause, and etiquette caused the man to snap his mouth shut.

"Now, if we were to join together," Maribeth offered, "we might bring to light more information that could put this entire tragedy to bed."

"I will not be engaging in the practice of spiritualism to solve a crime," Detective Poll stated firmly.

"Thank God!" George inserted, the thundercloud not having cleared from his face.

"Mrs. Van Hilton, Perliett, I must insist that you both go *home*," Detective Poll added, taking advantage of Maribeth's momentary pause. "Remove yourselves from this investigation and from the Withers family. Your interference will only muddy the waters and make things far more difficult."

Maribeth and Perliett exchanged looks. Perliett could see irritation in the depths of her mother's eyes. The lack of tolerance for her practice of connecting with the afterlife insulted her. Perliett knew precisely how her mother felt. She dared a glance at George, whose thunderous expression had settled on her. She blinked again. The hot tears pressed in where they were not welcome. She wasn't a *hobbyist*! Her intentions were quite pure. Her studies were self-taught, yes, but then for centuries humankind had been learning and exploring and teaching themselves ways of healing. Why couldn't an average person help when another was ill? Were all illnesses *only* to be treated by a doctor now? To be disregarded so coldly—for her mother to be cast aside as a witch of sorts? It was hurtful.

George's eyes narrowed.

He'd seen her tears.

Very well. Let that be the case. He needed to know what damage his words could cause.

"Detective, I will accept your admonishment, though I cannot agree with it." Maribeth's acquiescence was in word only. Perliett knew this as she watched her mother stalk away toward their carriage, which was hitched close to Detective Poll's automobile.

"Perliett," George began.

Perliett eyed him, aware that the detective and his wife were watching as well.

"Your mother—"

"My mother's intentions are as well-meaning as my own."

"Be that as it may—"

"You believe she's a fraud, don't you?" Perliett looked between the two men. "That she does what she does for monetary support? Engages in trickery?"

"Doesn't she?" George challenged. "Be honest with yourself, Perliett. How often have *you* connected with a ghost? Talked to them? *Seen* them?"

"Do you wish to make it your life's mission to discredit the Van Hilton women, *Dr.* Wasziak, or would you rather we assist in making Eunice's death as manageable as possible?" Perliett cursed the wobble in her voice. George did not understand! Spirits didn't just waltz into the room at the bidding of a live human and have a cup of tea while chatting about their deaths.

"I would be more concerned—" George stopped, and Perliett didn't miss the transfer of looks between the men—"with what Mrs. Withers said to you. She believed you to be Eunice, but what did she mean?"

"That I'm to die soon," Perliett responded as flippantly as she could, merely because if she didn't, she was certain to burst into a full-out river of tears. She didn't want George, of all people, to know how unnerving and painful all of this had been.

"Dear Perliett," Evangeline interjected as she reached for her, "we will protect you. Won't we?" She placed naïve and assured confidence in the supremacy of her law-enforcing husband.

Detective Poll offered his wife a thin smile, but when he met Perliett's gaze, there was a solemn concern buried in the crevices of his face. "If Miss Van Hilton does as we've asked, she should remain out of danger."

Should?

Perliett didn't miss his implication the word signified. She didn't miss the way George's stern visage had softened to a similar one of concern. Concern he had no right to offer her now that he had burned every shred of a bridge between them.

Detective Poll ignored the tension between them and continued, "You *are* aware, Miss Van Hilton, how similar you look to Eunice Withers? It's no wonder Mrs. Withers mistook you for her daughter."

Taken aback, Perliett was without words. She'd never—no—Eunice Withers was a beauty. She, on the other hand, was a dark-haired, average-looking woman.

"You are so beautiful, I'm sure you know this." Evangeline could articulate openly what her husband was subtly attempting to communicate.

"And beauty," Detective Poll finished, "draws attention. If Eunice's killer fancied her . . ."

Perliett grew cold. Miserably so. She didn't need George to finish the thought for her, but he did anyway.

". . . then the killer might fancy you."

12

Molly

A knock on the door alerted Molly to a visitor she was not expecting. She pushed herself off the floor, where she was unpacking another box of books. Her hand slipped as it knocked in a Pepper Basham romance. Romances were the only things she could read nowadays without having her heart split into two or her mind race as she felt the breath of a dead soul breathing over her shoulder.

Molly tiptoed around piles, feeling proud of herself for finally unpacking the boxes. She eyed the form standing outside the door. A man, black pants, a nice polo shirt. He had a badge clipped to his waistband.

She opened the heavy wooden door of the farmhouse. "Can I help you?" Molly eyed the man.

He couldn't have been much older than she was. Mid-thirties. Reddish-blond hair with green eyes and a smattering of freckles on his upper cheeks, the rest of his face hidden by a beard that was a darker shade of red than his hair.

Molly noticed another person behind him on the lower step. A female officer. Dressed in full uniform.

Foreboding climaxed quickly in Molly's stomach, and she

grappled for the doorframe. Trent. Dear God, she couldn't take another loss. She knew they weren't close right now, that there were wedges between them, but she loved her husband. She did. God *had* to know that!

"Molly Wasziak?"

Molly wanted to sit down before she passed out. Instead she nodded, white-knuckling the doorframe.

"I'm Detective Carter. This is Officer Hammish. We were wondering if we could ask you a few questions."

Questions. *Questions*? A flicker of relief spiraled through Molly. "Um—" Molly fumbled to right her mind back into a center of normalcy. "Um, sure. Yeah." She stepped onto the small cement porch. Trent had always told her never to invite strangers into the house. Of course, seeing as they both sported badges, she was probably safe. Nevertheless. "What can I help with?"

Detective Carter offered her a kind smile. "I'm sure you've heard of the unfortunate circumstances last week and the body that was found at your neighboring farm?"

"Of course. My husband found her body. He was helping with chores there."

"Trent Wasziak is your husband, correct?" Officer Hammish interjected. Molly wasn't sure she was comfortable under the other woman's sharp, assessing stare.

"Yes?"

"Ma'am, we've taken your husband down to the station for some questioning in connection to the victim."

Molly reapplied nervous pressure to the doorframe. "Connection? How?"

Detective Carter skirted her question. "Do you know a January Rabine?"

"Who?" Molly stared at him.

"Please answer the question," Officer Hammish commanded.

"No. I don't. I've never heard of her."

"Are you familiar with your husband's family?" Detective Carter asked.

"My in-laws. Yes, of course."

"How about his extended family? Aunts, uncles, cousins?"

Molly looked between the law-enforcement officers on her front porch. She fumbled for an answer. "I-I, maybe? Wasziak is a common Polish name in the area. I mean, Trent has a lot of cousins."

"What about family from out of state?"

"A few. His uncle. I think. Maybe Trent's cousin?"

"Which cousin?"

"I don't know." Molly couldn't remember. Not under this type of pressure. She recalled Trent having said something about a cousin he'd skateboarded with a lot in high school. But it wasn't as though they'd maintained a close relationship. "Some guy, I . . . his last name was Wasziak too, I think." Molly knew the information she'd offered was paltry. "What's going on?"

"Ma'am, we've identified the victim as January Rabine. She's from Artesia, New Mexico, and is a distant cousin of your husband's."

The image of the dead girl in the ditch washed over Molly, and this time she sagged against the wall. The young woman's name was *January*. She remembered Trent staring down at her. Calling the police. But the idea he had anything remotely to do with her death . . .

"She's his cousin?" Molly attempted to piece together the information she'd just learned.

"Distant," Detective Carter acknowledged. "We've contacted her family. They will arrive from New Mexico soon. In the meantime, we have reason to believe she was here to meet with your husband."

"I don't know anything about that," Molly supplied.

"Clandestine meeting maybe?" Officer Hammish asked.

"My husband doesn't keep secrets from me." Molly immediately bit her tongue. Famous last words of an ignorant wife, not to mention it wouldn't take much digging for the police to find out how disconnected she and Trent had become since the last miscarriage.

"We will need you to stay in the area, ma'am," Detective Carter instructed.

Molly eyed him. "I've nowhere else to go anyway." She struggled to maintain her composure as her emotions swung between shock and irritation at the conjectures being made. "January Rabine," she stated, trying out the name.

Detective Carter's eyes sharpened.

Molly met his look straight on. "I saw her. I saw her dead body in the ditch. Trent didn't do that. He had nothing to do with it, and if January is related to him, it's circumstantial."

Circumstantial. She'd read enough crime novels to know that word was filled with guts and power when trying to argue innocence in a case.

Detective Carter cleared his throat. "Well, we'll see, Mrs. Wasziak."

"Molly. My mother-in-law is Mrs. Wasziak."

"All right, Molly." Detective Carter turned, as did Officer Hammish.

"When will Trent be released?" Molly asked after them.

Detective Carter turned back, his face expressionless. "He's not under arrest, ma'am—Molly—just being questioned."

"What was January Rabine even doing here?" Sid came over as soon as Molly called. Her two younger kids in tow, they were tossing a football back and forth in the yard as Sid stepped over a pile of books on the living room floor.

"I don't know." Molly rocked back and forth on the couch, holding her coffee mug between her hands as if the liquid itself would magically erase today.

"This is so weird." Sid plopped down next to her, the couch

sagging. "She's a distant cousin *and* they found her body down the road from your place?"

Molly took a sip. It was hot. Her tongue stung. "Too coincidental. If Trent killed someone, why would he drop the body at a neighbor's farm?" Her question was rhetorical and intended to imply the ludicrous nature of the suspicion.

"He was interrupted?" Sid answered anyway.

"Sidney."

Sid had the decency to look appalled that she had disassociated so much from Trent that she was solving the crime instead of defending her friend. "Sorry. I was just—"

Molly leaped from the couch. "I need to find the Wasziak family tree. Trent's mom gave me one a while back. Who the heck is January Rabine?"

"She's very dead, that's for sure," Sid joked inappropriately. "And why didn't Trent recognize her when he found her?"

Molly stood in the middle of the room at a complete loss. Boxes were stacked on boxes. She had no idea where she'd put the family tree before they moved, let alone what box it was in now. "I need the family tree," she repeated, ignoring the blaring question from Sid.

"Maybe it's online?" Sid offered. "Or call Trent's mom?"

"She's in Greece with Trent's dad right now. Fortieth wedding anniversary trip, remember?" Molly retrieved her phone and ran a quick search on the internet. It was amazing how many Wasziaks there were in the world. "Trent's mom mentioned once that Trent's grandfather's name was Gerald. That's about all I know."

Sid peered over her shoulder. "Try that site." She pointed to a genealogy site, and within a moment, a Wasziak family tree popped onto the screen. "There. Gerald."

"Looks like the main family tree is here," Molly muttered. She followed the names. "Trent being the only child in his family, his dad and his grandfather, Gerald. Gerald had three boys. Trent's dad and his two uncles."

Sid followed the tree with the tip of her finger. "Right, and the one uncle, Roger, married and had a daughter, who was the only female cousin. Tiffany Wasziak, and her married name of—there! Rabine!"

"Whose daughter is January," Molly finished. "So, January is what? A second cousin once removed?"

"I dunno." Sid shrugged. "I can't ever remember how that cousin-to-relative ratio goes."

Molly tabbed to another screen and typed *January Rabine, Artesia, New Mexico* in the search box. Soon some matches appeared. Mostly old news articles from high school track teams. "She must have been a runner."

Sid squeezed in closer to see the year January graduated. "My gosh, she was only twenty when she was killed."

They met each other's eyes, and Molly knew hers reflected the same as she saw in Sid's. Sadness for a life not lived. The young weren't supposed to die.

Molly refocused her attention on the task at hand. "I need to find something to clear Trent."

"He's not being charged with anything," Sid reminded her.

Molly winced. "It makes me nervous all the same, like I need to be prepared to defend him."

"You won't find that on the internet." Sid's words struck with their logic. "*Who* January Rabine was to Trent means little right now. He would need an alibi."

Molly pocketed her phone. "I'm going to the station. I need to be there for Trent."

"Good." Sid patted Molly's knee, and Molly knew that Sid was affirming such an action primarily because it was something to do, if not at all helpful.

Molly jumped from the couch and hurried to the kitchen. She snatched up her purse and keys, then slipped her feet into flip-flops by the door. "Can you lock up when you leave?"

Sid stood in the doorway between the kitchen and the

carpeted dining room. "Sure. Drive slowly. We don't need you being in such a hurry you get in an accident."

"Right." Molly flung the door to the mudroom open, then reached for the screen door. A shriek yodeled through her throat as she almost ran into a man, who was reaching for the screen door from the outside stoop. "Trent!"

Sid's "Oh, thank God!" chimed in behind her.

Trent staggered into the mudroom, pushing past Molly.

"Are you okay?" Molly followed him. He bent and untied his work boots, kicking them off. When he straightened, Molly shuddered as his eyes, so empty, swept over her face and then moved to look beyond her.

"Is there any coffee?" he grunted.

"Yes." Molly followed him, feeling a bit like a puppy trying to get attention from its master.

Sid laid a hand on Molly's arm, her hazel eyes filled with understanding. "I'm going to grab my kids and we'll head out. Call if you need anything."

"Thanks." Molly wanted to reach out and beg Sid to stay. She was a buffer. A voice of reason. Stability. Everything Trent wasn't or hadn't been in what seemed like forever. But it was unfair. Unfair of her to put that pressure on Sid. So Molly let her go.

Moments later, Trent eased his body onto the bench in the corner kitchen booth. It was a kitchen addition inspired by someone who'd run a restaurant once maybe? Molly didn't know. She didn't care. She just stared at the man she'd once been barely able to talk to because of the butterflies he'd caused in her. Now he was sprawled on the gray vinyl seat of the bench, his hands cupping a large mug of black coffee, staring into it.

Molly pulled a chair opposite him and settled into it. "What did the police want?"

His shoulders rose and fell in a shrug. "Just to ask questions."

"Didn't you recognize her? Or know she was your cousin?" Molly's stomach settled with a pit in the bottom that was like a lead weight.

Trent shook his head and ran his callused finger around the rim of his mug. "I'd only seen her when she was a toddler. Years ago at a Wasziak family reunion."

"Have you stayed in contact with her parents? Your cousin Tiffany?"

Trent lifted his eyes for a moment before lowering them again. A brief glimpse into blue orbs flooded with defeat. "Dad wasn't close to my uncle Roger. So, any of Roger's kids—my cousin Tiffany? Nah. We didn't stay in touch."

Molly eyed Trent's hand, which now rested beside his coffee mug. She wanted to reach out to lay hers over his. To comfort him. Most of all, she wanted to not doubt him. She wanted to believe they were so bonded, she knew beyond any shadows or questions that Trent was in the clear. It haunted her that they weren't.

"The cops drilled me about my family," Trent continued.

Molly chose not to reach for him.

"They wanted me to repeat everything all over again from the day I found January's body." Trent grimaced. He took a long draft of his coffee. When he set his mug down, some of the black liquid sloshed over the side. Trent ignored it. "They wanted to know where I was the night of January's death. Apparently, her time of death was sometime after midnight."

"What'd you tell them?"

Trent gave her a look that she had somehow missed the obvious answer. "That I was home. In bed. With you."

She was Trent's alibi. "That makes it simple then," Molly affirmed. "I'd know if you weren't next to me."

"Sure. Tell that to the cops. The wife of someone they suspect isn't always the strongest alibi, Molls."

"What on earth would have been your motive to kill her?" Molly heard her voice rise in frustrated disbelief that her husband was even being questioned beyond being the unfortunate soul who'd discovered the murdered corpse of his own cousin!

"Nothing." Trent slapped the table. His expression was stormy, his face haggard. It seemed the last few hours had deepened the crow's-feet at the corners of his eyes and hardened the set of his jawline. "I don't have a motive, and they know that. They're just asking questions. I'm not under arrest."

"But you're under suspicion," Molly argued.

"Half of Kilbourn is under suspicion right now." Trent glared at her. It was rare he lost his patience with her. But now his irritation was written plainly on his face. "If you'd leave the house now and then, you'd know there's a town just down the road with people in it." His sarcasm slammed into Molly. "We have a population of about a thousand people, and a young woman was just murdered. You're exploring a *chicken coop*, for all the blamed good it'll do the world."

Trent's reaction was uncalled for. Unfair. Rude actually. Molly reared back. "What's wrong with cleaning out the coop?"

"Nothing. In theory. But how about try *living* in the real world?" Trent clenched his teeth and stared at her. "Doing something *other* than hiding?"

"You're the one who bought this place." Molly's words hit their mark. She could tell as Trent stiffened. It didn't stop her. "If you wanted me to socialize more, then you should've bought a house in town. You should have *been there* for me."

Trent gritted his teeth, his eyes squinting. In stubbornness? Maybe. Wasziak men were known for that, known for not mincing their words, for being factual and unemotional and—

"That's unfair." Trent's words grated through his throat.

Molly blinked back at him. "Is it?"

He closed his eyes. His forefinger tapped against his coffee mug. When he opened his eyes again, there was resignation in them. Anger. Hurt. "You're really gonna bring that up now? Today?"

"There's never a good time for you." Molly remained stalwart in her grief. She'd borne it all but alone. "You have your work at Clapton Brothers Farms. What do I have?"

"You could get a job." Trent's suggestion made Molly bristle. That wasn't the point, and he knew it. She wasn't clamoring for a career. She was grateful she didn't have to drag herself out of bed every morning to go to work. But their dream had also been that the privilege of her staying home would come with the honor of raising their children. That dream was dead.

"Listen." Trent drew in a steadying breath. He didn't look at her but instead fixated on his coffee mug. "You know I had chores when it happened."

"Four times." Molly's mumble interrupted any justification Trent was going to offer. "Four times I miscarried. Four times by myself."

"I can't help it if I was at the farm!" Trent swung at his coffee mug, and it slammed against the wall, splattering black liquid against the yellowed paint.

Molly froze. Stared at him. He wasn't demonstrative—*ever*. Trent let his head fall back as he stared up at the ceiling. He raked his hand through his hair, his hat falling off and clapping onto the floor.

"I can't do this now." His words sliced through her. She understood today had been hellish for him, finding out about January Rabine and the family connection. Sitting at the police station being interrogated. But he had to understand that the last several *years* had been hellish for her, and in ways she could never describe. The voices. The sights. The outright terror sometimes. He didn't know about that. He only knew that she was burdened with grief. Postpartum depression was as real after miscarriages as it was after a child's live birth, yet many didn't take that into consideration. Miscarriage was the ghost pregnancy. The type that didn't get calculated into grief like the loss of a stillborn or a baby through other means. Miscarriage was that haunting, hovering happenstance that was shared by the couple. Or *should* be shared by the couple at least.

"Fine." Molly bit her tongue. "Don't deal with it now. What's another year? Or two? There's not going to be any more babies anyway. We have the rest of our lives to talk about it."

"Molly." Trent's voice was dangerously low.

"No." She swiped at rebel tears that ran down her face. Sniffing, Molly ran her arm across her eyes. "Never mind. Your cousin is dead, and that is what's important now."

She didn't intend to sound so "woe is me," but it came out that way.

"Yeah. That's what's important now," Trent repeated.

Molly felt her entire being sag under the weight of his words. "Then what do we do?" she asked. It was the only thing she could think of to say.

Trent's shoulders lowered, and he began to gather up the shards of broken coffee mug. "There's nothing *to* do," he stated baldly.

Which was unfortunate. But it was also the repeated answer to the many issues they had stuffed in between them over the last few years.

13

No matter how hurtful and difficult it was to admit, Trent *was* right about one thing. She didn't leave home very often. This was evidenced by Molly having turned down the wrong street so that now she was backtracking her way to the farm supply store. She was buying chickens today even if it killed her. Not to mention the farmhouse felt stifling to her. All she could see in her mind were images of January Rabine lying dead in the ditch, and the little girl in the chicken coop attic, and that creepy sensation that someone had been in her bedroom. Watching her.

She had picked at the scabs of their mutual frustration and grief, and Trent was talking less than he already did. It was a wall between them, the babies. The four little Wasziak babies they'd lost early enough to not even know their genders. Early enough that many didn't even know or realize, or worse, recognize.

She was on emotional pins and needles today. She'd needed to get out of the house. Or do something like unpack more. But Molly hadn't had the gumption to haul the empty plastic bins to the basement for storage after she'd unpacked the last of her novels. The last thing she wanted to see was the basement walls with the carved memorials of dead people whose memories were vaporous at best. Home was unsettling, and that was not how a home should be. The warm, comforting haven Molly craved had begun to dissipate after her first miscarriage. It'd been dissolving ever since.

She finally pulled into the parking lot just as her phone pealed. Molly answered it, knowing from the caller ID that Trent would be on the other end.

"Hey," he began. His tone was matter-of-fact, as if nothing had happened yesterday. Life was going to proceed as normal for him. Molly could hear farm machinery in the background. "Uncle Roger just called," Trent continued. "January's parents and sister are arriving from New Mexico. My cousin Tiffany and her husband, Brandon, want to see us right away."

"Why?" It was the first word that popped into her mind. She felt defensive. Were they going to suspect Trent as well? Verbally attack him for somehow being to blame for their daughter's—his cousin's—death?

Silence.

"I mean," she said and tried to cover up her curt response, "we barely ever see your uncle Roger, and I've never even met your cousin."

"I don't know." Trent sounded impatient. "But I can't get away from work until later tonight, you know that. There's the milking and then one of the heifers cut her hindquarters on the jagged edge of an old metal fence post, so I need to treat it with meds again before I leave. Uncle Roger said he's bringing Tiffany and Brandon to town. They're getting a place to stay at the hotel, but I was thinking—"

She interrupted quickly before Trent had the audacity to suggest offering his extended family free housing. "Sure. You want me to have them for supper," Molly concluded.

"They're family," Trent stated.

"I know." She tapped her foot on the floor of her truck, attempting to gather her wits, stuff her emotions, at the very least be a relatively *nice* human to her husband. She didn't want to be like those women in the Proverbs who were compared to "clanging gongs" or "rain on a tin roof" . . . did they have tin roofs in biblical times? She was probably paraphrasing, but still, she didn't want to go down in their marriage history as completely embittered. She was already verging on nuts. Yes. Nuts. She knew some people were offended by flippant terminology, but she called it what she felt it was. She had married a Wasziak after all, and they didn't mince words.

"Molly? Are you there?" Trent's voice interrupted her thoughts, which bounced off the walls of her mind like a ricocheting bullet.

"Yeah. Yeah, I'm here. I can make hamburgers on the grill. I'm in town now, so I'll pick up potato salad and some carrots and dip or something."

More silence.

"Molls?"

"Yeah?"

"Thank you." They were two very simple words, but tears sprang to her eyes. There'd been a time just hearing Trent Wasziak's voice on the other end of her phone would have sent her emotions into a euphoric spiral. Their high school had been small, he'd been popular. Not a jock, but just the all-around nice country boy any Michigan girl from a rural area would drool over. And she'd claimed him. No. Molly reconsidered. Trent had claimed her. He'd been dogged in his persistent attention, and while she'd been elated, Molly had worried at some point he'd lose interest. But he hadn't.

"You're welcome," she answered belatedly.

He didn't hang up.

Neither did she.

"I'll be home as soon as I can," Trent finished.

"Okay."

Molly fixed her resolve. She needed to prepare to make hamburgers on the grill. Because that was what she did. The daily task of surviving when she felt the overwhelming cloud of death surrounding her. That gut-aching despondency that left her staring aimlessly ahead with nothing to hope for.

Except chickens. Chickens. Hamburgers on the grill. And welcoming another set of grieving parents.

January's parents.

Death came in all shapes and sizes, but it always left the same catastrophic damage behind, along with the scars that would last an eternity.

Tiffany and Brandon Rabine were at least ten years her senior, but tonight they appeared to be well into their fifties. Grief-worn faces were drawn with lines that sagged with sorrow. With them was their elder daughter, Gemma, whose own demeanor seemed more stoic than emotional. It appeared it was Gemma who was keeping her parents together.

Molly glanced at the clock on the dining room wall. She'd hung it there earlier, after she'd quickly unpacked the nice dishes and hung a couple of paintings so at least the dining room was halfway inhabitable for guests.

She never had gotten her chickens. She'd left the farm supply store feeling the task of getting chickens *and* grilling out for company was almost insurmountable.

Now a half-eaten supper lay on the table before them. Hamburgers were consumed, but there was a large amount of the store-bought potato salad and Jell-O salad Molly had picked up. A basket of chips was stationed in the middle of the table with a few on Brandon and Gemma's plates. The vegetable tray was void of cucumber slices—apparently they were a hit with the otherwise not-eating-much family.

Uncle Roger sat at the end of the table. He resembled Trent's father, and while Molly hadn't met Roger more than a few times in the last five years, he made himself at home with Midwestern ease. Now he leaned forward on the table, his elbows propped on either side of his plate.

"Trent really knows nothing?" His question was laden with disbelief.

Molly shifted uncomfortably in her chair. She glanced out the window, just over Uncle Roger's shoulder. Leave it to the Clapton brothers to keep Trent hung up at the farm until well into the evening. Story of her life.

"I'm sorry," she responded, mentally chiding herself for saying sorry for the tenth time that night. "Like I said, we only—*he* only found January. That's all. We didn't even know she was in the area."

"She hadn't reached out to you?" Gemma's blue eyes were sharp. Assessing.

"No." Molly shook her head.

"I can believe that." Roger sighed. "I'm her own grandfather and she hadn't even called to let me know she was here."

Tiffany retrieved a clean paper napkin from the holder in the middle of the table. She dabbed at renegade tears that left track marks through her haphazardly dusted-on makeup. Brandon reached over and gripped her hand, but his blue eyes—like Gemma's—landed on Molly.

"We had to identify January today. At the county morgue."

Molly bit her tongue before she said *I'm sorry* for the eleventh time.

"Why on earth was she here in Kilbourn?" Brandon voiced the question they all wanted to know. "Why not tell us she was coming? Talk to you, Dad, or reach out to family like Trent and Molly here?" Brandon swept his hand to encompass them in his speech.

Gemma reached for a potato chip, snapping it between her fingers. "If the police would let us see her things, then we'd be able to understand. January *always* kept a journal. They're probably scouring her private thoughts for clues." There was an edge to Gemma's voice. Molly couldn't blame her. The idea of losing a sister to murder was incomprehensible. Not to mention the police hadn't released the details of how she'd died or what might have occurred before her death based on the autopsy report. That left open-ended questions that were unsettling. Had she been assaulted? Brutalized?

Molly reached for her can of Coke and took a swig. Gosh, she'd give anything for Trent to make a heroic entrance now and save her from the horridness of this dinner.

"She didn't keep her journal in the Cloud?" Molly's question came without censuring it first. She regretted it the moment she said it, but it surprised her when Gemma's head shot up and an anticipatory light glowed in her eyes.

"I never thought of that!" She pushed away from the table. "I need to get my iPad from the car. I'm sure I can figure out January's email password and then access her Cloud drive. If her journal isn't on there, she may have left notes. Clues."

"*That's* why the police asked me if I knew January's passwords," Tiffany mumbled.

"They asked you that?" Brandon frowned.

Tiffany nodded.

"They must think similarly," he concluded.

The screen door slammed off the mudroom as Gemma made a hasty exit.

Tiffany sniffed. She crumpled her napkin, then addressed Molly. "I'm sorry," she began in a watery voice. "Do you have any tissues?" Tears were brimming again.

"Of course. Just a sec." Molly was eager to leave the table, and she shot out of the room like a guilty man from a courtroom. She didn't know why she felt guilty.

Sagging against the hallway wall, Molly tried to focus on where she'd stored the extra stash of tissue boxes.

Who saw him die? I, said the Fly.

She froze. The words were a hissed whisper in her ear. Molly shrank into the wall as if she could merge with it. She heard the murmurs of her guests' voices in the dining room. But the whisper. It was in her ear, hot breath on her neck, but it also came from . . .

Molly looked to her right. Into a back room where the

laundry was located, a back door exit, and the stairs leading to the basement.

With my little eye, I saw him die.

She took a tentative step into the room.

Who caught his blood? I, said the Fish.

Molly's feet were at the top step leading to the basement. How she'd gotten there so quickly, she couldn't explain. But the crooked, narrow wooden stairs beckoned her downward. The basement was a cavernous hole, dark at the bottom with cool, damp air that met Molly's nostrils—a moldy scent of moisture mixed with age.

A stair creaked beneath her weight.

Molly realized vaguely she'd not been downstairs since the day they'd first toured the house. Her hand gripping the stair rail, Molly stopped on the bottom step. The whisper had ceased. Her skin prickled at the basement cold. She reached, fumbling in the dark for the string to the lightbulb. Finding it, light flooded the gloomy basement.

It spanned the length of the kitchen and dining room. Spiderwebs collected in the rafters. A water heater stood in the far corner. A few crates were stacked haphazardly. Empty. Leaning against the wall where she saw—

Merlin Bachman

b. October 1, 1890, d. Otober

They had scrapped the tombstone after someone had misspelled *October*. Now it helped to hold up the foundation. The memorial marker to a dead man who no one remembered anymore. A lifeless story.

This basement was anything but dead. It was alive. She could feel it. Sense it. Alive with the untold stories of the dead carved into the foundation, mistaken names and dates causing them to be cast aside. What if no one had remade their markers? What if their graves remained unheralded to this day, and these tombstones in her basement foundation were the thwarted efforts to remember them?

Who caught his blood? I, said the Fish.

Molly repeated the words soundlessly, even though her mouth moved. Something was off. Dreadfully wrong. This place—this basement—this *farm*. She could feel it lurking in the air. A secret sin, something so dreadful that time was disguising it, but reality was trying to expose it.

She lunged for the stairs.

She had to get away from it.

Too much death.

All around her.

It pressed in on her lungs, stealing her breath. Suffocating her sense of reason, her sense of being *alive*.

Stumbling up the stairs, her knee struck the edge of one and she slipped.

. . . with my little dish, I caught his blood.

Molly grabbed for the stairs to regain her balance. As she did so, she looked up toward the light coming from the room above.

Her scream strangled in her throat as she stared into the lifeless eyes of January Rabine. She stood at the top of the stairwell, her stringy hair hanging over her shoulders, brushing her torso. Her hand was outstretched, her eyes a glassy white.

No. It couldn't be.

January was *dead*!

Molly clawed for the railing, her fingernail splitting as it connected with stone wall instead.

"Go away." Her command scraped from her throat as a hoarse whisper.

January's body blurred as Molly's vision made the dead woman double, then merge, then double again, like an awful shadow that wove and dodged through Molly's reality.

Molly scrambled to get away from her, and as she did, the stairs gave way beneath her. Falling into the dank basement, surrounded by gravestones, felt like falling into a grave. She would be buried alive as January watched from the grave's edge.

14

Perliett

Why did everything awful happen at night? In the darkness? Where ghouls and goblins lurked in the deep places. It had been nighttime when Eunice Withers was murdered. It was nighttime again, and while she appreciated being recognized as a caregiver—if not a bona fide *doctor*—Perliett wasn't particularly keen on midnight runs.

Perliett hooked her laces on her shoes and gave Maribeth a reassuring look. "I'll be fine, Mother."

"Fine doesn't keep you *alive*." Genuine worry marred Maribeth's face. "I wish I wasn't feeling so ill." She sniffed, holding a handkerchief to her running nose. Her eyes were watery from congestion. "Summer colds are miserably inconvenient, and I truly hate your rushing out in the middle of the night. Detective Poll has given me insufficient reason to believe the killer isn't still roaming about like the devil on the prowl."

"I'm not alone." Perliett tilted her head toward the carriage that waited outside, driven by young Brody Hannity—the grandson of another local farming neighbor.

"A nine-year-old boy is certainly not a knight in shining armor," Maribeth observed. She withdrew her handkerchief from her face and straightened with resolve. "I will come as well. We'll take our own carriage."

"Ain't no time, ma'am," the boy inserted, hopping from one foot to another. "My sister is awful sick."

Perliett exchanged a glance with her mother. "Awful sick" just might be beyond even Perliett's admitted purview.

"You may spread germs," Perliett said and waved her mother off. "I will be fine. Really. Go back to bed and rest before you become 'awful sick' too."

Maribeth's eyes narrowed at the instruction.

Perliett smiled at Maribeth, knowing full well that as much as her mother cared, she also preferred to coddle herself. Not to mention she had three sittings scheduled for the week and would be loath to put them off. Maribeth's gifts were becoming something of a marvel since word of the shattered window and Eunice Withers's supposed angst had spread through town.

Brody said little on the way, passing his grandparents' farm, with his own family home their destination a few miles past. His lanky body hardly looked ready to be manning a rig, and yet he did it with familiar expertise, even in the midnight glare of the moon.

Perliett craned her neck to look at the Withers farm as they wheeled by. The two-story farmhouse was square and solid-looking, and there was a large white barn with a cupola. It appeared to be a peaceful place. Perliett hoped it could return to such a state.

She settled back in her seat. Evangeline Poll had stated emphatically that Perliett resembled Eunice. She'd never noticed and still didn't quite believe it. The idea was altogether unnerving in some ways, while in others complimentary. However, Perliett could clearly recall what Eunice's poor dead body looked like lying on the table underneath a white sheet, and it wasn't a pleasant premonition of what she herself might look like someday. Not now. *Absolutely* not now.

George and Detective Poll were hypervigilant in their suspicions. There was no hunting killer on the loose. Merely someone who had taken a knife to Eunice Withers and—

"Here we are, Miss Van Hilton." Brody interrupted Perliett's musings. She didn't expect a nine-year-old boy to help her down from the carriage, so she saw to it herself.

Hurrying to the house, Perliett made quick work of the greetings. She was taken directly to the little girl's room where, after taking her temperature and listening to her cough, Perliett was almost certain she knew the remedy.

"Little Miss Patricia has the croup. It will pass, but we need to get her fever down. I recommend wetting one of her nightgowns in water from your well so that it is cold. We'll dress her in that. The coolness will be quite uncomfortable, but it should help bring down the fever. When it dries, she will sweat out the remaining illness."

And she didn't even need to use her apothecary chest for that solution!

After an hour of getting the little girl into the highly unpleasant wet nightgown, Perliett instructed the parents, "Be diligent. She will whine about the nightgown. Wouldn't we all? But it is for the best. I can check back tomorrow to see how Patricia fares."

Perliett waited.

The parents thanked her profusely and then both flanked their little girl's bedside.

Perliett stood in the doorway, a bit at a loss. Brody had gone to bed. It was two in the morning after all. Yet his father was making no signs of seeing her home. This appeared to be a habit forming with nighttime calls. Transport to the patient's bedside, followed by inadequate transport home. But Perliett could hardly blame them. Worry was etched into the parents' tired faces, and Perliett hadn't the heart to outright demand the little girl's father be a gentleman and see her home. Although, considering recent events, it was more than likely the more reasonable course of action. She shouldn't have been so quick to decline her mother's suggestion of accompanying her.

Stuck in the conundrum of politeness and consideration versus vigilance and caution, Perliett erred for what was most comfortable to her constitution. Blowing a soft breath from between her lips, Perliett gripped her apothecary chest by its handle and made her way through the dimly lit farmhouse to the front door. She opened it, pausing on the top stair of their porch.

"Well, this is unseemly."

Perliett eyed the dark yard, the darker shadow of the road ahead of her, and then she noted clouds had built up in the sky and become quite persistent at shutting out the moonlight. She adjusted her grip on her apothecary chest.

"Fiddlesticks," Perliett murmured. If she walked briskly, the distance could be traversed in under an hour. It was merely a few miles, and she wore a walking skirt and sensible shoes. Passing by the Withers farm would most assuredly conjure thoughts of murdered Eunice, but then one couldn't discount that Eunice had likely been flirtatious and coy and sneaking from her home in the middle of the night, which was not a recipe for good tidings. No. Perliett's reason for being out wasn't a clandestine meeting—or whatever had coerced the murdered young woman into the darkness. No. She was here for good reason, and fate would only be kind to her because of it.

Perliett adjusted her wool shawl around her shoulders and stepped off the porch. A nighttime hike would do her health good. She just wouldn't tell her mother that she'd walked home. In the dark. Under the surveillance of the crickets and the owls and the coyotes and raccoons.

Ten minutes into her walk, Perliett increased her gait as the Withers farm came into view. Truly, there was nothing ominous about the place itself, just the story of its inhabitants. If Eunice had been tempted to sneak from the home in the night, then her assailant had to have waited for her not far from here. Had she known him? Perliett certainly thought that would be a good possibility. Why else would a young woman leave her home in the middle of the night to mingle with a man she didn't know? Assuming that *was* what had lured her from her bed. A man. A lover? It was plausible considering it was the beautiful and coy Eunice Withers.

But maybe it *hadn't* been someone Eunice knew who had lured her from the safety of her home. Had Kenneth Braun? Perliett was certain there was a secret relationship between the two that was highly scandalous should it come to light. But she still warred within herself over her suspicions, and she'd yet to express them to Detective Poll. Her empathetic side certainly didn't wish to expose poor Kenneth to more trauma, considering his nosebleed and anxiety made for arguable proof that he wasn't to blame for Eunice's death.

Maybe it *had* been a stranger—a dashing stranger. Mysterious. Dark. Like Rochester from *Jane Eyre*. Or debonair like Mr. Darcy from *Pride and Prejudice* . . . Perliett glanced over her shoulder, certain she'd heard footsteps behind her. There was nothing but a dark road. "Oh, who am I kidding?" she mumbled to herself. "No female in her right mind would sneak out at night to meet up with the pasty, tongue-tied Mr. Darcy." No. A girl who was a romantic at heart would sneak out for someone far more enticing than a Mr. Darcy type of man.

Mr. Bridgers's visage flooded Perliett's mind. Now *he* was a mysterious, brooding Rochester sort. He was not at all what Perliett would have assumed—

She halted, tilting her head to listen.

For certain she *had* heard footsteps behind her! An overactive imagination could be to blame certainly, and playing Sherlock Holmes in the dark with a murderer afoot was reckless. But still . . .

Perliett whirled and instantly understood how a person could taste fear. She stared into the black deep of the night. Cornstalks lined both sides of the road. Cornstalks. Like the ones that had hid Eunice's body. She narrowed her eyes, straining to see in the dim light, the form, the outline, *anything* that could claim ownership to the footsteps.

A low chuckle filled the air. So quiet she wasn't sure she'd heard it. But then it drifted through the corn, combining with the thudding rhythm of her own erratic heartbeat.

"Who's there?" Perliett demanded, but the night swallowed her words.

This time, a throaty chuckle bounced off the stalks and wound its way toward her.

No. She'd no intention of being assaulted at knifepoint like Eunice. Lover, clandestine meeting with a stranger, or what have you, Perliett's reasons for being out were innocent. Innocent! She hiked up her skirts and ran, her apothecary chest dropping to the road like an abandoned child she could do nothing to save. Let the cornfield's laughter mock her as she fled. She had no plans of falling victim to a faceless predator.

The last person Perliett wanted to see the following morning was George Wasziak, who stood on her porch, hat in hand, fist poised to rap on the screen door.

Perliett jerked the door open before his hand could descend. She was, frankly, not in a fine mood. Not after last night. Why, she'd barely made it home without being slaughtered by the demon-like creature that had chased her down the road. Well, not literally chased her. Only his laugh. But truly, that laugh! No, it was a chuckle. The threatening kind. The kind that was laden with menace and evil intent.

I see you.

I could hurt you if I wanted to.

Only the chuckler hadn't. She'd run all the way home, leaving her precious box of goods behind in order to save her life.

"Missing this?" George hoisted her apothecary chest.

Perliett pursed her lips and grabbed it from his hand.

"No thank-you?" he goaded.

Perliett placed her precious box inside with a fleeting question in her mind about the welfare of Brody's sister. Had her fever broken?

"I see," George concluded.

Perliett turned her attention back to him. Perhaps *he* was the nighttime chuckler. The creeper in the corn. The murderous man who had ravaged a young girl.

"You're a pathetic piece of manhood," Perliett spat. Fine then. That her terror from the night before had made her irritable was an understatement.

George's eyebrows almost disappeared under the dark hair neatly combed over his forehead. "For what do I deserve that insult?" He didn't seem fazed. "You should herald me as heroic. I returned your paltry box of supplies, minus the heroin you pilfered to irresponsibly treat your patients."

"See?" Perliett shook her finger in his face. "This is the issue I have with you, *Dr.* Wasziak. You've no sense of decorum. Of decency. Of respect for a woman's intelligence."

"Don't I?" George challenged.

"Obviously not."

"And why would that be?" He crossed his arms, his suit coat sleeves tightening over his upper arms and distracting Perliett for a moment. "Would it be because you treated a little girl last night with the *wet blanket* treatment?"

"It was a wet nightgown," Perliett corrected.

"Or," George continued, "was it because you walked home in the wee hours of the morning *alone*?"

"They had to tend their daughter, not me," Perliett explained, excusing her actions.

"*And* it is apparent something frightened you or you

wouldn't have left said apothecary toys in the middle of the road for me to find this morning. Poor wee Patricia *worsened* during the night, you realize, because of a sopping wet nightie? They saw fit to invest in a practitioner with education and experience."

Perliett blanched.

"Yes." George's countenance was so dark, she was certain she could see a storm brewing. "You are going to hurt someone, Perliett Van Hilton, if you don't stuff this nonsense into that box of yours, lock it, and throw away the key!"

Perliett had nothing to say.

George eyed her. "I commend your desire to help others. There are different ways you can do so without risking their lives—as well as your own," he finished a bit lamely.

"My own?" Perliett already knew what George was about to say.

"How daft are you to walk home in the dead of night? We've already had that conversation!" He glowered. "Especially after what Detective Poll told you on Sunday."

Perliett hadn't moved from the doorway, and she hadn't invited George inside either. "What was I to do?"

"Ask for a ride?" George said.

Perliett pursed her lips again. She realized she did that a lot while George was present. "From whom? Their little boy had retreated to bed, and Patricia's father was quite vexed. Of course, there were no magnificent heroes at hand to rescue me either, such as you imagine yourself to be, I suppose? Or Mr. Bridgers?" She added Mr. Bridgers merely to irritate George, and Perliett smirked when it did.

George's countenance darkened at her mockery. "Jasper Bridgers. You *would* see fit to lump us together. I can only hope that your dislike of me means you feel thusly about him."

"Hardly," Perliett countered, folding her arms over her chest and tilting her chin up. "I barely know the man, who apparently has chosen Kilbourn to be his new place of residence."

George's eyes narrowed. "Because Kilbourn is such a destination for the citified airs of a man like Jasper Bridgers."

"Who do *you* believe Mr. Bridgers to be?"

"I've no idea who the boorish man is." George seemed offended she might suppose that he did.

"You're the town doctor, aren't you?" Perliett challenged. "Surely *all* the females with their medical concerns regale you with gossip during their treatments?"

George reddened. Whether blushing or angry, Perliett wasn't certain.

"I'm very curious who he is."

"Why?" George barked. "He's the epitome of who a good Christian woman should *not* be concerned with."

"Really?" Perliett teased him with a smile. "Am I a 'good Christian woman'?"

George raised a brow. "Aren't you?"

"Hmm, one might debate depending on whether they find my *mother* suitable to set foot in church on Sunday while exploring the spiritual realm during the week."

"You're baiting me, Miss Van Hilton." George's jaw clenched.

"And you're judging me, Dr. Wasziak."

They were at a standstill.

Then, "Fine. The benefit of the doubt. You *are* a good Christian woman," George conceded. "Mr. Bridgers is obviously not."

"A woman?" Perliett bit the inside of her lip to avoid laughing.

"A Christian," George seethed.

"You see." Perliett leaned casually against the doorframe, still refusing to invite George inside or to have him sit on the porch. "I find that to be juxtaposed with the Christian faith altogether. Don't the Scriptures say that we should love one another, even our enemies? And drawing such blatant judgment concerning another's faith should be left to the Almighty?"

"Surely." George nodded. "But not while throwing discernment to the wind! Loving another does not mean no discretion is involved. A mother can love her child while also not approving of their actions. I daresay even a mother could be wrathful were her child to act so arrogantly outside of her instruction so as to hurt themselves or another."

"And what has Mr. Bridgers done to warrant that extreme of a censure?" Perliett bandied about her debate. She enjoyed it too much, seeing George fluster, defend, and if she was being honest, he was quite good at it. Hard. Cold. But good at it. "I have a difficult time, George, seeing you as the loving sort of man."

Her words brought the conversation to an awkward halt.

George's eyes shifted from dark to darker to darkest.

Perliett suddenly knew she had pushed too far. His judgmental nature—as she saw it—was no different from her own aimed toward him. Both were censuring but in different ways. It was radical to accuse anyone of not being capable of love. Perliett knew that she herself had taken this argument to a far more personal sort of nature than George had. She'd challenged not only his faith but his aptitude to care for another human being out of love.

George worked his jaw back and forth. His nostrils flared for a moment. Then he garnered control. He opened his mouth to reply, but was cut short when Maribeth appeared behind Perliett, snapping the morning's newspaper with an emphasis that demanded the attention of both of them.

Perliett turned.

Maribeth's face was white, making her reddened and chapped nose appear redder. Her voice was husky from congestion, but her violet eyes were brilliant with concern. "Did either of you read the paper this morning?" She completely ignored the fact that George was not a regular morning visitor to their front porch and included him in the conversation without a second thought.

"I did not." George seemed to have no problem shifting his attention to Maribeth.

Perliett shook her head, still trying to recover from the whiplash-worthy exchange she'd just shared with the doctor.

Maribeth turned the paper so they could see the front page. "They've given him a name!"

"Who a name?" Perliett was perplexed.

"Eunice's killer! They're calling him the 'Cornfield Ripper,' after that English killer who brutalized his victims in the streets of London years back."

"Nighttime Chuckler is far more creative," Perliett muttered.

"What?" George scowled at her.

She realized she'd not expounded on her terrifying walk home the night previously. That George was right about the entire situation left her bereft of any argument. She felt it better if she held that minor part back or any arguments and debates she held would lose all credibility.

"'The Cornfield Ripper,'" Maribeth read, snapping the paper open so as to read it more clearly, "'guilty of the disfiguring and therefore the death of Miss Eunice Withers, has sought to contact the *Kilbourn Chronicle* by which he offers the police investigating her murder this message: "I found killing her to be part of me." The instructions provided to us here at the *Kilbourn Chronicle* are that we were to publish this at risk of another subsequent killing. We have therefore acted accordingly, and the public will see the Cornfield Ripper's message along with the local police simultaneously.'"

"He blackmailed the newspaper?" Perliett stared at the paper in her mother's hands.

"Not surprising," George said. "A man willing to take a life as violently as was done to Miss Withers will glory in lording the power of fear over this community. My guess is, Mrs.

Withers's public spectacle on Sunday awakened in him the notion of this manipulative gesture. Implant fear and one can be entertained long after the thrill of killing has subsided."

Perliett looked sideways at him. "You seem to know a great deal about the mind of a killer."

"If one studies humankind, one can conclude this rather swiftly."

"Well, now the police are being manipulated by him!" Maribeth folded the newspaper in half to obliterate the pompous words printed on the front page. "All the more reason we *should* engage Eunice in resolving this. She has much to say. Her spirit is restless and aggrieved."

Perliett nodded in agreement.

Dr. George Wasziak, on the other hand, remained stoic. He didn't say a word, though he seemed to contemplate many of them by the way his lips pressed together.

Maribeth was oblivious to the tension. She caressed the paper as if it were a portal to another world. "If only Eunice could speak to us . . ." Her eyes strayed in the direction of the study window that was boarded up now because of its being shattered the last time she'd attempted to contact Eunice. "Such distress . . ." Maribeth choked back emotion, blinking to usher away her tears. "You do not know, do you, Dr. Wasziak, what it means to be bound and gagged by death and unable to convey your desperation? You stand there, and I can sense your disapproval. I know Detective Poll disapproves too. But do I intend to bring harm? Is there personal gain from my endeavors?"

"You *do* charge your sitters, or so I've heard." George apparently found it impossible to remain silent any longer.

Maribeth held the newspaper to her chest, her eyes sparking. "And you profit from the illnesses of others. *I* make a pittance, Dr. Wasziak. I do not *need* to make myself wealthy from others' grief. My husband left Perliett and me in good financial stead. Accusations that I do this simply to profit from the grief of the ones who have lost connection with their loved ones are abhorrent."

"And yet you offer thin hope, Mrs. Van Hilton." George avoided Perliett's gaze. He also disregarded her rather sharp heel kick against his shin as he still stood half behind her.

"I offer more hope than you, Doctor," Maribeth shot back. "When your services are rendered useless as death claims a life, mine become next in line. We both have good intentions. Yours to heal the body, and mine to heal the rift between death and life."

"So, you are God then?" George's blunt inquiry caused Maribeth to pale.

Perliett turned full toward him, wondering if she glared hard enough, if the man would dissolve right there on the porch.

"I would never claim such arrogance." Maribeth's voice was thin with irritation. "As neither would you, I assume, and yet you still attempt to heal. What is the difference, then? Heal and raise a spirit from the dead? Both are miraculous in a way."

Her challenge was met with a moment of silence.

George shifted his feet and then cleared his throat. This time, his voice was gentler. It stirred something in Perliett she had not expected. His words stunned her, aggravated her, and startled her all at once.

"What need do we have of God if we can build our own bridges to eternity?"

While Perliett knew there were many more defenses her mother could raise in response to that question, her silence was the stronger indication that for Mrs. Maribeth Van Hilton, the conversation was over.

15

A summer night breeze wafted through her open bedroom window, lifting the gauzy curtain as if it were a ghost floating in the room. Perliett watched it from her place in bed, thankful she was not traversing the road tonight as she had the night before. The day had been rife with tension. Her mother had spent most of the day in her father's study, sniffling and coughing as she nursed her cold. Perliett could hear her mother in the room. She smelled the incense. She sensed the heaviness in the air that came with the visitation of the dead. But she dared not interrupt Maribeth.

All Perliett could do was consider George's accusation that her mother was toying with abilities that belonged to God alone. Yes, she recognized that while some mediums did indeed employ trickery to turn a profit, here her mother was at the moment beseeching Eunice Withers to come. And for no reason other than to bring reconciliation with her death and to help Eunice rest in peace.

Maribeth had not left the study yet, and Perliett had retired without interrupting her. Now she rolled onto her side and reached for the photograph displayed on her nightstand.

"PaPa," she whispered. At twenty-four now, it had been six years since he had passed away. Perliett could never forget the morning she'd waltzed into his study, ready to take on the world with him, only to find him slumped over his desk. Dr. Wasziak had not established his practice yet, and so it had been the now-retired Dr. Hempshaw who had hurried to the Van Hilton home only to pronounce Perliett's father dead. They'd already known that was his state, yet hearing the doctor declare it was still heartbreaking. Perliett had held some irrational hope that the doctor could revive him. That PaPa was not fully dead, and that they could urge his heart into beating again.

Perliett held the photograph tilted toward the window so the nearly full moon could shine its light over her father's face. His gray beard, his neatly combed gray hair. His beloved lined face with his right eye slightly slanted downward. It was the day that had changed her forever and in so many ways.

God had become more distant, since He had chosen not to answer her pleas for her father's life.

Mother had become devoted to her study of the spirits in hopes of connecting with PaPa and remaining tied to him in the afterlife.

Perliett had devoured tome after tome of old medicine books, remedies, ancient potions, and natural solutions so that she could help others not experience the grief she now bore every day.

Six years. She had hid her grief well. Behind a sharp wit, a sure intelligence, and a forthcoming smile.

Perliett stroked her thumb across the image of her father.

Six years, and nothing. She was older. Unmarried. George consistently challenged her and seemed intent on proving her methods not only impractical but unhealthy. Her mother had yet to conjure PaPa from the other side, and it left Perliett with no communication from him. Nothing to offer her guidance.

Here, a true spinster who lived with her mother, lay Perliett Van Hilton. Abandoned by death and by spirits. She might argue that at times she felt abandoned by her mother, who seemed to prefer ghosts over the living. Abandoned by . . .

Perliett sighed and rested PaPa's photograph back on her nightstand.

She knew the argument would be that God had not abandoned her. But that was because people believed that God never told an untruth, His Scriptures were holy, and His promise of eternal faithfulness usurped the physical world. That God crafted an eternal one filled with some sort of hopeful dream should one choose to accept the grace He offered. Of course, one could discount the opposing option of hellfire and brimstone if one went their own way, and that hardly seemed in line with an all-loving, gracious God.

The truth was, she was lost. Perliett swiped at a lone tear that trailed down her cheek toward her pillowcase. She was grappling with questions that offered no satisfactory answers. She could argue that the churchgoers in town—excluding those like her who abided it as their Christian duty merely because of tradition—were short on tolerance of her. But then, if she was being honest, she was short on tolerance of their intolerance. So, didn't that mean she also was intolerant? Was humankind merely a bucket of souls, pointing fingers at one another instead of at themselves and refusing to reconcile that they were innately not good to begin with?

PaPa had told her once, *"Perliett, all of mankind groans because we are trapped here without the fullness of the purity of God. Until we meet Him face-to-face, we are paltry excuses by ourselves. We should be humbler, we as mankind. We are nowhere near as magnanimous as we believe ourselves to be."*

PaPa had not been a theologian. He had not been a vocal man of faith either. He'd been a quiet man. Leading a quiet life. A quiet owner of a lucrative enough business to leave her and Maribeth in good financial stead. But therein lay the root of the problem. He had left them. To go where? To heaven? To hell? To an in-between place? Did he hover in the corners of their home like an angel watching over them, or did he plead with them from the shadows of the walls, a ghost begging for release?

In her dreams, she heard him. Chuckling. The low timbre of ominous laughter rolling in his throat. Mocking her. Boasting of his ability to take her. To brutalize her. To hold her beneath his will and bend her until she broke. Until she begged for mercy. Until she pleaded for grace and the chance to continue living. All before he plunged his blade into her, twisting her insides around the razor-like sharpness, laughing as her lifeblood drained from her and corn silk brushed her face as she—

With a gasp, Perliett shot straight up in her bed. Hadn't she just been pondering God and man and all that lay between them? She glanced at her nightstand. PaPa's photograph stared back at her, but for a moment she would have vowed she saw him shake his head, ever so slightly, in a warning to stay still.

Never obedient, Perliett flung the covers off her sweaty body, swinging her legs over the side of her bed. It was complete darkness now, the moon having taken a respite behind a thick cloud covering. Thunder rumbled in the far distance, mimicking the growly chuckle that echoed in her mind.

"You will not have me," she whispered into the darkness. Not sure why she whispered it, Perliett rose and reached for her wrap. Slipping her arms into it, she tied the ribbon at her neck. Detective Poll and George had weaseled their way into her subconscious, making her afraid Eunice's killer had somehow drawn designs on her, merely because of what? They were both brunette? They both had blue eyes? They both were . . . beautiful?

Perliett padded across the floor in defiance of her fear and of the warnings given to her. She was perfectly safe in her bedroom. In this house. There was no one here. No one lurking in the corner, chuckling in a taunt.

The window was open, and Perliett pushed aside the flimsy curtains. She leaned out the window, eyeing the familiar dark shapes of their yard. The weeping willow tree and its dancing branches that, even in the night, floated like fairies and brushed the earth. The large boulder that sat at the end of their drive. A wooden barrel filled with flowers that in the darkness had lost their color.

No. There was no one there.

Only her dreams flitting about, weaving in and out of the willow tree. A chuckle that reverberated only in her mind but threatened another night without solid sleep.

She pulled her body back inside, closing the window for good measure. No sooner had she straightened the curtains than a *clink* against the window made Perliett startle. She remained rooted, staring at the window through the curtains as if whatever apparition had administered its bell-like knock against the glass would become visible.

Another *clink*.

This time, she saw the distinct shadow of stone bouncing off the window.

A stone.

Inspired by a throw from a human arm.

For a brief second, terror paralyzed Perliett. The Cornfield Ripper was outside her window! He had found her! He had thrown a stone at her window to get her attention?

Rolling her eyes at her exaggerated imagination, Perliett pushed back the curtains and reopened the window.

"Who's there?" she hissed into the darkness. God have mercy if it was George Wasziak pulling some schoolboy stunt and—

"Perliett?"

"*Millie*?" Perliett made out the form of a woman lurking beneath the window. "I'll be right down!" she assured Eunice Withers's younger sister.

Perliett made quick work of traversing the hallway, tiptoeing down the stairs, and reaching the front door. She pulled it open just as Millie scurried onto her porch, gripping a knitted shawl around her chest. Her dark hair was hanging around her shoulders, but other than that, she seemed put together and healthy.

"What is it, Millie? Why on earth didn't you knock on the front door?"

Millie cast a nervous glance over her shoulder, then settled large blue pools of worry onto Perliett. "I didn't want to wake your mother."

Perliett had no idea how Millie knew which window was her bedroom, but she shrugged off the thought. "Here." She extended her arm to the porch swing, and Millie agreed, lowering herself onto it. Perliett sat beside her, holding the swing still with her foot braced against the floor.

"Is your mother ill?" Perliett asked.

Millie shook her head. "No. No, she's not. I . . ." She peered out into the yard and seemed satisfied when she didn't see whatever she was looking for. She turned her attention back to Perliett. "I didn't know who else to turn to."

Perliett reached for Millie's hands, and when Millie returned the grip, her fingers were ice cold. The summer evening was warm—stuffy, even though there was a breeze. There was no reason for Millie to be cold.

"Millie, what is it? What's wrong?"

Millie drew in a shuddering breath. "Has it happened to you? Do you *feel* him?"

"What are you talking about?" Perliett hoped Millie wasn't going mad like her mother.

Millie's grip tightened. "The Cornfield Ripper. You saw his letter in the paper, didn't you?"

"Less a letter and more of a sentence, but yes. I did."

Millie nodded as if Perliett understood. "He's watching us, Perliett."

"What?" Nonplussed, Perliett shifted in her seat.

"My mother—I know she's half out of her mind, but she says things, Perliett. As if she knows. Knows he isn't finished."

"Finished with what?" Perliett hated to sound so obtuse, but she was struggling to understand what exactly had Millie so spooked, and why she was bringing it to Perliett's bedroom window in the wee hours of the morning.

"With *killing*." Millie's fear-filled words came out in a watery gasp.

"You don't know that." Perliett shook her head. She needed to calm Millie.

"I *do*." A tear slid down Millie's cheek. "Did you know Eunice had several suitors? Not just Kenneth."

Perliett figured half the town suspected this about Eunice. "I pondered the idea. I know she and Kenneth were very close."

Millie grimaced. "I was going through her things to pack them away. There's too much around to remind us of Eunice and it sends Mother into fits. I found letters. Several of them were from her suitors, a few from Kenneth, but there was one . . ." Millie pulled away from Perliett's grasp and rummaged in the small handbag that hung by strings on her wrist. "This." The paper was crumpled, and Millie all but shoved it at Perliett.

Perliett received it and unfolded the letter. It was too dark to see clearly, but she held it just beyond her nose to make out the words.

Who killed Cock Robin?
I, said the Sparrow,
with my bow and arrow,
I killed Cock Robin.
Who saw him die?
I, said the Fly,
with my little teeny eye,
I saw him die.

"Well, that's just a nursery rhyme." Perliett attempted to disregard the shiver that ran through her. A horrible nursery rhyme, whether it was about an actual robin bird or some notable person from history. "No mother would recite this to their child at bedtime, but—"

Millie snatched it back from Perliett. "No *suitor* would write it in a love letter either."

"How do you know that was the intent?" Perliett inquired, not trying to negate Millie's concern, but also trying to understand what it even meant and, again, why Millie would bring it to her in the dead of night.

"Because," Millie said as she folded it hastily, stuffing it back into her handbag, "I found it *with* Eunice's love letters. Not with general correspondence. They were all tied together with a ribbon." She lifted her eyes. "I think it's a threat. I think Eunice's killer was taunting her. I believe Eunice was hiding this . . . this horrid letter from the family. She was *afraid*, Perliett. It is a threat, veiled by a child's nursery rhyme, but a threat nonetheless."

Perliett considered her words before responding too hastily. "You believe Eunice knew her killer."

"Yes." Millie nodded emphatically. "I believe he arranged a rendezvous with her. It's the only explanation as to why she wasn't in the house during the night."

"As you are now?" Perliett couldn't resist pointing out the irony.

Millie nodded. "Yes. Exactly."

"A poem about bloodletting would not inspire me to leave my home at midnight to meet up with a young man," Perliett said, challenging the girl's theory.

Millie nodded again. "I thought so as well. But then this evening, when I put my mother to rest in bed, she started *reciting* 'Cock Robin.' Why? She never recited it to us as children. I've never heard her even acknowledge the nursery tale's existence."

"Your mother wrote the letter perhaps?" It was farfetched, but Perliett was straining to find connections.

"Of course not!" Millie scowled in frustration. "It's not her handwriting. It's not *anyone's* handwriting that I'm familiar with!" She pressed her fingertips to her forehead. "I'm sorry. I'm not explaining this well at all. Eunice received that letter, then she was killed. Now my mother is reciting it *after* mistaking *you* for Eunice in the churchyard. Mother mistook *me* for Eunice the other day as well. She keeps saying she's seen Eunice, and at first I assumed it was you or I and she was confusing us with Eunice. But I'm uncertain now. Our mother knew nothing about Eunice's letters. So how would she know to recite the same nursery rhyme? Eunice *has* to be speaking with her! Your own mother would understand this!"

Perliett met Millie's desperate expression with her own strained smile. Her bedtime thoughts plaguing her with new doubts as well as new devotions. Why couldn't it *all* be true? Spirits visiting and God in His supremacy? A marriage of the two? For some reason, that idea seemed to offend both realms.

Millie continued, "What happened here—during the evening with your mother—my sister and brother-in-law told me about the window shattering. Eunice is unsettled because she's trying to warn *us*! You and me! *We're* next, Perliett, don't you see? Eunice is speaking from the other side!"

Unwelcome chills ran through Perliett. Ones that gave further credence to her mother's beliefs and challenged Perliett's own confused faith.

"Have you spoken to the police—to Detective Poll? Take him the letter about Cock Robin. Why come to me?" Perliett leaned in earnest toward Millie. "It's the middle of the night. Why put yourself in danger by walking alone in the dark when you can speak with Detective Poll in the morning?"

Millie gave her a look of bewilderment that implied she couldn't understand why Perliett couldn't see. "You truly believe the police will put any credibility in this letter?" She held up the missive. "Do they offer such to your mother?"

Perliett pressed her lips together in silence.

Millie leaned forward, fervent and urgent. "I came to save you, Perliett. *He* comes in the night. I couldn't live with myself if I didn't warn you in time. Now I'm so glad I did!"

"What do you mean?" Perliett drew back. She was wondering if Eunice's death had aggravated Millie's own senses. While she didn't discount that Eunice might attempt to make contact, Millie's erratic behavior was concerning.

"Because of the danger!" Millie waited expectantly for Perliett to realize whatever it was Millie assumed Perliett knew. After a moment, Millie's face fell, and her shoulders sagged as awareness flooded her eyes. "You haven't seen it, have you?"

"Seen what?" Perliett frowned. She wanted to go to bed and sleep away this confusing night's visit. She couldn't rightly allow Millie to walk home now. Not even if Millie was completely wrong. It wasn't safe. She knew that from personal experience.

Millie closed her eyes tight for a long moment, then opened them. "There." She stretched her arm out, pointing toward the top stair of the porch. "It's the true reason I avoided knocking. I didn't want to pass by it until you made me come to the door."

Perliett noticed a small dark lump at the top of the stairs. Her throat tightened with a wariness she couldn't explain, even as she rose to investigate. Her bare feet padded across the porch until she came to the mass. Bending her knees, Perliett lowered herself to see details in the depths of the night.

Her hand clamped over her mouth.

The small, broken bundle lay prostrate. Feathers twisted and ruffled. Beak partially open. The dead robin stared up at

Perliett in death. An omen deliberately placed at her doorstep.

"Who killed Cock Robin?" Millie whispered from the porch swing.

Perliett closed her eyes against the gruesomeness of the dead robin. She had washed Eunice Withers's dead body, but this? The bird was symbolic of her. Perliett knew this now. Someone was watching her.

Who killed Cock Robin, indeed.

16

Molly

"I'm fine." *Embarrassment* was too nice of a word for what Molly felt.

"Hold still." Gemma Rabine leaned over her as Molly sprawled on the couch. "I need to clean this." She dabbed at the scrape on Molly's knee where it had connected with the basement step. "You're lucky you don't have a concussion."

Molly looked past Gemma, whose ministrations, while welcome, were detached and unemotional. Uncle Roger stood over her, his hands at his hips. Brandon and Tiffany hovered just behind him, staring down at her as if her fall in the basement had awakened them from their grieving stupor.

"Do you need help?" Tiffany offered Gemma.

"She'll be all right." Gemma flicked on a penlight and checked Molly's eyes again. "She's responding fine. I don't see any signs of anything serious."

"I'm fine." Molly tried to push herself up. She heard the mudroom screen door slam, and sure enough, Trent barreled into the room, tossing his car keys onto the coffee table.

"Is she okay?" He ignored any greetings to his extended family, who had heard Molly fall in the basement.

Molly squeezed her eyes shut against the observations of the group gathered over her.

"She's fine," Gemma reassured Trent, and Molly hoped she left it at that. She'd no idea that Gemma was a nurse, and she really hoped Gemma didn't start drilling her for more details. A fall. That was it. Molly's explanation that she'd slipped on the stairs seemed to satisfy. There was no way on God's green earth she was going to recount the vision of Gemma's murdered sister, January, standing at the head of the stairs, ghoulish and haunting. Everything had gone black. Molly had fallen. The next thing she'd known, Uncle Roger was hoisting her up with Brandon's help.

Trent edged past his uncle and cousins. He knelt beside Molly, concern radiating from him. "You sure you're okay?"

"I'm fine." Though she said it for the thousandth time, Molly could read the doubt in Trent's eyes. "I slipped on the stairs. I was getting tissues for Tiffany and—" she looked beyond them toward the dining room just off the living room where they'd gathered—"there's still a hamburger for you if you're hungry."

Uncle Roger dared a laugh at Molly's diversion tactic. He clamped a hand over Trent's shoulder. "If she's thinking about the welfare of your stomach, boy, then I'd say your wife will be A-okay."

Trent eased from his position on the floor.

Gemma gathered the bandage wrappers and snapped shut the first-aid kit she'd apparently retrieved from her car.

Molly moved to sit up and succeeded, not mentioning to anyone that her head was pounding. She'd hit it, she was sure of it. But worse than that, she was sure that January Rabine had somehow floated down those stairs and infiltrated her psyche. Molly could sense her presence—or at least she was afraid she could. She dared a look at Tiffany, January's mother. Even in death, January held a resemblance to her. She also had the Wasziak chin and jawline. Molly shot a glance at Trent. He had it too. That stubborn, determined set that spoke louder than any words. Molly had seen it in her vision of January as well, whose ghost had not looked friendly.

"Molly?" Trent reached out to help her from the couch. The rest of the family had moved back toward the dining room, leaving them somewhat alone. He searched her face as if to reassure himself she wasn't injured. His brows drew together. "What happened?"

"I slipped," Molly insisted. She avoided his eyes.

"But what's wrong?" he pressed, lowering his voice.

Molly shook her head. "Nothing."

A stiff silence built between them, the kind that reflected their relationship. *Nothing*, *okay*, and *sure*—they were all words that silenced any real conversation. Squelched their going deeper.

At one time, Molly would have craved to have Trent study her with such devoted concern. But now? She shied away from him and moved toward the others, who seemed to be waiting for them anyway. Waiting for Trent. To ask him questions about their daughter, their sister, their granddaughter. Now wasn't the time for her and Trent to resolve anything, and Molly preferred it that way for now. There was no way to explain what she had seen in the graveyard of their basement. There was no way Trent would accept the truth without taking drastic measures to get her help.

She wanted it to stop, didn't she? The whispers, the sightings, the *feelings* that they weren't alone? Yet to stop it took more than increased faith and a prayer. Molly knew that. And the idea of the medical world becoming involved and psychoanalyzing her condition? That scared her almost as much as January Rabine's ghost.

Molly rummaged through the closet, where their clothes hung together in a jumbled mess. She chose an oversized

T-shirt emblazoned with the logo of Clapton Bros. Farms on it and slipped into a pair of cotton bike shorts. Glancing in the bedroom mirror, she took a brief second to re-messy-bun her hair, then pulled a few tendrils down by her ears so she didn't look so severe. She eyed her own brown gaze.

"You're a mess."

Saying it out loud didn't make Molly feel any better. Even *she* didn't want to hang around herself. She could hardly blame Trent.

Padding across the wood floor, Molly made her way downstairs. The smell of coffee permeated the air. A glance at the wall clock she'd hung last week stated it was 8:00 a.m. Trent must have made coffee before he left for work three hours ago. Which meant it was probably burnt coffee now if he'd left the pot on.

Molly rounded the corner into the kitchen and stumbled to a halt.

A lone sunflower had been stuck in a mason jar and placed in the middle of the booth's table. There was a plate, utensils, and a paper napkin lying empty but ready. A glass of orange juice was already filled. A box that looked like Chinese take-out sat to the right of the plate.

Molly turned to the small galley kitchen stove and stared in surprise at Trent. He was wearing a pair of old shorts and a T-shirt, and his hair was damp from being freshly showered. His feet were stuck into a pair of moccasin slippers.

"What are you doing here?" Perhaps the lamest question she'd ever asked, but it was all Molly could think to blurt out.

Trent looked up from where he was flipping an egg in a cast-iron pan. His expression was straightforward. "Making you breakfast."

"What about work? The farm? The *milking*!" A person didn't just not go to work in the morning when there was a dairy farm of cows mooing to be released of their heavy udders.

"I talked to Jerry. He said he could manage."

Jerry. One of Trent's co-workers. "Okayyyyy . . ." Molly dragged out the word because she wasn't certain it *was* okay.

"Have a seat." Trent waved the spatula toward the booth.

Keeping her quizzical eye on Trent, Molly slipped into place. "What's this?" She tapped the white Chinese takeout box. "Orange chicken?"

Trent's mouth twisted in a surprised sideways smile at her attempt at sarcasm. "Sort of."

Molly scrunched her face in skepticism. "Chinese chicken for breakfast?"

"Why don't you open it."

She reached for the box and was surprised when it felt lopsided and not at all the solid weight of orange chicken. Molly reached for the top to unfold it, wary when she heard scratching inside. Then a little squeak. Her gaze flew up to meet Trent's.

"No," she said.

He smiled softly. "It's *not quite* the same type of orange chicken you were thinking."

Molly pulled open the box, and sure enough, orange chicken was inside in the form of a baby chick. It stared up at her, its enormous eyes frightened and curious all at the same time. There was a distinct waft of chicken—the live sort—and the chick cheeped, its beak opening as though Molly were about to feed it.

"Trent . . ." Molly breathed. She felt suffocated with emotion. The kind she hadn't felt in—forever. She bit the inside of her lip to keep her tears at bay. Trent's thoughtfulness was unexpected. "Why?"

Trent scooped the fried eggs onto a serving plate that was already holding a few sausage links. He brought the platter over and set it on the table. "Just 'cause." He returned to the counter and filled a mug with black coffee, just the way Molly liked it, and returned to set the mug next to her plate.

Molly studied the little chick scratching at the bottom of the container, its scrawny wings fluffed with the beginnings of orange feathers. "Is it a boy or a girl?"

"Girl," Trent answered as he poured himself a mug of coffee.

"How do you tell?" she asked, reaching out with her finger to stroke the chick's back.

Trent smiled. "Do you really want to know?"

"No." Molly couldn't help but offer a little laugh.

Trent sat down in a chair opposite her. He cupped his hands around the mug. "There's more. Outside in the coop."

"What?" Molly knew her eyes were probably wider than the moon.

"Yeah. Sid picked them up for me last night after everyone left and you went to bed. I called her and asked if she would. We wanted—*I* wanted you to have something to look forward to."

"But . . . all the baby chicks out there! Nothing is set up. I don't have warmers, or feeders, or even fencing yet, and what about predators? Keeping out fox and coon and—"

"Hey, hey." Trent held up his hand. "I've got it covered. Your chicken coop is ready enough for now, and Sid said she'd help this afternoon. Plus," he added, "there are adult chickens too. We didn't just get chicks."

"And a rooster?" Molly was shocked at the level of excitement she felt over the stupid birds.

"Of course."

"Oh, good." Molly nodded in confirmation.

Silence captured the moment. Molly forked an egg, keeping her eye on the chick, almost too shy to look at her husband. Trent.

No, she hadn't expected this. A little TLC went a long way . . . Molly's eyes lifted and met Trent's. She just prayed, for both of them, that it wasn't too late.

17

Molly tossed handfuls of grain on the ground. She had eight chickens. *Eight!* And the rooster, and five chicks—not including Myrtle, who was tucked into the pocket of her waist apron as she threw goodies to the "girls."

Three days and she'd not lost one fowl to a predator. Three days and she and Trent had lived in a tentative but balanced existence. Three days and she'd found a tiny spark of joy. Or maybe it was just a tentative peace before a bigger storm. She wasn't sure, and she didn't want to ask.

"What'd you name them?" Sid rounded the corner of the barn. Molly had heard Sid pull up in her truck.

Molly offered a lopsided smile as she flung another handful of grain. "You won't approve."

"Try me," Sid challenged, squatting down to reach for a Bantam that sidled away from her.

"Well, that one there that won't let you pet her, that's Izzy. She's shy but super affectionate."

"And you know this after three days, huh?" Sid teased.

Molly shrugged. "It's more fun than unpacking boxes. The four Ameraucana there are Sue, Alex, Sylvia, and Chloe. Myrtle is in my pocket. I need to think of the others' names yet."

"Really?" Sid laughed. "Human names?"

"What else should I call them?"

"Mother Hen? Henrietta? I don't know, Goldilocks?" Sid stood. "And the rooster?"

"Oh. I'm calling him Orville. After one of the Wright

brothers, who tried to fly, sort of flew, but never really got the full use of wings."

Sid studied Molly for a moment, a softness in her eyes. "You seem . . . happier," she observed.

"I've been happy." Molly brushed off Sid's perusal of her.

"Sure" was Sid's unbelieving reply.

"Can you help me haul a few things into the coop attic?" Distract and divert. Molly was going to overfeed the chickens if she wasn't careful, so she set the bucket of grain back in the feed bin and shut it. Myrtle chirped in her apron pocket. Molly pulled her out and set the little fluff free. She couldn't rightly make Myrtle a house chicken—or could she?

Sid was willing to help and so they entered the coop. Molly had spent some time stacking some old unused items that had been left behind in the coop in the corner. A few flowerpots. A crate of odds and ends. Some old tools.

Molly hiked up the tools first, climbing the ladder steps. Sid lagged, and when Molly returned, her friend was going through the crate.

"Are you saving all this stuff?" Sid seemed genuinely interested.

Molly nodded, even though Sid wasn't looking at her as she leaned over the opening into the attic. "I haven't had a chance to go through it and maybe never will. I've got too much to unpack in the house, but the—"

"The chickens. I know." Sid's voice was filled with mirth. "The chicken house is top priority." She bent and pulled out a coffee can with a plastic lid. "This looks like an old Hills Bros. coffee can from the eighties." She turned it. "See? I was right! I know these things!" Sid pulled off the lid and held the can up and out toward Molly as if in victory. "A canful of old screws and nails! Bonus points for not needing to hit up the hardware store anytime soon."

Molly winced. "Probably dumb to haul that stuff up here, huh?"

Sid didn't answer. She had already set aside the can and was digging through a wooden cigar box that held various trinkets like a rusty screwdriver, an unused patch meant to be ironed on someone's work coat, a pair of pliers . . . "Look! It's a lady's nylon stocking! Gosh, I remember my grandmother wearing nylons!"

Molly made quick work of descending the ladder. "Nylons?"

"Thank God for the invention of leggings!" Sid laughed.

"But why would there be nylons in there?"

"Maybe the farmer who lived here before used it to strain something. My grandfather used Grandma's old stockings and would fill them with acorns and use them as a ball for the dog to play fetch with. They ripped them up pretty fast, but it's that old-time practice of recycling used items."

Molly reached deeper into the crate. "There's more stuff in here." She pulled out a rope. It was old, weathered, and a bit dirty. The dust had settled into its hemp threads, making residue stay behind on Molly's hands. She set it aside and reached in again. "Leather gloves." Made sense. Every farmer needed leather gloves.

Sid was pulling out an item, and Molly noticed a weird look on her face.

"A roll of duct tape?" Sid held up a well-used roll, also dirty with age.

"Is that odd or something?" All the items so far made sense to Molly. A farmer needed things. Practical items.

"It reminds me of a serial killer's kit." Sid sat back on her heels, dropping the duct tape and reaching in again.

A wave of eerie heaviness washed over Molly. "That's not funny."

Sid pulled an item out. Black, knit, and soiled. She met Molly's gaze, her mouth set in a thin *told-you-so* line. "A stocking cap?"

"Farmers get cold." Molly yanked it from Sid.

Sid nodded. "Mm-hmm. But they keep hats in the house. Ted Bundy kept his with his killing kit."

"Sid. Ew." Molly tossed the hat onto the pile of growing items. It hadn't been her intention to go through the stuff left behind by previous owners. She should have known, though, that Sid's curiosity wouldn't be able to just haul it into the coop's attic and forget about it. She did, after all, use her metal detector as a hobby.

"A *flashlight*?" Sid shrieked with surprise as she held out a silver flashlight that looked like it was from the 1970s. Scuffed, dulled, and rusted where the top screwed off to receive batteries.

"Farmers need flashlights too," Molly stated.

"Do they need a belt?" Sid held the buckle end of a leather belt and pulled it from the bottom of the crate as if she were lifting a dead rotting snake from the innards.

"Yes." Molly nodded, but now she was unsteady on her knees. She shifted so she could sit firmly on the floor.

"It's a murder kit, I swear it." Sid looked deliciously intrigued.

"Would you stop that?" Molly was doubtful. No one found a serial killer's murder kit in a chicken coop. That was the stuff of that channel on cable TV, where crimes were concocted and made into cheesy murder-mystery films for women.

"Still, it makes you wonder." Sid shifted on her knees, then started returning things to the crate. "All this stuff is decades old and not exactly going to solve any crimes anyway."

A chill ran down Molly's spine. She shot a glance at the stairs, afraid she would see that little girl in her translucent gown, or worse, that awful vision of January Rabine and her glossy, dead eyes.

"There's never been a serial killer in Kilbourn—has there?" She begged the question of Sid, who was packing the last of the odds and ends back into the crate.

Sid flipped her curly ponytail over her shoulder and out of her way. "Not that I know of. We leave them to Wisconsin to produce. Gein, Dahmer . . ."

"Funny," Molly mumbled.

Finished, Sid gave Molly a wink. "It's okay. It's not like you have murder victims buried all over your property."

"No, but with January Rabine's murder . . ." Molly contemplated telling Sid. Telling her what she hadn't told Trent—that she had seen January in the house. That she had seen . . . things. People. Or visions. "Sid?"

"Hmm?"

"Do you think when people are murdered—like January—their souls haunt places?"

Sid shot her a searching look. "You've been watching ghost-hunting shows lately?"

"No." And she hadn't, so at least that was the truth. "I was just—well, I've heard that theory before and wondered."

"My grandpa always used to say, 'Absent from the body, present with the Lord.'" Sid stood, wiping her hands on her jean shorts. "Of course, people's beliefs vary from church to church on whether it's immediate, or purgatory, or if there's a temporary heaven before—"

"Okay, okay." Molly managed a laugh. "I'm sorry I asked."

"No, I don't think there are lost, incomplete souls wandering the earth, waiting to pop out of the closet at night and beg for help to cross over." Sid eyed Molly. "Why do you ask?"

"I know people claim to have seen them, that's all. It seems enough people have talked of having sightings, that it's . . . well, it's hard to discount as all a ploy or a myth or so many people going cuckoo."

Sid nodded. "I don't argue there's a spiritual world out there."

"I tend to think—" Molly broke off and waved her hand toward Sid. "Never mind. It doesn't matter. Let's just get this stuff up in the attic so we can play with the chickens."

Sid bent and hoisted the crate in her hands. "Okay, sure. But I *can* tell you this. I think the line between life and the spiritual world is thin. I think it's also something that engages our curiosity and could be extremely dangerous if we're not cautious. Remember King Saul in the Bible? He could conjure the dead spirit of the prophet Samuel, but it wasn't blessed by God."

"Why is that?" Molly felt she should know, only she didn't.

Sid was making her way cautiously up the ladder. "Probably," she grunted as she hefted the box onto the attic floor, "because we're not supposed to seek after the dead. What can they do? They're dead, and they're not God."

"But they *can* haunt us?" Molly pressed, regretting it instantly when Sid shot her a confused look. "I mean, if King Saul could conjure a dead prophet, then the dead *can* be communicated with."

"Molly"—Sid seemed to choose her words carefully—"you can also play with fire, and it can permanently scar you."

"Or it can follow you like you're a trail of gasoline and you can't escape," Molly challenged, then reapplied her attention to the task at hand, effectively shutting down any further conversation about ghosts, the spirit world, God, or her own personal hauntings.

It was disconcerting to even consider that Sid's overimaginative assumption that they'd stored some killer's kit in the chicken coop attic could be true. Molly made her way down the canned food aisle of the grocery store. Each person she passed, she examined. January's killer hadn't been caught—they hadn't even released a suspect or a composite drawing of a potential subject. It was as though the girl in the ditch near the farm was just a name with no one to bring to justice on her behalf. And the worst part was that Molly wanted to forget January. Forget the unexplained visit from Trent's cousin. Forget that she had been killed just a mile from them. Forget that the police had called this morning asking for Trent. Forget that the cloud of suspicion hanging over Trent ruined the thin thread of unity they had rediscovered in the past few days.

Molly reached for a can of baked beans. She liked them. Trent didn't. She tossed them into the cart, the tin can clanging against the metal side.

"That's right. Throw it. I always feel better when I throw things."

Startled, Molly looked to her right, only to lower her eyes as a tiny hunchbacked elderly woman wheeled her cart next to Molly's.

"Oh." Molly mustered a smile. "Hello."

The woman's white hair was permed—or maybe it had been in rollers—and the curls fell in rows on her head. Her face was wrinkled, friendly, with cheeks that were the soft color of a pink rose. Her hands gripped the cart in front of her, and her shoulders barely rose over it. Cloudy brown eyes smiled at her.

"When I was young like you, I used to throw chicken eggs against the side of my husband's barn just to annoy him and to get out my frustrations." The woman laughed, more to herself it seemed. "It did wonders! Although the *hours* my husband spent looking for the neighborhood pranksters who threw eggs . . ."

Molly realized she was staring at her without saying a word. The lady reached out and patted Molly's hand.

"It's okay, dear. This is why I don't watch the news. Puts me in a tizzy. We can hardly handle life anymore! It's so tiring."

Molly nodded. Yes, yes, it was.

"I'm Gladys. And you are?"

"Molly," she answered, a bit reluctantly.

"Are you a Wasziak? You look like a Wasziak."

Molly nodded, although she didn't know what Gladys meant. "I married a Wasziak."

"Oh yes! That boy—what's his name? Toby? Tyler?"

"Trent."

"Trent! Yes. I used to be good friends with his grandmother, Norma. A fine family. The Wasziaks have been upstanding citizens of Kilbourn for decades."

Molly had heard that often, known it since she'd started dating Trent in high school, and now she bore the name too.

"You know, we don't live far apart from each other. If you hike across the back field of yours, you'll run into my daddy's old fields. I lease them out now, but back in the day, that was all worked by my family. You can probably see the roof peak of my farmhouse. The blue roof?"

Molly could picture the roof, though she hadn't taken much notice of it, or any of the neighboring farms. She nodded politely, glancing at her cart. She still needed to get bread, butter, cheese, and eggs—to get them by before the layers started producing.

"It's a shame," Gladys sighed. Her sweater was too hot for the summer day, as it hung to the back of her tiny knees. "All these years, all this history. Kilbourn was such a lovely farming community, and now no one seems to want community. It's each to his own. People think they can find fulfilling relationships online. *Online*. That wasn't even a thing when I was your age." Gladys patted Molly's hand again. "Well, dear, here I am chattering your ear off, but you're probably one of those who like to be alone."

She was, but she felt rude nodding.

"I think—" Gladys was interrupted by a flurry of footsteps behind them and the rough wheeling of a grocery cart in their direction.

The wheels of the new cart almost banged into Molly's heels.

"Hey!" She jumped to the side.

Gladys had straightened her barely five-foot frame, surprise written in the creases of her face.

"We need to talk," Gemma Rabine announced, looking every bit the older sister on a mission of justice. "Please." The polite additive came a bit too late.

Molly hadn't seen Gemma—or Tiffany or Brandon, January's parents—since the evening she'd blacked out. Molly assumed they'd either been in communication with Trent or simply had resumed the distance between cousins since none of them were close. What Gemma and she needed to talk about so urgently was a mystery.

Gladys edged her way between the end of Gemma's cart and Molly, as if her petite and aged frame were some sort of armor.

"In my day, we greeted one another with a polite 'How do you do?'" Gladys's reprimand seemed to bounce off Gemma, who was obviously preoccupied with her mission and not particularly glowing with friendliness. Molly noted that the nurse's eyes darted to her skinned knee and then back to her face. So, Gemma wasn't totally uncaring, but for the moment, she was definitely erring on the assertive side rather than the caregiving nurse-like side she'd offered Molly the other night.

"I was going to call you as soon as I was finished here." Gemma's statement glossed over Gladys and landed squarely on Molly. She held up a bottle of headache-relief medication. "For my mom." Her words were supposed to make a point, Molly could tell. She just wasn't sure what the point was. Gemma dropped the boxed medication into the cart and picked up another one. "Also for Mom." A box of acetaminophen with sleep aid rattled. "And I have to stop at the pharmacy for her scripts. My sister is *dead* and everyone is going about their business like nothing's happened!"

Molly glanced around at the other customers in the aisle as Gemma's voice rose. "I'm sorry, I—"

"Don't you apologize." Gladys held up a palm toward Molly and with a sharp look communicated to her to be silent. "You shouldn't be assaulted while buying your beans."

"And yet my sister can be assaulted and left in a ditch?" Gemma's high-pitched question silenced even the music on the grocery store speakers. At least it seemed to. Everything in the store grew curiously quiet. Gemma gripped her shopping cart, emotions ranging from anger to hurt to panic splaying across her face. "Please, Molly. You and Trent have to know *something*."

"I don't know anything." Molly found her voice.

Gemma tilted her head in disbelief.

"I think you're right." Molly lowered her voice to bring an element of calm to the situation before security was called. "We need to talk. But not here."

"Not here is right," Gemma spat.

"Not without me," Gladys inserted.

"Who are you?" Gemma eyed the elderly woman.

Molly, for reasons she couldn't explain even to herself, put her hand on Gladys's shoulder. "She's my friend."

"Fine. Bring her." Gemma waved them both off. "My grandpa's house. In an hour."

Molly shook her head. "The coffee shop. Pickles' Place." She had no intention of traveling a half hour out of her way to be confronted on Gemma's territory in her grandfather's—Trent's uncle Roger's—home. Not that Gemma was a danger, but a conversation could turn intense, and Molly wasn't sure she was up for being alone.

A warm hand with papery soft skin reached for hers. She looked down into Gladys's eyes.

"Don't you worry, dear. Families have tiffs all the time. I'll be with you, and we'll settle this." She ended her proclamation with a squeeze of the hand.

Molly regretted claiming the elderly woman as hers. She'd invited a stranger into her life with no hesitation, and yet she wouldn't visit Uncle Roger's home and he was family.

A family tiff?

Molly wondered how Gladys would feel once she realized theirs involved a brutal murder.

18

Perliett

She had boxed the dead bird up and now set it on Detective Poll's desk at the Kilbourn jail. He rose from his chair to look down into it, his face visibly horrified.

"What is—?"

"A dead robin." Perliett planted her hands on her hips. "It was left on the top stair of my porch, poor thing, and it doesn't appear that it died by slamming its head into a window."

Detective Poll gave her a quick glance, apparently a bit surprised at her blunt description.

Perliett let him live in his surprise. She was a nervous wreck inside, but outside she was determined to maintain her decorum.

"See here?" She snatched a pencil from the detective's desk and used the lead point to push back some feathers. "Its neck has been wrung, literally wrung. And then here." She used the pencil again to flip the bird over. "Its innards—" Perliett cleared her throat to avoid gagging—"they've been removed."

"Someone gutted a robin like a deer?" Detective Poll leaned

down, studying it, his surprise turning to morbid interest. "Why a robin?"

"Cock Robin." Perliett hadn't forgotten Millie's story and the idea that Eunice was attempting to save them, nor was she discounting the fact that Mrs. Withers had indeed interacted with her dead daughter and therefore the nursery rhyme truly was a message about the crime itself—and its criminal.

"Pardon?" Detective Poll lifted an eyebrow.

"A nursery rhyme." The door closed behind Mr. Bridgers as he entered the police station, and both Perliett and Detective Poll jumped, startled by his sudden appearance. Mr. Bridgers's dark countenance took in the occupants of the room in a swift sweep of his gaze, and it landed on Perliett, whom he continued to observe while addressing the detective. "The rhyme was first penned in 1744. A sort of re-penning, to be truthful, as there was an old English story titled 'Phyllyp Sparowe' that had originated back in the fifteen hundreds."

"You seem to know quite a lot about an obscure poem." Detective Poll drew back from the dead bird. He leveled an open stare on Mr. Bridgers, who didn't seem flustered in the slightest.

"Do I? I thought perhaps most knew of the rhyme's origins. We all know, for example, that 'London Bridge' was written because they rebuilt it several times—and it also *had* most certainly fallen down at one point. And we're not unclear at all about Jack and Jill, are we?" Mr. Bridgers paused, and at the blank look on the detective's face and mirrored on Perliett's, he concluded, "King Louis XVI and Marie Antoinette. Of course, he was beheaded, and she died after the Reign of Terror . . . Truly, *neither* of you knew this?"

"I always found Jack and Jill to be quaint," Perliett admitted sheepishly.

"There is nothing *quaint* about aristocracy, unfortunately."

Mr. Bridgers offered her a forgiving smile. "Or most nursery rhymes, for that matter."

"Mr. Bridgers, what brings you here?" Detective Poll attempted to regain control of the conversation. "I'm sure you didn't come to discuss nursery rhymes."

"I find literary history quite fascinating actually. Especially those limericks with English heritage. There's brutality behind almost all of it—or tragedy." His dark eyes twinkled ominously.

Perliett rethought her previous attraction to him for a moment, until a smile split his face, elongating the creases in his cheeks and strengthening the cut of his jaw.

"But I realize we are in the presence of a lady. That being said"—he turned to the detective—"I stopped by to deliver this." Mr. Bridgers handed the detective a piece of stationery. Average stationery, from what Perliett could see, with a message written in a scrawled handwriting that wasn't definitively male or female.

"And this is?" The detective took it warily.

"It was left outside my boarding room door. I daresay the person who left it is insane at the very least."

"Why?" Perliett was curious now as Detective Poll held the mysterious stationery hovering over the dead bird.

"Read it," Mr. Bridgers said.

Detective Poll cleared his throat and read, "'She sang as she was tied. She cried. And when she finally said she'd lied, then she truly died.'" The detective's head shot up. Incredulous, he stared at Mr. Bridgers. "Good glory, man! What is this?"

Mr. Bridgers shrugged. "I was hoping you could tell me."

"Is it about Eunice?" Perliett interjected.

"One wonders, doesn't one?" Mr. Bridgers seemed awfully unmoved by the limerick.

"Do you have any idea who left this?" Detective Poll eyed Mr. Bridgers sharply. Perliett noted that the detective's typically friendly persona had deepened to very distrustful. She couldn't blame him. Mr. Bridgers popped up at the strangest times, in places most unrelated to him, and yet . . . how did one question a man whose innocence seemed protected by a sheer lack of evidence to imply otherwise? One couldn't accuse a man of a crime or of being suspicious merely because he had questionable timing and interests.

Mr. Bridgers shook his head. "I have absolutely no idea who left it at my door. As you both know, I'm new to the area and so I wouldn't have expected anyone to know me, let alone single me out to be the recipient of such melodramatic prose. Still, I felt it necessary to report it, seeing as"—he cast a sideways glance at Perliett—"there *has* been a death recently."

"And you're certain the person meant for you to receive this? It hadn't fallen from someone's pocket by chance?" the detective pressed.

Mr. Bridgers remained unflustered. "Someone deliberately wedged it between the doorframe and my door so that when I opened it, I would see it."

Detective Poll drew in such a deep breath, Perliett was afraid his diaphragm would balloon out further than his ribs would allow. He released it before he suffered any rib cracking, and she tapped the desk with her fingernail.

"Consider, Detective, the dead bird that was left for me last night. Now this poetic atrocity for Mr. Bridgers? Perhaps Eunice's killer continues to seek attention? He did write to the paper."

"Perliett—I mean, Miss Van Hilton," Detective Poll began.

"Perliett is quite all right," she nodded.

"Fine then," he agreed. "I am not clueless. Your observations are common sense. The only problem I have is that you're involved at all."

"I stopped chasing down clues, sir."

Detective Poll issued Perliett a stern look.

"Well, I did, until I was gifted with a dead robin! You must admit, this is all quite difficult for me to simply sit back and ignore since the churchyard scene with Mrs. Withers."

"Churchyard scene?" Mr. Bridgers interjected.

Perliett waved him aside. "I'll explain later."

"You'll do no such thing," Detective Poll commanded. "Your involvement in this matter must be treated carefully. Don't you see, Perliett, someone brutalized a robin and left it on your doorstep? There is a message there, and I don't like its implications. As for you, Mr. Bridgers, receiving this— this *note* makes my head spin trying to figure out how you could be involved."

"Aside from the evening with Mrs. Van Hilton and the Withers when we attempted to connect with Miss Withers's spirit, I've nothing to do with it at all," Mr. Bridgers responded placidly. "I've made no mystery about who I am." A sideways glance at Perliett told her he assumed she understood that as well as the detective. "Have I?"

Detective Poll cleared his throat. "Well, we've only just become acquainted, so for all sakes and purposes—"

"Yes, yes. I see." Mr. Bridgers nodded, his deep voice rumbling in his chest with understanding. "I understand why one may assume me to be circumstantially curious if not questionable."

Perliett studied him for a moment. He was hatless and also missing his jacket. The fact that he was in white shirtsleeves was bordering on disrespectful for a proper call, even if it was to the local police. But she had to admit that it was wickedly attractive as well. He had rolled the cuffs of his sleeves so that she could make out the cords on his forearms. His bare arms that on a farmer in a field while plowing would barely raise an eyebrow, but here, with a gentleman . . .

She blushed, and she knew it.

Mr. Bridgers knew it too, and the corner of his mouth tilted up in a smile that tempted.

"*Do* you know the Withers family?" Detective Poll's question broke into the brief unspoken moment of heady tension between them.

Mr. Bridgers lazily shifted his focus onto the detective. "I don't. Not really. Rather, I became acquainted with Eunice's brother-in-law, Errol, the one who accompanied Miss Withers's sister and father to the meeting. Errol invited me to come with them, so I did."

"Why?"

"Why what?" Mr. Bridgers countered.

"Why attend with them? What interest do you have in Eunice Withers?" Detective Poll was not giving up, and Perliett admired him for it, while at the same time she wished he'd interrogate the dead bird just as hard and determine why it was on *her* porch, and what interest the killer might have in *her*.

"I have little interest in Eunice Withers," Mr. Bridgers replied. "My interest is in Maribeth Van Hilton."

Perliett drew back, half appalled by the casual nature in which the man spoke her mother's name, and half intrigued as to why he was so interested in her mother.

"Mrs. Van Hilton?" Detective Poll responded.

"Mm-hmm." Mr. Bridgers nodded, not avoiding the detective's forthright stare. "I find the spiritualist movement quite interesting. Even Doyle, the author of Sherlock Holmes himself, has found it to be of great intrigue. To decipher the beyond is to take part in an extended universe. Wouldn't you wish to be included in that, if you could, Detective?"

Detective Poll coughed, cleared his throat, and then sniffed. "No. No, I'd rather leave additional universes to God. There's enough to deal with here."

"But if those who have passed can assist those here, and us them? Why should we discount it?" Mr. Bridgers asked.

Perliett looked between the two men. Mr. Bridgers, progressive and creative, and Detective Poll, traditional and . . . boring?

"I don't discount it," Detective Poll replied gravely. "I merely leave for God what is His to know, and trust that He has not revealed it to me for my own good—and even my own safety."

"Respecting your position," Mr. Bridgers said with a dip of his head, "I politely disagree."

Detective Poll had warned her to always have a chaperone. To avoid night calls to homes. To lock her doors and windows, which was a tad impractical considering it was nearing the end of August and hot and sticky even at night.

Perliett adjusted the fingers of her gloves as she stepped onto the sidewalk outside the police station. She sensed Mr. Bridgers's presence behind her, and she waited politely as he shut the door and joined her in his rolled-up shirtsleeves, as if they were two very familiar friends with a relaxed intimacy between them. She averted her eyes. He really should wear a jacket, but then he was also practical since she was already sweating in the small of her back from the late summer heat.

"Disconcerting, isn't it? All the suspicion and fear being raised by one unnamed person with a violent tendency."

Perliett glanced to her right at the man and nodded. "I'll be honest, I *am* unsettled."

"As you should be!" He nodded, a strand of dark hair falling rakishly over his left eye. "Anyone brazen enough to leave a dead bird on a woman's porch deserves to be tarred and feathered. No pun intended."

Perliett stifled a giggle. "Tarred and feathered? It's been some time since anyone resorted to that old practice of discipline."

"Wrongdoers should be punished aptly." Mr. Bridgers grinned.

Perliett returned it, then dropped her gaze. The man made

her almost as nervous as the Cornfield Ripper, only it was a far different sort of nervous. It sent her stomach into little swirls of pleasure, and she quite liked it. In moments such as these, she quite liked Jasper Bridgers, for all his mysteries. Besides, his own explanations made him a tad less dangerous now that he had grouped himself in with the likes of her mother. Those involved in the spiritualist movement were often misconstrued for something other than they really were—which was simply a curious lot with a great respect for the afterlife.

"Mr. Bridgers?" Perliett ventured.

"Jasper," he responded.

"Yes. Jasper." Perliett dipped her head in acquiescence and allowed Jasper to steer her away from a bicyclist who was riding on the walk. The cyclist rang his little bell, but it didn't stop Jasper from admonishing him as he rode past.

"You should be on the road and not running young women down with your contraption."

Perliett offered Jasper a grateful smile, both for protecting her and for calling her *young* instead of something that made her feel more rightly the spinster that she was.

"Where are you from, Jasper?" Perliett eyed a beautiful navy-blue hat in the window of a store they passed. She attempted to be more interested in that than truly agonizing over the questions that were becoming stronger and more necessary to know about Jasper Bridgers.

"Ah, you finally ask what has been on your mind for some time." Jasper had a way of calling out the unspoken so blatantly it caught her off guard. His fingers touched her elbow, and he steered her toward the small green yard of Kilbourn Park. It had a cast-iron bench resting beneath a large oak tree. Someone had planted pots of flowers at each end, and their perfume wafted in their direction. A sweet beckoning to come and rest amid sheer chaos.

Perliett was surprised Jasper didn't answer her question.

He seemed intent on leading her to the bench, so she went along, lowering herself onto it when they arrived and arranging the draping of her emerald dress.

Jasper settled next to her, crossing his legs, his arm casually stretching across the back of the bench and behind her shoulders. Surprised at his familiarity, Perliett's instinct was to resist, but her nature conflicted with both propriety and reason, and she found it to be a bit exhilarating.

"I was born in Massachusetts," Jasper offered, "but my father moved our family to Chicago when I was quite young."

Perliett nodded. Chicago. It explained why he had no discernable accent, seeing as he was from the Midwest. It also explained his more polished airs. He wasn't a farmer or a country boy. He was obviously accustomed to socialization and interaction on a scale much larger than small Kilbourn. Still, the cavalier attitude he exuded intrigued Perliett, while she determined simultaneously that the name of his home city could probably explain it. Chicago. To each his own, and yet a melting pot of a bit of every culture known to man, not unlike a smaller version of New York City.

"Do you have a family?" Perliett ventured.

Jasper's mouth twitched in a slight smile. "My parents have both passed away. I have an older sister, who returned to Boston after she married. I myself am not married." He turned and leveled his eyes on her, and Perliett inwardly protested the blush she felt creeping up her neck.

"Why Kilbourn?" she asked.

"Why not Kilbourn? It's such a quaint little town." Jasper swept his arm through the air as if to encourage Perliett to take special note of where she lived and had grown up. "A farming community, the simple quiet of country life. Even the businesses are small and don't require boardrooms to run them. The buildings go no higher than two floors unless they're a barn. And no one is attempting to outdo the other by adding more levels to their structures. Your biggest boast are the acres of cornfields and your cows and little churches."

"You almost mock Kilbourn, Jasper." Perliett eyed him. She couldn't interpret whether Kilbourn sincerely captivated him or if he found it to be beneath him.

"On the contrary. I admire Kilbourn. Small treasures are hidden in small places. Like your mother."

"My mother." Yes. He had expressed his fascination with Perliett's mother.

"She is gifted." He seemed to search her face for something, although Perliett wasn't certain what. "She knows how to communicate with the beyond. It has honored me to be a sitter for her twice now, and I daresay I'd like another go at it."

"Why are you so intrigued by those who have passed away?" Perliett toyed with the edge of her glove, noting a thread had come loose from the decorative tatting at its edge.

"I fail to understand how one could *not* be intrigued by the afterlife. Take your Dr. Wasziak, for example."

"He's not mine."

"No, but he is Kilbourn's."

Perliett bristled. "I too offer medical services."

"Of course," Jasper said in a patronizing tone, making her bristles become sharper.

"I *do*!"

His dark eyes deepened. "I never insinuated you didn't, my dear Perliett."

She blushed again—curse it.

"Now," Jasper continued, "Dr. Wasziak believes in an almighty God."

"As do I," Perliett said.

"As do most. Or many, I should say. But those who do often discount the other elements of the spiritual world that are just outside our reach and our understanding. In their pursuing the knowledge of God, they dispense with the pursuit of the other. That limits what they know and narrows their perspective so that all is filtered *through* the aspects of a triune God instead of through the panoply of other possibilities, which also hovers just out of reach."

Stunning. His way with words was both poignant and terribly twisted. Perliett understood what he was saying, and at the same time it somehow sounded wrong. Which one was wrong, she wasn't sure. The pursuit of God or the pursuit of a spiritual world.

"And why are you so persistent in exploring it that you seek out a small-town spiritualist like my mother? Surely you can find some in Chicago?" she challenged.

Jasper laughed. A deep, rumbling laugh that sent shivers through her. "Of course I can. I have. In fact, I've sat with Doyle, and together we've explored the spirit world. He's tested it quite aptly. Some he has debunked as mere trickery, while others there is simply no explanation but that it is real. But that is my experience in Chicago. New York. London. I want to know how it transposes into the world of common man."

"Common man?" Perliett raised an eyebrow.

Jasper had the decency to look apologetic. "I simply mean those outside the influence of big cities, big business, and big money. Does the spirit world have the same effect? Is it needed to the degree it appears to be in the upper echelons of American society? Or are men—common laborers, the bread and butter of the economy—in as much need for the same veil to be seen behind? Do they have that same insatiable desire, or are they somehow content with their lot in life as it is? Death included."

Perliett studied Jasper for a long moment, and he remained steady under her frank gaze. Finally, she determined to speak her mind, because—well, that was what she normally did. "You give the 'upper echelons' far more credit than they deserve. They are not unique, Jasper. We all wish to connect with ones we have lost."

"What about you?" His voice lowered. "Who have you lost, Perliett?"

For a moment, she was certain she was floating, maybe even sinking into the soft depths of his eyes. They were dark pools, not unlike—well, not unlike George's—but somehow his were different. They compelled her instead of repulsed her. They made her very aware that she was a woman, that he was a man, and that—

Jasper took hold of her gloved hand and, with presumptuous assertion, gently tugged at each finger of her glove, coaxing it off.

Perliett swallowed. She watched as he removed it boldly and laid the glove across his knee. Then he threaded his fingers through hers, and his thumb explored the soft skin between her thumb and index finger.

"Who have you lost?" he repeated, his voice soft, understanding. Jasper's eyes narrowed with emotion—with a caring—that Perliett hadn't experienced since PaPa passed away.

She found her eyes welling up with tears, and she blinked them away.

"The pain lurks behind the façade you portray to all," Jasper observed.

His thumb was purely intoxicating as it stroked her hand. Back and forth. Perliett found it hard to catch a proper breath.

"My father," she admitted, almost in a whisper. A breeze lifted some tendrils of dark hair and swept them across her face as the oak leaves above them rustled like a tiny musical number playing in the background. "When he passed, nothing was ever the same again."

Her admission aloud seemed like a betrayal to her mother. Perliett wished to declare that her mother had fulfilled the areas in Perliett that had broken when PaPa had died. "I want nothing more than to speak to PaPa. Even if it's only to hear him say my name."

"And you've never felt his presence before?" Jasper pursued.

"Once." Perliett nodded. "Once, in his study, when my mother—well, I felt his hand on my shoulder. But nothing more. He is gone and . . . it's his silence that makes me question the most."

"Question?" Jasper's eyebrow rose.

Perliett looked down at their hands. She would undermine her mother to admit it aloud. But sometimes—sometimes she burst to share it. To hear herself say it and then have someone explain why she was wrong. Why she shouldn't doubt. Why she was right to believe.

"It makes me question whether she really *can* reach the other world." Perliett's words came in a jumble. Flowing over each other like a wellspring that couldn't be stopped. "She seems to connect with others. Why can't she with my father? He was why she became who she is in the first place—because we wanted to connect with PaPa. Now? She won't even try."

"You've asked her to?"

"Yes!" Perliett was aware of how her voice rose. "Yes, I've *begged* her! Now we simply don't discuss it. PaPa is off-limits. Why should he be, unless she knows she cannot reach him? She doesn't wish to admit it. Are there elements of the spirit world that prohibit people with my mother's abilities to make the connection? Or is it—?" She stopped, her emotions making her words trip thoughtlessly over themselves.

"A ruse?" Jasper supplied gently.

"Yes!" Perliett was embarrassed by the word as it escaped her lips. "Oh, I don't believe my mother resorts to trickery. I *don't*. How do you explain what happened when she summoned Eunice Withers and the window shattered? Still, there are gaps. Pieces. Unfulfilled hopes . . ."

"So then you question if perhaps the narrow pursuit of God alone is truer?"

"Could it be? Are we merely muddying the waters by trying to broaden the scope of things? Isn't it difficult enough to understand God, let alone to understand a world of deceased spirits lingering and hovering with incomplete lives?"

Perliett pulled away from Jasper, grabbing her glove from his leg and yanking it onto her hand. She had said too much. She had opened herself to this stranger too much. Somehow he drew it out of her, and still all she knew of him was that he was from Chicago and he had a sister. He was still a stranger. For all she knew, he was the Cornfield Ripper flirting with her before he speared her with his blade and left her to bleed out amongst the corn spiders and corn silk.

"I need to go." She looked toward town, then to the river that ran through the park behind them, only a quick jaunt down a manicured path. The solitude of the river beckoned her. Reason pointed her toward town. "I need to go," she mumbled again, and her feet urged her toward the body of water instead.

"Perliett!" Jasper jumped to his feet as she hurried away. She heard his voice carry over the breeze behind her. "You shouldn't go alone!"

She waved him away. "Please." Perliett turned, stopping in her tumultuous and now-embarrassing display. "Please," she pleaded, "I will be fine." It was daylight after all. No one struck with murderous intent in the sun's glare.

Perliett hurried down the path. She thought she heard Jasper shout once more. She was tempted to look behind her and see if he followed. Part of her wished he would. Wished he would overwhelm her womanly outburst and, in a fit of male passion, manhandle her into his arms and kiss her senseless. She'd never been kissed. She'd never been held. She was lonesome and lost and . . .

The river was a gentle current, muddy and brown. It wasn't beautiful. But the greenery on either side made it come alive like a pretend world, and Kilbourn merely a wisp of a memory behind her. Perliett left the trail and pushed through the grasses, looking up at the oak and maple that lined the riverbanks. Daisies spread their white faces and yellow smiles throughout the long grass. Moss grew on rocks that lined the river and edged the rotting tree that had fallen into the river's path years before.

Perliett halted, her long dress tangled in the weeds. She pulled the greenery from its claw-like embrace of her embroidered dress that skimmed her hips and hung narrowly to her ankles. She tugged off her gloves so she could grab at the weeds. A ladybug flew from its hiding place and bumped into her elbow. Perliett brushed it away just as a black fly announced its annoying presence.

Always. Always there was something evil to ruin something beautiful.

Always there was something pressuring peace to float away as chaos consumed.

Always—

Perliett froze. Her eyes focused on something in the weeds. White. Smooth. She strained to see over the bank. Whatever it was, was half in the river, and something like soaked chiffon floated just beneath the surface.

She stumbled a few steps forward until her vision grasped what she saw. The woman's hand was curled in death around a bunch of daisies. Her skin was pale—almost translucent—and her dress was torn, soiled in a dark brown stain Perliett closed her eyes against.

Perliett drew in a steadying breath. She leaned over and saw the woman's legs in the river, the chiffon of her torn skirt drifting back and forth in the current as it stuck to her body by a seam twisted around her bare white leg.

She knew before she even mustered the courage to look at who it was. And when Perliett allowed her gaze to settle on the woman's face, there was no scream, no words, no tears. Just the whisper music of the leaves as they moved and danced in the breeze. Just the tinkling notes of the river as it rolled over itself on its journey.

Millie's eyes were open. They were vacant. Still, they stared at Perliett as if to accuse.

I told you.

Perliett heard the words float through the air.

I told you.

19

Molly

Gladys was a warrior in polyester. She plopped next to Molly at the coffee shop table, dropped her purse on the floor next to her, and pushed her plastic-framed glasses up her nose.

"It was wise of you to meet that woman in a public place."

Molly offered Gladys a tolerant smile. She hadn't really expected the elderly grocery store woman to follow her to the coffee shop to meet up with Gemma, mostly because she didn't think the older woman would *want* to. It was awkward sitting next to her, a stranger, and even more awkward feeling as if she would panic if this tiny old lady chose to leave. Gladys had adopted Molly as her own to protect. Her mind seemed sharp enough, but a stiff breeze could blow the poor lady down the street, and Molly wasn't confident that Gemma wouldn't become that stiff breeze.

"Speak of the devil," Molly muttered as Gemma tugged a chair out from the opposite side of the table and sat down. She hadn't bothered to order coffee, but then neither had Molly.

"I'm going to try to stay civil," Gemma announced.

Gladys looked between them.

Molly wasn't certain her cocktail of antidepressants would be strong enough to help her endure the madness that was to come from this conversation.

Gemma leaned forward, her athletic arms tanned from the New Mexican sun. "I found January's journal online."

"Like I suggested." Molly couldn't avoid the barb.

"Right before you *slipped* in your basement," Gemma quipped in return. "Anyway," Gemma continued, "you know why January was here."

It was a statement, not a question.

"No, I don't." Molly shook her head.

Gemma snorted and smiled, but it was lopsided and only half friendly. "Fine, I'll humor you with the reasons. Ancestry. That's why she was here. She wanted to learn all about our lovely Wasziak roots." The sarcasm was so unexpectedly thick, Molly would've needed a chainsaw to cut through it.

"The Wasziak name goes way back in Kilbourn," Gladys added.

"I'm sure it does." Gemma's lips thinned. "Along with the murders."

"The murders?" Molly's uneasiness only intensified. She shifted in her chair.

Gemma tilted her head and studied Molly for a moment. "I almost believe that you know nothing about this. But January wrote she'd met with the family in Kilbourn several times and discussed just that."

"I have no clue what you're talking about."

"The Cornfield Ripper of Kilbourn, Michigan. Look it up. It's folklore and legend around here, and our grandfather, with however many greats you want to attach to it, was smack in the middle of the whole thing."

"Oh, *that* tale!" Gladys clapped her hands together like a happy child. "I love murder mysteries. Have either of you watched *Murder, She Wrote*? Angela Lansbury is fabulous in it!"

Molly looked between them. "We never met with your sister, Gemma."

Gemma lifted her phone and swiped her thumb over the screen. "'Met with M today. Stated that Trent was purchasing the farm where the murders occurred.'" Gemma looked up. "Explain that."

"That's an initial. That's not my name!" Molly protested.

"But it's Trent's name."

"I know nothing, Gemma. I raise chickens and try to stay out of people's way." She sounded like a defeated martyr, and Molly knew that her own issues with mental health would not contribute positively to this conversation. She could already feel herself spiraling between intense anger, shortened breaths, and the onset of a full-on panic attack.

Gladys's warm hand slid over hers. She squeezed, and Molly met the rheumy eyes. "It's okay, dear. Let's deal with this calmly." She turned to Gemma. "I'm not new to the area, and I know a bit about the farms around here. If you're talking about the farm associated with the Cornfield Ripper, that's the old house and barn off Highway 34."

Molly felt her insides curdle. "That's where we live."

Gladys gave her a sympathetic look. "Well, dear, you're living in a murder house."

Gemma slapped the table. "I knew it!"

"Wait. No. No. The real-estate agent would have said something." Molly's mind spun with the finality of Gladys's pronouncement. "Maynard knows the area well. He's a Clapton, and they own practically everything anyone else doesn't!"

"Whether you knew about it or not, January was murdered while she was investigating our ancestors, who apparently were *very* involved in a historical set of murders," Gemma protested. "Murders that also involved your farm."

Gladys gentled her voice. "I'm so sorry for your loss."

"The police have questioned Trent," Gemma said, ignoring Gladys's sympathies.

"Questioned and charged are two separate things," Molly retorted.

"Girls." Gladys laid both of her wrinkled hands on the table, and they silenced like reprimanded children. "I have been alive for over eighty years. I've lived through World War Two, I lost my brother in Vietnam, and I've suffered my own losses—especially when my husband, Kendrick, passed away thirteen years ago. And if there's one thing I've learned, it's that what you think isn't always what *is*. There are stories behind each of us, and until we shush up and listen, we'll never hear the truth of it. Do you understand?" Her last question was pointed.

Gemma nodded.

Molly nodded.

They exchanged looks laced with a tentative truce.

Gladys shifted in her chair, and Molly caught a whiff of the elderly woman's menthol joint rub mixed with what she thought might be honeysuckle hand lotion. The older woman searched Molly's face for a moment before her eyes softened and the wrinkles that lined her face grew deeper with understanding.

"It wasn't a mistake, our meeting in the grocery store today." She reached over and took Gemma's hand, squeezing her fingers. "And now you too. All right? Let's start over with what we *do* know. Gemma, you've lost your sister. Molly, you've lost someone too. I can see grief in your eyes."

Molly regretted the tears that sprang to the surface.

Gemma sniffed back her own emotion, looking away and out the coffee shop window.

Gladys released them both, her hands shaky with age. "Grief is a shadow man that follows us into our futures and swallows it up if we let him. Just like it did back in the day when the Cornfield Ripper roamed Kilbourn." She tapped the table and directed her words at Molly. "My mother was friends with one of his victims. Millie Withers was her name. She was the second girl to be killed—after her older sister. The Withers family saw more grief than most of us in this lifetime."

"I've not even heard of them," Molly inserted lamely, more for Gemma's sake than anything. It was important to her that Gemma realized she truly wasn't hiding any secret knowledge of some vintage killer no one cared about anymore.

Gladys smiled, but there was an edge to it. Almost a warning. Her eyes narrowed with caution. "You *should* have heard of the Withers family."

"Why?" Molly wondered if anything in this conversation would ever make sense.

Gladys's smile was thin, sad, and a little troubled. "Well, because of what we've already established. You and your husband bought their farm. The Withers farm. You live in their house. The house of the murdered sisters."

"Did you know about this?" Molly struggled to temper her voice. She didn't want to engage in a full-frontal attack on Trent, but her nerves were raw. She noticed her hands tremored, and she slipped them into the front pocket of her hoodie.

The evening was blessedly cool. A breeze had dropped the humidity significantly and pushed the almost ninety-degree temps into a more manageable eighty-something. They sat on the front porch, iced tea in glasses perched on a wicker table between them. Trent was freshly showered, his hair damp with waves in it that at one time Molly would've assaulted with her fingers, and he would have tickled her sides to get her to quit.

Not anymore.

Her chickens pecked at the yard. She noticed Sue, her orange feathers glossy and fluffed, poke under a stick and flip the stick with her beak. Chickens had such purpose. Such central focus. She envied them. She envied Sue the chicken.

Trent stuck his finger in his paperback to save his place. He chose his words carefully, and Molly could tell that, yes, he *had* known this was the house of the historically murdered Withers sisters.

"I knew," he admitted. He didn't look at her, instead choosing to aim his vision at the broadside of the barn. "Maynard told me when we were first looking at the listing. It's one reason the place was on the market for as long as it was."

"Because people don't like buying a house someone was murdered in?" Molly heard the quaver in her voice.

Trent gave her a quick glance. "Technically, the Withers sisters weren't murdered *in* the house. They just lived here."

Molly drew her knees up to her chest, attempting to perch her feet on the edge of her chair. She realized she couldn't do it anymore—curse that extra twenty pounds. She shoved her feet back to the porch floor.

"Trent, I can't—" She stopped. What? She couldn't what? Live in a house that was haunted? What should she tell Trent?

Hey, so the other day I saw a ghost moving in our bedroom when I was watching from the chicken coop?

Hey, remember when I collapsed on the basement stairs? Yeah, so January Rabine is back from the dead.

Did you know I hear voices . . . ?

"Molly."

"Trent."

Nervous laughter between them.

"You go first," Trent offered.

Molly noticed he was thumbing the pages in his book. She couldn't interpret whether it was because he was antsy to return to the escapism of his story or that he was apprehensive about something.

"Please be honest with me," Molly started, refusing to look away from Trent but instead allowing her gaze to drill into him with earnestness. "Did you talk to January before she died? Did you know who she was when you found her in the ditch?"

Trent looked away.

That wasn't a good sign.

"Trent." Molly leaned forward, her voice cracking with emotion. "Trent, please. You know the police are suspicious of you. I'm being accosted by your family in the grocery store. I can't do this. I can't live in the middle of a *murder* saga and question whether you're being honest with me. That morning you found January's body, you *knew* it was her? And you never told me? Never said anything to me or to the police or . . . I'm at a loss as to what you are and aren't telling me! I wish you were honest with me."

He jerked his head toward her, and Molly drew back at the glint in his eyes.

"*I'm* not being honest with *you*? How about you be honest with me? You lie to me that everything is all right and you don't tell me what's going on with you. It's obvious you're not okay. But you won't talk to me."

"Don't turn this on me, Trent." Molly lowered her voice, as much to control her tears as to convince Trent she was gravely serious.

A swift thrust of his arm and Trent hurtled his paperback across the porch. The book hit the porch rail and bounced into the bushes. Sue and the rest of the girls clucked and flustered in a flurry of feathers and chicken panic. Trent surged to his bare feet, hands at his waist, and looked out over their farm. The Withers Farm.

"I'm trying, Molly, to make it so you don't have to worry about *anything*. You don't have to have a job. You don't have to worry about bills. I've spent the last few years trying to relieve you of *any* stress that will make things worse for you. So maybe that means protecting you from the truth of harsh realities." Trent spun and glared at her. "What more do you want from me?"

"I want you to be *honest*!" Molly drew back into her chair even as she half cried the words at him. She knew she was being duplicitous, but she couldn't avoid it. "Did you talk to January Rabine before she died?"

"Yes!" Trent threw his arms up. "*Yes!* Is that what you want to hear? Is that what's important to you?"

Molly leaped from her chair. It was hard to breathe. Finding air that had been verbally sucker-punched from her was a tremendous task. She crossed her arms over her chest, more to gather her strength and not cry. Oh, she wanted to cry. To rant, to weep, to wail! There was nothing likable about her right now, or Trent, or this entire sordid mess they called life!

"You're lucky she was your kid cousin or I'd have *other* questions." Molly heard the words come from her lips and instantly regretted them.

Trent's expression darkened. His lips set in a grim line. "That's going too far."

"Well?" She couldn't stop herself. The emotions were causing her to be impulsive, thoughtless. "And she's dead now! If you're lying to me about having talked to January—if you lied to the police and let them think she was a Jane Doe—why? What else aren't you telling me?"

Trent stalked toward her, and Molly shrank back. She wasn't afraid of him so much as she was intimidated by the hurt in every line of his face. *She* had hurt him.

Molly could feel his breath on her face when he answered. "January is my cousin Tiffany's daughter. She reached out to me for whatever reason, I don't even know. She was here to research our ancestry. That's all, Molly. Innocent ancestral research."

"Trent, I didn't mean . . ." She didn't question whether

he'd had an affair with his twenty-year-old cousin. She could sense how sick and ridiculous that was.

"I told the police that too, Molly," he snapped. "That day. I didn't hide it from them. They know. They know I talked to January. They know I *found* her! The cops didn't blast the news all over, and especially not until they got ahold of Brandon and Tiffany to tell them their daughter was dead." Trent's voice was strained. "Not to mention, *you* didn't need to know. You're not able to handle stress anymore, Molls. I was only protecting you."

A sickening, guilty sensation flooded her. The realization of how brutally disgusting her selfish inner focus was. Tears of remorse sprang to her eyes.

Trent ignored the regret that had to be clear in her demeanor. He raked his hands through his hair before letting them fall with a slap to his sides. His eyes were stormy, tortured . . . desperate.

"I can't do it anymore, Molly."

"Do what?" She was afraid to ask but did so anyway.

"This." Trent's voice shook. "Having you doubt me. All I've tried to do is take care of you. Since the . . . since we lost the babies, I *know* it ripped you apart, but you won't talk to me. You just pulled into yourself and left me. You're punishing me for not being there. For not being some sort of Superman. So I'm trying to make a life, Molly. I'm trying to pursue *life* and not just *die* while I keep breathing. You're like a dead person just walking around, and I can't do it anymore. Between you and now January's murder, I—" He swore. Ran his hand over his forehead. Agitated. "There's not a place in Kilbourn that isn't touched by its history. We *all* are touched by our own histories, Molly. But we have to either get over it and move on or die with it."

Molly sank into the chair. Her knees were weak, her body trembling. Trent was right. But she didn't want to admit that while she *heard* death, while she witnessed spirits hovering in the corners, and while she worried it would continue to lick at her heels until it claimed her too, she was afraid to live. Because living was sometimes far more terrifying than staring death in the face and accepting one's fate.

20

To make the morning even worse than it already was after having awakened to an empty house, Molly stood at the top of the basement stairs looking into the spider-infested abyss. Trent had slept on the couch. Molly was sure she'd heard him sniffing, but she couldn't fathom the strong farmhand of a husband of hers lying on the couch, crying. Still, she couldn't erase the sound from her heart. She was helpless. Helpless to know how to drag herself out of the mire of depression, through the current world of tragedy and unanswered questions surrounding January's murder to a healthy, loving place once again.

Of course, it would help if Trent tried too. Where was the impasse? That point when it was no longer her fault but his too? Or perhaps it was his fault and she needed to take less responsibility? Or maybe—maybe they'd just dealt with their grief so differently a sort of Grand Canyon had been carved between them without their fully realizing it? Regardless, Trent's sleeping on the couch was a new one. She didn't like it. It indicated further separation, and she'd hoped—with the gift of Myrtle the chick and the chickens, and Trent staying home that morning to make breakfast—that maybe something would change.

And now she needed toilet paper.

Why Trent had to store paper goods in the disgusting dungeon of a graveyard that was the basement, she didn't know. Her last foray downstairs had been disastrous.

Molly mustered the gumption and hurried down the stairs. At least she wasn't feeling woozy this time—or *seeing* things. Yet. She jerked the string, and the lone light flooded the basement with its rays, which only created unearthly shadows. The fieldstone and gravestone foundation hadn't changed. It still cried out the incomplete and erroneous names of people who had decomposed decades ago.

She hurried across the basement to the far wall, where Trent had put up some plastic shelving. Tugging at a pack of toilet paper, she dislodged it from the shelf. Thank goodness. Now all she needed to do was make it up the stairs successfully and her journey into the pit of despair would be over.

Molly adjusted the package in her arms and turned, her foot stubbing against the concrete slab that jutted a few inches above the floor level. She eyed it. Eyed its wooden pallet-style cover. The opening to a pointless crawl space. She wasn't convinced it wasn't the doorway demons came from.

Still, curiosity was a beast. Molly lowered the toilet paper to the floor and crouched by the cover. The concrete had to have been added in later years, long after they had put the crawl space in. Probably to stabilize it. Molly looked around and saw a screwdriver sitting on the bottom shelf. Snagging it, she jammed it between the wood cover and the concrete, lifting it an inch.

Blackness met her. She'd need a flashlight to see inside the crawl space. And why put a crawl space in a basement? No one was going to store canned goods in there. Molly glanced up, and a gravestone in the wall greeted her with its dulled, etched name.

Samuel Mes—

Gah. She needed to get out of here. The basement was an entrance, and that crawl space a crypt. Molly jerked the screwdriver back and let the lid fall back into place. Its thud was louder than it should have been. She froze.

No. The thud wasn't the cover.

She heard it again. Above her.

Not again.

That cold sensation washed over her, prickling her skin and raising the hairs on the back of her neck.

It wasn't footsteps she heard.

There was a random movement.

Shuffle.

Molly backed away from the crawl space, staring up between the floor joists as if she could see upstairs. She shot a panicked look at the staircase. There was no one there.

Shhhhhhhhhhhhh

Molly jerked her head to the side. The voice had come from the corner. No. From the crawl space? She curled into herself and scooted on her backside farther away from the crawl space opening.

Shhhhhhhhhhhhh

"Stop it." She shook her head from side to side, covering her ears with her hands. She couldn't. She couldn't do this again. Couldn't—

"Go away!" Her voice broke the inhuman atmosphere.

Stillness answered.

A type of silence loaded with the unheard presence of another. She could feel them. Sense them. She hated this basement. Hated this place.

Crawling across the floor, Molly managed to brace her hand against the wall, her fingers rubbing against the carved edges of a dead person's name. She pushed against it, rising to her feet.

There was more here.

More in this house.

On this property.

She could sense it. Feel it. Like a wickedness that had been buried years ago but was coming alive again. Raising its head and stretching its skeletal arms from the grave to visit the current day. It was what haunted Molly. She knew that now. It was what killed January.

The only way to shove it back into its grave for good was to confront it. Reveal the ghostly remains of the past so that the dying present could be restored.

"Where are we going?" Sid waved at her kids as Molly drove out of Sid's driveway. It was such a benefit that Sid and her husband shared child duty. Allowing Sid these middle-of-the-day interactions made Molly feel less alone.

"The library," she answered.

"The library?" Sid quirked an eyebrow as she moved to buckle her seat belt belatedly.

"I want to look into the Cornfield Ripper, and I need your brains to help me sift through the information."

"The Cornfield Ripper?" Sid's curiosity was piqued. "Well, that's digging deep into the past. Is this because of Trent's cousin?"

"January?" Molly gripped the steering wheel tighter than she'd anticipated. "Yes. I need to know why she was here. Why she was poking into the family ancestry, and why she was researching the old killer."

Sid finally wrestled the seat belt buckle into place. "Is her sister still bugging you?"

"Gemma hasn't talked to me since the coffee shop fiasco. But some of what she said—it makes sense. I mean, she has legitimate questions. What if January stumbled onto something? What if that's what got her killed?"

Sid looked doubtfully at her. "The Cornfield Ripper lived over one hundred years ago. No one alive even cares about that story anymore, outside of historians, conspiracy theorists, and people who like to tell creepy stories."

"January did. Enough to figure out that Trent and I bought the house the victims lived in."

"Really?" Sid's voice squeaked. She composed herself and shook her head. "Happenstance." Sid clucked her tongue.

"Everything and everyone in Kilbourn is connected. Small-town curse, you know?" She laughed. "Heck, if we dig deep enough, we'll probably find out *we're* cousins."

Molly couldn't discount that. They drove in silence until they reached the library. Once inside, they reserved a station, and within moments they were skimming through microfiche newspapers from the 1900s.

"Oh, there's a report on a local boy killed in a farming accident." Sid stopped Molly's intensive scrolling to point at the screen.

Molly paused and skimmed the article. "It's not about the killer." She continued scrolling.

"Hold up." Sid's hand settled over Molly's, stilling her. "What exactly are we looking for? What is the primary goal here?"

"I don't know. I . . . I'm not sure, but I feel like there's got to be something. January didn't just *die* for no reason."

Sid scrunched her lips in question. "I'm just trying to wrap my head around this. The police are obviously going to be investigating anything that's connected to January's death. Why do you feel you have to?"

It was a fair question, though not an easy one to answer.

"There are ghosts," Molly began.

Sid's head shot up in surprise.

Molly quickly continued, "I mean, the past always seems to collide with the present. One affects the other. The problem is, we can't always understand why or how."

"But a century-old murder case?"

"Maybe?" Molly shrugged. "I honestly don't know. But it seems January found it important that Trent and I bought the old Withers farm."

"You think she stumbled onto something?"

"Maybe," Molly said again, feeling more defeated the more questions Sid asked. This really was a pointless goose chase.

"Who *was* the Cornfield Ripper?" Sid's question prompted Molly to lean back in her chair.

"According to what Gladys told me, he was never identified. He killed and then disappeared after he had fun stalking and taunting the town of Kilbourn."

"Right, but what do actual historical facts say? Not the stories handed down by the people of Kilbourn."

"Funny meeting you here." The voice made Sid jump and Molly wince, knowing instantly who had come up behind them.

"Gemma." She turned in her seat.

The younger woman eyed her, hugging a notebook to herself. "I'll tell you what the facts say," she said and directed her attention to Sid. "The Cornfield Ripper claimed the lives of the two Withers sisters in the course of one month. After which he continued to contact the local newspaper, laying claim to the girls' deaths. They may attribute other deaths to him, but he didn't specifically claim them, so there was an ongoing search to find the Cornfield Ripper, until he went dormant and was never heard from again."

"So that part of the story *is* true." Sid seemed oblivious to the tension between Molly and Gemma.

Gemma edged around them and dropped her notebook on the table by the microfiche monitor. "Yes. My sister found out that a George Wasziak—who I've already mentioned to Molly was our distant grandfather—was directly involved in the investigation. It seems he may have even been a suspect at one point."

"Him and probably everyone else in Kilbourn," Sid acknowledged.

Gemma seemed to warm to Sid's engagement. Molly opted for silence. It was probably better that way.

"Not a lot was recorded about the murders outside of the newspaper reports."

"What about police reports?" Sid inquired.

Gemma shrugged, shooting an indistinguishable look at Molly. "None on record. They've been lost over the years."

Molly frowned. "How do you lose police reports?"

Gemma seemed to welcome her question. She plopped down on a third chair, rolling her eyes. "Handwritten records in 1910? Easy to lose track of. I mean, they could be in archives somewhere, but nothing is digitized back that far."

"You asked the police about it?" Sid picked some lint that hung on Molly's sleeve. Molly gave her a grateful smile.

"January asked." Gemma's voice dropped. She rubbed her eyes. "Sorry. I . . ." She hesitated, then met Molly's eyes. "I'm trying to—"

"I know," Molly cut in, acknowledging Gemma's pain. She had to. She felt grief every day herself. Where she wallowed in it, however, Gemma was surging forward, looking for a resolution to her sister's murder. Coping was what they were both attempting to do.

Gemma sighed, taking a moment to pull her shoulder-length hair back into a ponytail. Molly noticed how tired the girl looked. Twenty-eight years old should not look that haggard. That exhausted. But then she felt the same way about herself in her early thirties.

"I don't understand why January was so consumed by this part of the Wasziak ancestry." Gemma's admission resonated with Molly. Their eyes met. Gemma continued, "I mean, I understand our great-great-grandfather lived during that time. He was a doctor, going by what January wrote in her journal. He probably pronounced both the Withers sisters dead. But there were other people involved. It's not as if George was ever seriously suspected or investigated. At least not that January wrote about or that I've found. So why her fascination with the Cornfield Ripper?"

"Why is anyone fascinated by crime?" Sid interjected with a questioning twist of her mouth. "Think about it. Someone goes missing on television and we're riveted by the clues. We watch documentaries about serial killers all the time."

"*You* do," Molly teased.

Sid grinned. "Okay, fine, but the point remains. Maybe January was simply intrigued by the history and the potential familial links to it."

Gemma reached for her notebook and opened it. "I took notes of my sister's journal."

How Gemma could even complete a sentence without getting emotional was beyond Molly. They were so very different in how they approached grief.

Gemma tugged at her lavender T-shirt, adjusting the rounded neck by her throat. Molly noticed a thin gold necklace with a J hanging from it. Her throat clogged. Her own insensitivity toward Gemma and her loss struck Molly with sudden force. She'd been so self-focused, so—

"The officer listed as the primary investigator was a Detective Poll. A few persons of interest—or who knows why January wrote these names down—were Perliett Van Hilton, Maribeth Van Hilton, and Jasper Bridgers."

Molly stiffened. All thoughts of grief fled from her. "Who? What was that name?"

Gemma glanced at her, a furrow of question between her brows. "Jasper Bridgers. Why? Do you know who he was?"

Molly and Sid exchanged glances. Sid bit her bottom lip, and that was never a good sign with Sid. It meant she was hesitant. Had lost some sort of confidence. Or else she was worried. Molly bit at her thumbnail and then dropped her hand to her lap. There wasn't any reason to be worried, just . . . confused. Really. It was Kilbourn after all. A small town. Where everyone was connected.

Gemma was getting impatient with the silence. "Who is Jasper Bridgers?"

"He was *my* great-grandfather," Molly admitted hoarsely. "Bridgers is my maiden name."

21

Perliett

"Perliett."

The voice sounded distant. It echoed as though she were in a long hallway, and at the other end someone was attempting to summon her. She sensed the warmth of a blanket as it descended across her shoulders. A woman's hand pushed hair back from her face, held a glass of water to her lips, and urged her to speak.

She was dead.

No.

Millie was dead.

Millie.

Perliett snapped to her senses. She took in the long grasses. The heat of the afternoon smothered her, and she clutched at her blouse, buttoned appropriately to her neckline.

"Miss Van Hilton," the woman interjected, trying to stop her from unbuttoning.

Perliett batted the woman's hand away. Forget propriety, she was dying. *Dying!* She could feel the choking hands around her throat. She knew in an instant she would be next.

That he was looking for her. Watching her, maybe even now. She had to run.

Scrambling to her feet, the scorching hot blanket probably meant to offset shock fell to the ground. The woman, who Perliett vaguely realized was Miss Petra, Dr. Wasziak's nurse, fell backward into the weeds.

"Someone stop her!" Miss Petra cried.

Perliett stumbled on the riverbank, her foot sliding and submerging into the water. She pulled it out and clambered to her feet.

He would find her. She was next. She was dark-haired and looked like the Withers sisters. Millie had warned her.

Cock Robin.

"Who killed Cock Robin?"

She could hear Millie in her ear.

I told you, Perliett. I told you he would come.

She clawed her way up the embankment to the path that had first led her to the river. Her left shoe leaving a wet footprint, Perliett catapulted her way up the trail. She needed to return home. Lock the doors. The windows. As Detective Poll had instructed.

Arms grabbed her from behind and yanked her half off her feet.

Perliett screamed, kicking with her heels and jabbing with her elbows. She would not die! She would not surrender!

"Perliett!" The male voice shouted sternly in her ear, demanding she cease her struggle.

It only encouraged her to fight harder. She dug her fingernails into the man's hands that gripped her waist.

"You little minx!" he growled. Instead of releasing her, he forcefully spun her around, pinning her to his chest.

Perliett's frantic gaze collided with George Wasziak's. The doctor appeared to have no patience for her shenanigans. Well, why would he? Her fingernails had all but skinned him alive.

"You're in shock, Perliett. Now stop struggling before you make me smack you across the face!"

She froze. Drew back. "You wouldn't!" she hissed, skewering George with a glare.

"I have known it to be effective against overreactions of shock. So please, do not make me strike a woman for the first time in my life."

Perliett palmed his chest and pushed against it. If anything was shocking her back to her senses, it was how firm his chest was. How strong he was. How oddly comforting it had been to be stilled from her fear by a man who was stronger than she was. A man with good intentions, even if he was high-handed.

George released her. He brushed the front of his white shirt, now soiled from the dirt on her hands. "Woman, you will be the death of me."

"If I don't pass away first." She cast a nervous glance toward the river.

Men mingled there. She glimpsed Detective Poll. She noticed Jasper was there as well. A few others. They were wrapping Millie's body in a blanket. She caught little snatches of it through the weeds and trees.

"What killed her?" Perliett attempted to right her emotions. She'd made a ninny of herself in her shock. She knew that now. Any credibility—well, not that she had any, but still—with George would be toasted and eaten for breakfast now. Dry toast. Difficult to swallow. Maybe it would choke the man as it went down.

"She was stabbed. The same as her sister."

At least George didn't withhold the gory details from her as if she were a child needing to be mollycoddled. "As many times too?"

"I won't know until she's taken to my office. I will examine her there."

"I'll help," Perliett announced, shaking leaves and brushing mud from the skirt of her dress. Her beautiful emerald skirt. So pretty . . . so damaged.

"No. You'll go home to rest under the care of your mother." George examined her, and Perliett could tell that while she wasn't wounded, her screaming and her descent into hysterics as she called for help had made her shaky. Even so, George had no right to lord his authority over her now that she had calmed herself.

"I will come. A woman must be present to clean the body."

"I have Miss Petra."

"But you called for me when Eunice died," Perliett challenged.

"Because Miss Petra was away for the day." George lifted his face toward heaven as if to pray for extra patience. "Perliett, for once, don't argue with me."

"I never argue with you." She knew she sounded petulant. Perhaps she hadn't completely recovered from her shock.

"Perliett—"

"I can see Miss Van Hilton home," Mr. Bridgers offered as he approached them. Concern practically emanated from him and warmed Perliett. She did a quick and completely inappropriate comparison between the two men and was surprised to note that George's chest appeared broader, but Jasper's arms stronger. Or maybe that was because he was in shirtsleeves and George was wearing a coat, regardless of the thick humidity in the air.

It surprised Perliett to catch George rolling his eyes in an uncustomary childish approach to addressing Jasper.

"*I* will see that Perliett returns to her home safely." George put a definitive period at the end of the argument as he raised an eyebrow and glared.

Jasper's mouth twitched a little. He looked past George. "Perliett, who would you prefer to see you home?"

"She's not in a state of mind to make those decisions—"

"You," Perliett said, interrupting George with a pointed

look. "I mean you, Jasper." She realized saying *you* while looking at George gave the wrong impression.

"Very well." Jasper stepped forward as if he were going to take her arm, but George moved in front of her and effectively blocked them from being together.

"I am her doctor, Mr. Bridgers, and I must insist I see her home and converse with her mother regarding any follow-up care that should be given to Miss Van Hilton. Which, incidentally, is none of your business."

Jasper bowed slightly. "I submit to your vast knowledge and expertise." Mockery was thick in his words, but George ignored him. He turned instead to Perliett.

"Come with me."

"What nonsense." Perliett waved him off. "I can administer my *own* care, thank you very much, and my mother hasn't . . ." She broke off before she revealed that for all the love she had for her mother, the nurturing side of Maribeth Van Hilton was lacking.

George looked as if it was all he could do not to take her arm and manhandle her to his carriage for the ride home.

Jasper met her eyes. "Go, Perliett. Dr. Wasziak has good intentions, even if his delivery leaves much to be desired. I will stay behind and see if I can be of assistance in this matter here." He looked over his shoulder, muttering, "The poor girl. I pray she didn't suffer."

"Prayers that have come too late," George inserted.

"Did *you* pray prior to her death?" Jasper asked.

George glowered, his eyes darkening to that familiar deep shade of fathomless black. "I haven't ceased praying." He eyed Perliett for a moment, just long enough to make her squirm beneath his gaze—almost knowing, almost intimately acquainted with her soul. "And I will continue to pray until all are safe."

She *was* still shaken. But wild horses couldn't drag her body across the plains long enough for Perliett to ever admit that to George.

George.

He sat stiffly beside her in his carriage, ignoring the wheezing clack of a passing motorcar. She had the fleeting thought that George Wasziak was too old-fashioned to own a motorcar. He would use a horse and buggy until his gravestone boasted his name.

Perliett linked her hands together to disguise her trembling fingers. What had upset her so much more about Millie's death than Eunice's? She had studied Eunice's body. Honestly, she'd been *intrigued* by the mystery of it, despite the awful circumstances. But Millie? Perhaps it was because she'd just been on Perliett's porch. Last night. They'd discovered the dead robin. She'd been so adamant they were in danger.

She had been so right.

"When you return home, I would recommend you have some chamomile tea with lavender. It will help calm your nerves."

"I know," Perliett responded to George with a curt nod.

"I could administer a small dose of sleeping powders if you—"

"If I were a porcelain doll, *George,* I may welcome this sort of delicate attention, but really, I'm made of far stiffer material." It annoyed Perliett when her voice broke. Tears were her nemesis, but when they did come, at least she and George were in the privacy of the carriage. The tears were impossible to stop.

"Mmm." His low growl was almost mesmerizing and insinuated he'd noticed her chin quivering.

George snapped the reins, and the horse trotted faster. Soon the Van Hilton home came into view. Its two-story white structure, front porch laden with massive potted ferns

. . . it was home. Yet it felt strangely empty as George steered the buggy into the drive.

Her mother was absent. Where, Perliett did not know. But this should solve any worry that George would stay and belabor them with instructions for Perliett to follow, as if it were she who'd been attacked and not poor, dead Millie Withers.

"My mother is not home. I can tell because the front door is closed. She always leaves it open during the day if she's home. So, you may drop me off here. I will see myself inside." Perliett swung toward the outside of the buggy, but George's hand on her arm stopped her.

She turned, giving him her full attention in spite of herself.

His black eyes had softened, only they were edged with concern and not a little caution. Even the hand on her, while firm, was gentle. Coaxing almost. No, pleading. She wasn't accustomed to this side of George Wasziak.

"Perliett . . . I don't feel it is safe to leave you here alone."

She swallowed back her nervousness. "I'll be fine." She waved off his concern with a tremor in her voice. Her justification was paltry and silly in light of what had just happened. Foolhardy, really.

George shifted in his seat and it brought him closer to her. He maintained his grave expression, only somehow he seemed more vulnerable. It was as if he was wrestling with something.

"We don't know who is responsible for the Withers sisters' deaths. But Mrs. Withers is correct in that you are similar in appearance to them. If the killer is selecting a victim merely based on appearances, then you are likely to be on that list."

"This isn't a new concept, George." Perliett tempered her voice. He seemed to care—at least in this moment—and as long as he wasn't being arrogant, she could appreciate human kindness.

"I realize that, but I'm not certain you are aware of the dangers of men."

There it was. That insult that her womanly constitution made her somehow innocent of all concepts—especially medically. "Of course I am!"

"Are you?"

"I know what atrocities can be committed against a woman's wishes."

George colored, and she was surprised at that. For a second, he blustered then shook his head. "That's—that's *not* what I was implying, though potentially accurate. I was referring to man's *innate* wickedness."

"Men in general terms, or do you include women?" Perliett couldn't help it. Baiting George was what she was best at.

He smiled grimly. "Contrary to what people wish to hear, I believe we all have a nature to do evil."

"Even babies?" Perliett challenged with a teasing smile, thankful for the distraction.

"Even babies."

"Heartless brute." She had no qualms calling the man out for his condemnation of an innocent soul.

George drew back slightly, quirking a black eyebrow. "You've never seen an infant scream in a fit of anger?"

"I would hardly call that evil."

"A foreshadowing then? Of what is coming. That imperfect person whose primary motivation is to satisfy one's own pleasures."

"That's a bad thing?" Perliett thought of her morning coffee and was fairly certain she'd be willing to follow in the footsteps of the Cornfield Ripper if someone were to threaten that pleasure.

"It is when it hurts another."

Perhaps she'd been too flippant about her retaliation in the face of her coffee forfeiture. But still . . . "Most men and women do not act on the basest of carnal motivations, though. You can hardly compare a child's tantrum to the Cornfield Ripper's brutality."

"Certainly not the outcome. Or the consequences. And not even the impact on those around them. You are correct. But in the end, both land on the same side of the scale regarding right or wrong."

"What does any of this have to do with right now?" Perliett grew agitated. George was simply an intellectual who had married his intellect with his faith, and that became annoying because of its arguable truth.

"Do not put your trust in anyone right now."

Perliett tilted her head. "Even you?"

"My argument includes everyone, if you take me literally."

"So, I should be afraid of my mother?"

"I didn't say to be afraid. I said to not put your trust in a person right now."

"But—"

"Kilbourn has proven to not be a safe place. Think carefully. There are no strangers here—except for Mr. Bridgers, another topic altogether—which means one of us has a propensity to act on the great violence in our heart."

"But not my mother," Perliett said.

"I merely am saying to be wise."

Perliett scowled. "You are talking in circles. I have this feeling you have something else you're trying to say and you're avoiding it."

"Because you'll accuse me of being high-handed."

"Perhaps."

George rubbed his chin with his hand. Perliett heard the scratch of stubble against his palm. He took a deep breath and then released it. "I . . . Never mind." He shook his head, deciding against saying whatever was on the tip of his tongue.

"George . . ." Perliett surprised herself by reaching out and resting her hand over his.

He jerked as if her touch burned him. She realized her

gloves had come off sometime between finding Millie's body and now. Skin on skin, the heat that rose surprised her, but it also stunned her enough that she couldn't remove her hand.

She couldn't move.

They locked eyes. A long, silent moment.

George cleared his throat but didn't pull away. "Be cautious. In everything. You play with fire until it burns you, Perliett, and you still go back for more. It keeps me up at night."

"Worrying about me is not your responsibility." Perliett was amazed at the warmth that flooded her. She hadn't expected that. Not from George Wasziak.

He drew back his hand. His scowl returned, and he sniffed. "No. You are *not* my responsibility."

For some reason, Perliett felt George stated it more so to remind himself than to assure her.

I am a beast.
Kills the robin.
Save a feather.
I stroke my face with its softness.
I remember.
Feeding the beast will keep it content.
For now.
Until another robin decides to fly.

22

Molly

"It's not possible." Molly climbed the ladder steps into the attic of the chicken coop.

Sid followed but with less enthusiasm. Caution seemed to envelop her, and Molly was very aware that they were swapping roles. Typically, Sid was the adventurer and Molly wallowed. But now she was motivated. Motivated by the reality that maybe Gemma Rabine was righter than she wanted to admit. That seeking justice for January would illuminate secrets long buried that perhaps haunted them in the present. Not that the past could answer for her and Trent's personal losses, but resolving the past and the present seemed to promise some sort of undefined hope she couldn't explain.

And hope wasn't something she'd had for some time. Even if this was more desperation than anything, it was something. At least she was *doing something*.

"I can't believe it truly is a killer's kit," Molly emptily reassured both herself and Sid as they entered the attic. She crossed the floor and approached the crate that held the items

Sid so brazenly had dubbed a serial killer's kit a few days before.

"Even if it is," Sid argued, "it has nothing to do with the Cornfield Ripper. That was in 1910. They didn't have duct tape in 1910."

"What did they have then? Someone could've tossed a roll of duct tape in later. Maybe it's a clue." Molly sorted through the contents again. She pulled out the leather belt strap and studied it. "See? This could be vintage."

"A clue to what? What are we looking for?" Sid toed the corner of the crate.

"I don't know." Molly didn't want to admit it, but she felt as directionless as she felt invigorated. "But if it involved our grandfathers in the Cornfield Ripper killings even a little bit, then that ties to January's ancestral research, which could lead us to why she was killed."

"I almost expected Gemma to say a ghost killed her." Sid chuckled, crossing the room to duck and look out the small window.

Molly stilled and eyed Sid's back. "What if it did?"

"Molly." Sid turned and leveled a look on her that left Molly pretty sure she'd just about revealed her hand as far as what she believed when it came to spirits.

Believed? That was too strong of a word. What she was afraid was true about spirits? Maybe that was more accurate.

"Well, think about it." Molly wasn't quite willing to let it go. "People have said ghosts have scratched them in the night. Cut. Sometimes strangled even. Who's saying that—"

"Molly!" Sid half laughed and half twisted her face in disbelieving laughter. "You can't seriously think there's any credibility to the idea that January was killed because she was researching an old murder case? By a ghost, no less. Do you know how many people have researched the Cornfield Ripper before? It's a cold case—just like Gemma indicated. That stuff intrigues people. Looking into it doesn't get a person killed."

"Is this a killer's kit, though?" Molly dangled the leather belt. "Coincidence?"

"Then take it to the police," Sid concluded, her hands at her hips. "If you really think those items are somehow tied to January's death, then you need to call the cops."

"I'm just saying . . . there are a lot of unanswered questions here." Of course, that wouldn't make sense to Sid. She wasn't aware of half of what Molly could sense. Could *feel.* She hadn't seen the ghoulish remains of January Rabine in the basement. She hadn't been haunted by the vision of the little girl in the coop attic. That this was the old Withers farm? Why would a killer target two sisters? And had other deaths come after? If so, who were they?

"Earth to Molly." Sid was waving her hand in front of Molly's face. She'd returned from the attic window and now crouched beside her. Concern was very apparent in both her body language and her words. "I don't deny that things are weird. Even scary, what with January being murdered just down the road."

Molly ignored her as an idea struck. She tugged out the duct tape and looked at the logo on the internal cardboard core. Current enough that she recognized it. She tossed it aside and reached for the gloves. Unmarked, no tag. She leaned over the crate. There had to be something to date the items by.

"What are you looking for?" Sid asked.

Molly didn't answer but instead gave a quick yelp of joy. She reached in and lifted the newspaper that lined the bottom of the crate. "A date!" She drew the stiff yellowed paper toward her. "A clue or something to tell us how old the stuff in this crate is, and whether it's a killer's kit."

"It's not," Sid replied.

Molly side-eyed her. "You were certain it was a few days ago."

Sid offered a sheepish smile. "Well, yeah. Back when it sounded fun, and I didn't really believe it."

Molly skimmed the newsprint, then flipped the paper. She shot Sid a victorious smile. "The paper's from 1982."

"See? This cannot be the Cornfield Ripper's kit."

"No. But what happened in 1982?"

"Do we care?" Sid quirked an eyebrow.

Molly read the paper's headline. "I don't know. Do we?"

"What does it say?" Sid leaned over her shoulder to read.

"Nothing all that interesting. Stock market report. Weather forecast. High school sports team scores." Molly sat back on her heels. Disappointment was something she was very familiar with, and she didn't like the way it crept in so quickly after her euphoric high that somehow this crate would provide answers. It was a long shot. Just a crateful of random items that could be found on any farm, and they shed no light on January's murder or the century-old cold case.

"You know," Sid began, her curiosity returning, "the Cornfield Ripper has never really made the news. I mean, not the *news* per se, but the list of national serial killers. It's like he never existed."

Molly let that sink in, even as she laid the newspaper back in the crate.

"Of course," Sid continued, "they didn't call them 'serial killers' back then. That term was coined later, as recently as the seventies with the appearances of Ted Bundy and the BTK Killer. Actually, you have to kill three or more people to be considered a serial killer, I think . . . *Man,* I watch too much crime TV." Sid laughed.

Molly sensed Sid's attention falling on her as her chattering waned. She couldn't explain it, but Sid's words had triggered something inside her. A *feeling*. Molly peered into the corners of the attic. Nothing. No one was watching them.

"The Withers farm," Molly mumbled.

"What's that?" Sid asked.

Molly pushed herself off the floor. "This is the farm where the Withers sisters lived. Gladys called it the 'murder house.'"

She hurried across the attic to look out the window. Her flock of chickens were pecking the yard, busy and oblivious to the world around them. The rooster, on the other hand, marched around like a sentinel. But she looked beyond them now. Toward the house. Toward her bedroom window.

The Withers sisters. Had it been the spirit of one of them she'd seen moving in the room from this very window? What if the little girl was the ghost of one of them, only as a child? What if the farm still held secrets about their deaths?

"I have to uncover them." Molly's mutter was more to herself than to Sid. She had almost forgotten Sid was there. She placed her hand on the glass and stared toward the bedroom window of the farmhouse, allowing her eyes to rove the side of the building. Had the killer watched them before they died? Had January's killer watched her? She should ask herself why—why it was suddenly so important that she knew. That she finished whatever it was January had discovered. January Rabine's murder was anything but random. It was tied, somehow, to the Withers sisters. It *had* to be. To the family's history, and ultimately to Molly's new home.

Trent eyed her from across the room. It was nighttime, but Molly was sitting up in bed, her laptop perched on her lap. She could feel Trent's inquiring gaze. He'd watched her retire to bed by seven o'clock for so many nights, the fact that it was going on nine was an anomaly in her behavior.

"What are you working on?" He extricated himself from his T-shirt, pulling it over his head and tossing it into the overflowing dirty-laundry pile.

Molly hesitated, momentarily distracted by his muscled back, his toned biceps, his ridiculously funny farmer's tan. She hid a smile, both out of respect for the man's ego and because she was a bit surprised she'd noticed. Noticed *him*. After their last confrontation, they hadn't spoken much. She was willing to bet on all her new chickens' lives—except Sue. Sue was her favorite, or maybe it was Myrtle, or Chloe, or heavens! She loved them all now! But anyway, she was willing to bet that Trent wouldn't be happy with her internet search history.

He unbuttoned his jeans.

She dropped her gaze to her laptop, heat rising to her cheeks. Well, this was unexpected.

There was silence as Trent tugged off his jeans and then slid into a pair of shorts. The bedroom was stifling with summer humidity. Yes. That was it. Humidity. He crossed the room to the window and hiked it up until it was fully open.

"I'm going to put a fan in the window."

Molly nodded.

Their inane conversation was as stifling as the air. She dared a glance at Trent. His back was already glistening with sweat. His shoulders were—*wow*—Molly distracted herself with her research. She'd forgotten how broad they were. She'd forgotten about the birthmark on his right shoulder that she used to kiss over and over until he'd pay attention to her. It'd been months since they . . .

She jammed the enter button on her computer a little too hard.

Trent sank onto the edge of the bed, swung his legs on top of the covers, and leaned back against the headboard. "You're up to something." His voice was gravelly with tiredness yet touched with curiosity.

Molly managed to give him a small smile. He was trying, in his awkward way. Peacemaking. That was a good place to start.

Making a quick decision, Molly turned her laptop so Trent could see.

He leaned over, his bare shoulder brushing hers. She'd put a tank top on for bedtime. She felt his skin on hers, and suddenly the butterflies returned. Trent had showered. He smelled like soap. That fresh scent of soap filled with toxic chemicals that were all synthetic and so delicious smelling . . . like the ocean mixed with rain and citrus and—

"You're researching serial killers?" Trent's confusion was clear.

"Not serial killers so much as their patterns," she answered.

"Well, your interests have changed." There was humor in his voice. Teasing.

She glanced at him.

Flirtation in his eyes.

Where that came from, she had no idea! But he was male. All male. So, there was that.

Debating, she lost the battle against her desire to keep her distance from Trent. There had been a time before loss when they'd talked about everything. *Shared* everything. And she meant *everything*!

Quickly, before the warmth in her turned into a hot blush, Molly continued, "Gemma said that January had been looking into the Cornfield Ripper." Molly watched Trent's face to gauge his reaction.

He nodded, completely unsurprised. "Yeah. That's what we'd talked about."

"You did?" Molly straightened in anticipation. "What did she say? Why was she researching it?"

Trent eyed her for a moment and then answered carefully. "She ran across it when she was reading family history. My great-grandfather—"

"George," Molly supplied.

"Yeah. George. He was involved in the investigation because he was a doctor. He helped the police at the time determine the cause of death."

"And my great-grandfather, Jasper Bridgers?" Molly asked.

"What about him?" Trent appeared genuinely at a loss.

"Gemma told me that January was looking into him, and a family called the Van Hiltons."

"I don't know—I just—January called me up and said she was in town. That she was spending the summer doing family research and wanted to know if I knew any old stories to help fill in the blanks. I guess she was writing some sort of family memoir. She said she was going to get ahold of her grandfather—Uncle Roger—but that things were strained, and she wanted to talk to me first."

It made sense. If she was compiling a memoir, throwing in George Wasziak's inclusion in a murder investigation would add intrigue.

"Did you know that most serial killers have an M.O.?" Molly offered.

Trent smiled a little, and to sabotage Molly's nerves, his fingers brushed her bare leg. "Most criminals do, Molls."

"Oh?" she heard herself tease back. Really? She was flirting with her husband. Over serial killers. That had to stop.

Trent's smile broadened. "Yeah," he said and wagged his eyebrows. "And they keep souvenirs, and they're psychopaths with no conscience, and they often start their fascination with killing by targeting animals."

"But did you know that there's a difference between planned and compulsive killers?"

"Sure." Trent stretched his arms out, then bent them behind his head, his elbows sticking out. She felt the absence of his fingers against her thigh. He continued, "And they rarely switch modes. They're one or the other."

"Right." She was distracted.

"Your point?" His eyes were warm.

Gosh! This reminded her of before. Before it all happened. Before they lost the babies. When they were friends. Lovers. How could they go from being so emotionally distant to suddenly, tonight, the heat in the room being far more than the summer's temperature gauge?

Molly jabbed at the laptop screen with more force than needed. She blinked a few times to clear her senses. "When I looked up the Cornfield Ripper—and there's not much online about him—I also found that after the Withers sisters were murdered, there was another attack. But it wasn't tied to the Cornfield Ripper. He didn't claim it."

"Doesn't mean he didn't do it."

Molly smirked. "Well, maybe it does."

Trent yawned lazily, although Molly could tell he was listening. "Hey. I'm glad something's got your interest, but—why this? It's not exactly calming bedtime reading."

Molly shut her laptop and set it on the bedside table. "We live in the Withers house." Dare she curl into his side like old times? She hesitated.

"I know." His voice dropped. He was expecting an argument. Molly could sense him bracing for it.

"January was murdered."

"Yeah."

"Do the police know why?"

"They're not saying anything, but that's typical in an investigation."

"What if she stumbled onto something—about the Cornfield Ripper?"

"Molly, the Cornfield Ripper didn't come back from the dead to kill January." Trent looked pained as he said it. Molly could tell he was recalling finding his cousin—in the ditch—by a cornfield—stabbed . . .

"There's no correlation." Trent reached over and flicked off the light. He nestled into his pillow. "Something else happened to my cousin."

"I'm sorry," Molly whispered.

"What?" His voice was equally as soft.

The darkness enveloped them in a warm, intoxicating embrace.

Molly dared to roll onto her side. She reached out and laid

her hand on his abdomen. Trent's muscles twitched beneath her touch. "I'm sorry." She whispered the words again. For exactly what, she wasn't even sure. Empathy for January's death? Apologies for her standoffish behavior? Mutual grief for the babies they would never know.

Trent's chest rose and fell in a deep silence. "Yeah. Me too."

Those words. So incomplete and yet so full.

It was a start, wasn't it?

Death required resolution in all aspects of life. The only problem was, often that resolution never came, or its answers and reasons why fell far short of satisfactory.

Maybe that was why death fascinated people. It was the not knowing why. Why did someone kill? Why did someone die? Why did God allow evil to exist? Why . . .

Why. The unanswerable question of the ages.

Molly started as Trent rolled onto his side. In the darkness, he reached for her. Maybe there was hope after all? At least a possibility?

23

The chickens were perturbed about something.

Molly tugged on her rain boots and trudged across the yard toward the coop. Sue and Alex were squawking like they wanted to raise the dead—and Molly didn't need more of that!—and the others were flustered, a flurry of feathers dotting the yard.

"Oh no." Molly increased her pace. If a fox or a raccoon had gotten into the coop . . . She had locked the chickens and her "boy"—the rooster—in last night, but she knew Trent would have let them out before he left for his job at Clapton Bros. Farms.

Fox and coon didn't hunt during the morning hours, did they?

She hoped not.

Counting chickens, Molly noticed only Sylvia was missing. Chloe, check. Izzy, check. Myrtle would be in the brooder with the other chicks. The gate to the chicken yard was open, which was normal for the daytime. The coop door was open as well. No sign of a struggle, no copious amounts of feathers to indicate a war between predator and prey.

"Sylvia?" Molly called. She ducked through the coop's doorway. The brooder was intact. Trent had wired it so Myrtle and three of the other chicks could be safe beneath a heat lamp. "Sylvia?" she called again, fully expecting the Ameraucana chicken to answer. Silly. For all the craziness of late, Molly found herself roaming the yard with her chickens.

Getting to know their personalities. They were becoming friends.

Something had definitely disturbed the chickens, though they were calming now. Still, Molly peeked into the nesting boxes. No Sylvia. A scratching sound at the far end of the building captured her attention. An empty five-gallon bucket had overturned but was bouncing as if something was inside it. Molly hurried to the bucket and attempted to lift it. It was tipped in such a way that the metal handle had popped out on one side and wedged between part of the building's wooden frame and siding. It made it awkward to release the trapped chicken, as the space the bucket was wedged in provided little room to pull it free.

"How did you get stuck in there, Sylvia?" Molly scolded her chicken with the gray feathers that Sid said were called blue. "Did you do gymnastics?" Molly continued to tease. Sylvia scuffled inside the bucket as Molly worked at releasing the handle so she could remove the bucket.

The handle broke from the plastic, and Molly was finally able to lift it. Sylvia flew out in a proud and offended fluster of feathers. Molly shouted after the retreating chicken, "Chloe is a more grateful Ameraucana Blue than you are!"

Sylvia clucked.

Molly laughed. It felt good to laugh.

Needing to get the bucket's handle extricated from where it was jammed in the wood frame, Molly squeezed herself between the wall and the nesting box to get a better grip. She tugged and twisted, and the handle finally released with enough of a jerk that Molly's ample backside banged into the nesting box. The resulting crack as it dislodged from the wall stole Molly's momentary joy at rescuing her chicken.

"For goodness' sakes!" she grumbled, opting to sound like her grandmother instead of cursing like her dad always had. Molly dropped the handle and focused her attention on the nesting box, now half torn off the wall. She hefted the box with her knee so it didn't pull out from the wall any farther. Thankfully, there were no eggs in it that could've rolled out and broken since this was an old unused nesting box void of straw. She examined the wall where the box was pulling away from. A shadow caught her attention, and Molly frowned. That was odd. She ran her hand along the back of the nesting box, and her palm felt the distinct feel of old, cracking leather.

"What the heck?"

Allowing the box to hang haphazardly, Molly squeezed both hands behind it and tugged at the object. There was a slight ripping sound as the item gave up part of its cover.

This was unexpected. Molly drew the old book toward her. Who attaches a book to the back of a chicken nesting box?

The remaining part of the cover was indeed cracking leather, dried from time and age. The remnant of a decaying black silk ribbon bookmark stuck about an inch above the cover. Cautiously, Molly opened the cover. Its spine crunched from the movement, and she hesitated, only opening it halfway for fear of ruining it. A quick glance confirmed there was no title on the front of the book.

Molly tilted it to peek at the page inside. Handwriting. Thicker cursive in lead pencil scrawled over the page. It was difficult to make out with the book only half open.

May 13, 1910

Moon is in first quarter phase.

1 dead sow. Coyote?

The recorded year immediately snagged Molly's attention, for 1910 was the year of the Cornfield Ripper. She eyed the writing. It was a journal of sorts. A farmer's log of the weather? The moon phases? Happenings on this farm? A thrill shot through her. What if one of the Withers family members had written this?

She tried to nudge the journal open wider to allow for further browsing. The spine cracked again, and this time the book gave in to the pressure without sending pages scattering.

Molly leaned against the wall. The handwriting looked masculine. Broad strokes with a firm edge. The person writing had pushed hard against the paper.

She turned the page.

More weather reports. Mention of a purchase of grain. Sale of three dozen eggs. The writer had penned a preferred forecast on one page, indicating the hope that rain wouldn't hinder the first cutting of hay.

It was interesting for the purposes of farm history. For anything else, it was boring words of information that were of little use. An almanac of sorts. She recalled back in the day her grandmother mentioning they'd lived by the *Farmers' Almanac*. Weather predictions, farm reports, crop indicators. All of it was critical to running a farm before the days of phone apps with their instant and regularly updated weather reports, stock reports at one's fingertips, even streaming music to play in the tractor while cutting hay.

Molly closed the journal, careful to make sure she didn't damage the pages further. The book had held up remarkably well, considering it was written starting in 1910. Who knew when the owner had stashed it behind the nesting box, or why.

She pushed off the wall of the coop. The chickens had gathered near her, probably hoping for grain. Molly gave them all a motherly smile.

"Later, girls."

She stepped around the clucking fowl and made her way from the chicken coop. Molly carried the journal with her, thumbing the edges of its leather binding.

1910.

Withers Farm.

The journal had been hidden the same year the murders of the Withers sisters had occurred. It sparked an urgency in

Molly. She hurried to the house and nestled into the booth in the kitchen.

She laid the journal on the table. Anyone keeping a journal would have *had* to have written about the sisters' murders. Of course, if every page contained only farm records, then maybe it wasn't a private record of the Withers farm life, but still . . .

Molly opened the book as her phone rang. She tugged it from her pocket. "Hello?"

"Molly, is that you?" It was Gemma Rabine.

"Yes."

"I need to find Trent. How do I get ahold of him?" There was an urgency in her voice that put Molly on edge.

"Why?"

"Because I need to. He's not answering the number Grandpa gave me for him. How do I find him?"

"What do you need him for?" She wasn't trying to protect Trent from Gemma, but she wasn't going to just dole out information as to how he could be tracked down via Clapton Bros. Farms, not until Gemma fessed up to what she was after.

"The police pulled some DNA off my sister." The wobble in Gemma's voice made Molly still, a foreboding settling in her gut with the weight of a heavy lead anchor. Molly sagged against the booth.

"They haven't been able to identify who it belongs to, but it's male."

"They told you all this?" Molly was trying to wrap her head around the information.

Gemma's laugh was tainted with a bitter edge. "I'm persistent when it comes to my sister. Anyway, I need to talk to Trent. I need to see who else January was in contact with. She had to have told Trent more than he's shared."

Molly felt a small measure of relief. Gemma wasn't indicating it was Trent's DNA on January's remains. She was pursuing an unknown person.

"Gemma—"

"Trent knows more than he's saying."

Molly hedged giving Gemma his cell number. It felt like a betrayal of Trent, and after the other night, she didn't want to undermine the fragile truce that had formed between them. "If Trent's not answering his phone, then I don't know how to get ahold of him right now."

"Sure." Gemma's tone told Molly she clearly didn't believe Molly. "Listen to me, Molly. If I were you, I'd be more concerned about what my husband was up to. Like I said before, the Wasziak family history isn't as clean and innocent as they would have us believe."

"There's nothing to indicate that Trent—" Molly started, but Gemma interrupted.

"You know what else I found?" Gemma asked. She didn't wait for Molly to reply. "I found out that George Wasziak, the hallowed great-great-grandfather of mine, wasn't that nice of a guy after all. He actually *refused* to cooperate with the police when he was accused of attacking a woman shortly after the second Withers sister's murder. Remember that name, Van Hilton? Apparently, he did a number on her."

"Gemma . . ." Molly stared at the old book on the table. It held little intrigue now, not in the wake of such stunning news.

"Do your own search, Molly. Look up the Wasziak name in the county record and see what they're hiding. Do it. I dare you."

Weather is promising.
It will be a full moon.
I would see her face.
Who will dig her grave?
Will she watch me while I dig?
Reminder: need to buy nails to fix chicken coop.

24

Perliett

She shouldn't be surprised. Not really. Her mother poured tea into a cup, her face set in that solemn, contemplative way it always took on whenever she'd had an "encounter."

"It was so . . . surreal, Perliett." She slid into a chair at the kitchen table, resting her teacup on the table. "I looked up and there she was. Beside my bed."

The lantern cast a warm glow through the kitchen. Perliett noted that the back door was shut, but Maribeth had left the window open over the washbasin. She would need to close that before they retired. George's warnings—the memory of Millie's corpse half floating in the river . . .

"She just stood there. Staring down at me." Maribeth took another sip of tea, her eyes fixed on the distant wall as if she were being transported back to the night before when in her bed and she was awakened by an apparition.

"Eunice visited you?" Perliett took the chair opposite her mother. Her heavy curtain of dark hair fell over her shoulder and her nightdress. They were preparing for bed, but Maribeth was apprehensive about going. She'd asked her daughter to join her for tea. They needed to talk, she'd said. Perliett expected her mother to ask questions regarding the shocking afternoon. About Millie. Instead, she was elaborating on her own experience from the night before.

Maribeth nodded, her black hair pulled into a thick braid. "Eunice. She was so pale. Ethereal, really." Maribeth raised her eyes to meet Perliett's, and Perliett saw in their reflection a sort of awe and fear swirling together. "Her eyes were—they were empty. I could see through Eunice as if she were a mist."

"She spoke to you?" Perliett couldn't deny the way her throat tightened and her breaths shortened. It was one thing to know her mother summoned communication with the spirits in their study, but it was entirely different to learn they roamed the house. Shifting through walls and observing them in their sleep. The sacred aloneness of one's room at night, curled beneath the covers, was violated when a spirit lurking in the corner became a reality.

Maribeth nodded. "She did. A strangled whisper. Her hand—so white—kept grasping at her throat. Her windpipe seemed as if it had been mangled beneath the hands of her killer." Wide eyes made Maribeth look almost creepy herself. The hot tea passed through her lips with a cooling sip, making a bubbling sound that reminded Perliett of the woman she'd sat with last year, who had taken her last gasping breaths of life.

"But Eunice wasn't strangled, Mother." Perliett's correction brought an awareness into Maribeth's expression.

"Are you certain?" Maribeth asked.

"Yes. I helped clean her body." Perliett wished her mother hadn't raised this topic tonight. She desperately needed a good night's rest. An opportunity to gather her wits after a shocking day. Now she couldn't help but cast wary glances into the corners of the room. Was Eunice there? Was she listening to them discuss her demise?

"Regardless," Maribeth said, brushing aside Perliett's

correction as to how Eunice had died, "she's trying to tell me something, and I can't . . . I can't interpret what it is!" Perliett noticed her mother's hand shook as she set the teacup back on the table. "I need to make a connection again." Maribeth pushed off the table.

"*Now*?" Perliett drew back.

"Yes. Come with me." Maribeth motioned for Perliett to follow her as she passed, leaving the familiar aroma of rosemary wafting behind her.

Perliett ignored the twist in her stomach. Her bare feet padded along the carpet runner as she followed Maribeth to the study. It wasn't lost on her that Maribeth was intent on contacting Eunice but had never shown the same urgency to connect with PaPa. Dare she ask? Could her mother attempt to summon more than one spirit tonight?

After today's events, Perliett ached for the steady presence of PaPa. He wouldn't have been so oblivious as her mother was or even preoccupied by the murdered instead of giving his attention to the living. To Perliett. Whose life was supposedly in danger, according to Mrs. Withers, Detective Poll, George, and even the killer himself, if the dead robin was any indicator.

She cast a nervous glance at the windows in the study. The one that had shattered was still boarded up. Was it secure enough? Would it keep out the Cornfield Ripper if he tried to enter? If he and his cackling nighttime chuckle of mockery hunted her inside her own home?

Maribeth lit three candles in the middle of the table, blowing out the match so that a tendril of smoke drifted in a curling dance toward the ceiling. She went to the shelf at the edge of the room—PaPa's shelf—and lifted a heavy crystal rock. Tucking it in her left arm, she selected a pencil from a cup and retrieved a piece of stationery.

"What are you doing?" Perliett hadn't seen her mother with pencil and paper before, not during a summoning.

"Shhh." Maribeth rested the crystal near the candles and laid the stationery and pencil in front of her. The flickering of the candles made the crystal almost glow. "Sit." Maribeth waved at a chair as she brushed her hand behind her to smooth her nightgown as she sat.

Perliett obeyed. It was difficult to swallow. To breathe. An oppressive air—not unfamiliar—settled in the room. She watched in silence as her mother closed her eyes and drew in a deep, steadying breath. Then Maribeth opened her eyes, focusing on the crystal. She lifted the pencil with her right hand, but instead of gripping it with her fingers, she balanced it against her knuckles.

The room fell into a dark silence. Perliett could hear the steady breaths of her mother. A clock on the wall ticked its seconds.

One. Two. Three. Four. Five. Six. Seven.

Maribeth fixated on the crystal. Perliett watched as her mother's eyes seemed to glaze over, her blinking slowed.

Perliett opened her mouth to ask her mother if she was all right, then realized Maribeth was falling into a trance. Her breaths came slowly, a deep and silent intake and then a drawn-out release. The exhaling through her nose made the candle flames dance.

Grasping the material of her nightgown, Perliett clenched it in her fingers below the table. Her hands were trembling. Why something so powerful, so miraculous as connecting with the afterlife would feel so unnerving and dangerous, Perliett couldn't explain.

The pencil moved.

Perliett's gaze flew to Maribeth's hand, which moved along the paper, the pencil lead leaving a light trail behind it. Words were forming on the page, although Perliett couldn't read them from her seat across the table. It was strange how the pencil stayed balanced against her mother's knuckles, how her wrist moved so gracefully and so quickly. The words seemed to come almost faster than Maribeth could write. Maribeth kept her focus on the crystal and not the paper. Her breaths came faster now, louder. Perliett leaned in, watching her mother's face for signs of distress.

Something was wrong. Maribeth hadn't blinked for over a minute. She was still in a deep trance as the pencil in her hand continued working its way across the page. The candle flames flickered faster, and Perliett sensed cold air creeping up her nightgown, wrapping itself around her legs. Her throat constricted as the sensation of hands clamping down on her neck became very real.

Maribeth's eyes widened, her stare shifting to just above Perliett's shoulder. Her mouth moved but remained wordless. Perliett tried to twist in her chair, even as she drew her hands up to her throat to fight off the stranglehold that didn't exist.

A low moan gurgled in Maribeth's throat, rising with insistence.

Perliett shoved back in her chair, her body colliding with empty air that somehow felt occupied by something or someone. Her feet tangled in her nightgown and she fell to the floor, the chair overturning with a clamor. The candles were snuffed, plunging the room into blackness. Maribeth's scream rent the air with a nerve-shattering impact. Rolling to her knees, Perliett fought against her clothes.

"Mother!" She grasped the edge of the table, squinting in the darkness. "Mother!" When Maribeth didn't answer, Perliett stumbled to the doorway and ran her palm against the wall until it met with the switch to ignite the gaslights around the room.

When the lights flared to life, her gaze landed on Maribeth's form, slumped over the table, the pencil rolling until it fell off the edge and landed with a clatter on the floor.

Her smelling salts didn't revive Maribeth. Perliett had propped her mother's head on a pillow as she sprawled on the study floor.

"Mother, please," Perliett urged as she rummaged through her apothecary chest. She pulled out a bottle wrapped in a small velvet bag. "I'll pour you some of this." Talking to Maribeth gave Perliett hope that she'd soon regain her senses. A small glass was tucked in her box. Perliett lifted it and poured some brandy from the bottle. She held it to her mother's lips, but the alcohol dribbled down her chin, running onto her neck. "Mother, you need to drink this. The brandy will help."

There was no response.

Perliett patted her mother's cheek. "Please." When there was continued silence, Perliett emptied her box in a panic. Bottles of this and that, powders, tablets, and syrups. Her chin quivered, and she swallowed down tears. Tears that now strangled her more than the invisible hands had.

"God help me." The impulsive prayer did nothing to lighten the room. Nothing to strike her with medical inspiration. She had reached the end of her paltry knowledge. Perliett had a moment of disdain for herself. For her pretense and pride that she could pretend to be anything more than someone with home remedies. That she could compete with the knowledge of George Wasziak and the medical field. Her mother was comatose, lying on the floor beside her table that was the bridge to the other side, and Perliett was helpless to care for her!

She needed assistance. Immediately. Perliett shoved bottles away from her, and they rolled on the floor. Useless. Useless treatments when it truly mattered!

Perliett leaned close to her mother's face, holding her finger beneath her nostrils to assure herself that the woman still breathed. "Mother, I'm going for help."

There was no reaction. No blinking of her eyes. No trembling of her lips.

"I'll be back," Perliett whispered, smoothing Maribeth's hair from her face. Scurrying to her feet, Perliett's hip bumped the table. She glimpsed the stationery.

Who'll make the shroud?
I, said the Beetle,
with my thread and needle,
I'll make the shroud.
Who'll dig his grave?
I, said the Owl,
with my pick and trowel,
I'll dig his grave.

The Cock Robin nursery rhyme.

Terror flooded Perliett. The sort of panic that sent reason warring with unadulterated fear. She spun and ran from the room.

The moon was full and thankfully shed its luminance across the road, dancing on the tops of the cornstalks in the fields that bordered it. Perliett ran, wishing she had at least put on her slippers. Stones cut into the bottoms of her feet. Her nightgown twisted around her legs, and she hiked it up with her hands.

Should-haves raced through her mind. She should have stopped long enough to hitch the horse to their buggy. Originally, it seemed it would take too long, but now the tradeoff of time to hitch up the horse showed her foolishness that she now ran on foot. Her father's choice to live outside of town was a curse tonight. That George Wasziak's home bordered the town was a blessing. He would know. He *had* to know how to revive her mother.

But the circumstances replayed in her mind, circling and taunting her. The candlelight going out. Her mother's shriek.

The feeling of being strangled. The nursery rhyme penned almost supernaturally across the page.

It was too eerie, too unexplainable. Too *paranormal.* George would not approve. She could see his glower now. His deep dislike for all things her mother did. But he wouldn't deny her care. Care that she—as Maribeth's daughter—*should* have been able to give. She stumbled and cried as she ran down the country road. Helpless. Alone. Thoroughly and completely broken of any vestige of pride.

This was not right. The summoning of Eunice. The murder of Millie. The messages of omen in the form of a child's nursery rhyme. Birds. Just creatures fictionally grieving over a dead robin. A dead robin that had showed up on her porch. Jasper Bridgers getting anonymous messages at his room. The newspaper receiving a taunt it was all but coerced into printing. Mrs. Withers convinced she was hearing from Eunice. Warning them. Trying to communicate—

Perliett cried out as her foot slammed onto a sharp stone. Her ankle twisted, and she skidded to the ground. Her knees scraped across the hard-packed dirt. Tears broke through her resolve, trailing down her face as Perliett pushed against the ground with her torn palms.

"Help. Please help." Her voice shook as she cried to no one. To nothing. To the abyss that was the sky, filled with only a moon that stared down at her as if intoxicated by what might happen next. At what might happen under the spell of its glow that should comfort but instead was shifting across the earth as though tempting evil to come out to play.

Perliett willed herself to her feet, reaching out with her left arm to find something sturdy to stabilize her. She wobbled, the bottom of her foot bruised. She couldn't run now, only limp. She needed to get help. George was too far. The Withers farm. It would be closer. Perhaps Mr. Withers could take a horse and go fetch George.

A whistle pierced the night air, colliding with the crickets' song and stilling their tune. Perliett froze, standing on her right foot as she tendered her left, touching only its toes to the ground.

She recognized the tune. Its haunting melody shifted through the cornfield.

"London Bridge."

A lonely, mournful song with an edge of trauma and an aura of mocking fun.

No. *No.* Awareness spread through Perliett. She had run straight to the cornfields. Straight into the blackness of the night. She had done precisely what they had warned her against. Only—her mother needed her.

Panic chilled the blood coursing through her veins. She needed to run. To sprint. Safety.

A chuckle followed her stumbling steps down the road.

Then the whistle filtered over the breeze.

A cloud drifted in front of the moon.

The light went out.

25

Molly

She wrestled from the sleep that made her thoughts foggy. Molly opened her eyes, rubbing them. The afternoon light splayed through the bedroom window, and it all came back like a brick being thrown through the glass.

Gemma's call.

The Wasziak family secrets.

Oh yes. A bit of internet searching and it wasn't hard to uncover the history of the Wasziak men. But none of it was as shocking as Gemma had made it out to be. Molly had known that Trent's dad and his brothers were trouble back in the day. Uncle Roger had a few misdemeanors on his record. Before that, Trent's grandfather had been arrested back in the sixties for assaulting a man outside a bar. But those were typical Midwestern Friday nights around here. Sure, the Wasziaks had a habit of rabble-rousing. Then Trent's dad had found God, so had his brother Roger, and while still somewhat estranged, their generation had seemed to reconcile with right-versus-wrong behavior. Regardless, the Wasziaks still had a good reputation in Kilbourn. Gemma's insinuation that they were hiding dirty secrets didn't match with the county records Molly had seen. Maybe Gemma's perception of *good* was clean slates without any sin.

Molly cringed. She'd done what her body craved. Sleep. It was all so exhausting. So overwhelming. January's murder made little sense, and Gemma's accusations toward her own family name and reputation felt exaggerated. Sid was right. So was Trent. The Cornfield Ripper of 1910 made even less sense than everything else.

It was more comforting to succumb to her dead emotions, the sensation that nothing was right, but she couldn't really feel the grief that was supposed to come with that. Sleep. Sleep would put it all into oblivion. It would knock the mysteries, the deaths, the depression into oblivion.

Molly rolled onto her side and sat up, swinging her legs over the edge of the bed. Her knit shorts pulled up high on her thighs. She stared at the cellulite on her hips. She wasn't obese, but she wasn't thin. She was a typical curvy Midwestern woman who ate too many carbs and cheese.

"Blech," she muttered. The awful pit was growing in her stomach again. The one that made her sick. She glanced at the prescription bottle on her nightstand. She'd taken her medicine that morning, right?

A thud downstairs made Molly still. The clock read one o'clock in the afternoon. Too early for Trent to be home. She stood and padded to the window and peeked out. Sid was probably here. She probably let herself in . . .

Molly frowned. Sid's truck wasn't in the driveway. The place was empty of any signs of life other than her chickens that scrounged in the gravel for bugs.

"Who killed Cock Robin?
I, said the Sparrow,
with my bow and arrow,
I killed Cock Robin."

The nursery rhyme that had haunted her in the basement coursed through her memory. Molly wrapped her arms around herself. Curse that poem. Where had it come from anyway? Molly questioned whether she'd really heard the whispered words. It had been subliminal, hadn't it? In her mind?

A shiver ran through her. Molly reached for one of Trent's sweatshirts hanging over the back of a chair. She shrugged it on.

She was alone.

Here in the Withers house.

Another thud jerked Molly's attention to her bedroom door. She squeezed her eyes shut.

God, please take them away.

The presence of the dead. The ones she wanted nothing to do with. She wasn't a medium. She didn't have some special talent that psychics would rejoice over if they knew. This was different. This was . . . a *needing*. Purpose. Connection. Her babies. The ones she'd lost. The little ones she was supposed to be holding, raising. They were ghosts. But just because they were ghosts didn't mean she could hear other ghosts. See other ghosts.

The curtain at the window lifted, its filmy lightness brushing her shoulder and cheek. Molly shrieked, jumping away from it.

The window was closed.

There was no breeze.

The curtain was like a manifestation of another presence.

Molly ran from the bedroom, grabbing at the doorframe to keep from falling as she turned into the hall. The staircase leading down to the main level loomed before her, carpeted in an old shag, its rail marked by chipped white paint.

Her bare feet pounded down the stairs.

She swore if she looked over her shoulder, she would see the curtain, having dislodged from the window, floating down behind her, the form of the dead beneath it, reaching toward her, its arms begging for the conclusion to their life.

Limbo.

Lingering.

"No, no, no," Molly whimpered. She reached the kitchen and backed against the sink, grasping the edge of the counter. Her eyes scanned the dining room through the doorway beyond. She glanced into the hallway that also opened into the living room.

No one was there.

She'd give anything to find an intruder. A masked man. Someone intending to steal or attack. A *human* entity was far preferable than an elusive spirit that dodged her and toyed with her.

"Go away!" Molly shouted. Her words echoed through the house.

She heard the floor creak.

"Go away!" Her voice was wobbly as she shrieked. "Oh, please—" sobs caught her breath—"please, just go away."

Nothing. Silence.

Then, "I saw her die."

It was audible. The voice. It shattered the silence with a violence that sent Molly scampering away from the sink, pressing her back against the refrigerator.

"I saw her die."

"Oh, God, help me." Molly bit her lip. Tears streamed down her cheeks. She held her hands out to ward off the voice. The sound of the gravelly tone that resonated in her ears. She needed to call someone. She needed help.

Molly shot a look at the table, but her phone wasn't there.

The floor creaked again. A door slammed, the air becoming stifling as the breeze from the open mudroom door was shut off as it closed against the screen door. Molly couldn't see it, but she could feel it.

Spinning, she raced from the kitchen away from the front door. She needed to get herself out of the house. It was haunted. The Withers sisters—the dead who owned the unfinished gravestones in the basement—God only knew who was dodging her, teasing her mercilessly.

Molly turned into the side room with the basement stairs to the left and the door to the outside straight ahead. She ran for it, grabbing at the doorknob. It twisted, but the door wouldn't open.

Molly darted a terrified look over her shoulder.

She heard another door slam. That would be the living room door. The only other main level exit to the outside. It was as if a poltergeist occupied the house with only her and was determined to shut her inside.

Molly tugged at the door. "Open up!" she screamed at it.

The door refused to give, and Molly looked wildly around for a tool or something to break the window beside it. She was desperate now. Desperate to get out of the house.

A crowbar! She remembered seeing one on a shelf in the basement.

Fear ironically gave Molly the courage to run down the stairs. The gravestones in the wall seemed to move. The unfinished names and dates swirled as if she were suffering from astigmatism and seeing double. Molly's foot caught the edge of a plastic bin. She sprawled onto the floor, her fingers jamming into the concrete edge of the covered pit in the basement floor.

Molly scurried away from it on her hands and knees. She caught sight of the crowbar and grabbed for it, pulling herself up by holding on to the plastic shelving Trent had installed.

Twisting around, Molly rushed back to the stairs. Her feet met the wooden step, and hope pushed her up the first few stairs. She lifted her face to look at the door she was about to bust open, but she was instead met with the back of the basement door. Closed? The poltergeist had shut the basement door!

Molly twisted the doorknob, shoving the door with her shoulder. It refused to open. It wouldn't budge. It was a heavy door, the old kind that wasn't hollow but solid. Something had either wedged it shut or held it shut from the other side. She couldn't recall a lock on the door. Molly banged on it with her palm.

"Let me out!" She banged again, then hefted the crowbar and tried to hook it between the door and the jamb. It didn't budge either. Of course, the basement door would be more solid than anything else in this place!

Molly bit her lip, tasting blood. She rammed the crowbar against the wood of the door, hoping to bust through. It bounced off as if she were hitting rock. What was this door made of? Molly lost her balance and grappled for the wall before she fell down the steps.

Her backside hit the top step. Molly lost her grip of the crowbar and it clattered down the stairs.

Tendrils of fog drifted through the crack between the floor and the bottom of the door. They were coming for her. A spirit seeping through the seam, and it would float upward, morphing into the form of, who? January Rabine? Was she the one haunting? Angry? The Withers sisters from 1910? Had they never left this place, or did they—?

Molly stiffened.

Her delusions cleared for a moment. The fog was no ghostly apparition. It was—smoke? It was coming in stronger now. Thicker. She heard footsteps pounding on the floor above her.

"I watched her die." The words replayed and cut through the terrorized and delusional haze of Molly's brain. "I watched her die," she repeated aloud, grounding herself in reality. It had been a human voice. An admission. A final confession. Not an otherworldly entity but someone all too real, all too dangerous.

And now they would watch her die.

Here in the gravestone basement.

26

Perliett

The sky was dark, and Perliett blinked groggily. Her head was pounding, the pain shooting from her neck through her scalp. Her back was sore, lying on uneven ground. Cornstalks rose on either side of her, blocking out the moonlight. Leaves, sticky with their sharp edges, scraped at her face.

Perliett groaned, flexing her left shoulder that felt as if a fist had bruised it. She couldn't remember what had happened, but her mother—she was at home, unconscious—that was it! She'd been trying to get help. The whistling. The chuckle . . .

Her eyes flew open. Tassels from the stalks hung over her. Perliett tried to sit, but everything in her ached. She moaned, wiping at her face with the back of her hand. When she pulled it away, she saw darkness smeared across it. Blood?

She'd been attacked. Perliett knew it now. She frantically ran her hands down her body. She was still clothed in her nightgown, but it was torn at the hemline and under her arms. She pulled her legs up, feeling them. They throbbed with the pain of being beaten by something hard.

A memory pulled at her.

Tough hands grabbing her from the road, dragging her into the corn as she screamed. A hand clubbing the side of her face to silence her.

Now Perliett screamed again, this time a shortened version of the long one she recalled ripping through her throat and leaving it sore. She batted the spider away that was crawling on her leg, its hairy legs tickling her skin. Perliett managed to get to her knees. Further inspection of her body brought her relief that she was only bruised, battered, but not violated and no broken bones.

She sucked in a shaky breath. The cornfield stretched like dark sentinels in rows. The road was nowhere in sight, yet Perliett sensed she was not alone.

"H-hello?" she whispered. Using a full voice felt too startling, too dangerous.

The wind blew across the cornstalks that rose over her head. The corn rustled. Something snapped.

"London Bridge is falling down . . ." A child's singsong voice filtered through the stalks.

Perliett whirled, trying to see through the shadows and rows of corn.

". . . falling down . . ."

She spun in the opposite direction. Darkness.

". . . falling down . . ."

Perliett's breath caught in a horrified sob. What sweet child would be out in the middle of the night, singing nursery rhymes in a cornfield?

"London Bridge is falling down . . ."

A cornstalk snapped just beyond Perliett's right shoulder. Jerking her head up, she froze, fear invading every part of her and pinning her to the ground.

The girl was scrawny. Her dress hung from her body like a flour sack. Her head tipped to the side, studying Perliett, the whites of her eyes making them piercing.

"Help me," Perliett whispered. She tried reaching toward the girl, but pain shot through her shoulder at the attempt.

The little girl smiled. It was not friendly. She tilted her head in the opposite direction.

"Please," Perliett tried again.

The child studied her, the night's breeze lifting tendrils of dark hair to brush across her face. She opened her mouth. "'Who'll dig his grave? I, said the Owl, with my pick and trowel, I'll dig his grave.'" The girl lifted her hand, and Perliett pushed herself backward with a whimper.

Fingers wrapped around a handle. The strange girl held up a small gardening shovel.

"I'll dig your grave," she whispered with a grin.

Stalks slapped her face as Perliett plowed through the corn. She fled, praying that the darkness would hide her, begging for God to keep the clouds in place, obscuring the full moon. What could a girl, no more than ten or eleven, do to her? But what *had* been done to her already?

Energy surged through her, masking the pain from her earlier assault. Perliett held her arms in front of her, pushing the corn away. The road had to be nearby. It *had* to be!

She looked wildly over her shoulder and saw no menace behind her, no child chasing her. Her feet were unsteady on the rutted, dry earth. The smell of mold and corn slammed into her senses with a persistence that made it impossible to forget where she was. Lost in a Michigan cornfield, in the middle of the night.

Perliett was certain she'd run for hours by the time her body broke free from the prison grid of stalks that surrounded her. It had probably been minutes, but regardless, Perliett burst into a shuddered sob as she spotted the road before her. In the distance, she saw the peak of a roof.

The Withers farm? It didn't appear to be. Where was she?

She didn't care. Perliett aimed for the house, barely noticing the congestion in her lungs that made breathing difficult, not paying attention to the bottoms of her feet that throbbed with pain.

The night was eerily still. The breeze had settled down as if finally retiring for the night. The crickets seemed to have hushed in reverence of Perliett's attempt to flee the frightening child with the shovel.

Dig her grave?

It was a garden spade, but how morbid! What terrible words to come from the mouth of a child! But whether in the form of a child or something far worse, death licked at her heels, and it was the thought of death that catapulted Perliett up the porch steps to the door of the house. She brought her fists down with urgency again and again, pounding against the wood until her hands ached.

She heard a man holler from inside, "I'm coming! I'm coming!"

A light flicked on. She heard the sound of the latch turning, and then the door opened.

An older man peered through the screen door at her, holding up an oil lantern to see her better.

"Please let me in! I beg of you!" Perliett clutched the front of her filthy, torn nightgown.

"Laura!" the man yelled as he pushed the screen door open. "Come in, come in, child!"

Perliett stumbled through the door, vaguely recognizing the man as Mr. Hannity. A local farmer. He had a small farm just up the road from George Wasziak's place.

Mr. Hannity grabbed on to Perliett as her legs gave way and she collapsed. He held her up, steering her past a parlor and into another sitting room, where he lowered her to an overstuffed chair.

"Laura!" he barked again.

An older woman's voice responded, "Coming!" Then she

appeared, tying the strings of her wrapper around herself, her gray hair hanging in a loose braid flung over her shoulder. Her eyes widened at the sight of Perliett. "Oh, good gracious!" Laura—Mrs. Hannity—rushed to Perliett's side. "Are you all right?"

Perliett was shaking uncontrollably and couldn't formulate an answer. She was more familiar with Mrs. Hannity, who was a friend of her mother's. *Mother!* Perliett grimaced in pain as she opened her mouth to speak.

"My mother. She's—home. Unconscious. Needs—a doctor." Perliett let her head fall back against the chair. She heard, rather than saw, Mrs. Hannity give directions to her husband.

"Go retrieve the doctor right away! Send Mikey to check on Mrs. Van Hilton and to fetch us if a doctor is also needed there."

"We've only got one doctor." Mr. Hannity seemed at a loss at how to divide George Wasziak into two in order to service both emergencies.

Mrs. Hannity must have urged him to go, because when Perliett opened her eyes, Mr. Hannity's form was retreating from the room.

"Not—me." Perliett reached for Mrs. Hannity's hand. "I'll be fine. My mother."

Mrs. Hannity leaned over her, clicking her tongue in astonishment. "You need a doctor, Perliett." Her voice was soothing, nurturing. She pulled a crocheted blanket off a nearby sofa and wrapped it around Perliett's shaking body. "Something awful has happened to you, dear. Who did this to you?"

Perliett shook her head. She had little to say to the woman. She had the memory of being attacked. The memory of being pushed to the ground. Hands on her body, and then . . . nothing. Absolutely nothing until the little girl singing a nursery rhyme in the corn had stepped forward and offered to dig her a grave.

27

Molly

Smoke was supposed to rise, not fall. Which could only mean that the house was already filled with the suffocating fumes as they squeezed through every crack in the floor and began to fill the basement. Molly waved her hand in front of her face to clear away the dusky haze. The electric light hanging overhead was flickering. She could hear crackling overhead, worse than a campfire, the heat infiltrating to the cave-like abyss she was holed up in.

Willing herself not to panic, Molly scanned the basement for something that could help bust open the door to the upstairs. The crowbar had been a dismal failure, but it was probably her best option. Snatching it off the floor, Molly crawled up the stairs, coughing against the smoke that filled her lungs the higher she climbed. Wedging the crowbar between the bottom of the door and floor, she pushed down on it, praying that it would cause the door to crack, split, or—anything that would release her from this prison.

The door stood solid.

With an angry wail of frustration, Molly flung the crowbar down the stairs and reached for the doorknob with the irrational instinct to rattle it and hope it would miraculously open. She tapped it with her fingers. It wasn't hot. Not yet anyway. A good sign the fire wasn't directly outside the door.

She needed to get out of here and call 911 to save their home—if it wasn't too late already—but that was nothing if she didn't make it out alive! Molly clambered back down the steps, the damp basement providing little reprieve from the fear that was consuming her. Like an idiot, she'd left her phone upstairs by the bed. She could see it in her mind's eye, possibly melting in the flames now.

With a whimper, Molly raced to the plastic shelving Trent had put up. She rifled through its contents. There wasn't much there of worth, let alone anything that would contribute to an escape. Paint cans, a milk crate filled with rags, various rolls of tape and other adhesives. Some unpacked moving boxes claimed her attention. Molly ripped them open, disappointed to find they were filled with trophies from Trent's high school football days, and a few souvenirs from some vacations he'd taken as a kid. No wonder he'd stuffed them downstairs. They were artifacts of a life that seemed eons ago. Carefree. Hopeful. Dream-filled.

Smoke rolled down the stairs, and Molly cast a look upward to see smoke squeezing through cracks in the joists and floorboards. She took another wild spin around the basement. She needed something stiff to jam against the door and bust it free.

Molly dragged her fingers over the gravestone walls. Half-completed names and dates boasted their demise to her in stone. Invitations that she would join them soon. Trent would return home to find the house charred in smoking ashes. The floors would probably collapse on her long before she died of smoke inhalation. Would they even find her body complete? She'd read once about a house that had gone up in flames in the early 1900s, and it had been so hot it consumed all the family's children, leaving only tiny, unidentifiable bone fragments behind.

She kicked at a five-gallon bucket that was empty and went catapulting across the floor. Dying was not a possibility Molly had entertained. For all her depression and darkness, the idea of going away from Trent was akin to the ultimate betrayal. A desertion of sorts. Now someone was attempting to make the decision for her.

There had to be a way out of here. Unwilling to be defeated, Molly attempted the door again. This time, smoke gagged her, slinking its way up her nose and down her throat. She was able to get some of the wood on the door chipped away, but even as she pushed on the door, Molly could sense there was an object behind it, holding it in place, as if the intruder had wedged something there to prevent escape.

Unable to catch a clean breath of air, Molly retraced her steps back into the tomblike basement. She was going to die here. Die against a foundation of grave markers.

"Please," Molly begged aloud. She knew God was listening. But listening and actually doing what she wanted God to do was another matter. She had prayed and begged before. Miscarriages still happened. Distance between her and Trent still happened. God was on His throne—but it felt like He wasn't.

Her gaze fell on the boarded-up concrete slab in the floor. She knew it wasn't a cellar door or they'd have seen the entrance on the outside of the farmhouse. But could it provide a way of escape? A source of oxygen or maybe even a strong enough support overhead if she could fit into a crawl space, so that when the house collapsed she would have a shot at survival?

Molly retrieved the crowbar. If she couldn't bust down a door, she'd be pathetic if she couldn't pry apart a boarded-up hole in the floor! She coughed as a cloud of smoke assaulted her, burning her nose with its acrid scent. The crowbar made quick work of the first board. Whoever had built the cover had merely placed it here for protection so no one would accidentally fall through and hurt themselves.

The smoke continued to grow in its insistence, so Molly peeled off her T-shirt, leaving her in her bra and shorts. She wrapped the shirt around her nose and mouth even as she cast a futile look around the basement for water to soak it in. Finding none, Molly returned to prying up the boards in the floor.

The last one gave way just as the light from the overhead bulb flickered and went out. Plunged into darkness, Molly refused to give in to the tears that wanted to rip at her throat and spiral her into helplessness at her fate. She dropped to her knees, feeling the edge of the cement border and sticking her hand into whatever lay beneath the now-open hole in the floor.

Molly stretched her arm downward until her armpit connected with the concrete. She still couldn't touch bottom. This was definitely a crawl space, which was what she'd hoped. Something crashed overhead, sending Molly to her backside as she swung her legs over the side of the hole. Pushing herself off, she braced for a fall. Instead, her bare feet landed on a hard-packed dirt floor.

Unable to see, Molly dropped to her hands and knees, feeling the ground in front of her, the walls, and the ceiling. Cool, damp air enveloped Molly as she crawled in. A thousand spiders probably scurried away from her, yet the infested crawl space was preferable to the smoke-filled, burning house above her.

Assuming the crawl space went only a few feet, Molly braced herself to run into earth. This must have been used as an in-ground cellar back in the day. There was no way she could stand. The dimensions of the space had to be less than four feet high and wide, giving her enough berth to go forward but not to turn around easily.

Five feet or so inside and realization dawned on Molly that the crawl space had to have already extended beyond the foundation of the farmhouse. She was legitimately underground. If the house were to collapse, it would trap her in this tight space, the basement filled in with debris, and odds were good there was no way out. The crawl space was a literal earthen grave. The idea sent claustrophobia coursing through her.

"Oh, God, oh, God." It was a prayer. Truly. Molly tilted her head back to look up but saw only blackness. It surrounded her, hemmed her in, and behind her the smell of fire choked the air. It was a physical depiction of how life had been the last three years. Closed in. Oppressive. Heavy. Suffocating. Dismal. Void of life and of hope.

Whispering clichéd prayers of "Save me" or "I promise I'll do this, if you'll do that" ran through Molly's mind, but they felt hypocritical now. All those stories of God rushing to the salvation of people in the Bible via fiery bushes, or mastering the fangs of lions, or tsunamis that swallowed Egyptians—she didn't challenge Scripture's authority, but she also didn't think He worked that miraculously anymore.

She'd take a tsunami now. She'd take an angel. She'd take anything. She'd even take a whisper if it meant she could live.

Someone was shouting. It echoed in her mind like a voice cutting across an English moor. In fact, wasn't that where she was? Molly could see the rolling landscape, the fog wisping along the earth. She could feel the damp spray of the air at that moment when the rain was a mist before it became a drop that turned into a torrent. She felt the boorish hands of Heathcliff as the literary male dragged her toward him, enveloping her in his cloak like a tarp that—

"Molly!" The voice cut through the dreamlike imagery

that made Molly drop her head back, letting it hang because she didn't have the energy to lift it.

"Get her out of there!" another voice commanded.

My, my, Heathcliff was bossy. Maybe it was Rochester. Wait. Were Heathcliff and Rochester heroes in the same Brontë sister novel, or separate? She hadn't read one in eons. No. Not read. She was there, wasn't she? But the English moors smelled like a firepit, with the soggy thick scent of wet ashes burning her nostrils.

"Get her over here." It was a woman. "What's her pulse?"

Someone answered.

Her body jostled like she was dead weight in someone's arms, and they were trying to hoist her out of a pit.

"Get the oxygen!"

Molly tried to open her eyes. They burned. Stung. Tears flooded them as she strained to see.

Her body settled onto a soft mattress. She was rolling. She could hear the creaking of metal springs, the crunch of wheels on gravel. Lights flickered behind Molly's closed eyelids. Red lights. Blue. Men were talking. She could hear water spraying.

"Molly!" This time the voice was familiar. It was close.

She realized she was gripping a hand so tightly that her own was feeling pricks of nerves beneath the skin.

"C'mon, Molls, wake up." He was urging her. A frantic undertone startled her.

Reality crept into the edges of her consciousness. No English moors. It was Michigan. Michigan farmland. This was the aftermath of—

Someone lowered a plastic cup over her nose and mouth. Air, purer than anything she'd breathed before, whooshed up her nostrils, filling her sinuses, her lungs, and startling her into awareness.

Molly's eyes flew open and instantly locked with Trent's. His face was sooty, his blue eyes hazed with emotion she couldn't interpret. He was holding her hand and stroking her hair away from her face.

A quick glance around and she realized she was on a stretcher in the back of an ambulance, Trent squatting beside her. "Trent," she said, trying to speak through the oxygen mask the EMT had placed on her. She struggled to push herself up on her elbows. "The house—"

"Molly, lie back, please." The EMT smiled at her. Molly recognized the woman's unmistakable air of calm authority. She was in charge.

Molly obeyed but reached for Trent's shirt. He leaned over her, and Molly noticed his eyebrows were scorched. His cheeks were tinged bright red, as if he'd been in the sun too long. Ashes flecked his hair. Soot dotted his nostrils and colored his face.

"Are you okay?" Worry for Trent flooded her senses.

He gave an exhausted chuckle and ducked his head for a second before lifting it. "Yeah. Yeah, Molls, I'm fine."

"The house?" This time, she didn't try to sit up to see whatever remained of their house. Of the historic Withers farmhouse. The murder house.

Trent grimaced. His brows drew inward, and the muscles in his jaw flexed. "We'll have some work to do."

"Did it burn to the ground?" Molly felt a band on her upper arm tighten. The EMT was taking her blood pressure.

"No." Trent shook his head. "But there's a lot of damage. I barely got you out before that side of the house—the living room wall gave in, and part of the second floor collapsed."

Not burned to the ground, but practically destroyed anyway.

Molly closed her eyes.

The EMT spoke over her to Trent. "Her blood pressure is high. That's expected. We're going to take her in. She'll need to have her lungs examined to see how much damage the smoke left behind. There're no burns, thank goodness." A pause. "Sir, I'd like to see to your arm."

"Just get my wife to the hospital." Trent was firm. Commanding.

Molly opened her eyes, unaccustomed to that tone in his voice. He rose and stared down at the EMT, who was looking out the back of the ambulance.

"Head out," she shouted.

The ambulance doors shut, and Molly felt the vehicle lurch forward.

"You might need oxygen too." The EMT was still addressing Trent.

"I'm fine." He waved off her concern.

"Why?" Molly asked, even though her voice sounded like a cross between Darth Vader and an oxygen machine. "What's wrong with Trent?"

"Nothing!" he barked.

"He pulled you out of the fire," the EMT replied at the same time.

Molly's gaze flew to Trent, and then she looked back at the EMT, who nodded.

"You're married to a hero," the EMT said. "The firefighters weren't particularly pleased he put himself in such danger and didn't wait for them to go in first." A laugh and then the EMT added, "But no one argues with a successful rescue. Still, he was pretty reckless. You're both lucky to be alive."

Trent remained silent.

Molly observed him for a long moment.

The EMT checked her vitals again. Fingers on Molly's pulse, her blue eyes sparkled, relief mixed with admiration. "That's quite a man you have there." She smiled. "How he knew about that crawl space? No one would've known to check it. And right before the floor collapsed? Yeah. Heroic."

28

The hospital was keeping her overnight for observation, even though her tests had come back clear. Minor smoke inhalation. No internal injuries. No broken bones. No burns. Nothing. She wasn't averse to admitting God had maybe pulled through as per her prayers begging Him. She just wasn't sure yet how to process it, considering the times He'd remained so dreadfully quiet.

"You knew I was in the basement?"

"I figured it out." Trent gave her a weak smile.

"How?"

"I hoped? Prayed?" Trent settled on the edge of the bed, the mattress sinking beneath his weight.

"How did you know to come?" Her throat was sore. Probably from the smoke she had inhaled. But she needed to know. To understand. Someone had tried to kill her. Did Trent and the authorities even know this yet? Had they realized it? Molly had been so preoccupied with the ambulance ride, the tests, that even now the truth of what had happened was still seeping in.

Trent made a tent with his fingertips and stared at his callused hands. "One of the guys at the farm saw smoke coming from the direction of our place. I tried calling you, and you didn't answer, so I left the farm to come check. I called 911 on my way, and when I got there, flames were shooting out the living room window. It looks like the fire started in there somehow."

"And then the fire department came?" she prompted.

Trent gave her a sideways look. "Yeah, but not before I went in. I tried to find you. I could get through the kitchen to the stairs. I made it up about halfway up and was shouting for you." He stopped. Molly noticed his Adam's apple bob as he swallowed hard. "When I came back down, I saw the washing machine was tilted out, like someone had tried to move it. The dryer was pushed just far enough that it lodged in front of the basement door."

The dryer! The heavy object that had kept the door from opening.

Trent shook his head. "I don't know what happened, Molls." His eyes drilled into hers, questioning her. His doubts were reflected in them. Concern too. He was as confused and in shock as she was. Molly could see it written in his expression.

"Someone locked me down there."

Trent worked his jaw back and forth, and his body stiffened. "Do you know *who*?"

"No." Molly wasn't ready to admit that it had taken her getting locked in the basement before she believed the person to blame was actually human and not a paranormal entity.

Trent finished his recounting of what had happened. "The fire department arrived by the time I got the dryer pushed back so I could unlock and open the door. They tried to keep me back, but I went down and saw the pallet boards you'd pried up. Then I found you, and . . . well, we got the heck out of there as soon as I pulled you out."

"I don't remember . . ."

"You wouldn't." His expression darkened. "You were passed out. I thought maybe from oxygen loss, but they think it was probably a mixture of that and panic."

"I was stuck in a crawl space," Molly said, defending herself weakly.

"No one blames you," Trent reassured her.

"We've lost everything, haven't we?" The enormity of what had happened hadn't fully sunk in yet.

Trent shifted on the bed so he could look directly at her. "Listen, Molls. I don't care about that. It's all just stuff." He took her hands. "You're alive. That's what matters. Nothing else."

Molly felt the warmth from his fingers saturate her hands. She noticed his forearm was bandaged. She reached out and touched it. "You burned yourself?"

"I'm fine." Trent ignored it and gave her hands a little shake. "Who did this to you?"

Molly met his eyes, which were laden with controlled fury and worry that created lines in the corners of his eyes. "I don't know." And she didn't.

I watched her die.

The memory of the words that had been hissed behind the door stung her, and Molly's eyes widened. She'd thought it was a ghost at first. A ghost admitting to watching decades' worth of death. Maybe even the Withers sisters' murders in 1910. That whole historical serial-killer thing seemed eons away now and so unimportant.

"As soon as the doctor releases you, the police are going to question you to get your account of things." Trent hadn't let go of her hands. "If you know anything—anyone—or why—" Trent squeezed his eyes shut and took a deep breath, apparently willing away his anger. When he opened his eyes, Molly could see a war being waged inside him. He stroked her hand. "First January—now you. Something's going on, Molls, with *my* family."

"I know," she nodded. She could agree with Trent on that. It was why she'd been looking at old newspapers per Gemma's account of January's ancestral research into the serial killer of 1910. It was why she'd been scrounging through Sid's so-called killer kit they'd found in the chicken coop. And it was why she'd questioned the contents of the journal she'd found this morning behind the nesting box . . .

Molly bolted upright, startling Trent, who reared back at her sudden movement.

"The journal!" Molly fixed her eyes on Trent. "I found a journal in the chicken coop!" Why it still felt so important made no sense to her. Moon phases, grain prices, and weather reports had nothing to do with her house being set ablaze and someone trying to kill her.

"What are you talking about?" Trent pressed.

Molly allowed him to push her back onto the pillows, but her body was tense. She could feel the tension in every muscle. "This morning I found a journal. From 1910. Some farmer's notes about his crops and stuff."

"And that's important because?" Trent urged, obviously wondering where Molly was going with this.

She drew in a steadying breath. "I don't know if it's important, but January was researching the Cornfield Ripper of 1910."

"Yeah. January had asked me some stuff about our mutual great-grandfather—well, for her it was great-great, but anyway—George Wasziak."

"And?"

"And nothing, Molls," Trent said with a shrug of his shoulders. "January seemed to think he was somehow involved. But no one ever talked much about him. He was just a name on a family tree. I don't know why she was so fixated on him. And then she mentioned your great-grandfather, Jasper Bridgers, but she made him sound like a nice guy. But then why he was even part of it, I don't know . . . but everyone in Kilbourn is connected somehow, you know?" Trent shook his head. "It was like January was looking for a juicy story that wasn't there."

"And yet someone killed her," Molly finished.

Trent met her eyes. His were troubled. "Yeah." He fidgeted with the edge of the blanket that covered Molly. She watched his callused fingertips play with the seam. He appeared to argue with himself, then opt for complete transparency. "She called me the afternoon before she was killed. She was going on about the Wasziaks being secretive. About a history of family violence—I couldn't make sense of it. And then she brought up something about a missing woman from 1982. I just let it go. Stories. That's all they were."

The year 1982 echoed in Molly's head as Trent spoke. She'd just seen that year. She'd seen it somewhere . . .

"The paper," Molly whispered.

"What?" Trent tipped his head in confusion.

"The paper in the kit was from 1982," she said. Her breaths came quicker now. "Who was the missing woman from 1982?"

"I don't know," Trent answered. "January didn't say."

"We need to find out." Molly stared her husband in the eyes so she could gauge his response. "Trent . . . your dad, was he ever violent toward you?"

Trent pressed his lips together. His eyes darkened. "Why on earth would you ask that?"

"Is it true?" Molly ventured gently. "Are the Wasziak men . . . is there a history of violence?"

Trent shook his head vehemently. "No."

"I know *you're* not," Molly quickly inserted.

Trent didn't smile at her letting him off the hook. He stared past her at her pillow for a moment before finally meeting her eyes. There was a bit of apology in his. What for, Molly didn't know, so she waited and listened.

"My grandpa wasn't exactly a warm guy. My dad tried not to be that way, but none of us are good with emotion. Grandpa was all about rules, truth, and God. You didn't cross him. He was a tough man, but he was devoted to his faith too. I'm guessing Grandpa's father—George Wasziak—probably wasn't that much different. Heck, it takes a strong woman to love a Wasziak man." Trent's eyes softened for a moment when he looked at her. "But January was trying to turn family problems into some sort of murder history book." This time, there was a firmness in Trent's voice she had no intention of arguing with. "The men in my family may not be great with feelings—we're factual, sometimes even a bit harsh—but Wasziak men aren't violent, Molly. January was twisting history to fit her narrative, and—" Trent paused to suck in a deep breath—"I'm afraid she royally ticked someone off."

"But not a Wasziak?" Molly led with caution.

Trent didn't answer for a moment. He worked his jaw back and forth, winced, then set his mouth in a grim line. "No. Not a Wasziak. I can't believe—no. I don't know who, but it wasn't one of us."

29

Perliett

"You've all lost your minds!"

Perliett awoke to the stern baritone of George Wasziak. His words pierced through the pounding in her head as she lay on the guest bed in the Hannitys' farmhouse.

"Now, George, all I'm saying is, you were seen . . ." It was Detective Poll's voice.

"Are you arresting me? Is that it, Detective?"

Perliett tried to reason through the conversation she was overhearing. They were just outside her room. She was alone for the time being and did not know where Mrs. Hannity had gone and whether anyone had checked on her mother, who, for all Perliett knew, was still in the throes of a hypnotic unconsciousness.

"No. I'm not." Detective Poll's response was grave.

"Then leave me to see to my patient."

"Not alone."

"Fine!" The bedroom door opened with an unintentional slam against the wall. George barreled in, the dark hair hanging over his forehead unkempt and wild, his black eyes that intense darkness as a storm hit.

Perliett shrank back into the pillows, but George froze as he neared her, Detective Poll stationing himself in the doorway like a guard on watch.

George's jaw flexed as he stared down at her, and Perliett couldn't tell if he was incredulous, horrified, furious, or bewildered. Perhaps all four. He swallowed hard, sniffed, and seemed to be attempting to gather his wits.

If she had created this effect on Dr. Wasziak, what must she look like? Still, the very reason she was here in this bed was a consequence of the necessity to get help for her mother.

"My mother—"

"Is being tended to," George interrupted.

"Miss Petra has gone to tend to her," Detective Poll added from the doorway.

George cast him an irritated glance.

"Is she all right?" Perliett tried to rise on her elbows.

"She's fine," Detective Poll answered, either ignorant of or choosing to completely ignore George's continued ire. He continued, "Mikey, Hannity's son, helped fetch Miss Petra and returned here a bit ago. He said it appears your mother fainted."

Fainted?

Perliett lowered herself gently back onto the pillows. She'd risked arm and limb and everything else for something smelling salts could have resolved? But she'd tried those! She'd tried brandy! Her mother hadn't responded to any of them. Not even a flicker of an eyelid.

"It's impossible. She was unconscious when I left." Perliett's argument hurt her lips. They felt swollen and bruised. So did her face. She reached up to touch her cheek.

"You're a sight." George regained command of the conversation from Detective Poll.

"I need a mirror." Perliett tried to look around for a hand mirror in the Hannitys' guest room.

George stepped in front of her view of the dresser and

blocked it. "You don't want a mirror. Now hold still and let me tend to you."

Perliett wanted to resist, but truthfully the knowledge that her mother wasn't in some critical state had relieved her. With that relief came a flood of awareness of her own throbbing pain from the attack in the cornfield.

George leaned over her, his fingers finding her pulse at her wrist.

"I'll be all—"

"Shh," he demanded.

"George, I—"

"Silence."

Silence. Overbearing, heavy-handed oaf.

He examined her, and she felt her skin warm beneath his fingers. They brushed along her neck, feeling both sides. Pushed hair from her hairline. Trailed down her bruised arm, turning it ever so gently—which seemed so out of character for the annoying man—and noting the marks.

"What happened?" Detective Poll asked the inevitable question.

George ignored him as he continued to examine her. He lowered the blankets so he could access her bare legs and feet. They were coated in blood and dirt. Her nightgown was still ripped and soiled. Perliett turned her face toward the wall, away from George—away from the humiliation of having him see her bare skin.

"Miss Van Hilton?" the detective pressed.

Perliett drew in a shuddering breath, hoping that George didn't notice. He must have. His hands stilled for a moment before continuing to examine the bottom of her feet, which were cut and scratched.

"Talk to him." The direction from George spurred Perliett to raise her eyes and meet his.

Terror was seeping into her as what had occurred became real all over again. The road, the cornfield, the . . .

"London Bridge," she whispered.

"What's that?" Detective Poll stepped into the room.

Perliett locked eyes with George. His eyes narrowed, listening, contemplating her next words as he weighed them against her injuries.

"There was a little girl . . ." Perliett tore her gaze away from George to look at Detective Poll, who had arrived at the end of her bed.

He frowned. "A little girl did this to you?"

"I-I don't know," Perliett half sobbed. "I was fetching help. I couldn't rouse my mother. I heard 'London Bridge,' only . . ." She paused, recalling while simultaneously wishing she could block the memory of it. "It sounded like a man, humming it, and then someone grabbed me." She bit her lip, squeezing her eyes closed against the memory. Against the humiliation of George taking a wet cloth from the nearby washbasin and wiping it down her legs to better assess the wounds. Where *was* Mrs. Hannity? It was indecent to be in the room alone with the doctor, let alone with the detective as well. Two men? Two men and only her?

Fear rose in Perliett's throat, choking her. "Get Mrs. Hannity," she croaked, followed by a frightened whimper.

"Go," George directed Detective Poll.

"You know I can't leave you here—"

"Can't you see she is about to be overcome with panic? Go, man, and fetch the old woman before God himself comes down and claps you on the side of the head for being an absolute nincompoop!" George and Detective Poll stared at each other.

Perliett waited for the detective, who finally spun on his heel and marched from the room, obviously vexed by George's high-handedness and, it seemed, something else. Yet being alone with George didn't lessen her anxiety. She knew—she *knew*—it had been a man who had attacked her in the field. She didn't feel safe. Not with George. Not with Detective Poll. Not with . . .

"Jasper!" Her eyes locked onto the form that barged into the room just ahead of a flustered Mrs. Hannity and an even more perturbed Detective Poll. A sense of relief washed over her, though it made little sense considering Jasper was as male as the two other men in the room. Something about his self-confident demeanor calmed her. He pushed past George and grabbed for her hand.

"Perliett, I—"

George stiff-armed Jasper so the man was forced to drop his hand from Perliett's.

"Excuse me!" Jasper leveled an affronted glare at George. "You can see she needs comforting."

"I am her physician and I will say what she needs," George retorted.

"Posh, both of you!" Mrs. Hannity pushed her own way in. She settled her plump form firmly between them, crossing her arms over her ample bosom. "Mr. Bridgers, I must insist that you leave. You too, Detective."

"How about you question *him*?" George interrupted, jabbing his thumb in Jasper's direction. "He always seems to pop up at the most convenient moments. Does no one else find it suspicious that women started *dying* when Mr. Bridgers came to town?"

"I'm offended!" Jasper roared.

"Now wait one moment!" Detective Poll's expression turned beyond irritated.

"A moment ago, you all but accused me of being suspect in the brutalization of Miss Van Hilton." George was incensed, and even through the fog in her mind, Perliett found some reason in his words, loath as she was to admit it.

"Because you were seen on the road—" Detective Poll was cut short by Mrs. Hannity's loud and exaggerated clearing of her throat.

"I realize you need all sorts of information from this young woman and perhaps both of these men." Mrs. Hannity rested her cool hand on Perliett's arm. "But she is not well. She has been mistreated in some of the vilest ways, and until she is tended to, your questions will need to wait."

Detective Poll opened his mouth to speak, but Mrs. Hannity held up her hand.

"Ah, ah, ah!" she interrupted. "Go now. Take Mr. Bridgers with you. Why he was summoned I have no idea."

Jasper dipped his head in response, offering a brief explanation. "Miss Van Hilton's mother sent for me to be by Miss Van Hilton's side in her mother's stead."

"Pishposh." Mrs. Hannity waved the man off. "The woman doesn't have her full senses—my apologies for being rude, Miss Van Hilton—and sending for you in the middle of the night is complete and utter poppycock. What relation are you? Have you taken oversight of the Van Hilton women? I think not. And I, for one, *would* know because I make it my business to know these things. Now, Miss Van Hilton needs a good *Christian* woman to care for her, along with Dr. Wasziak—"

"Who is under suspicion for—" Detective Poll interrupted, to which Mrs. Hannity skewered him with an elder's glare.

"Under suspicion for assaulting Miss Van Hilton?" she countered.

Perliett widened her eyes.

"Yes!" Detective Poll affirmed sternly.

Mr. Bridgers whirled on George with a look that communicated he might engage in war if not stopped.

"Poppycock!" Mrs. Hannity laughed. "Have you looked at him? His shirt is crisp and white, his trousers pressed, why—he even has clean hands!"

Detective Poll heaved a frustrated breath, his chest rising and falling with annoyance. "A man can clean himself up."

"I was merely out for a walk," George protested, entering the fray. "Have you never walked a country road at night for leisure?"

"No. I have not." Detective Poll raised an accusatory eyebrow. "And you were spotted—"

"The cows spotted me and, who else, a handyman hired by the Withers family?"

"Mikey too," Detective Poll reminded George. "He ran into you when he was on his way to retrieve you."

"Mikey and the handyman. Reliable sources. And the handyman is half blind—I've treated him myself."

"So have I," Perliett inserted weakly.

George glowered at her.

Detective Poll pursed his lips. "You're trying to convince me you *happened* to be on a midnight countryside stroll at approximately the same time Miss Van Hilton was being attacked by the Cornfield Ripper?"

"*Was* it the Cornfield Ripper? Oh, I read his letter in the paper!" Mrs. Hannity gasped, clutching at her throat.

"We don't know yet," Mr. Bridgers added, almost seeming irked that he wasn't being paid attention to.

"By tomorrow morning, I will be the talk of the town if you continue to accuse me of doing this to Perliett." George gritted his teeth. "My reputation as a physician is at stake here."

"Was it Dr. Wasziak who did this to you, Miss Van Hilton?" Detective Poll asked the question that would have solved the entire mystery.

Perliett winced. She couldn't remember what had happened between the time she was on the road and when she awakened in the cornfield to the leering face of the little girl. "I don't know," she whispered, which did nothing to exonerate George, who shot her a desperate look.

"Perliett—"

She looked beyond him to the detective. "But I don't believe it was Dr. Wasziak." Did she? Was she certain her word bore truth? Could it be that George Wasziak in his blustering, aggravating person was responsible not just for her assault but for the murders of the Withers sisters? It seemed ludicrous. "It couldn't have been. There was a little girl."

"You said this before." Detective Poll took the opportunity to press for more information before Mrs. Hannity interrupted again. "A little girl? Who was she? Did you recognize her?"

"No." Perliett needed brandy. She could sense it. A swig from her brandy bottle in her apothecary chest would do wonders to calm her nerves.

"How old was she?" the detective asked.

"I don't know." Perliett closed her eyes against a wave of throbbing pain that streaked across the top of her head. "Ten, eleven years old maybe? At most."

"There's no one in the neighborhood with a child that young," Mrs. Hannity provided.

Perliett wanted them all to leave. To go. To allow her to bathe herself, cleanse her wounds, take medicine powders for her horrific headache, and to wallow in the nagging premonition that all of this was far from over. That chaos was just beginning. That Eunice Withers, in her dead spirit state, truly *had* tried to warn them.

He was not finished yet.

Because Perliett was still alive.

30

Molly

Gladys poured Molly a cup of coffee and set a plate of cookies on the table.

"There," she said. "Drink up. It'll warm your insides."

That it was already ninety degrees at ten o'clock in the morning on this late August morning apparently didn't affect the old woman.

Molly reached for a cookie and eyed it. It looked like a sugar cookie with a date or prune smashed in the middle. She took a tentative nibble of it, even as her eyes strayed toward the south. She could see, just beyond the hayfield, over the tops of a line of maple trees, the peak of her and Trent's barn.

Gladys had seen the smoke from the fire a few days ago, and she'd checked in on them the following day, when Molly and Trent stood side by side in the yard, staring at the remaining half of their farmhouse. They were planning on staying with Sid—until Sid had called in a panic, saying the stomach flu was running rampant through her children. Stomach flu in August? Leave it to Sid's kids to catch it. The call came through when Gladys was chatting with them. Nosing her way into their business, Molly felt, but Trent found her, what was the word he'd used, *sugar-sweet*? In the space of a few minutes, Trent had accepted Gladys's invitation to stay in her farmhouse. She had four guest rooms, she'd said, and she was old, living alone on her family's farm when she should be either in assisted living—or dead. She'd added that last part with a chuckle.

Molly felt bad she didn't share the sense of humor. Trent needed humor to snap out of the fog of trauma that came with a house fire and the beyond-blaring reality that someone had tried to kill Molly. Molly, on the other hand, was pretty convinced she'd never—*never*—sleep again. It was bad enough to be haunted by the dead and never know when you'd hear them singing nursery rhymes in your head. But to know some flesh-and-blood person was vicious enough to lock her in a basement and set it ablaze?

"You don't like dates?" Gladys was staring at her from across the table.

Molly snapped out of her thoughts. "Oh!" She looked at the cookie. She'd been nibbling the edges, leaving the date in the middle. "I-I do." She didn't.

"You're lying." Gladys tapped the table with her index finger and offered an understanding smile. "And you don't need to eat the date. My mother used to make date cookies, so I've always had a partiality for them."

Grateful, Molly set the cookie on a napkin in front of her. She was fine. Really. She had to convince herself of that after spending hours with the police recalling the events of the fire, having fire investigators confirm evidence of accelerant in the living room area, and being told that if Trent had arrived much later, she would have been trapped in the crawl space and probably died of smoke inhalation.

Trent hadn't wanted to leave Molly with Gladys and return to work, fearing for their safety. Gladys insisted they would be fine. Trent's expression this morning when he left the house to resume his duties at Clapton Bros. Farms, a thermos of coffee made by Gladys in hand, told Molly he was anything but convinced. The police assured them they would do frequent drive-bys. It'd been four days since the fire and Molly was as edgy as in the moments following in the hospital.

What was worse, Gemma had been calling. Leaving messages. Texting. Molly ignored them. She shouldn't, but she had to. Her mind was still reeling from the trauma. She could barely close the bathroom door to do her business without panicking because she was closed in. The thought of Gemma's persistence, partnered with her sense of justice, made Molly cringe.

"My mother"—Gladys was still chattering—"and my father inherited this farmhouse from her parents. My grandparents were farmers and friends with the Withers family. You know, they used to tell stories about the Withers sisters, poor girls. And their mother? She lost her mind after her daughters were killed."

Molly tried to calm her frayed nerves. Gladys was a dear. She truly was. And a kinder, more generous soul, Molly was sure she would never meet, but she really didn't want to discuss the Withers murders of 1910 any more than she wanted to recount the events of the last few days.

But Gladys seemed to be tripping down memory lane with the carefree nature of a little girl. She chewed on a date, swallowed, and continued, her lips wrinkled and thin and almost as pale as her skin. "I find it interesting that your cousin, Gemma, was so adamant that you all look into the Withers murders, seeing as they were over a century ago. But then you're all so connected to the family line, I suppose it makes sense. Trent being a Wasziak and all. I vaguely remember Dr. Wasziak. George, they called him."

Molly perked up. "You knew Trent's great-grandfather?"

"Mm-hmm." Gladys smiled. "He passed during the war. I was, oh, probably nine when he died? So I recall a little.

Occasionally, Dr. Wasziak would stop by our farm here and shoot the breeze with my grandfather. I remember he was intimidating." Gladys's smile didn't seem to coincide with the memory of an intimidating man. She seemed fond of the memory. "He was tall and glowered like a grumpy old man. But I could see right through him. He had a good heart—it was just buried under his crankiness."

"Do you think Gemma could be right?" Molly ventured.

Gladys's eyes sparked. "About Dr. Wasziak being a killer? Oh, heavens no. If he was, then he lived with it his entire life, and it wasn't as if he could get away from it." Gladys set her cookie down and adjusted her pink cardigan. "My dear, think about the community here, all these neighboring farms. They've been around for decades, passed down from family to family. My family farm—we're the Hannitys. Then there is the Withers farm. Then the Wasziak house beyond on the outskirts of town—that's where George lived as a boy, and later when he was an adult bachelor. The Withers family sold their farm because they had only one more daughter, and she was already married and moved away by the time they were ready to scale back. There was no one to hand the farm down to. So they sold the farm to the Clapton brothers, whose family business owned it until you bought it."

Molly tipped her head in bewilderment. "We bought it from a real-estate agent. Maynard."

"Yes." Gladys nodded as if Molly would understand. "And Maynard is a Clapton, and his cousins, the Clapton brothers, were the owners."

Nonplussed, Molly sagged back in her chair. "So, the Withers family sold their farm to the Claptons. Why would the biggest farming business in the county want to sell it off? Wouldn't they want the land?" Molly was trying to piece together the different connections.

Gladys gave a thin-shouldered shrug. "It's only a few acres.

I mean, they kept most of the land and just sold off the house and the barn and enough acres to make it salable."

Molly reached for her coffee cup. "But back to George Wasziak. He was accused of attacking another woman?" She gave a little laugh.

"Mm-hmm. Perliett Van Hilton."

"Yet he wasn't convicted of it? Did they think he was the Cornfield Ripper or that it was unrelated?"

"No conviction, God bless the man. Like I said, I was a little girl when he passed. I just remember a few things my daddy told me about the doctor and the murders." Gladys took another nibble of her cookie.

Molly felt lost.

Gladys smiled. "Remember, my dear, this is a small town. You can probably find out more by asking a bunch of old folks like me."

"Anyone who tries to find out winds up dead." Molly shuddered. She didn't have the fortitude to stand in the face of another fire. There was no resolution to whoever had attempted to take her life. The idea that murders from 1910 had anything to do with today was too coincidentally intertwined to be ignored anymore.

"So, we let it rest then." Gladys nodded.

"No!" Molly stated emphatically.

"I suppose." Gladys shook her head as if clearing her thoughts. Her eyes clouded a bit, and then she frowned. "We just need to keep you safe." She reached across the table and patted Molly's hand, her gaze sincere and encompassing. "And you need to heal."

Molly lifted her eyes.

Gladys nodded, knowing. "If there is one thing I *know* Kilbourn is good at, it's hometown loving and coming together. Sure, there are the bad apples—rotten ones obviously—but there are good ones too. Masquerading in costumes we don't expect them to wear."

"What do you mean?" Gladys was touching places in Molly's soul that were raw and sore.

Gladys took a sip of her coffee and tilted her curl-coiffed graying head. "Oh, my dear. There will *always* be agony in the living. But it is in the agony that we discover our roots, and so often what we thought we needed wasn't really what we need at all. It's *who* we needed."

For now, they were unsolved riddles, and yet they fanned the small flame of hope again in Molly's heart.

"I'm confused." Sid plopped down on a tree stump in the front yard, staring ahead at the remains of the Withers farmhouse—Molly's burned-out shell of a home.

Molly glanced at her friend. "Gladys doesn't always make sense, but I think what she remembers is pretty clear. She's been gracious to Trent and me the last few days."

"Still . . ." Sid made a face. "The Withers farm. The Clapton brothers owning it before you?"

Molly nodded. "Well, as Gladys says, 'Welcome to small-town life.' It shouldn't be a surprise that the Clapton brothers owned this place. I guess I just wasn't paying attention. Trent said he didn't think it was important enough to mention. How else would Trent have found out they'd put it up for sale? They're his employers, so it makes sense."

Sid slapped her knees and stood, leaving the tree stump deserted. "Well, you and Trent can come and stay with us now. The kids are better, and you've been with Gladys long enough. Besides," Sid added, "Trent will relax more if you're with us and not relying on a little old lady to protect you."

Molly was well in agreement with moving in with Sid and her family. Her husband, Dan, working from home added an extra layer of security. Maybe then she could sleep at night. At least at Gladys's place she hadn't been hearing voices or seeing things, not since they'd left this burnt shell of a haunted farmhouse.

"So, what's next? Are you bulldozing this or what?" Sid didn't beat around the bush.

Molly reached down to fluff Sue's feathers as the Ameraucana Gold pecked at the earth by Molly's feet. "We have to see what the insurance people say. Trent wants to rebuild. He thinks the other half is salvageable."

Sid grew serious. "Are you all right with that? I mean, staying here after—"

"After someone tried to kill me?" Molly offered a lopsided smile. "No. And yes. I don't know. Sid . . ." She looked to the sky and folded her arms across her chest. Tears burned her eyes. She wanted to just spit it out—all of it. The voices, the depression, the grief of the miscarriages, the distance between her and Trent, and now all the added drama with January Rabine's death and the fire.

"Molly?" Sid came to stand next to her and rested her hand on Molly's arm. When Molly met her friend's hazel eyes, she wasn't able to hold back the tear that rolled down her cheek.

"I'm just . . ." Molly gave a watery laugh and rolled her eyes. "You all will think I've lost my mind." She shook her head. Nope. Not saying another word. But the weight of it—all of it—was breaking her.

Sid patted Molly's arm. "Honey, we thought you lost your mind a long time ago."

They shared a laugh at Sid's good-natured teasing.

Molly nodded. "Yes, well, it's worse than you think."

"Is this finally confession time?" Sid winked. But there was a seriousness and an anticipation behind her eyes that told Molly her friend hoped for—probably prayed for—her to open up about what was troubling her.

Molly walked away a few steps, fixating on a blackened stud that rose from the ashes of the house. "You know there were the miscarriages."

"Yes," Sid said quietly behind her.

Molly hugged herself, grasping her shirtsleeves. "Trent has never . . . he acts like they're just something that happened. Not that we lost *children*." Tears. Yep. They were coming. She was a wreck. The fire. The fear? They had ended her resolve to hold it all inside. "And then he buys this . . . this *farm*. I mean, we had dreams—you know we did—to have a hobby farm. Chickens. A dog. Cats. Maybe even a goat." Molly half laughed and half sobbed. "But I just—it feels like the last four years I've been living in a funeral." Her chin quivered. "You know?" Molly spun. Sid was just standing there, compassion in her eyes. No pity. Just compassion.

"I know." Sid nodded.

Molly smiled weakly. "How do you live with such grief? The loss, the feeling every morning when you wake up that someone else may die, or worse—you don't *care*! You don't *feel*. You're a combination of anxiousness and purposelessness. It's so hard even to get up in the morning, let alone go to bed and let your thoughts just take over."

Sid licked her lips and rolled them together as if fighting off emotion on Molly's behalf.

"And when you're married to someone who just *gets over things*? I don't know. Maybe Trent's faith is stronger than mine? Maybe I don't *have* faith. God doesn't explain himself. He doesn't explain away bad things happening, and He doesn't stop them either. And when good things happen, I'm convinced He cares again, but then something else happens and it's this spiral downward. I hate myself for doubting and for being weak, and then I hate myself for questioning God." Molly's torrent of words couldn't be stopped. "I think I *am* losing my mind, Sid. I *hear* things. I *see* people. Who aren't alive!"

There. She'd said it out loud.

Blatant and bold.

Or maybe so over the top, Sid would take it as an exaggerated description of Molly's depression.

She was thankful Sid didn't twitch, or blink, or even move. Only the breeze lifted her burgundy curls and brushed them across her T-shirt-clad shoulder. Sid waited. Silent. Compassion still in place.

Molly squeezed her eyes shut and tears dripped out. When she opened them, Sid was still there. Waiting.

"What's wrong with me?" she whispered through tears. "What's wrong with me, Sid?"

In an instant, Sid had covered the ground between them and pulled Molly into her arms. "Molly Wasziak, there is *nothing* wrong with you. You've gone through grief, you've bottled it up, and we've been waiting to help."

Molly sucked in a gulping breath and pulled away to look at Sid. "But I do *see* things, Sid." Oh gosh, it sounded so melodramatic. "I hear things too."

Sid's eyes shadowed. "Okay." There was no judgment in her voice. She rubbed Molly's upper arms. "Okay, so we need to figure that out. We need to get you someone to talk to, to help you work through this. To make sure the medications you're on are effective. And someone to help you with your questions. This isn't a lack of faith, Molly. This is *life*. And we don't always understand why things happen the way they do. And you're right. God doesn't explain everything. But the fact that you're asking and seeking *is* faith. Because you're choosing to believe there *is* a purpose even when you don't feel like there's one."

"But the voices? The sightings?" Molly challenged. She wouldn't accept a dismissal now that she'd confessed it aloud. Sid wouldn't dismiss it unless she thought it all figurative. Well, it wasn't, and Molly needed her friend to realize that.

Sid took a deep breath and then went for it, her eyes sincere and full of concern. "We know you've suffered postpartum depression after having a miscarriage, and what you're explaining to me fits."

"Seeing ghosts fits with postpartum depression?" Molly gave a crooked grin.

Sid laughed weakly. "Well, I'll be honest—I'm not a doctor, but after I had my last kid, you know I had a hard time."

Molly nodded. "For a month."

Sid offered a wobbly smile. "A month, yes. I couldn't sleep. And when you don't sleep, you hear things and see things and—"

"You saw ghosts?" Molly didn't mean to sound challenging, but she couldn't help herself.

Sid shook her head. "No. But I kept hearing the baby cry, and when I'd check on him, he was sound asleep. A few times I thought I heard Dan outside in the yard, but he wasn't there. Physical and emotional exhaustion—honey, they wreak havoc on your ability to process things. You're already on medication for your mental health and to help you sleep. Who knows what else is going on in your mind."

Molly tried to take an inventory of the voices she'd heard, the sightings, the feelings . . . what if they were imagined. She wasn't sure if she'd actually heard the voices or if they were only in her mind. The little girl in the coop—she'd passed out right afterward and had done the same thing with January Rabine. What if her mind *was* tired? What if the visions hadn't been real but were manifestations of what was in her subconscious?

Sid interrupted her thoughts. "We need to get you back to the doctor. Are you taking your medications regularly? Have you mixed them with anything else?"

Molly hesitated. She recalled before the fire how she'd questioned whether she'd taken her medications. The other night she'd taken her sleep aid and then took it again at midnight when she couldn't recall the first time. So doubling that up, and then taking her antidepressant . . . a sliver of hope broke through. "Do you think it's my medications? Could they cause hallucinations or . . . or other things?" If it could be explained that simply. Exhaustion. Bad reaction to her medications. Depression. Maybe it wasn't a psychotic break or some sort of mental telepathy with dead people!

Sid was speaking. "Molly, the mind is a tender, fragile thing. Don't discount that maybe you're not crazy. You're not insane. You're not nuts. Your mind is tired. Molly, your heart is tired. *You* are tired. We need to get you back to your doctor, first and foremost, but *after* you tell Trent this."

Trepidation latched back on to Molly. She shook her head. "I can't. I can't tell Trent."

"Why?" Sid challenged.

"I've already disappointed him." Her voice cracked. Maybe that was it. The root of it all. Not that he had not been there for her during the miscarriages—oh, certainly, that was part of it—but the fact that she hadn't been able to give him the children they'd dreamt of. Then she'd become a hopeless excuse for a wife, wallowing in her mental anxieties and grief. To admit to seeing things, hearing things—even if there was a medical explanation? It was just another failure.

Sid squeezed Molly's hand. "You've both disappointed each other." Sid's words were telling and drove truth deep into Molly's soul. "This isn't the responsibility of just one of you. Trent needs to come to terms with your feelings of grief and loss, even if he's able to move on with life. And you need to rediscover that you can trust him, because he *loves you*, even if he can't meet all your emotional needs in the way that you want. Heck, the man ran into a burning house for you—he's got protector ingrained in every blood cell in his body!"

More tears. Molly swiped at her face, but it was useless. "I'm so tired," she admitted.

"Yes," Sid agreed, "and it's okay to be tired."

Once again her friend's words were like a balm to Molly's soul.

31

Gemma pulled her car to an abrupt stop on the gravel driveway and was out of her vehicle before Molly and Sid could pull themselves together. She didn't seem to notice Molly's tears or Sid's serious demeanor as she approached them. Her long tan legs covered the ground with purpose, and she looked equally intense in her expression.

"Whoever did this to you killed my sister," Gemma stated without any sort of greeting.

Sid reached out, but Gemma stepped away. "Gemma, now isn't—" Sid started.

"Now *is* the time," Gemma interrupted. Her eyes had a slightly wild look to them, yet she also seemed genuine in her concern. "Why were they trying to kill you, Molly?"

Molly stared at Gemma. The younger woman was asking the question the police had asked her. The question that *I don't know* felt like such a horribly paltry answer to. "The police haven't figured that out yet." Molly would not offer any other theories.

Gemma crossed her arms. "No motive? Nothing? Sounds like January. Do you know the Kilbourn police are thinking of calling January's death a 'random assault'? *Random*? And a random house fire? In a town with a population of cows and chickens? I don't think so." She pursed her lips. "We need to combine what we know and piece this puzzle together, because the police certainly aren't helping."

Sid stepped between Gemma and Molly. There was protectiveness on her face Molly loved her for. "Gemma—"

"I filled this with everything I could gather from January's online journals." Gemma had a backpack slung over her shoulder that she shrugged out of. Unzipping it, she tugged out a notebook.

"And?" Sid asked.

Gemma's face darkened. "And Molly may have information that she doesn't even realize is important. If we can piece it together, I'm hoping we can come up with a map that will lead us not only to the motive, but maybe even *who* is responsible."

Molly could tell the idea intrigued Sid. She was hiding it well, though. Molly could hardly blame her, for didn't they all want answers? And yet something about digging into the past frightened her. Gladys's stories and timelines had left Molly more confused than before.

Gemma looked between her and Sid and seemed to struggle to find that one key component that would gain her Molly and Sid's cooperation.

"He'll come back," Gemma said. "You know the killer will come back."

Molly stared at her. She was right. Trent knew it. Sid knew it. Molly knew it. In the depths of her denial, she knew that running from the truth would not be possible. Not from her own depression, not from the truth about her hallucinations or whatever they were, and not from the circumstances that had upended her world and threatened their peace and safety.

She eyed the remains of the farmhouse. It felt as though she were looking at a picture of herself. Half ash and half salvageable.

"Molly?" Sid prompted, sensing Molly's struggle.

Molly squared her shoulders and drew a deep breath. One truth was glaringly clear to her. Resolution would not come from hiding. She just needed the strength to face it. Face her depression, face her struggling marriage, face the unreal events of late, and face, more than anything, the knowledge that faith wasn't something you achieved, it was something you fostered. Maybe that was the first truth she needed to come to terms with. To have the faith to move forward, she needed to have faith there was stable ground beneath her.

She looked at Sid, then at Gemma. She thought of Trent, working at Clapton Bros. Farms today and worrying about her safety. She considered her parents in Florida, who had offered repeatedly to fly up to help. She thought of blessings. For the first time, Molly thought of the other side of truth. There was loss, yes, and helpless grief and fear. There was also stability and hope, family and friends. It was that fine balance in faith. Trusting that nothing was purposeless while believing that purpose wasn't always apparent at the beginning. A tangle of threads in a tapestry that when completed and turned around, revealed a beautiful pattern that made sense only at its woven completion.

"We need to finish this," Molly stated.

Gemma gave a satisfied smile of victory that she'd gained Molly's cooperation.

"Are you sure?" Sid pressed.

Molly nodded. She took in the shell of what once was, now burned and brutalized by the violence of life, and her eyes lifted above the roofline to the blue sky above, the white clouds, and the swallows that dove through the air. Life was waiting to be discovered from the ashes. It was time to stop burying herself and to live.

They sat at Sid's dining room table, Gemma's notebook open, Molly's laptop, and a big poster board Sid had taken from her kids' craft supplies. Pens, pencils, highlighters . . . Molly felt as if she were in an office-supply store.

"Okay." Gemma was definitely taking charge. "We need to bullet-point what we know on the timeline since January died and the fire occurred."

Molly exchanged looks with Sid. There were moments like these when Gemma was so unemotional about her sister's death that she oddly reminded Molly of Trent. Maybe not showing emotion *was* really a Wasziak family trait. But that didn't mean they didn't care, but that they were realists. Fix-its. Doers. Whereas emotion ran through every cell in Molly's being and made her a feeler. A helper. An empath of sorts.

"January came to Kilbourn at the beginning of this month." Gemma made a mark on the poster board with a purple Sharpie. "I last talked to her here, and then Trent found her—" Gemma cleared her throat—"Trent found her this day." Gemma scribbled in the date of January's death and looked away.

Molly shifted in her seat. "Trent talked to January the afternoon before she died."

Gemma jerked her head up. "I didn't know that. What'd they talk about?"

Molly modulated her breath so she wouldn't succumb to the anxiety that toyed with her. "He told me she was asking questions about your mutual great-grandfather, George Wasziak."

"Great-great-grandfather," Gemma corrected.

Molly nodded.

"Okay," Sid interjected. "So, a common denominator might be George Wasziak of 1910." She wrote that down with a green Sharpie.

Gemma tapped her capped marker against her cheek. "January's notes indicate she was building a family tree and got very tied up and interested in 1910 and Kilbourn's Cornfield Ripper."

Sid wrote *Cornfield Ripper* on the list of common denominators.

"Trent said she was also asking him about some woman who was killed in 1982," Molly offered.

Gemma stilled, raising her eyebrows. She grabbed her notebook and flipped through a few pages until she found her own notes. "Okay, so *that* makes a little more sense." She pointed at her writing. "January had mentioned in one of her journal entries that Kilbourn wasn't a quiet, innocent town like everyone thought, that the 1910 murders set the stage for future violence. Then she wrote '1982' in the margin along with a name."

Sid perked up. "What's the name?"

Gemma curled her lip. "I never heard of this name when I was looking up people here in Kilbourn, but the name was Tamera Nichols."

Molly and Sid both shook their heads. "Yeah, that's a new one," Sid agreed. "There aren't any Nichols in the area that I know of."

"Write it down." Molly sighed, waving toward the list. "Tamera Nichols."

"Of course," Gemma added, "January had written the other names involved in the 1910 scenario—Jasper Bridgers and Perliett Van Hilton."

"Van Hilton. That name sounds familiar," Sid mused.

Molly nodded. "She was the third woman attacked—only she wasn't killed." She recalled Gladys's recounting.

"Correct," Gemma said. "The funny thing is, when I research the Wasziak family tree, there is mention of a Perliett Van Hilton."

"Wait. George Wasziak had a thing for Perliett?" Molly asked.

Sid's eyes were wide with concentration. "Ooh, what if it's a tale of thwarted love?" She drew lines between the names on the poster board.

"Let's focus on one situation at a time." Molly leaned forward and traced Tamera Nichols's name with her finger.

"Realistically, 1982 is more likely to have an impact on today than some old cold-case mystery from 1910."

"True." Sid nodded.

Gemma sat back in her chair. "But how?"

"Who's Tamera Nichols?" Molly asked.

Gemma reached for her laptop and ran a search. As she typed, she explained, "I've already searched that name and date, along with Kilbourn. Here's what I found." She turned the laptop toward Molly.

Molly leaned forward to read the text. "'Wisconsin woman, Tamera Nichols, was reported missing on the second of May. She was last seen in Kilbourn, Michigan, on April thirtieth.'" The online news article was dated 1982. Molly squinted to read some of the smaller print. "They included this on a blog post written ten years ago by a Brianna Nichols."

"We should try to contact her," Sid suggested. She looked between them. "Think about it. Your sister"—she looked to Gemma—"was researching the Wasziak family ancestry. She stumbled upon a murder case from 1910. That would intrigue me if I were her—enough to search for other serious crimes tied to Kilbourn in the past. Now fast-forward to her finding out about a missing Tamera Nichols in 1982 . . ." Sid raised her eyebrows as if Gemma and Molly should understand where she was going with her reasoning.

"And?" Molly prodded.

"What if we have this all wrong?" Sid asked. "What if the Cornfield Ripper story has nothing to do with what happened to January and to you, Molly? What if it's all about Tamera Nichols?"

"My sister was digging into a more current missing-person case out of curiosity, which started when she discovered the tale of the Cornfield Ripper, and then someone caught wind of it?" Gemma raised an eyebrow.

Sid nodded. "And they don't want it investigated by anyone. Even an amateur."

"But why come after me?" Molly had to ask. It wasn't as if she were an amateur sleuth of historical crimes. She was a depressed woman in her thirties who seriously needed therapy. "I have only been looking at the 1910 Cornfield Ripper facts. If what happened to January was motivated by Tamera Nichols's disappearance in 1982, that's unrelated to anything I've researched. So why me?"

"Yes." Gemma studied Molly. "Why you?" She wasn't condemning Molly so much as asking it as a genuine question. "I was thinking it was the Wasziak connection, which was why I kept focusing on 1910."

"There's a crate in my chicken coop," Molly started.

"The killer's kit!" Sid straightened, snapping her fingers.

Molly smiled shakily. She really was an emotional wreck right now. "Yeah. And the newspaper that lined it was from 1982."

"Okay, so what?" Gemma looked lost.

Sid caught Gemma up on their finding what resembled a killer's murder kit in the chicken coop.

"Wait. What if that's the missing link? What if it's the farm?" Gemma asked.

"I don't get it." Molly sagged in her chair.

Sid got it. Molly could tell by the look on her face. "Yes. What if whoever was involved with Tamera Nichols going missing left their stuff at your farm? What if there are clues there? So, January was digging into the story about the Withers family and their farm and she ran across Tamera Nichols's disappearance, then threatened to open up a cold case, and to top it all off, you moved in to the Withers farmhouse that hadn't been occupied for a long time and were messing around in the outbuildings, discovering stuff that was supposed to stay hidden?" Sid stopped to suck in a breath after her excited revelation.

"I found a journal." Molly held up a hand as Sid and Gemma jumped forward with excitement. "It was from 1910, though, not 1982. It was just a bunch of random farming notes. But it *was* hidden in the chicken coop."

"Where is it?" Gemma was smiling, hope lighting her features and erasing the intensity.

Molly scrunched her face in apology. "It burned. With the fire."

Gemma's shoulders drooped.

Sid waved her finger in the air. "Awww, no. I refuse to accept defeat! Where there's one, there's gotta be more. We need to rip that coop apart and find out what else is hidden in there!"

"That could be a wild goose chase," Molly countered.

"Or it could bust two old cold cases wide open," Gemma concluded.

32

Perliett

For the first time since she'd met him, Jasper was wearing on her nerves. His dark confidence was smothering, as he'd posted himself at their house like an unwelcome guardian. It had been two days since Perliett's attack and her mother's dramatic engagement with Eunice Withers's supposed spirit. Maribeth was doing well. Perliett, on the other hand, was curled into a ball at the end of the sofa, a blanket over her lap. She sipped tea with calming chamomile while she tried to forget that awful, leering face of the child and hoped to heaven she never heard the song "London Bridge" or the nursery rhyme "Cock Robin" ever again.

The all-consuming feeling that this wasn't over and she wasn't safe was only emphasized by Jasper's presence. Her mother was accepting of him, too much so in some ways. She was feeding him lunch and dinner, serving him tea, and holding long discussions on the front porch about the movement of spiritualism, mediums, the impact of spirits on the living, and so forth.

And what about his involvement? George seemed to not trust him at all, while Maribeth absolutely did. Jasper had raised questions in Perliett's mind from the moment she'd met him, yet he'd also enchanted her with his enigmatic nature. His dark charm.

Detective Poll had only just informed them yesterday that he'd found no further insight as to who had left the dead robin on her porch, nor any connection as to why the Cornfield Ripper would leave a message outside Jasper's door. That was perhaps the most befuddling part of it all. What had Jasper Bridgers to do with any of this? Whether innocent or guilty?

Perliett wanted nothing more than to have faith in her mother's confidence and her own preoccupation with Jasper. But in light of George's constant glowering and challenging, she found herself questioning all of them.

Now Perliett heard Jasper's and Maribeth's voices filtering through the open window, and she found herself nauseated. Perhaps it was from her head injuries. Seeing her reflection in the mirror had been shocking. A split lip, a black eye, a cut at her temple. That wasn't considering the bruises on her arms and legs. Thankfully, she had only been battered. Murdered would have been final, and violated would have made living unbearable.

The screen door slammed, and Perliett heard footsteps. She looked up, fully expecting her mother or Jasper to enter, but instead it was George. The look on his face was one of irritation, and there was a glimmer in his eyes that Perliett couldn't interpret.

"Your mother granted me entrance. I'm here to check on your wounds," he declared, tossing his hat onto a chair and standing over her.

Perliett looked up from her cuddled position on the sofa. "I've already applied my ointments to the cuts. You know I'm perfectly capable of—"

"Of botching your own healing process with your quackery." George pulled up a chair and sat down. He leaned forward, resting his elbows on his knees and lowering his voice. "If I could burn your apothecary box, you know I would."

"Maybe you are a violent man after all?" Perliett quirked an eyebrow.

George narrowed his eyes. "I am appalled that anyone would accuse me of—"

Perliett waved him off. "Oh, I know it wasn't you." And she did. Her nerves would have tingled differently if she felt she was in danger. As it was, the tingling was altogether unwelcome anyway. For the first time today, she experienced a lift of her spirit, and it had occurred when George walked into the room, which was entirely unacceptable.

"Let me examine the stitches." George pointed to the cut on her temple that he'd stitched. Not unlike her cheek when the glass in the study had shattered. He must find some sort of glee in sewing her up.

"I look like a science experiment."

George's small smile made her stomach flip unnecessarily. His face was close to hers as he examined his stitchery. This wouldn't do. He never smiled. Why begin now? When he was inches from her?

"You don't need to inspect the stitches." Perliett resisted, pulling back. "It's unnecessary."

"It *is* necessary." George ignored her and moved to the edge of the couch, his gaze falling on the stitches at her hairline. His fingers pushed back some errant curls, and Perliett shivered. He looked at her with concern. "Are you in pain?"

"No." Perliett tugged the blanket higher against her chest.

They stared at each other. Silent. Then George dropped his hand and turned for his medical bag. "I am going to apply an ointment I feel will help with the healing and—"

"I have already put aloe on it." Perliett pointed to the aloe vera plant by the window.

George eyed it, then Perliett. He grunted. "That's what I was going to recommend."

Perliett bit back a smile.

George did as well.

Silence again stretched between them.

"Your bruises?" George finally asked. "I would like to see them."

Perliett obediently extended her arms. There was no use arguing with him, and if she showed him her arms, then she would have a better opportunity to resist when he asked to see her bare legs. Absolutely not. Never again would George Wasziak lay eyes on the bare skin of her legs and feet.

George took hold of her wrist and pushed her sleeve up.

Perliett watched his face instead of his hand. His fingers were scorching and probably branding her skin, and she did not know why her stomach was reacting so curiously toward him. It never had before. Or had it? And she'd only had the strength at that time to argue back in order to still it, unlike today when she felt completely defenseless?

George was studying her bruises—clear blue ones made by fingers. Whoever had attacked her had manhandled her. The same marks were on her other arm as well. He rubbed his thumb over them absently, as if he'd forgotten she was watching him.

"George?" Perliett asked softly.

George started and cleared his throat, resting her arm back on the blanket. "They're healing well."

"What is it?" Perliett could read something on his face. Something that showed he was pondering her bruises.

"Those marks," George said, pointing to her arm, "were not made by a little girl."

"Are you questioning what I saw?" she challenged him.

"Not at all." George didn't even try to apologize. "I question instead who was with the little girl that night. *How* is a girl involved, and *why*? Detective Poll is turning Kilbourn upside down and shaking it, but nothing is falling out. Not even a crumb."

"If you ask my mother, she would be happy to contact either of the Withers sisters, and perhaps you can ask them yourself—if something horrific doesn't happen like shattering windows or my mother losing consciousness."

George must have heard the slight edge to Perliett's voice. He glanced at the open window. They could hear the murmurs of Maribeth and Jasper Bridgers as they discussed—enthusiastically—just that topic.

The doctor's eyes narrowed. "You're skeptical, aren't you? You have to be—I can see it in your eyes every time we spar with words."

Perliett looked away from him.

George waited a moment and then said, "It's all right if you don't believe as your mother does."

"That's just it!" Perliett's gaze flew to meet his, and for once she didn't see censure in George's eyes. "I believe there's an otherworld."

"As do I," George said.

"I thought you didn't?" Confusion spiked through Perliett.

"I just don't believe in trying to connect to anyone in the otherworld besides God. And why would we seek a sadly limited perspective of a dead person instead of an unlimited one of a very much alive Being?"

"But if He were to use the spirit of Eunice—"

"To what end? To shatter windows?" George laughed skeptically. "I hardly believe God is limited to using any spirit but His own."

"Spirits were used in the Bible," Perliett challenged.

"Mmm, yes." George nodded. "At detriment to the kingship, the throne, and also to the man's soul."

"King Saul, you mean?" Perliett knew her Old Testament, thanks to PaPa.

"Summoning the spirit of the dead prophet Samuel did not please the Lord," George concluded.

"But Samuel's spirit *was* there to be summoned." Perliett

wondered if they would continue to debate or find some resolution between them.

"True," George conceded. "But again, it was ill-advised, unapproved, and condemned. We are not to seek the spirits unless it be the Spirit of God."

"Why?" Perliett had to ask. Even though he'd already supplied his answers, she felt them lacking. Narrow-minded. No, hurtful. He discredited her mother's beliefs while espousing the same faith in God that PaPa had. Could they not both be merged and be compatible?

George's eyes were heavy-lidded, and he studied her as he brooded. "If your father were to be summoned by your mother, would you continue to pursue meeting with him, or would you instead pursue an understanding of God?"

"What a silly question," Perliett laughed.

"Why is it silly?"

"Because!" She laughed again, then paused as the question became more poignant. PaPa. What she wouldn't give to be with him again. To converse with him. To have his influence helping her. Guiding her. Teaching her and . . . "Oh!" Perliett's eyes widened, and she stared at George.

He tipped his head and waited.

Perliett considered for a moment. "I would need my PaPa—"

"More often than God?"

"More often than God."

They both spoke in unison, George with a grim set to his mouth, and Perliett with an aching feeling in her heart that was quickly threatening to overwhelm her. Which was totally unacceptable, especially in front of George.

"Or perhaps it would complement my faith?" Perliett offered.

George was kind enough to give her a small nod. "Perhaps. But I daresay, and I know you will battle me on this, that perhaps not all of the spirit world your mother dabbles in is as real as you believe. While I believe some could be, I know even devoted spiritualists have questioned the validity of some of their practices."

Perliett stiffened. "You're accusing my mother of trickery?"

"No different from my accusing you of quackery."

Perliett bristled, the warm tingling subsiding. "And you're wickedly rude."

"I never claimed otherwise, but at least I'm truthful with myself about it."

"Not all of my ministrations of medicine are quackery," Perliett added, feeling justified.

"No."

She looked down at her fingers, still clutching the blanket. "I concede that heroin may not be the wisest of treatments."

"And that you're ignorant of new advances in medicine?" George prompted.

Perliett met his eyes. "Not ignorant. I study."

George grinned. It broke through the storm on his face and stunned her. He had long creases in his cheeks. "You study?" He laughed. "Study what?"

"You." Perliett smiled sheepishly.

George nodded. "Ah."

And it was painfully true. She *did* study him and his techniques. In fact, Perliett despised admitting how much George Wasziak had influenced her daily life.

"Well then." George rested his hands on his knees. "I can do no more for you today. Continue to rest."

Perliett's hand shot out and grabbed for George's shirtsleeve without thinking. He stiffened, looking down at her. She dropped her hold. Dropped her gaze. She dropped what she was going to say too. It was foolhardy, impulsive, and ridiculous.

"What is it, Perliett?" His voice was husky, and she dared to lift her eyes.

"I'm frightened." There. She admitted it to the one person she thought she would never admit weakness to.

George had no reaction.

"I miss PaPa." She sounded like a child, so she added, "He knew what to do. Always."

Still nothing from the doctor.

Perliett tried again, feeling as if she were digging a hole and getting ready to bury herself in it. She probably would soon—of embarrassment, if nothing more. "My mother is convinced Eunice Withers is warning us. She has three sittings this week with others in the community who wish to contact their dead relations. Her existence is consumed now by contacting the dead, and I don't—I can't—I feel alone," she ended weakly.

George studied her for a long moment. "And what would you wish of me, Perliett?"

She bit her bottom lip, not even sure how to answer that. George's eyes lowered to her lips, then rose back to meet her eyes. Perliett swallowed. "I think—I want . . ."

"What do you want, Perliett?" George's voice deepened.

Perliett was certain he'd leaned closer.

The air between them grew thick, surrounding them, enveloping them, warm like the summer breeze and stifling like the humidity. She couldn't breathe.

"What do you want?" he whispered.

"You." The word escaped her before she could reason through the realization that defied every thought she'd ever entertained about Dr. George Wasziak.

~

"He's written the paper again!" Maribeth flew into the house, Jasper close on her heels. When he entered the room, he took in George, who leaned away from Perliett with a speed that implied some sort of guilt.

Perliett felt her cheeks warm. *She* was warm. She was bewildered and not a little horrified at what she had just said to George Wasziak.

Now he sat there stoically. Unmoved. Masked. Glowering like he always did, the absolutely wretched, wretched man! And, at the same time, she couldn't hate him. Perliett stifled a sigh at her own inconsistency.

Maribeth shook the paper. "The Cornfield Ripper quotes the 'Cock Robin' nursery rhyme. Whatever for? It makes no sense. And then he says, 'I will dig a grave and bury them. I will show her that the monsters inside will never stay buried. They rise. The robin rises. Who killed them, you ask? I did. And she danced on their graves.'" Maribeth lifted incredulous eyes. "Whatever is he talking about?"

"It's laden with intentional nonsense," Jasper stated.

"Or is it laden with intentional meaning?" George asked.

Maribeth folded the newsprint and set it on a side table. "I find it repulsive. That the paper would even print it and give him the time of day."

George shrugged. "It's the sort of thing that sells papers."

"It's abhorrent," Maribeth stated.

"It's chilling," Perliett interjected. She nervously fingered the blanket on her lap and looked at each of the observers who stood over her. "Certainly and utterly chilling. 'Cock Robin'? Mrs. Withers had been reciting the nursery rhyme to Millie before she died. There was a mutilated robin left on my porch. This is not happenstance writing from an insane person. There's a reason he quotes the nursery rhyme."

Jasper grimaced. "He is purposeful. He left his calling card outside my own door as well."

"What if . . . ?" Perliett sat up straighter on the sofa. The idea was swirling in her mind and mixing with the emotions of moments before. It was difficult to even think under George's impassive expression, and under the very apparent toggling Jasper was doing as he looked between them, attempting to uncover what had transpired. "What if," she tried again, "the 'she' he refers to isn't Eunice or Millie or *me*. What if it is her? The little girl I saw?"

"When he says, 'I will show her that the monsters will never stay buried,' you're saying he's speaking of the girl?" Jasper repeated for clarification.

Perliett nodded.

"Who *is* the girl, then?" Maribeth mused. "She is the key. She has to be!"

"What if we never find out?" Perliett asked the question that lay in the darkest parts of her.

George met her eyes. So did Jasper.

Maribeth stilled.

None of them had an answer. The idea of the Cornfield Killer never being identified was terrifying.

For when they're gone, my mind stills.
She looks at me with expectation.
I must awaken my mind. Because she asks me to.

33

Molly

"This is where I found the journal." Molly crouched next to the nesting box that was still hanging precariously from the wall. Sid leaned in to look, as did Gemma.

"Did you look behind the other boxes?" Gemma asked the obvious question, and Molly shook her head.

"No. I didn't have a chance to, because of the fire." Molly straightened.

"And you said the Clapton brothers owned this property after the Withers family sold it to them?" Gemma was getting all the records straight in her mind, and Molly couldn't blame her. It was a typical small-town farming community. One property ran adjacent to another, families intermarried, and history became a conglomeration of the past and the present.

"Gladys said they did," Molly affirmed. "And Trent told me last night that no one lived in the house for quite a few years. I guess they bought the property for the acreage, not the buildings."

"So they sold it to you guys because Trent works for them?" Sid was attempting to fill in the blanks.

Molly shook her head. "Not really. The Clapton brothers had listed the farmhouse with a real-estate agent, along with a five-acre parcel."

"Then it was almost forty years since anyone lived in the farmhouse before you bought it?" Gemma inquired.

"There was a renter once, back in the nineties. They did a little renovation but it didn't last as a rental," Molly explained, thankful she'd asked Trent clarifying questions last night when they'd gone to bed in Sid's spare room.

Gemma raised a well-groomed eyebrow. "An empty farmhouse in 1982. Sounds like a perfect habitat for a killer."

Sid lifted her metal detector from where she'd leaned it against the coop's wall. "Time to look for clues," she announced. She patted the detector lovingly and smiled. "This is my baby. You both can look behind the nesting boxes."

Molly wasn't keen on ripping the nesting boxes from the wall, but at least they were the unused boxes and not the ones near the end of the coop where the chickens were already making their eggs in the straw-filled compartments.

Sid began sweeping her detector over the coop's floor. It was beeping incessantly, and she bent multiple times to pick up nails and toss them into a bucket. "This is going to take forever if this place is filled with old nails."

Molly led Gemma to the attic, where she showed her the crate of items that resembled a serial killer's kit. Gemma handled each item, then eyed the newsprint lining the bottom of the crate. She pulled it out and scanned it.

"I see nothing in particular about Tamera Nichols," Gemma said, "other than the year the paper was printed—1982."

Molly nodded her agreement.

Gemma placed the paper back in the crate. "You know, people get really into this serial-killer stuff." She glanced at Molly. "I saw cereal bowls for sale online, and at the bottom of the bowls were the different faces of killers. Throw pillows with their mug shots on them too."

Molly curled her lip. "People shouldn't glorify them like that. It's disgusting."

Molly noticed Gemma's expression change to one of grief, a dark cloud passing over her eyes.

"Gemma?" Molly ventured.

"What?" Gemma looked up, her blue eyes sharp again.

"I'm sorry about January." She'd never really expressed that to Gemma. Or to Gemma's parents, Brandon and Tiffany, or Uncle Roger. "I really am," she added. No one should have to experience the violent death of a loved one, knowing their life had been stolen from them. Drained against their will. Murder was a theft that way, and no amount of punishment could make up for the loss.

Gemma nudged the crate with her shoe. "You don't need to apologize. It wasn't your fault January was killed." Her voice was tight. She was hiding tears. Molly could tell because she'd made a practice of it over the past few years.

"I know it's not my fault. Still, I'm sorry you have to experience it. I'm sorry on behalf of the person who *should* have remorse for what they did."

Gemma put her hands on her hips, sniffed, swiped at her eye, and shook her head. "We move on." The frankness of the statement stung Molly. She stared at Gemma for a long moment before deciding to challenge her.

"How?"

Gemma looked up, eyes wide with honesty even though there was a thin sheen in them. "You have to move on, Molly. There's nothing else to do."

Maybe that was the truth. But she didn't have to like it.

Gemma reached up to run her fingers along one of the exposed beams of the roof. "Moving on doesn't mean forgetting." She dropped her hand, wiping a cobweb onto her shorts. "It means living with their memory until God reunites us. It means finding a resolution to their death so you can keep on living. January would want that from me. Life.

She always said she'd live forever because death wouldn't be able to catch up to her. I guess it's my turn now, huh? To outrun death?"

Molly offered a lopsided smile. "I don't think you'll have much luck."

"I won't." Gemma was so matter-of-fact, it made Molly both jealous and uncomfortable that someone could be so at peace with the murder of her sister.

Gemma met her confused eyes. "Don't forget, Molly. My mom was a Wasziak, which means Wasziak blood runs through my veins. We may have a reputation for being aloof and harsh and even uncaring, but sometimes—" she looked away—"sometimes that just hides the truth."

"What truth?" Molly asked, seeing Trent in her mind's eye and wondering if he would relate to Gemma's words.

"The truth that we care so deeply it hurts to even show happiness. Because we know that even the smallest of joys is a gift—a momentary gift from God—but that this world will inevitably steal it away, because that's what happens in a broken place. So even joy hurts because we love hard." Gemma rubbed her dry eyes as if they were flooded with tears. "Wasziaks are tough people. But not emotionless. We're tough *because* we feel so deeply, and it's the only way we can survive."

"Ummm, ladies?"

Sid's call snapped the moment between Molly and Gemma like a rubber band. For the first time, though, Molly had sensed a genuine understanding between them. While there were differences in who they were and how they were made up, they had connected in a profound way. All was okay.

Molly wanted to text Trent. It was impulsive—the old Molly. The Molly who didn't mind that Trent lived behind a reasoning self-confidence of calm, while she was a hurricane of emotional torrents. They needed each other, perhaps for those very reasons.

"Get down here!" Sid called again.

Gemma was already climbing down from the attic, so Molly followed suit, but not before she tugged her phone out and sent Trent a quick emoji text. A smiley face with hearts for eyes. Too much? Sheesh. She felt as if she were dating all over again.

Her feet landed on the straw and dirt floor. Gemma was rubbing her tennis shoe-clad toe in the dirt to remove some chicken poop she'd stepped in.

Izzy and Sue ruffled their feathers and scattered, leaving Sylvia and Chloe behind, who seemed rather oblivious to the world for chickens. The rooster chortled his warning that Molly and her friends were usurping his territory.

"It's okay, Orville." Molly waggled her finger at him, knowing better than to pet him. "I won't steal your girls—even if they like me better. Besides, I think Sue has a crush on you," she couldn't help but add.

"You gave your chickens human names?" Gemma's pretty face struggled against a smirk.

Molly raised her nose in the air a bit but softened it with a smile. "Animals deserve dignity too."

"Until they're made into chicken nuggets." Gemma's sarcasm stung a little, but Molly gave her the benefit of the doubt that she meant to be funny.

"Shhh." Molly bent and placed two fingers at the sides of Chloe the chicken's head as if the hen had ears there. "Don't listen to her. You'll never be a nugget."

"Stop chatting with the chickens and get over here." Sid sounded a bit more urgent as she posted herself at the far end of the coop.

Gemma and Molly exchanged looks and made their way to her in a few quick steps.

"What is it?" Gemma asked.

Molly was distracted as Sue waddled after her, her feathers ruffled.

"Look at this." Sid leaned her metal detector against the wall, then kicked straw away from the floor. She kneeled and used her hands to clear the area. "I found a coin—a 1922 quarter."

"That'll be worth something," Gemma inserted. "Back then, quarters had silver in them."

Sid looked uninterested. "When I picked it up, my detector was still going off. So I poked around and found this." She fingered a round metal loop on the floor. "When I went to pick it up, it didn't budge. See?" She demonstrated for them.

"And?" Gemma didn't seem to follow, but Molly did.

Molly dropped to her knees, ignoring the way the dirt and straw pressed into her bare skin. Sweat ran in rivulets down the small of her back from the midmorning heat swamping the chicken coop. Sue pecked around Molly's feet, then flustered and took off, clucking in the opposite direction.

"Is it a trapdoor?" She helped Sid to clear the area around the ring.

Sid nodded. "I think so." There was excitement that twinkled in her eyes, but also a hesitation that reminded Molly this wasn't a treasure hunt anymore. It was linked to a missing-person case from forty years ago, a hundred-year-old murder, and arson.

Gemma was more cautious as she knelt, getting a piece of cardboard that was lying in the corner to rest her knees on. "A trapdoor. Was that common in an old shed like this?"

"Maybe," Sid replied. "Back in the day, a lot of old buildings had cellars or earthen basements. Odds are, this wasn't always a chicken coop."

"I thought it seemed bigger than a normal coop," Gemma acknowledged.

"It's not Pinterest-cute," Molly admitted. "Just a converted building. Eventually I'd like to have a lot more chickens. Maybe forty or—"

"Hey." Sid commanded their attention. "Check it out." She ran her finger along a very distinct edge in the floor, indicating the confirmation that it was indeed a trapdoor. "It's not large, though. I mean, a person could hardly fit through it."

Molly squelched a nervousness that started playing with her insides. She looked over her shoulder at the door. Chickens. Rooster. Nothing out of the ordinary. But it didn't satisfy that chill that raced through her and caused her to shiver.

Gemma noticed.

So did Sid. "You okay?"

Molly nodded.

Sid pulled a jackknife from her back jeans pocket—because that was Sid, to carry a jackknife—and flicked it open. She ran it along the edges of the trapdoor, loosening the dirt and debris. Closing the knife, Sid slid it back into her pocket and hooked her finger through the metal ring. "Ready?" She looked from Gemma to Molly.

"Why do I feel like there's a dead body down there?" Molly swallowed.

"Not funny," Gemma retorted.

"Sorry." Molly realized she was in danger of reverting to her open-mouth-insert-foot days of speaking before she thought.

"I'm just going to open it." But Sid didn't move.

"It's probably just hiding old cans of nails or something," Molly reasoned against the *knowing* that was growing inside her.

"This is silly," Sid resolved, and gave the door a yank. It creaked, releasing finally, dust puffing into the air, followed by an instant scent of old straw and mold.

They all leaned over the hole, which wasn't much bigger than the size of a milk crate.

"There's a tin box." Sid stated the obvious.

Gemma looked at Molly expectantly. "It's your property."

So, it was Molly's duty to extricate the box from the cavern of time and open it? She grimaced, wiped her hands needlessly on the sides of her jean shorts, then reached in. Touching the tin box sent jolts through her palms like the invisible touch of time reaching out and contacting her. Her skin tingled for no other reason than the anticipation mixed with trepidation about what they would find. Was it possible to have that awful premonition that, in opening this box, she would release spirits from the past? Ones that were better left alone, in the captivity of a tin box in a secret hole in the chicken coop?

"Are you going to pick it up?" Gemma prodded.

Molly nodded, gathering gumption, and pulled the box out of its grave. She set it on the floor with a thud.

"There's no lock on it," Sid observed.

No. She was right. Just a latch. A simple latch that, once flipped up, would make accessing the box a walk in the park. Old artifacts were supposed to come with booby traps, weren't they? Or ghoulish, whirling poltergeists that swooped in and sucked your soul out of your body?

"Molly?" Sid's concern prompted Molly.

She flipped the latch and lifted the lid without saying a word. There was a solemnity to the moment as the hinges fought against the movement of the lid being pushed upward. Then it was open. The box revealing its treasure with stark reality.

"A book of nursery rhymes?" Gemma sounded disappointed as she stared at the vintage book, its binding frayed, its cover faded—which was a colored image of a goose with a massive ruffle around its neck. Mother Goose? Maybe. Yet it looked more neutral, nondescript.

"Maybe it belonged to a kid, who hid it out here," Sid offered, even though she didn't sound as if she believed it, or as if she wanted to believe it.

Molly gently lifted the book and wiped her palm against the picture. "It doesn't list an author's name. Not Brothers

Grimm." The word *Rhymes* was the only script on the cover, in faded blue that had once been brilliant but now resembled washed-out denim. She opened the cover.

Copyright 1873.

"It's way older than 1910," Gemma noted.

Molly still didn't respond. She knew, even before she turned the page, that what lay inside was evil. She could sense it oozing through the pages, licking at her soul with the demand of wicked taunting. The little girl in the chicken-coop attic became a clear vision in Molly's mind. She remembered her. A spirit, a vision, a ghost, a premonition before she lost consciousness, Molly had no idea. But somehow, she knew . . .

Jacqueline Withers.

The name was scrawled on the following page in pencil lead, with the tentative cursive of a young child.

"Was this one of the Withers sisters who was murdered by the Cornfield Ripper?" Sid ventured, a bit of awe mixed with leery caution lacing her question.

"No." Gemma shook her head. "The Withers sisters were Eunice and Millie. I've never heard of a Jacqueline."

"But they had an older sister, right?" Sid adjusted her body on the floor so she could better see the open book.

"Yes," Gemma said, "but her name was Angelica."

"Her daughter maybe?" Sid hypothesized.

Molly cringed. Daughter. Young girl. She closed her eyes, her hand splayed on the page of the book. Drawing in a steadying breath, Molly spoke. "There was a little girl. Here."

"What?" Gemma frowned.

Sid had a cautious expression on her face.

"I saw her." Molly's admission came with a degree of doubt—in herself and in what she thought she'd seen.

"A ghost?" Gemma drew back.

Molly shrugged. "I don't know. I've been struggling with . . ." She exchanged a look with Sid, then addressed

Gemma. It seemed unfair to mention her struggle to Gemma before ever confessing it to Trent, but the moment seemed to call for it. "I've been struggling. And, sometimes, I pass out."

"Like the night we came for dinner, Molly?" This time, Gemma seemed more empathetic.

"Yeah. But when I do, I tend to see things. I'm not saying it's a ghost, but maybe a premonition?"

"Do you believe in those?" Gemma's question was frank.

"Do you?" Molly countered.

Gemma nodded. "Sure. I think we can have intuitions. I don't know that they usually come with *seeing* things, but everyone's mind is different."

"Do you believe in God?" Sid interjected.

Gemma looked between them, to the book still open to Jacqueline's name, then back to Sid. "Yes."

Sid accepted her answer with a smile. "I believe that sometimes God uses our circumstances to reveal things to us. Not necessarily in a vision, but who's saying He couldn't do that? My uncle lost his wife about twenty years ago. He was beyond grief and couldn't sleep. He was worried about her eternal destination. He had no peace. And then one night he said he woke up, and she was in the corner of his room, surrounded by light and smiling and nodding at him to reassure him she had chosen the way of faith. That God was personal to her. That—"

"She recited the Nicene Creed?" Gemma teased dryly.

Sid smirked, clearly not finding Gemma's remark funny. "No. But the sight of her was enough for my uncle to wake the next morning and give God the glory for saving my aunt."

Gemma looked thoughtful. "And you believe that?"

"I do," Sid responded solemnly.

Molly stared at Sid. She'd never heard Sid speak of her uncle's vision before. But the idea that God was behind it—that it was a gift and not a spiritual manifestation or visitation or even interaction with the dead . . . "I do too," Molly added quietly.

Gemma eyed them both as if she were interrupting some deeply important moment. And she was, Molly realized, but that was all right too. Funny how when a person took a step back from all the expectations they had on themselves, that grace stepped forward and picked up the pieces that made no sense. An explanation might not even be offered, but then faith meant you believed without fully understanding. Ignorance? Molly shook her head to herself. No. No, it wasn't ignorance. Not when so much had been proven and so much evidence existed to affirm her belief that God was real, God was interactive, God *was.*

"Anyway." Gemma gave Molly a direct look. "You saw a little girl. For whatever reason. What's your point?"

Ignoring Gemma's edginess, Molly ran her finger along Jacqueline's name. "I want to know who she was. Was *she* Jacqueline?" Without waiting for an answer, Molly turned the page.

The ink sketch of a robin covered the first half of the page. A scrolled title swirled in beautiful print. And then the words . . .

"Who killed Cock Robin?
I, said the Sparrow,
with my bow and arrow,
I killed Cock Robin."

Directly below the nursery rhyme, someone had sketched—in adult handwriting—the words "watch them die."

A terrible silence wrapped itself around the three women. Molly could hear Gemma's breaths, slow and even. Controlled. Sid's were shakier, filled with nervous anticipation. Molly dreaded turning to the next page. She recognized the handwriting. It was identical to the writing in the farmer's journal she'd found behind the nesting box. Only this? This was horrifying and real and sadistic.

She flipped the page, its yellowed paper revealing another rhyme, and the margins were filled with more scribbling.

Darkness will be pivotal.

Expect her to scream.

Drink the sound into your soul.

They had found it. The darkest secret yet on the old Withers farm. An almanac of sorts. A killer's almanac.

Molly had frozen, unable to turn more pages. Gemma gently tugged the book from her hands and inspected it.

Gemma gasped softly when a lock of hair slipped from the pages, landing on her bare leg. She scurried backward, raising the book in the air and eyeing the hair as though it were a spider ready to bite.

"What the heck is that?" Sid did the opposite of Gemma, surging forward to retrieve the errant lock of dark hair. It was tied in the middle with a silk purple ribbon.

"Hair." Gemma stated the obvious with a curl of her lip.

"A souvenir." Molly knew she was saying what they probably all wished to avoid. She eyed the book in Gemma's hand. "Let me see that."

Gemma handed off the book with a nod, as if glad to be rid of it.

Molly thumbed through its pages. She curled into herself, sucking in a shuddering breath. She saw pencil sketches of women's profiles. Some of the pages contained more entries. Dark entries. One looked as if it had been written in brown ink—stained, blood maybe?

Molly closed the book almost reverently, not out of respect but out of fear. Her eyes met Sid's across the hole in the floor. "I think," she whispered hoarsely, "we just found the Cornfield Ripper's diary."

It is a game.
This waiting.

When the moon is perfect.
When she is ready.
The monster inside awakens.
Who shall dig the grave? it asks.
Not I.
I like them to be found.
People should know that I rid the world of them.
The Temptresses.
I paint their epitaphs in their blood.

34

Perliett

The incessant knocking at the door made Perliett gather her strength, nerves, and gumption in order to answer it. She wasn't particularly keen on how jumpy she had become. One could put forth the argument that she had every reason to be. But Perliett didn't appreciate weakness in herself. It diminished her capabilities, and heaven knew she needed to keep her self-confidence, or at least the appearance of it.

Still, the knocking persisted, and the door needed to be answered.

Perliett opened the door finally, eyeing the person on the other side of the screen door, her stomach suddenly flipping with a terrible sensation of omen.

"Mrs. Withers?"

"Open the door." Mrs. Withers's command came out in a panicked hiss as she shot suspicious glances over both shoulders. She banged on the wood frame with the ball of her fist. "Open it. Open it. Open it."

As if she wanted to let an insane woman into her house.

Perliett subtly hooked the lock into place, eyeing Mrs.

Withers through the screen. "How may I help you?" Of course, this *would* be the one afternoon since the attack that Mr. Bridgers *and* her mother had left her alone at the house to go for an errand run into Kilbourn. A parcel had arrived for Mr. Bridgers, whose dedication to their oversight and guardianship had been both noble and suffocating. Her mother? Perliett didn't know why her mother wished to ride along, except the two had scarcely stopped discussing the elements of the dissertations in a New York newsprint by an investigator of the Fox sisters—now deceased but known for their interaction with the dead—and the fallacies in the investigators' attempt to debunk the various individuals like Maribeth, who now openly practiced sittings to satisfy the public's need to connect with the afterlife.

"Let me in!" Mrs. Withers pulled on the screen door, her countenance darkening as she met with the hindrance of the lock.

"Does your husband or daughter know where you are?" Perliett tugged her sleeves down over her wrists to hide the yellowing bruises from her attack. She didn't know what might set Mrs. Withers off into a worse tizzy than she already was.

"Let me in before he comes and slays us both." Mrs. Withers's demeanor changed from frantic demand to utter petrified terror. Her eyes widened, not blinking. Her face had the pallor of a dead woman, yet she breathed and gasped and almost choked in her panic.

Against her better judgment, Perliett fumbled with the hook lock. Slaying them both was not an outcome she wished to come up against. When weighing the consequences of inviting a woman in who was insane with grief or coming face-to-face with the Cornfield Ripper . . .

Perliett stumbled to the side as Mrs. Withers shoved into the entryway. She yanked the door shut, its solid wood providing a small bit of relief. She eyed the open windows in the parlor. "Close those windows." Her demand was met with her own action to push past Perliett and reach for the windows herself, tugging them down and locking them.

"Mrs. Withers!" Perliett braced herself against the doorway to the parlor. Dizziness had not completely dissipated from her assault, and she certainly wasn't up to her typical strength yet.

Mrs. Withers was wearing a black mourning dress, its collar buttoned high to her chin. Its long sleeves were stained beneath her armpits from sweat—goodness knows it was almost ninety degrees today!—and her forehead had little streams of perspiration trailing down her temples.

"You think he's gone, but he isn't." Mrs. Withers bustled to the other window she'd already closed. Staring out as if the menace had chased her here.

"Who?" Perliett harbored little hope that Mrs. Withers knew who their nemesis was, let alone that if she even claimed a name, it would be credible enough. The woman was crazed. Lost her mind. Addlepated. And could one blame her? Her two unmarried daughters, slain by the hand of a vicious killer?

"You barely escaped alive!" Mrs. Withers spun, crossed the room, and jabbed her finger into Perliett's chest. "Barely. The robin is dead, you know. Dead. I saw its grave. All the little graves. Mounds of dirt."

"What *are* you speaking of?" Perliett reached for Mrs. Withers, who was growing more agitated and making less sense by the minute. She glanced around the room. Where had George stuffed her apothecary chest? Doubtful her mother noticed, and so George had seen fit to hobble her medical practice by secreting away her options.

Brandy would be good. A better cure than tying a loaf of bread stuffed with ox brain to the woman's head, which had been done in days of old to cure the ailments of the mind.

Perliett almost laughed at that thought as she pictured George walking in as she tied said brain-stuffed bread to Mrs. Withers's head.

Mrs. Withers collapsed onto the sofa, wringing her hands. She rocked back and forth, even as her wild eyes fell on Perliett. "You haven't seen them, have you? All the little animals. All the little mounds. Dirt upon dirt. A nursery rhyme turned into a nightmare, I tell you."

Sensing there was some truth woven through the elements of psychological distress, Perliett forced herself to sit next to the woman on the sofa. She reached out, folding her hands over Mrs. Withers's hands, who startled, then froze, staring at Perliett.

"How did you live? *Why* did they let you live?"

Perliett didn't answer.

Mrs. Withers dropped her gaze only to begin a quiet sobbing. "My girls. Ohhh, my girls! I should have seen. I should have known. Nothing good comes from sin. It is wickedness. All wickedness." She surged to her feet and, without warning, fled from the room, turning down the hallway toward the study.

Perliett raced after her, nearly sending a decorative vase flying as her hip bumped into a table. "Mrs. Withers!" she called.

The woman planted herself at Maribeth's round table. She sat in Maribeth's chair, spreading her arms out, palms on the table, lifting her face to the ceiling.

"Eunice! Millie!" she cried.

Perliett stood horrified in the doorway. The room was swathed in a dusky midafternoon pall. Mrs. Withers ran her hands in small circles on the black lace tablecloth.

"Come to me!" Mrs. Withers petitioned the spirits in a way that was very different from Maribeth. "Come!"

Footsteps behind Perliett startled her. She spun to see Maribeth's stunned demeanor as she beheld the crazed woman at her table. Mr. Bridgers stood behind her, and his gaze collided with Perliett's.

"What is going on?" he demanded, his voice low and urgent.

Perliett bit her lip. "She shoved her way in here. She's trying to make contact with her daughters."

"She needs to stop!" Maribeth tried to squeeze her way past Perliett. "I have guests coming tonight. She cannot be here. She cannot tamper with my sitting area."

Perliett held her arm out to stop her mother. "Wait. She isn't stable of mind. Upsetting her more could be catastrophic."

"But my table—" Maribeth broke off as Perliett leveled a stern glare at her mother.

"Your table will survive. What is there to tamper with but the candles?"

Maribeth blanched.

Perliett ignored the niggling questions that arose at the look on her mother's face. Questions that made her wonder again why Maribeth always avoided summoning PaPa and yet would so passionately invest herself in the grief of others.

"Let me through. I will see to the woman," Mr. Bridgers stated.

"Stop. Both of you." Perliett turned so that her back was to Mrs. Withers and she could pause the intensity of their advances.

"But I can help her." Maribeth pushed Perliett aside. "If she wishes to connect with her daughters . . ."

"You!" Mrs. Withers stood abruptly, the candles on the table wobbling, one of them falling over. She leveled a glare at Maribeth, holding up a shaking index finger in accusation. "You said you could contact Eunice. You told my husband she would be there—"

"Mrs. Withers." Maribeth held up her hands, speaking in a soothing voice. "We did contact Eunice. Your husband

and daughter and son-in-law were here to see it—as was Mr. Bridgers."

As was I, Perliett thought sardonically, not appreciating that her mother was inching toward the hysterical woman and ignoring Perliett's warning. Mrs. Withers was not in a proper frame of mind. Grief had spiraled her into nonsensical displays of panic.

"What did she say?" Mrs. Withers's expression shifted from one of accusation to one of plea. "Did she tell you? Did she tell you it all?"

"What all?" Mr. Bridgers stepped beside Perliett. His hand brushed hers, and Perliett surprised herself by jerking hers away. He shot her a questioning look. "All will be well," he said under his breath.

Yes. All would be well. When the Cornfield Ripper was stopped. When the leering child from the cornfield was identified. When Mrs. Withers regained her right frame of mind. When Perliett herself could feel safe again!

"The robin falls," Mrs. Withers whimpered. "She falls. Eunice will tell you." Her eyes widened with earnestness as she met Maribeth in the middle of the floor. Maribeth reached out to take Mrs. Withers's hands. To calm her. To reassure her. Instead, Mrs. Withers swept her hand through the air, and it slapped against Maribeth's face with a crack.

Maribeth cried out, covering her face with her hands and bending over to shield herself. Mr. Bridgers launched into the study, intent on whisking Maribeth away from the violence at the hands of Mrs. Withers.

The woman sobbed. A maniacal, laughing sob. "Oh, Eunice. My Millie. We have betrayed your trust." She lifted her face to the ceiling, yelling as if her daughters' spirits lurked in the corners, hovering, waiting to hear their mother speak. "She would be better off if *she* were the one who were dead! Buried in a grave that cannot be found. Forever!" Mrs.

Withers collapsed to her knees, and Mr. Bridgers hauled a weeping Maribeth away from the woman.

Perliett took a few hurried steps toward Mrs. Withers, freezing in place as the woman wailed.

"I have borne a monster, and even the afterlife cannot hold her still."

Mr. Bridgers came up beside Perliett, his baritone voice resonating in her ear, his breath warm against her cheek. She flushed, stepping away. What had sent trickles of pleasure through her last week now made her wary. The trauma of her attack had stolen any thin remnant of romantic interest she had in her.

"I am going for Mr. Withers. He must come and fetch his wife. She is beyond reconciling with reason."

"I agree." And she did, only she wasn't sure that Mr. Withers would be any help considering he apparently couldn't keep his own wife at home as it was.

Mr. Bridgers sniffed, even as Maribeth sidled past him, casting Perliett an anxious look as her cheek blazed red from Mrs. Withers's slap. Jasper clicked his tongue in derision at the situation. "This is unfortunate. The woman has lost her mind. It would be good to appeal to the county court and have her committed."

"Committed?" Perliett whirled on him.

He gave her a nonplussed look, heavy-lidded eyes piercing and oh so handsome and suddenly dangerous. "If this isn't enough to convince you, what will it take, may I ask?"

Perliett darted a look at Mrs. Withers, who was rocking back and forth in a kneeling position on the study floor. "Well, I—"

"And surely her family won't take the necessary steps to do so."

"But—"

Jasper must have read the question in her eyes. "Where I was raised, there was a woman in town who continually sunned herself in her front yard, in full view of the community, dressed only in her petticoats."

Perliett blushed.

He continued, "It took the wisdom of one concerned male citizen to bring attention to her erratic behavior, and they committed her. For two years."

"Because she enjoyed the sunshine?" Perliett cast another nervous glance at Mrs. Withers.

"The species of humanity will either evolve, Perliett, or devolve." Jasper lifted his hand and brushed his knuckles down her cheek. There was gentle confidence in them, and for a moment, Perliett swayed against them, before a nagging irritation disturbed her. "Mrs. Withers shows that sometimes a portion of humanity is simply not to the, shall we say, standard of other humankind? They need assistance to exist, whereas we exist on our own purview."

"Our own purview?" Perliett repeated, realizing she sounded a bit like a parrot she'd read about once that mimicked its master.

"Mm-hmm." Jasper smiled thinly and graced Mrs. Withers with a quick assessment. "There is so much intelligence in man. Both here and after our souls cross over. We must protect it. The species."

"The species," Perliett repeated, hearing herself, almost hypnotized by the man and his darkly charismatic nature.

"Stand watch, Perliett. I will return shortly." With that, Jasper left in a bluster of spice and pine scents that left Perliett's senses reeling.

Fingers closed over her arm, clamping into her skin. "We must move her from my room," Maribeth murmured. "I am not comfortable with her disturbing the spirits."

"How can she disturb them here and not in the parlor? Are they restrained to one room of the house?" Suddenly,

Perliett wished the answer would be yes. The idea of lurking spirits of the dead wandering through her home no longer seemed all right or even comfortable.

"You know what I mean." Maribeth's eyes narrowed in a way that pled with her daughter to understand.

Perliett nodded. She did. The study was Maribeth's sanctuary of sorts. A private place into which she invited guests only by her bidding. Mrs. Withers was an intruder. A disconcerting intruder conjuring up memories of two frightful experiences.

"Eunice is not a safe spirit," Maribeth confided in a whisper. "I fear her mother's presence here will only exacerbate her angst. She is restless. Angered."

"And what has she revealed to you of her killer?" Perliett searched her mother's face, longing for resolution to her doubts.

Tell me something. Something I can grab hold of.

Maribeth looked pained, shaking her head. "She speaks in riddles. In writings manifested through me that make the puzzle only more complex."

"Then why seek her out?" Perliett hooked her arm through her mother's. The woman was still beautiful. Being in her forties had done little to diminish her youth. In some ways, Perliett felt more her equal than her daughter.

Maribeth leaned her head against Perliett's shoulder. She offered no answer but a distant affection. Perliett realized it was what her mother often did when she didn't know how to respond, or worse, when there was no answer to be given.

35

Molly

A solemn quiet fell over the foursome. After examining page after page of the diary, Gemma had reluctantly left. It was evidence of crimes long committed. A glimpse into the mind of a killer. Now Trent and Molly sat side by side on Sid's couch while Sid and her husband, Dan, lounged in their recliners.

"Do we turn it in to the police?" Sid asked quietly.

The diary lay on the coffee table between them. It was open, revealing ominous words.

Monster.

Blood.

Notes of observations of women that had to be speaking of the Withers sisters.

Perliett Van Hilton.

His victims.

"There's no statute of limitations in Michigan," Dan stated. He pushed his glasses up his nose. His hair was cropped short, his goatee trimmed. He reached across the distance between his chair and Sid's. They linked hands. Molly realized they probably didn't even recognize they'd done it. It was instinctual. Dan continued, "Murder can still be penalized."

"I'm going out on a limb in saying that the Cornfield Ripper of 1910 is dead," Sid said with a smirk.

Dan was a literalist. He nodded, missing the humor. "True. But there are generations of family who may still be seeking closure."

Molly glanced at Trent. There was about a foot between them. He was freshly showered from farm work. He smelled good. He hadn't said a word about her impulsive emoji text. Warmth crept up her neck. Now she felt as if she'd sent him something inappropriate. Guilty. Embarrassed rather. He could at least give her a wink. Just a wink.

"We owe it to Kilbourn to turn the diary in to the authorities." Trent's words held conclusion in them. "It's not ours to keep."

"But it was on your property."

Molly could tell Sid wanted to keep it. Ew. "I don't want it," she said and shook her head. Not in her fragile state. She still needed to find the gumption to tell Trent . . . well, *everything*. Until she told Trent, Molly knew she wasn't going to completely rest. But it was a confession that, while most would say was embracing her mental struggles and agreeing it was okay to not be all right, Molly felt was opening the Pandora's box they had danced around since their first miscarriage.

"Why is the killer's diary on the Withers farm?" Trent's question sliced through Molly's straying thoughts.

She jerked back to attention.

Sid straightened. "I've been wondering the same thing. Doesn't it mean the killer *was* on the Withers farm?"

"But what does any of this do in resolving your cousin's death?" Dan prompted, drawing them all back from the past's crime to the present. "You ladies were searching for clues about that missing woman January Rabine had been investigating. Instead, you once again stumble onto the murders of 1910."

"They have to be linked somehow," Sid concluded.

"How?" Molly bit her fingernail. She couldn't peel her eyes from that awful book of nursery rhymes. From the killer's pencil-sketched handwriting. That they were a few miles away and safely ensconced in a much more recently built farmhouse gave Molly relief from feeling like dead eyes were watching her from the corners, but still. A link?

"Linking murders from 1910 to a missing woman in 1982 to the murder of January today?" Trent blew out a huge breath, stretching his arms over his head, then draping his left arm over the back of the couch.

Molly could feel his hand on the cushion behind her neck even though his skin didn't touch hers. She could feel the warmth. Feel Trent.

Dan adjusted in his chair, reaching for a cup of decaf coffee and slurping it before he spoke. "I did some research for Sid today."

"My hero." Sid offered him a corny smile.

He returned it. "Well, it was a relief to take a break from coding. Anyway, I dug into Tamera Nichols's history—at least what I could find. She was a transient worker. Hailed from Madison. She had been waitressing at a diner in Kilbourn that's closed now. Apparently, she worked there for about three months before she disappeared. After a brief investigation, authorities concluded she had purposefully disappeared."

"But her family still reported her missing?" Trent squirmed. He was tired. Molly could sense it.

She stilled when his hand slid down the back cushion of the couch and his thumb touched the skin at the back of her neck. A light touch, but it sent electricity through her to her toes. A deep part of her ached. A longing. To be close again. To be his best friend again. To know Trent in the way she had when they had shared dreams instead of loss, happiness instead of bitterness . . .

"I contacted Brianna Nichols." Dan was still explaining, unaware of the sparks that were flying from Molly's entire being.

Good gosh! Trent's thumb stroked the back of her neck. Lightly. A caress that was absentminded yet so purposeful. Molly didn't move for fear the slightest twitch would somehow communicate a distaste for his touch. She'd shrugged him away so many times over the last few years.

Maybe that heart-eyed, smiley-faced emoji was the beginning of miracles.

"She wrote the blog post Gemma found?" Sid inserted.

Dan nodded. "Yes. Brianna Nichols is Tamera Nichols's younger sister. She's always believed that something happened to Tamera—not that Tamera disappeared on purpose. In her message to me, Brianna mentioned Tamera was a loner. She was independent, a drifter. But she was devoted to their grandmother. When Tamera stopped contacting her, Brianna knew something was wrong. The family knew it too. Only there was no evidence to go on. She simply vanished."

Molly couldn't breathe. Trent's index finger had joined his thumb, and now it was a mesmerizing massage of gentle strokes.

"I feel like we're missing something obvious," Sid stated.

Yes. Yes, so did Molly. She was missing the entire conversation because Trent's fingers were weaving into the hair at the nape of her neck. No one noticed either. Why would they? A husband absently caressing his wife's neck wasn't unusual. But for them?

Molly dared a glance at Trent.

His sky-blue eyes met hers briefly. His lid dropped in a wink.

There it was.

The killer wink. The wink that usurped any other killer's story of the night.

Trent shut the door.

His arm snaked around her waist and he pulled Molly against him, her back pressed into his chest. He lowered his head and nuzzled behind her ear.

"That was one sexy emoji," he whispered.

Molly was sure she had reverted back to her teenage years for all the butterflies exploding in her stomach. She twisted in his grip and lifted her chin. "You liked it?"

The expression on his face told her it had both stunned and thrilled him. "Just a little bit." He lowered his head, but before Molly could even process his movement, he had claimed her lips.

The kiss was desperate. Filled with the sort of agony that separation of heart created and the collision of renewed hope inspired. Molly reached up to wrap her arms around Trent's neck. The feel of him. The strength in him.

She had to tell him.

Had to be honest.

Molly pulled away, Trent protesting in his throat and following her, his mouth settling on the side of her neck. "Trent?" Molly gasped. God help her. Her nerves were going to make her throw up.

"Yeah?" Trent's voice was filled with the gravel of desire.

Molly hesitated.

Trent must have felt it. He paused, pulling back a bit to search her eyes.

What to say? Really. How did one summarize loss and grief and anger and melancholy and hope and faith and fear and haunting? She should have kept her mouth shut. He wanted her. *She* wanted *him*. For the first time in forever, things felt . . . better. God knew in her heart of hearts, everything inside her had pulled toward Trent's soul when his thumb had touched her neck. But now? How did one rectify the truth? The truth of who they were to who they had been?

It was grief that they shared. It was grief that spread its icy fingers on her skin, making her feel another presence in the room. It was that gut-wrenching, soul-agonizing emotion that mystified anyone not walking through it themselves. She was not alone, because grief never left her, and she had opened her heart to it like a home, enhanced by whatever physical detriments the pregnancies had left behind in her body to assist in the hospitality of such numbing despair.

Grief had taken up occupancy in the spare room of her soul and, like a spirit, haunted her with a rabid persistence.

Trent furrowed his brow. He threaded his fingers with hers. A solid lifeline for the first time in forever.

"I need help," Molly whispered. It was all she could say. All she could muster the strength to explain. She waited. She waited for the questions. She waited for him to tell her how much she had hurt him—hurt *them*. She braced herself for him to matter-of-factly remind her that life needed to be lived and the lost needed to be let go of. She willed herself to not react when his replies to whatever she would say next were placid. Void of expression. It was the Wasziak way. She could do this. She could get through this. By the grace of God she could—

Trent's caress was gentle. He kissed her slowly now, but it wasn't searching or seeking. It wasn't expectant of anything more. His kiss was an end to the chapter of her melancholy.

His whisper in her ear soothed her more than any other words could have. "I've got you."

Then, in the stillness, Trent's kiss turned to holding her. Simply holding her.

Accepting.

Of her.

In all her mess.

No questions asked.

He was finally here.

36

Molly knocked on Gladys's door, and when the elderly woman opened it with her warm, wrinkly smile, a huge part of Molly relaxed. Days might have passed since the fire, but this was the first day she was spending on her own. Sid had appointments with her kids. Gemma had texted saying she was trying to plan with her job back in New Mexico so she could stay longer and investigate her sister's murder. Trent was at work. The police weren't able to provide protective detail for her, especially since no further threats had been made on her life.

All was quiet.

Too quiet.

She felt this lull before the storm. Others seemed to think the storm had blown over and now it was cleaning up the aftermath. Trent wanted to go to his uncle Roger's tonight and meet with his cousin Brandon, Gemma's dad. Her mother had returned to New Mexico, a complete wreck. Dan had offered to take the killer's journal to the police, but not until after Sid had photographed every single page.

Molly? She was still swooning from last night. Eventually, their silent reestablishment had led to more, and then . . . gosh! She was still light-headed, and for the first time in forever, it was the good kind of light-headed.

This morning they'd had a straightforward chat. Instantly concerned about her visions, Trent had insisted they put a call in to their doctor. Within a half hour, he had returned their phone call, and with the promise of a scheduled visit, he had already identified the negative interactions of her medications.

"You're on a prescription to assist you with sleeping, and mixed with the strength of your antidepressant, hallucinations *are* definitely a possibility—especially if you've lost track of when you've taken your medication and perhaps even doubled up at times. We'll need to adjust the prescriptions, but we'll need to do it cautiously. You can't quit cold turkey, and we also need to make sure we stay on top of your depression and sleep." The doctor had given Trent some instructions to help Molly monitor her medications and pled for transparency going forward if she heard or saw things, blacked out again, or felt dizziness. "All of those are signs of significant side effects to the meds, and we need to stay on top of that. You don't bully through it, you hear?"

If honesty always came with such restful resolutions, she was all for it. She and Trent had hung up from the call and shared a long embrace before Trent had pulled away with intent to go to the farm. He'd tugged his hat onto his mussed hair and given her a direct and stern look.

"Keep your phone on you. In case you need anything."

"Yes, sir," Molly had smirked. It sounded so patriarchal of him, but it was more than she'd received from Trent in months. She'd take it.

Now her day had led her to Gladys's house, and Molly wasn't sure why.

"Come in, dear!" Gladys was wearing a cotton dress in a muumuu style covered in small pink flowers against a white background. Her curls hung loose around her head in a gray halo of sorts. Her cheeks were powder pink, her smile welcoming.

Molly handed her a bouquet of wildflowers she'd picked from Sid's garden. "A thank-you for letting us stay with you."

"Oh, how beautiful!" Gladys took the flowers and waved

Molly forward. "Come in, come in! I was just going to have my morning coffee. Will you join me?"

Molly nodded as she entered the cozy kitchen.

Soon, coffee in hand, Gladys tapped the table at which Molly sat. "Wait here. I have something I found you might be interested in."

She shuffled from the room, and Molly waited. She fingered a lace doily that adorned the middle of the table. Sipped her coffee. Listened to the wall clock tick.

"I was going through some things in my mother's trunk yesterday," Gladys called from the other room, her voice shaky with age. "It's time I do that. I won't be around forever. Recent events reminded me of that."

Molly frowned to herself. Recent events? If Gladys was feeling threatened by January's killer or the arsonist, Molly wanted to know.

"Are you all right?" she called back.

"Oh yes!" Gladys was returning, and her voice drew closer. "I've just been reliving memories. Thinking about your poor cousin and that fire." She rounded the corner, a photograph in hand. There was a fierce look in Gladys's eyes that warmed Molly. A nurturing defensiveness for Molly. "I'd like to roast whoever did that to you and your home."

Molly smiled. She had the sudden mental picture of Gladys wielding a flamethrower and letting loose the full rage of an eighty-plus-year-old grandmother.

"Here." Gladys slid the photograph across the table toward Molly. It was pasted to a vintage piece of cardboard with golden scrolls at the corners. A young woman was centered in the picture, dressed in the garb of the 1930s, she herself looking to be around the thirty-year mark. A man stood behind her, his hand on her shoulder.

"Who is it?" Molly lifted her eyes.

Gladys eased into a chair. "That is my uncle Mikey. He was engaged to this woman." She tapped on the woman's face but didn't seem to have any warmth to her voice. "A vixen, my mother said. She had a nature that would cool the heat off the devil himself."

Molly widened her eyes. The distaste in Gladys's voice was more than likely inherited from her own mother. "What happened?"

Gladys offered a wry smile. "Oh, they eventually broke off the engagement. My mother told me Uncle Mikey came to his senses before he made the most pitiful error of his life." Her eyes dimmed then. "Of course, the sad story is, Uncle Mikey went on to fight in the war. We lost him somewhere in France."

"I'm sorry," Molly murmured. She wasn't sure how any of this applied to her, but she was willing to wait. The coffee was good. Gladys was warm and gave the ambience of safety in numbers.

Gladys sipped her coffee, eyeing the photograph.

Molly studied the woman in the photograph. She had bobbed hair, curled, dark, with a beret on her head. Her dress was square-cut according to the style of the day, with buttons down the front. She was pretty. High cheekbones, long lashes, eyes that turned up at the corners in an almond shape.

"Who was she? Why did they break up?"

Gladys pursed her lips at the woman. "Well, she's dead now, thank the Lord. There were whispers about her, back in the day. Rumors, you know?"

Molly didn't know, so she waited.

Gladys took another sip of coffee. When she lowered the mug, she smiled a little. "They had advised Uncle Mikey not to marry the girl. My mother told me she had quite the reputation around town, and excuse my French, but she was a brazen hussy. Only Uncle Mikey was blind to it. She had a way about her, Mother said, that could fool the wisest of men."

"She sounds deadly," Molly teased.

Gladys didn't laugh. "Oh, you know, that was also a rumor. There's a look in a person's eyes when you're not sure they have feelings?"

Molly grimaced. She had accused Trent of that before.

Gladys waved her hand. "Not in a normal husband-and-wife argument—I'm talking the stone-cold sort of person who hasn't the ability to feel wrong."

"A psychopath?" Molly suggested.

Gladys nodded. "Yes. Yes, that's it."

"She was a psychopath?"

"From what I've been told, I would say yes. Anyway"—Gladys tapped the picture again, directly on the woman's image—"my grandfather confronted Uncle Mikey. Told Mikey that the Hannity name would not be tarnished by her and her reputation whispered by all. Mikey defended her, swearing none of the rumors were true. My grandfather vowed he would disown Mikey from the farm if he married the girl."

"Mikey broke off the engagement, then." Molly leaned forward, her interest in the story growing.

Gladys nodded. "And he was happier for it. Until the war, of course."

"And the rumors? What happened to her?" At some point, this had to wrap back around and apply, didn't it? Gladys had stated the photograph made her think of Molly, but so far there was no connection.

Gladys lifted the picture, studying it with her rheumy eyes. "She lived a long life and then died in the late seventies. She had a family, grandchildren and great-grandchildren. It wasn't fair really that she lived and Mikey died."

Molly eyed Gladys. It was a harsh verdict to wish death on a person, no matter how unfeeling or sinful they might be.

Gladys flipped the photograph over and laid it on the table. Then she locked eyes with Molly. "She was Jacqueline Withers. The younger sister to Eunice and Millie Withers, who were murdered by the Cornfield Ripper in 1910."

The nursery rhyme book! Molly stared at Gladys. "I didn't know they had a younger sister."

Gladys raised an eyebrow. "Neither did they, my dear, neither did they."

"Jacqueline Withers." Molly slapped the photograph that Gladys had willingly lent her onto the seat next to her in her car. Unfortunately, Sid was still in appointments and Gemma wasn't answering her phone. "Jacqueline Withers was the younger sister. How did they *not* know she existed?" The idea was ludicrous, and yet the pieces seemed to be dropping into place.

Molly steered her car out of Gladys's drive and headed toward town. If the killer's journal was originally Jacqueline Withers's childhood nursery-rhyme book, how did he ever get ahold of it?

More questions piled in Molly's mind as she drove. She should've stayed to ask Gladys more, but the adrenaline that had pumped through her on hearing Jacqueline's name was only just now wearing off.

She saw the outline of her half-burned farmhouse rising on the road ahead. The white barn standing guard over it. Her chickens needed feeding, but Trent said he would stop to feed them on the way to Clapton Bros. Farms. He didn't want her near the house alone.

But as Molly neared their shell of a home, her breathing came shorter and more rapidly as she considered its history. The Withers farm. This was it. This was where Eunice and Millie Withers had been raised. Where Jacqueline had grown up too? How was that even possible if no one knew of her?

Other questions swirled as if they were on a merry-go-round in Molly's head. How did this tie in to Tamera Nichols's disappearance in 1982? What had January Rabine found that had caused the taking of her life?

As Molly's car neared the house, the foreboding inside her increased in its intensity. Not now. No. She'd gone this long without feeling like she was going to hear voices. See things. But that dark hollowness was flooding through her. She looked at her hands gripping the steering wheel. They were trembling. Her skin felt clammy even while her body shivered.

Ominous. That's what it was. The Withers house had been built on gravestones. It was a physical premonition of the horrors that would visit them. The horrors of death, creeping in, brutalizing, stealing.

The burned section of the Withers—no, *her*—farmhouse was a black scar against the blue summer sky. One of the corner studs, charred and crumbling, pointed toward the clouds as if in one last plea for its life. The section of the house on the east side was open, and she could see inside to the remnants of their home. Going through the debris was going to be a chore. Insurance was counting it a total loss.

Molly let up on the gas, pressing softly on the brake, slowing the vehicle as she neared the house. A car was parked in the driveway. Was someone looting the ruins of her life? She saw her chickens pecking in the yard. She could see someone was poking around in the cavernous interior of the house. Molly reached for her phone, quickly dialing Sid as she pulled over just past the house.

Sid's voicemail answered. Molly left a message. Putting down her phone, she debated. Approaching the house alone was more than likely foolhardy. If this person were the arsonist . . .

The man straightened and spotted her in her truck. The cornfield that lined the road was a green backdrop to her black vehicle.

He waved, a broad smile on his face.

Maynard! Their real-estate agent. Relief surged through Molly at his familiar face. She shifted the truck into drive and pulled onto her property. Once parked, Molly opened her door and jumped out as Maynard Clapton walked up to greet her. He stuck out his hand, and she took it, the handshake friendly.

"Your insurance company called me about some assessments. I am so sorry about what happened here." He clicked his tongue, resting his hands on his hips. His khaki pants and polo shirt were smudged from his jaunt through the remains of the house. "I had no idea how bad it was." He shook his head. "I moonlight as an insurance adjuster, and the insurance agency sent me out to report on the extent of the damage."

Molly kicked a stone, and it went rolling across the drive. Izzy ruffled her feathers and squawked at it as if it were a predator. "Trent said they're calling it a total loss."

Maynard nodded. "Yes, they are."

"So, what questions do they have?" Molly tried to understand why he was here if the insurance agency had already made their decision on the claim.

Maynard chuckled as he walked back toward the house, and Molly followed. He pointed to the remains. "All of this needs to be inventoried—if there's anything salvageable, that is. But you don't need to worry about it." His warm brown eyes met hers. "I'm sure it's traumatizing to look at. That's what I'm for."

"I can help you if you want," Molly offered while trying to stuff down the annoying sensation that she would look into the open space of her old bedroom to see January Rabine's hollow-eyed ghost staring down at her as she had that day on the stairs. The doctor had said it might happen again until the medications were balanced out.

The hairs on Molly's arms rose as she neared the basement pit. Staring into it, she eyed the ashen remains. The plastic shelving Trent had installed was melted and warped. The gravestones intermingled with the fieldstone foundation were covered in soot, the names barely legible on some of them, with a few dislodged and fallen to the floor. Evidence of water damage was everywhere, a few remaining puddles still in the corners that were devoid of sunlight.

Maynard held up his hand, a concerned expression on his face. "Really, Molly, you should go. There's no need to put yourself through this."

No. There wasn't. He was right. Molly shot a longing glance at her truck. Maynard noticed. His hand tapped her forearm.

"Go ahead," he urged, "I've got this."

And he did. She managed one more glance back at the basement and froze. Her breath caught in her throat as her gaze landed on the crawl space. For a brief flicker of a second, Molly would have sworn she saw the form of a young girl, a leering smile . . . and then she vanished.

Molly blinked, attempting to regain focus.

"Molly?" Maynard prompted. "Are you all right?"

Molly took a few steps toward the basement, fixated on the crawl space. Why was there a crawl space? She remembered hiding in it, trying not to breathe in smoke. She didn't remember Trent pulling her out or the fire crew carrying her to the ambulance. Trent said she was unconscious by the time he'd gotten to her.

Those last conscious moments inside the crawl space during the fire became clearer now. Molly stepped around the real-estate agent, or insurance adjuster, or whatever Maynard was moonlighting as today and made her way to what remained of the stairs leading to the basement. She took them carefully.

"Molly, it's best you don't go down there. It's dangerous." Maynard's voice of caution sounded behind her, but she ignored him.

He was right.

There was no reason to go down there.

Molly's mind grew foggy, almost enough to forget that the real-estate agent stood behind her, concern etched on his features.

The smoke had seeped into the cracks of the crawl space. It was midnight-black inside and she could see nothing. Putting out her hands, Molly felt only the cold earth beneath her fingers, her nails biting into it. Were these the last marks she would make before she died? Would she suffocate or burn alive?

Horror made Molly push her way until her back was against the far wall of the crawl space. Her hand connected with a cool object. Her fingers ran across metal ridges. The smoke was getting thicker, burning her lungs. In a desperate, foolish measure, Molly turned and pressed her mouth against the cool metal of what had to be a barrel stored in the back of the crawl space. There was no cooler oxygen rolling off it than there was coming in through the cracks at the opening. The long intake of air left Molly light-headed. Her fingers trailed down the side of the barrel as she drifted, her lungs aching from the black smoke.

Molly blinked, awareness flooding back in. She had hopped into the crawl space. Crazy. Anxiety seeped into her marrow. She shouldn't be down here. Disoriented, Molly leaned against the crawl-space wall, her body in a crouch. Deep breaths. Deep breaths. The doctor had said if she started having an episode, the breathing would be helpful, just as in an anxiety attack. To rest. To log the episode.

Blinking quickly to clear her thoughts, Molly opened her eyes. Daylight flooded the crawl space from behind her. The basement was open to the air, a shell of what it had once been. Molly looked to where she'd hidden from the fire. From the arsonist. She saw an old barrel there. It looked to have been white at one time but was now a dingy gray, covered with rust. An old label clung to the side of the barrel, peeling off, damaged from smoke.

The sensation of danger struck her. This wasn't smart. Hairs on her neck and arms stood even straighter, little bumps rising on her skin. Molly moved to turn around and exit the crawl space. Trent would be furious if he knew she'd gone down here alone, with only Maynard as her backup.

Maynard. She didn't know him well, outside of his being from the Kilbourn Clapton family tree. Why was he here again?

As awareness continued to grow in her, common sense came back into play. This was stupid of her. She needed to get back in her truck and head home. If she was going to explore the crawl space—the memory of being slowly suffocated—all of it, it should be with Trent.

"Don't."

Maynard's voice over her shoulder startled Molly. She screamed, standing to her full height but instead colliding with the earthen ceiling. Tall enough to hold the barrel but not tall enough to stand in, Molly fell against the crawl-space wall.

Maynard held up a hand. "Be careful about touching anything. You really shouldn't be in here in case this space collapses."

"Yes." Molly nodded. "I was just going to leave. I need to go home. I'll come back with Trent. I-I just remembered that old barrel and the fire and—"

Maynard waved it off. "That barrel's old. Farmers used to keep stuff in barrels and store them in their basements. Now come on out of there." He extended his hand where he stood at the opening of the crawl space.

Something inside her resisted. Resisted his hand. Resisted moving.

Then it clicked. All of it.

"Jacqueline Withers," Molly whispered. "She's the one who sold this property to Clapton Bros. Farms, wasn't she? She was the last Withers to own the murder house of 1910?"

"What are you talking about?" Maynard frowned. "Come

on, Molly, let's get you out of there. We can talk in the sunlight."

Molly eyed the metal barrel. "Am I right? You should know all this since you're a Clapton and sold us this place."

"Yes," Maynard agreed. "Seriously, let's—"

"Why would Jacqueline Withers sell her family farm to your family? Were there no more Withers left to inherit it?"

Maynard bent and took a step into the cramped space.

Molly stilled. "I'll come out, Maynard." She eyed him, nervous that instead of waiting for her, he'd entered the crawl space, now blocking the way out.

"Jacqueline Withers had kids." Maynard nodded. "I would have told you and Trent that if you'd wanted to know."

"Okay." She motioned for Maynard to back out. "Let's get out of here." She'd been careless going into the crawl space, and with Maynard in the way of the exit, claustrophobia along with a sense of dread were growing inside her. "Maynard?" She snapped her fingers, and the sound made Maynard jump.

He stared at her.

"Maynard, let's go. You're right. I shouldn't be down here."

Maynard raised his brows as if he hadn't heard her. "Jacqueline Withers had lots of kids—and grandkids. She married a Clapton."

Realization spread its numbing fear through Molly. Jacqueline Withers was a Clapton, and Maynard was a Clapton.

Maynard crawled toward her. The concern on his face had been replaced with a strange expression.

"Maynard?" Now it was her turn to urge him out of the crawl space.

He ignored her. "Did you know that some people—like the Wasziaks—claimed my grandmother was responsible for the Cornfield Ripper killings?" Maynard snorted. "As if a small girl could have been responsible for *murder*."

He edged forward. Caught off guard, Molly scrambled back and cried out as her back hit the metal barrel.

Maynard's expression was growing worried once more, panicked. "Jacqueline Withers Clapton." Spittle flew from his mouth when he said the name again. "She married into the Claptons." He continued moving toward Molly. "You know, you're just like January Rabine. Nosy and stupid. Why didn't you listen to me? I told you not to come down here!"

"Maynard, please," Molly whispered, fear gripping her. Her disorientation had led her back into the crawl space, only this time, instead of being trapped by fire, it was becoming clear that she was trapped by January's killer.

37

Perliett

Jasper Bridgers had taken far too long. Perliett could see that Mrs. Withers's form was fast collapsing in on herself. She continued to rock back and forth in the middle of the study floor, her pallor changing as the minutes ticked by. It wasn't healthy for her. It wasn't reasonable to leave her there, alone in her suffering.

Perliett disentangled herself from her mother.

"What are you going to do?" Maribeth's worried voice followed Perliett into the room.

"I'm going to try to get Mrs. Withers home. She needs rest. This is disturbing her far too much."

Maribeth started after Perliett, then halted, probably realizing that Mrs. Withers's absence would mean her study could be reclaimed in peace. "Be careful," she advised.

Perliett hesitantly reached for the woman crumpled in a heap on the floor. "Mrs. Withers?"

Mrs. Withers looked at her with empty eyes. Tears traced rivers down her cheeks that were devoid of color. Her black dress was drenched in her sweat, and Perliett avoided taking deep breaths as she questioned the last time the woman had bathed.

"Let me get you home," she encouraged.

Mrs. Withers allowed Perliett to help her rise to her feet. In moments, she had led the woman from the house, Maribeth rushing ahead to make sure the carriage was still hitched and ready from her earlier errand with Jasper.

"I thought Jasper took the carriage to get help?" Perliett frowned at the sight of it.

"I . . . I don't know," Maribeth said after a long pause.

Perliett wasn't going to try to understand. She had Mrs. Withers's cooperation and wasn't going to squander it. Once they helped Mrs. Withers onto the seat, Perliett carefully climbed up herself, attempting not to bump any of the healing bruises on her arms and legs. Maribeth laid her hand on Perliett's knee, looking up from where she stood by the carriage.

"Be careful. Come home immediately."

Perliett noticed her mother didn't offer to assist her and, with her last statement of caution, was already heading back to the house, most likely to her beloved study.

The distance to the Withers farm did not seem so far in the daylight, driven by horse and carriage. It was the first time Perliett had traversed this road since the night of her attack. She eyed the cornfields bordering it, a frightened tremor passing through her.

Get Mrs. Withers back to the Withers farm and then return home.

It was that simple.

Where Jasper Bridgers had swept off to was beyond Perliett. He certainly hadn't *walked* or they would have come upon him. A nagging sense told her he had a different agenda than seeking help. How difficult was it to fetch Mrs. Withers's husband? Must they turn this into a complaint that the woman was mad? The family had suffered enough with Eunice and Millie's murders. To have their mother committed because she was . . .

Perliett gave Mrs. Withers a sideways glance. The woman

had straightened on the seat of the carriage, tilting her chin up as she appeared to strain to see something or someone.

"Robin . . ." she muttered.

Perliett frowned. "Who is Robin?"

The sound of her voice startled Mrs. Withers. The woman stared at Perliett, her eyes widening. Her icy hand flew out and landed on Perliett's leg.

"No. You mustn't come. Leave me here."

There was awareness in her eyes now. A strange validation that within her lived the mind of a woman that reasoned.

Perliett shook her head. "I'll take you to your home." She pointed. "I can see the barn there. And the house . . ." The roofline of the white barn and its cupola was bold against the sky.

"We have gravestones in our basement," Mrs. Withers admitted with a shudder. "I've long despised them. Randolph wouldn't replace them with more fieldstone. Even after I begged him."

Randolph. Mr. Withers. Perliett had to remind herself of Mrs. Withers's husband's name.

"But"—Mrs. Withers's face transformed into a warm smile that spread to her eyes—"Alden would. He said he would. For me."

Alden? Perliett had no idea who Alden was. She knew Mrs. Withers's eldest daughter and son-in-law, and the name Alden was not in the Withers line.

"Stop," Mrs. Withers demanded. Her fingernails bit into Perliett's knee.

Perliett tugged on the reins. The horse snorted, tossing its head, then halted, leaving them among fields of corn with the farmhouse and barn roofs cutting the horizon above the tassels of corn.

Mrs. Withers climbed down from the carriage, and Perliett realized her mistake.

"No, no, Mrs. Withers." She scampered down, banging her inner thigh on the runner. Wincing, she limped around the horse, dragging her hand in comfort along the horse's side and touching its nose as she passed.

Mrs. Withers was disappearing into the corn when Perliett reached the other side of the carriage.

"Mrs. Withers!" Perliett cried.

The cornstalks swallowed up the woman, hiding her from view. Fighting against fear and the need to help the obviously disturbed woman, Perliett forced herself to ignore her fright. She pushed at the stiff stalks of corn, waving her left hand as corn silk tangled with her fingers. She could smell the corn, its sweet, tangy scent mingling with the damp earth beneath their feet.

"Mrs. Withers?"

"Alden?" Mrs. Withers's shaky voice traveled through the corn rows.

Perliett increased her speed, glimpsing the woman, who moved remarkably fast through the cornfield her husband had planted months ago in early spring.

"Alden!" There was panic in her voice.

It urged Perliett forward.

Mrs. Withers cried out again, only this time there was a twinge of relief in her tone.

Perliett plowed forward, seeing the form of the woman coming into view. She stumbled, her foot tangling with a cornstalk that had been broken and lay across the path. Perliett put out her hands to catch herself as she fell, but two enormous arms shot out, hauling her to her feet.

She stared up at the man, who had appeared out of nowhere. His farm clothes were worn and dirty from daily chores. His left eye was cloudy, blinded from birth. His graying hair stood in tufts from the top of his head, and his beard was untrimmed.

It was the Withers handyman. She knew him. In the past

she had treated a farm injury he'd suffered. He'd been polite but withdrawn.

Hadn't Detective Poll mentioned that the handyman was seen the night of her attack? They'd dismissed him due to his being half blind.

"Alden?" Mrs. Withers curled into his side like a lost child. His left arm came around her and released Perliett.

She tripped backward, her shoulder hitting a stalk and the corn leaves scraping at her face.

Alden. The handyman was Alden?

"Where is she? Is she safe? Is she all right?" Mrs. Withers was frantic, clawing at Alden's shirt. Yet he was staring at Perliett with one cold blue eye. His expression was grave, his jaw set.

"You," he declared.

Perliett was frozen in place.

A snap from behind caused her to whirl around.

"Jacqueline!" Mrs. Withers cried out in relief.

But there was no relief in Perliett's heart. She stared into the face of the leering child from the night of her attack. The child no one seemed to know existed.

"My baby girl!" Mrs. Withers shoved past Perliett, gathering the child into her arms.

Jacqueline stood stiffly as her mother held her, her chin resting on Mrs. Withers's shoulder, with the same blue eyes as her father's staring coldly into Perliett's face.

Then the girl smiled.

38

Perliett had no intention of dying. Dying was a dreadful thing, and there was nothing appealing about the afterlife either. She charged back toward the carriage before Alden or the other two could stop her.

"Ho!" Alden shouted.

Mrs. Withers was weeping, holding on to Jacqueline tightly as the girl struggled to free herself from her mother's desperate grip.

Perliett ran through the corn, the leaves scratching her face. Never again. She would never set foot in a cornfield ever again.

Her ankle twisted on a rut in the ground, but she righted herself and kept fleeing. She could hear the corn busting behind her as the behemoth of a handyman chased her. Scattered thoughts raced through her mind.

Alden the handyman? A secret affair with Mrs. Withers must have resulted in a child. Jacqueline. But how did no one know except—?

Perliett batted away a spiderweb that stretched over her mouth and wrapped around her cheek.

She recalled almost a decade earlier when it was said Mrs. Withers had lost a baby. She had been almost full term. George had been out of town at the time. Perliett hadn't been attempting to practice any of her own medicine then, far from it. There had been a midwife. A baby's funeral.

Had the casket been empty all along?

Had Mrs. Withers faked her infant's death and secreted her away to be with her father, Alden?

It was altogether possible. Exceptional but possible.

Perliett burst from the cornfield, racing onto the road, where the horse still stood hitched to the carriage. She clambered onto the seat and slapped the reins against the horse's back.

"Hyah!"

Alden broke into the clearing. A deadly expression on his face.

Perliett whimpered as the horse startled forward, whinnying its surprise and shock at Perliett's unorthodox treatment. The carriage surged, Perliett barely holding on. She looked over her shoulder. Alden was running after her. She saw another carriage in the distance. Gaining on them.

If God had ever looked down and decided that she was His to protect, now would be a wonderful moment to do so! It was an abstract plea, but one Perliett found herself clinging to.

She managed another glance behind her.

Alden had collapsed onto the road. Mrs. Withers was screaming, rushing toward him as the big man rolled onto his side, clutching his arm. The young girl stood off to the side, yet her attention was fixed on Perliett.

Everything in Perliett told her to keep going. She could tell something had happened. Alden's heart perhaps? How timely for her and how awful for him! The caregiver in Perliett entertained the briefest moment of obligation to turn around and offer aid. But the survivor in her told her if she did so, she would be saving the Cornfield Ripper.

Perliett wasn't in the business of saving killers. Besides, George said her practice was all quackery anyway, and she was thrilled at the moment to believe him.

Molly

"Maynard." Molly held out her hands, reasoning with the man as if he were a child. "Let's go and talk about this in the sunlight."

"There's nothing to talk about!" He rubbed the side of his nose with his thumb. His agitation was growing, and he kept glancing at the barrel behind her.

Molly pushed down her fear, willing herself to be calm. Panicking now would be worthless.

"I didn't want to sell the farm. My cousins—they wanted to off-load it." Maynard leaned his back against the wall of the crawl space, sliding down until he sat in front of her, trapping Molly in. He ran his palms over his balding head, groaning. "All these years, it was vacant. I could *sleep* when it was vacant. But *sell* it?"

"W-why didn't you want to sell Jacqueline's farm?" Molly waited. Maynard didn't answer. "Was it because it has something to do with the Cornfield Ripper?"

Maynard's head jerked up, his eyes wild. "What? That old story? What does that have to do with anything today?"

"I don't know!" Molly's frustration and fear were growing palpable. Her outburst made Maynard's jaw clench. "I'm sorry." She held up her hand again. "I just—there's been a lot about the Cornfield Ripper and the Withers sisters coming into play of late." She wasn't sure she should mention January's name. Wasn't sure what he might do if Maynard truly had been the one who killed her.

Maynard snorted, shook his hands in fists in front of him, and stared at the opposite wall of the crawl space. "That stupid girl. It *started* with her researching the Cornfield Ripper. Researching the *Wasziaks*. Fine! Research it! What do I care? But then she had to get nosy about crime in Kilbourn." He scowled at Molly, and she shrank against the barrel. "Crime in Kilbourn? What, teenage vandalism? Oh yes, and what is that?" His voice rose in a mocking pitch. "A disappearance? The only other questionable occurrence in the Kilbourn history books. And your cousin January *had* to look into it."

"Tamera Nichols." Molly said the name before she could bite her tongue.

Maynard's eyes darkened. He leaned toward her conspiratorially, as if telling her a secret. "Your cousin figured out that Jacqueline Withers was my grandmother. That Jacqueline Withers was a Clapton, and that Clapton Bros. Farms owned the property you were buying. She nosed around and figured out that Tamera Nichols had a boyfriend."

"You," Molly stated. There was no reason not to now. It was obvious. January had inadvertently pieced together crimes spanning decades that were linked only by ancestry.

Maynard leaned into Molly, and she whimpered, pulling into herself. Then his hand reached out and slapped against the metal barrel. "How's it going in there, Tamera?"

Molly began to shiver, realization flooding every pore in her already-stressed body. Tamera Nichols had been buried in a barrel since 1982 in the crawl space of the Withers murder house of 1910!

Settling back, Maynard laughed. His expression was almost pitiful. He shrugged. "They blamed Jacqueline's father for the murders of the Withers sisters—and the attack on that other lady."

"Perliett Van Hilton?" Molly said.

Maynard snarled. "It doesn't matter. No one ever charged Alden, Jacqueline's father, for the killings because he died. Sudden-like. He had an all-too-convenient heart attack." A thin smile spread across his face, leering, not unlike the one Molly had seen in her exhaustion-induced dreams. "But they always underestimated my grandmother. Good ol' Jacqueline. You know, after I put Tamera in the barrel, I realized the answer to that old question of whether murder is in a person's genetics. What do you think, Molly Wasziak? Is there an inherited need to kill?"

Perliett

"Stop!"

The man's voice carried after Perliett, but she scrambled down from her carriage after racing into the front drive of her home. The carriage that had been behind her had followed, though she didn't care who it was now. She was home. She would lock herself inside and never come out!

Perliett flew into the house, slamming the door behind her, clicking the lock into place. She ran down the hallway, toward PaPa's study, intent on finding her mother. Together. They must be together and be safe and—

Perliett skidded to a halt, staring in outright disbelief. Her mother stood in the circle of Jasper's arms, the affection more than apparent in her swollen lips.

"Perliett!" She leaped away from Jasper, dabbing at her mouth.

Jasper's visage darkened. He lifted a hand to calm her. "Perliett, be reasonable."

"Reasonable!" Perliett was anything but, and if anger could rain down in drops of fire, perhaps that would be the most effective way of proclaiming her fury. "You were supposed to get help! Now I find you here with my mother while I'm fleeing for my life?"

"Oh, Perliett!" Maribeth moved to rush to her daughter's side, but Perliett stopped her with a glare.

"No. What is this?" She swept her arm to encompass the whole of her father's study. "For your sake, Jasper Bridgers, you best have a good explanation as to who you are once and for all and where you went!"

Jasper cleared his throat, straightening his shoulders, and looked down his nose at her with the patronizing expression of someone who believed the other needed to find their inner calm. "I am a journalist. From Chicago."

"A journalist?" Perliett spat. She would hog-tie the man and throw him into the cornfield with that horrible child.

Mr. Bridgers held up a hand. "This shouldn't amaze you. I already told you, I have been researching the rise of spiritualism in the cities. Studying it in rural areas has been enlightening."

"You've been studying my mother?" Perliett frowned.

Mr. Bridgers wagged his head back and forth. "In a way, yes. Or rather, *with* your mother. She possesses unique talents and, coupled with what I know of elements of illusion, I wanted to register the impact of the need to connect with the afterlife from a rural small-town perspective. If people of modest incomes would invest with the same passion and need as the wealthier."

"Illusions?" Perliett felt her throat closing in. Choking out whatever belief might have been hanging on.

Maribeth took a few steps toward her daughter. "Oh, not all of it!" she protested. "You know I've always been sensitive to these things—though your father was hesitant to approve—and Jasper had written to me after he heard of my abilities in that news article that was written last year, remember?"

"After your first sitting?" Perliett nodded, unimpressed. "Yes, I recall."

Maribeth smiled, hopeful about getting things resolved. "Yes, so Jasper wrote and proposed a study. We did not know that Eunice Withers would be killed, obviously—or Millie."

"Illusions?" Perliett repeated, the word grating on her tongue.

Now Mr. Bridgers stepped forward. "Only a few. To enhance what already comes naturally to your mother. This is why I'd yet to leave for help when you so courageously took the carriage with Mrs. Withers. I was safeguarding some of our supplies outside in the barn before people descended on the house to assist Mrs. Withers. We can't ruin your mother's reputation or gift on behalf of my curiosity, can we?"

"The window shattering—Eunice's visitation—it was a ruse, wasn't it?" Perliett was becoming wise, and the idea of Mr. Bridgers's scam and Maribeth falling under his influence was almost equal to the horrors she had just faced.

Someone was banging on the front door. It distracted them for a moment, but Mr. Bridgers took another urgent step toward her, extending his hand. "We meant no harm, truly! I merely applied pressure to the window with carefully placed nails, and then with a tug of a transparent line, they shifted and the window shattered—right on beckoning, I might add." A slight smile of pride touched his eyes.

"And your collapse? The night I was attacked, the writing in the book from Eunice?" Perliett leveled a look of disbelief on her mother.

Maribeth bit her lip. "Not everything I do is a ruse, honestly."

"But Eunice didn't write that poem, *you* did."

Maribeth looked a bit sheepish. "I wanted Detective Poll to allow me to help with the investigation. To prove I have a gift. If you had evidence to show him that Eunice had connected with me . . . well, I didn't know you'd rush out into the night for help! I thought you'd use your apothecary box and stay with me until I could feign coming to. I was hardly able to maintain my silence when you used smelling salts, but I did. You must understand, I have *four* sittings scheduled for next week as it is. The need is genuine, Perliett!"

"The need?" Perliett gave an incredulous laugh. "The need to be lied to?" She cast astonished eyes on Jasper. "You wrote that note from the Cornfield Ripper to yourself, didn't you? You staged it? It was never left outside your door. You wanted to insert yourself into the investigation to garner more curiosity for my mother?"

Jasper's lips tightened in affirmation of Perliett's accusation.

"And the dead robin?" She looked between them. "Was that even the Cornfield Ripper's doing?"

"It was!" Maribeth wrung her hands. "But I overheard you and Millie. I heard about the poem and—"

"And you used it to appear that you heard from Eunice." Disillusioned, Perliett shook her head. "You lied."

Maribeth's plea straightened into a sterner look. "I don't lie. I have gifts."

"Unproven ones!" Perliett cried. "And you turn it into a magic show? No wonder you wouldn't summon PaPa. You *can't* summon him!"

"Perliett, that isn't true!"

"That time you did try to summon PaPa, who squeezed my shoulder? I felt him. I felt the hand as physically as I can feel you now! The doors to the wardrobe opening? How do you explain that? Did you *summon* that, Mother?"

"I have been in Kilbourn for some time, keeping a low profile," Mr. Bridgers admitted. "When a person is partaking in a sitting, between the intensity of emotion and the fear of the unknown, they often miss the medium's assistant."

"Assistant?" Perliett looked between him and her mother. "You? You squeezed my shoulder? That was *months* ago!"

"There are certain elements that help make the sitting more real for the sitter," Maribeth explained, "and then I can connect with the actual spirit and . . ."

Perliett's chin wobbled. Tears burned her eyes and then trailed down her cheeks. "If you must resort to trickery to make your beliefs 'real,' then they are not the truth. You dabble in a world you know *nothing* about, and that is dangerous." She turned her angst onto Jasper. "And you enable it. You *help* it. You destroy faith."

"No," Jasper countered. "Rather, I help others gain access to experiences that are only enhanced. The experience itself is still real."

Perliett leveled a frank gaze on her mother. "You haven't connected with Eunice Withers at all, have you? You have fooled others and given them false hopes."

"But there *was* an influence here that night!" Maribeth insisted, her voice rising. "I saw Eunice by my bedside." Her voice grew eager to prove herself. "Remember? I saw her apparition!"

"Which you cannot prove," Perliett finished grimly. "And if there was, it is an influence I want nothing to do with." She spun on her heel, leaving her father's study behind. The mysteries of the spirit world—oh, they were real. But they weren't meant for entertainment, nor were they meant for profit. Her mother played a dangerous game to validate her beliefs, alongside her cohort Mr. Bridgers, whose toying with others' faith was a mere experiment in the psyche of mankind. It was a horrible, awful game, and it was not one Perliett intended to continue playing.

39

Molly

"You think Jacqueline Withers was behind the cornfield killings?" Molly breathed carefully. In and out. Having an anxiety attack in a crawl space while leaning against a barrel filled with the remains of a woman who had been missing for forty years would do her no good at all.

Maynard shrugged. He wiped sweat from his temples. "Who knows? Does anyone know? Does it matter? Alden. Jacqueline. People died. Just like Tamera." He glanced at the barrel.

"Why?" Molly whispered. "Why did you do it? Why did you kill her—and January?"

Maynard clicked his tongue, shaking his head. "Oh, come on, Molly. Don't be so dumb. January is obvious. She was going to uncover my secret. I was barely twenty when Tamera and I were dating. I was twenty when Tamera led me on and then went out with another man. But that wasn't right. She was mine. And when I told her, we fought. The only place I could think to hide her was here. No one lived in my cousins' old, deserted farmhouse our grandmother used to own. A renter was one thing, and I wasn't a fan of it when they did renovations to the living area. But renting was a waste of time. So then my family decided they wanted to sell and offered it to Trent before I had the chance to do a thing about it! I had to go along with it."

"You started the fire, didn't you?" Molly breathed.

Maynard offered an apologetic smile. "I had to. Twice I tried to get in here. I needed to see that you weren't disturbing the crawl space. I needed to make sure you didn't have January's notes on Tamera."

Realization, both blessed and terrifying, washed over her. "*You* were in our house? At night?"

Maynard gave a curt nod.

The ghostly steps she'd heard that first week in their home . . . "Were you ever in my bedroom during the day?" She thought of the movements she'd seen from the coop's attic window and attributed to a ghost.

Maynard shot her a look. "I thought you were gone. I didn't know you were in the chicken coop of all places!"

"Is that your kit in the coop?" Molly had to know now. She had to know everything.

Maynard raised an eyebrow. "What? That crate with duct tape and such? It's still in there?"

She nodded.

He waved her off. "I wouldn't call it a kit. After Tamera, I considered . . . well, sometimes a person has a monster inside, and when it wakes up, it's hard to put back to sleep."

"Maynard," Molly said, internally breathing a prayer, "you need to let me go."

He laughed. "What, so you can tell everyone everything?"

Molly didn't reply. She didn't know how to.

Maynard rubbed his eyes, defeat sagging his shoulders. "Ah, Molly, maybe we just end it all here, yes? The two of us. And Tamera." His eyes shifted to the barrel. "Just be done with living. It's not worth it anyway, is it? To live? All the darkness in the world. The beasts that live inside us. There's no redemption."

"But there is." Molly was experiencing it herself—the first glimmers of healing. The life that God could bring outside of the death that inevitably wielded its way through life. "We're just broken," she added.

"Ha!" Maynard wagged his finger at her. "There you are right, kiddo. We *are* broken. I saw her die."

His statement brought the memory of the day of the fire rushing back to her. She'd heard him. Heard him claim it. Heard the pride-like tone of his voice. He'd seen January die. He'd seen Tamera die. And he'd liked it.

There was a scuffle in the basement outside the crawl space.

A muffled shout.

Maynard's eyes turned wild. "Shut up!" He glared at Molly, his expression demanding she not make a sound.

She noted he carried no weapons, none that she could see anyway. He had nothing that could harm her—outside of his willingness to hurt others. A grossly hardened soul and a lineage of violent stories.

She, on the other hand, had hope. And for the first time, Molly claimed it.

Perliett

She heard the front door crack as whoever was kicking against it finally won. She saw her mother's face crumple in hurt and betrayal. She witnessed Jasper Bridgers turn his back to her and soothe Maribeth with the ignorant confidence of a man who was comfortable turning deceit into truth when it fit his needs. She felt arms grip her as her knees buckled, then swing her up awkwardly—because no man could carry a woman of any size with ease. This Perliett knew.

Stumbling into the parlor, George dropped her as gently as he could on the sofa. He kneeled in front of her, searching her for new wounds.

"You are mad," he scolded, lifting her hands and examining her wrists. He ran his fingers up her arms to her neck. "Your face is all scraped."

"It was the corn. George . . ." Perliett pushed away his hands and reached for his shoulders, taking them urgently. "Alden. The handyman. He—"

"I know. He was already dead when I came upon him and Mrs. Withers."

"And the girl?"

George frowned. "Yes. The girl. Who is she? How have we never seen her before in a place this small?"

"They've hidden her. Jacqueline. She is Mrs. Withers's daughter."

George's only expression was the raising of his eyebrows. "And she was in the cornfield when you were—"

"Yes." Perliett sucked in a sob.

"You believe it was Alden who did this to you?"

Perliett nodded repeatedly, choking on her tears and coughing.

George patted her back. "Try to compose yourself. I don't have my smelling salts with me."

"I do." Perliett gestured toward her apothecary chest in the corner. She had not noticed it there before, hidden behind a palm plant, but she noticed it now.

George's eyes narrowed. "Hmm, I'd prefer to burn it."

"You can burn the heroin," she replied and gave a watery laugh, relief breathing oxygen into her blood.

George chuckled. "I can, can I?"

"Yes." She wiped at her eyes.

George pushed a handkerchief into her hand. "Your house is a fine mess."

"I know." She couldn't argue with him, as George Wasziak

spoke the truth. "My mother and Jasper, they've been creating ruses . . ." Tears choked out the rest of her explanation, but George nodded his understanding.

"Do you see now why I was worried—cautioning you, attempting anything I could to get you to listen to me? Your mother and you were so set in your ideas, and I knew. I knew your father did not wish that for you."

"You've been a brute." Perliett scowled through her tears.

"Everything short of manhandling you." George nodded. "Yes. Your father was a man of faith. We attended church together. We spoke often of the things of the Lord, and you were following in the ways of your mother, which had your father quite concerned."

"You could have told me that." Perliett pushed his shoulder out of frustration.

George drew back. "And would you have listened?"

"Well, no."

"See?"

"You're an oaf." Perliett slumped back in the couch, clutching his handkerchief to her nose. "Where is Mrs. Withers now? And the girl?"

George frowned. "I hailed Mr. Hannity. He's fetched Detective Poll. Leave them to the authorities. Let them sort it out."

Perliett pursed her lips. "I will not just sit by and—"

"And what? What will you do, Perliett. Will you walk? No, no, will you run? Is that it? Into the fray of chaos with a dead man lying in the road, a child without a conscience born out of a love affair, and a woman who has been abused by the entirety of her life's choices?"

"Yes." Perliett nodded stubbornly.

"No." His dark eyes, bottomless pits of arrogant confidence. Resolute stubbornness. He was so sure he was right. So sure of everything. So sure of her.

Well, it was not to be!

Perliett sat up and leaned into the man kneeling before her. She leveled a strict eye on him. "Yes."

George's eyes narrowed. "God help me."

He kissed her then. Palmed her by the back of her head, threading his fingers in her already-mussed hair and yanking her into him. He didn't release her either. He made sure Perliett knew that his no meant no, but if she kept saying yes, then ohhhh my . . . that yes would most definitely lead to more kissable trouble.

Perliett whimpered beneath his kiss, his lips claiming hers with a possessiveness that fit his authoritative, irritating, God-help-her, fascinating and altogether intoxicating personality.

Finally, George pulled away. He leveled a look on her that made her shiver rather delightfully. Perliett licked her lips for the sheer need of it, and his eyes followed, then rose back to meet hers.

"Do you understand the answer is no?" He finished his argument a bit belatedly.

She would let him win. This time. And because she was letting him win, she didn't feel as though she was at all diminished or devalued in the slightest.

"Yes," she answered.

40

Molly

It had taken a few throat-scraping screams to bring Trent and the police barreling into the crawl space. To Molly's relief, and somewhat to her surprise, Maynard had done little to resist. Instead, he'd just sat there. His eyes and expression empty. She couldn't even say, in retrospect, that there was any remorse in him. He was just . . . cold.

They had retrieved Tamera Nichols's body from the barrel. Dan turned over the information from Brianna Nichols's blog, and the authorities were going to contact her family, forty years later, with word that their sister and daughter had finally been found.

Along with the closure of that case came the inevitable closure of January Rabine's. Maynard's DNA matched the unknown DNA they had taken from January's body. With Molly's recounting of her conversation with Maynard, the police had pressed charges against him for not only Tamera's and January's murders, but the attempt on Molly's life, breaking and entering, and arson.

Clapton Bros. Farms had given Trent three months' paid

leave. Molly had a feeling they were on tenterhooks, considering their own ties to the sordid family saga.

Now, Molly sat in the chicken yard, throwing grain at the chickens. Sid handed her a thermos of coffee. September had dawned, and with it the heat and humidity had stayed. Molly jostled the thermos, only to hear the clinking of ice.

"Oh good. Iced coffee."

Sid smiled. "It's too hot for anything else."

Silence settled between them, and then they heard a truck door slam. Sid stood. "Trent is here. You know you're both welcome to stay with Dan and me until you can rebuild."

Molly shot a glance at the newly leveled area where the Withers farmhouse had once stood. "Thanks, Sid." Their eyes met. She meant it. There was something special about friendship. The kind that didn't come with conditions. The kind that was willing to take you as you were. Messed up. Mixed up. Medicated up. Whatever the combination.

And she was doing better now. She'd had no more major episodes since her doctor had adjusted her medications. She was also seeking counseling, and Trent was coming with her. She was rising out of her fog of melancholy and seeing that there was the promise of joy on the horizon. There was faith. There was family.

Trent waved as he passed Sid. They exchanged some words, Sid laughed, then called out, "See you both at supper!"

As he neared her, Molly turned her attention back to her chickens. To Sue, Izzy, and Sylvia, who had somehow fallen onto her side, flipped her head over, and sprang up in a squawking flurry of feathers. The chicks were old enough to be let out, and Myrtle scampered about with the others while the rooster kept watch with intent to kill if a predator challenged them.

Trent stood beside Molly's camp chair. "So, I have the plans for the new house—if you want to see them."

Molly gave him a smile. "I'd love to. Just no gravestones or crawl spaces, please."

Trent laughed, reaching for her hand. She took his, and he pulled her to her feet.

"Do you think . . . ?" Molly let her question drop. "I know the medications were causing most of my issues, but how did I know about 'Cock Robin'? It was in my mind *before* we found the book of nursery rhymes. And the little girl in the attic? I wouldn't have known about Jacqueline Withers, but was it her?"

Trent looked over her shoulder toward the Clapton Bros. cornfield that abutted their property. When he spoke, his words were chosen carefully. "I don't have the answers, Molls. Maybe God gave you insight with the poem, with feeling like you were seeing things . . . to help bring closure to January's death. To Tamera's. Even to the Withers sisters."

"Maybe." Molly wouldn't discount it, but she found comfort in crediting God with the knowledge and the inspiration. "You know, I was doing some research into our families."

"Yeah?" Trent allowed her to change the subject. She would always wonder. Always be aware of that fine, filmy veil between this world and the spiritual world beyond. But she was content to leave it a mystery for God and God alone to reveal to them in His time.

"Your great-grandmother was Perliett Van Hilton."

Trent frowned. "The third victim of the Cornfield Ripper?"

"Mm-hmm. She escaped with her life—somehow—and then ended up marrying George Wasziak. So even though at one point he was suspected as her attacker, he ended up being her hero." Molly smiled up at Trent, praying he'd read her meaning in her eyes.

He did. His smile warmed. "You mean to say, unemotional and gruff Wasziak men aren't necessarily the beasts you females think we are?"

Molly smiled, biting her bottom lip.

Trent's eyes dropped to her mouth. He leaned forward, and for a blessed, glorious moment, Molly felt his kiss. Felt the emotion behind his placid face. Felt his soul and his love and his devotion in spite of it all. In spite of loss, and in spite of trials.

He pulled away, but Molly followed until she buried herself in his chest, breathing in the scent of hay and manure and fresh air and everything farm.

They didn't say anything.

But this time—for the first time in a long time—the not-saying-anything said absolutely everything.

Perliett

The funeral of Alden the handyman was a solemn affair. Mrs. Withers refused to condemn him for the murders of her daughters, and she had also refused to admit that he was the one who had attacked Perliett.

Perliett had attended the funeral with George, not because of grief but because she needed the closure it provided. Now she watched as they lowered the man's coffin into the grave. A fine mist fell from the gray sky. The air felt sticky. Her hand was hooked in George's elbow, and she glanced to where Maribeth stood. She had, to her credit, cut off communicating with Mr. Bridgers. Apparently, the man had no qualms about it, as he was at the funeral as well, standing beside a young woman Perliett recognized from town. Charmer that he was, he'd lost no time—and for some reason, Mr. Bridgers seemed to have no intention of leaving Kilbourn. That was fine, Perliett concluded. He could stay, he could marry, he could become part of the Kilbourn community and leave generations in his wake. Perliett could do nothing but avoid him from now on, and pray, for the sake of the Bridgers generations, that they could separate their spiritual lives from the otherworld of deceased souls and instead center themselves on the truths stretching through history by the hand of God himself.

There were things Perliett still couldn't explain. The fingers that had snuffed out the candles before the window shattered. Maribeth insisted that if Perliett *had* seen ghostly fingers, they were real. The very idea sent chills through Perliett. Perhaps. Yet she suspected Mr. Bridgers might have figured some way to create that illusion as well.

Perliett let her eyes roam until they fell on the girl, Jacqueline Withers, clad in all black, standing by her mother. A dazed look stretched over Mr. Withers's person. He would adopt the child, George had said. He had been given little choice. The Withers name was tarnished because of his wife's actions, and he couldn't add child abandonment to the list of sins now that the entire town of Kilbourn knew of Jacqueline's existence.

Perliett lifted her gloved hand to wipe a droplet of rain from her cheek. Her movement caught Jacqueline's eye, and the girl stared at Perliett, unblinking. There was calculation behind her eyes that assessed Perliett.

How she had survived the attack by Alden, Perliett was afraid she would never know. Even now, as she stared back at Jacqueline, allowing herself to soak in the girl's coldness, she wondered if Alden truly *was* the monster his letters to the newspaper made him out to be. Or had it been a vicious little girl who had influenced him? A girl who experimented with her violence toward birds? Who took her animals and buried them in graves, as Mrs. Withers had alluded to? She wondered if it was Jacqueline who had left them on others' doorsteps.

Perhaps.

Perhaps there would never be any answers to the questions.

Perliett leaned into George, hugging his arm now, sensing Jacqueline's stare that had not broken.

George's mouth moved against her ear. "Should we go?" he asked.

Perliett met the girl's eyes. She waited. Jacqueline looked away finally. Perliett shook her head. "No. There's no need to run."

And there wasn't. No matter what happened going forward in this small farming community, no matter what ghosts were left behind as generations passed, Perliett would stand on what she knew to be true. A burgeoning faith and a stability in the knowledge that no spirit was outside the supremacy of God.

George pressed a kiss behind her ear. Subtle but telling.

Perliett leaned against him, contentment growing inside her. Silly George. She would give up her apothecary box for him, and her own ruse that she was anything but a hobbyist dabbling in remedies. She would embrace truth. Truth was valuable and not to be trifled with. Perliett resolved to seek truth for the sake of her own future generations, even as Jacqueline Withers turned her back on her father's grave and walked away into the mist.

QUESTIONS FOR DISCUSSION

1. Perliett likes to practice old-time remedies that are considered quackery by the local doctor. What old-time remedies for various ailments have you either tried or heard of?
2. Molly struggles with depression and exhaustion. Think of a time when you've been at a low point. What helped pull you up from the depths?
3. Perliett is on a journey to define the truth in the various belief systems around her. How do you identify truth? What is the foundation on which your faith is built?
4. As Molly's best friend, Sid is concerned for her but is cautious in confronting the issue of mental health. What are ways we can come alongside those who struggle with depression, anxiety, and other such health issues? How would you want someone to approach you if you had similar struggles?
5. Spiritualism was at an all-time high in popularity at the turn of the last century, with the idea of contacting the dead the primary emphasis. How does faith affect your view of the concept of life after death?

How do you think that perspective impacts the way you grieve?

6. The nursery rhyme "Cock Robin" is connected with the murders at the Withers farm. Which nursery rhymes or songs have you found to be particularly creepy? Why do you think they became so popular? What purpose might they have served for those who sang or recited them?
7. Farming communities have been vital to American life since America was founded. What have been your personal experiences with our country's farmland? What was it about your upbringing, whether in a small town or big city, that caused you to view life the way you do?
8. Just for fun, since chickens play a big role in Molly's life, what would you name a chicken if you adopted one as a pet?

ACKNOWLEDGMENTS

When I started writing Perliett's and Molly's stories, I had no idea what the year would hold for me. Loss of employment was fast followed by the passing of my beloved, most precious momma. It was difficult to write a story in a fictional world, especially one about grief and postpartum depression, and also about that all-encompassing desire to *want* to see your loved one again.

What is eternity? What happens after we die? As I've been asked many times before, do you really believe in ghosts?

I believe in Jesus. The Author and Finisher of my faith. I believe that those who have run the race before us cheer us on, a great cloud of witnesses. I don't discount a spiritual realm far beyond our understanding. While I don't pursue it in the way of spiritualism, I pursue it in the way of knowing God. Pursuit of Him will result in an eventual *knowing* of what lies beyond the veil. God chooses to reveal himself in many ways, and He chooses to comfort in grief in various ways also. Like the day my tears came in torrents after my momma's passing and an American bald eagle swooped mere feet from my windshield in a calm soaring. Momma's favorite bird was the eagle. It reminded her that we will "mount up with wings like eagles," we will "run and not be weary, walk and not faint." So I thank the Lord for my eagle sighting, so rare in its low flying and methodical flight. In that moment, I was reminded that Momma still lives. And God? He's very much on His throne.

As for postpartum depression, that too is a personal journey. Many of us have experienced it. I have. I have experienced loss from miscarriages, the exhaustion that goes with this, the depression. For those of you who are walking this journey and feel alone, I encourage you to reach out. You are not alone.

I want to thank my Bethany House family, my editors Raela Schoenherr and Luke Hinrichs. Thanks to my agent, Janet Kobobel Grant, for her continued support of my career and through this intensely difficult year.

Special thanks to my beta reader Kara Peck, whose own loss this year mirrored my own. Our mommas sure are living it up in heaven, aren't they?

Much love to my dear friends who pick me up when I fall. Kimberley Woodhouse, Natalie Walters, Anne Love, Kara Isaac, Tracee Chu, and Jerilyn Finger—you all are buried deep in my heart.

An extra thanks to Andrew Baerlocher for helping me navigate the world of spiritualism, both past and present, and for helping me align it with the perspective of my faith, anchoring it in the Truth.

And finally, to the Polls. Especially to their chickens. All forty hundred of them.

Jaime Jo Wright is a winner of the Christy, Daphne du Maurier, and INSPY Awards and is a Carol Award finalist. She's also the *Publishers Weekly* and ECPA bestselling author of three novellas. Jaime lives in Wisconsin with her cat named Foo; her husband, Cap'n Hook; and their littles, Peter Pan and CoCo. Visit her at jaimewrightbooks.com.

Sign Up for Jaime's Newsletter

Keep up to date with Jaime's news on book releases and events by signing up for her email list at jaimewrightbooks.com.

More from Jaime Jo Wright

Wren Blythe enjoys life in the Northwoods, but when a girl goes missing, her search leads to a shocking discovery shrouded in the lore of the murderess Eva Coons. Decades earlier, the real Eva struggles with the mystery of her past—all clues point to murder. Both will find that, to save the innocent, they must face an insidious evil.

The Souls of Lost Lake

You May Also Like . . .

In search of her father's lost goods, Adria encounters an eccentric old woman who has filled Foxglove Manor with dangerous secrets that may cost Adria her life. Centuries later, when the senior residents of Foxglove under her care start sharing chilling stories of the past, Kailey will have to risk it all to banish the past's demons, including her own.

On the Cliffs of Foxglove Manor by Jaime Jo Wright
jaimewrightbooks.com

In 1928, Bonaventure Circus outcast Pippa Ripley must decide if uncovering her roots is worth putting herself directly in the path of a killer preying on the troupe. Decades later, while determining if an old circus train depot will be torn down or preserved, Chandler Faulk is pulled into a story far darker and more haunting than she imagined.

The Haunting at Bonaventure Circus by Jaime Jo Wright
jaimewrightbooks.com

Mystery begins to follow Aggie Dunkirk when she exhumes the past's secrets and uncovers a crime her eccentric grandmother has been obsessing over. Decades earlier, after discovering her sister's body in the attic, Imogene Grayson is determined to obtain justice. Two women, separated by time, vow to find answers . . . no matter the cost.

Echoes among the Stones by Jaime Jo Wright
jaimewrightbooks.com

BETHANYHOUSE